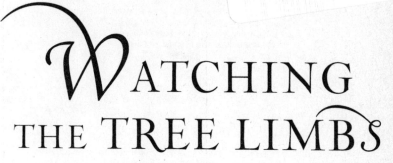

# WATCHING THE TREE LIMBS

## MARY E. DeMUTH

# NAVPRESS®

### BRINGING TRUTH TO LIFE

NavPress
P.O. Box 35001
Colorado Springs, Colorado 80935

ISBN 1-57683-926-5

Cover design by Kirk DouPonce, DogEaredDesign.com
Cover photo of girl by ShootPW.com
Author photo by David Edmonson

Creative Team: Terry Behimer, Lissa Halls Johnson, Kathy Mosier, Arvid Wallen, Angie Messinger

This novel is a work of fiction. Names, characters, places, and incidents are either the product of the author's imagination or are used fictitiously. Any resemblance to actual events, locales, organizations, or persons, living or dead, is entirely coincidental and beyond the intent of either the author or publisher.

Unless otherwise identified, all Scripture quotations in this publication are taken from the *King James Version* (KJV). Other version used: the *New American Standard Bible* (NASB), © The Lockman Foundation 1960, 1962, 1963, 1968, 1971, 1972, 1973, 1975, 1977, 1995.

**Published in association with the literary agency of Alive Communications, Inc., 7680 Goddard Street, Suite 200, Colorado Springs, CO 80920 (www.alivecommunications.com).**

Library of Congress Cataloging-in-Publication Data
DeMuth, Mary E., 1967-
  Watching the tree limbs / Mary E. DeMuth.
     p. cm.
  Includes bibliographical references.
  ISBN 1-57683-926-5
  1. Girls—Fiction. 2. Rape victims—Fiction. I. Title.
  PS3604.E48W37 2006
  813'.6—dc22

                                    2005033680

Printed in the United States of America

1 2 3 4 5 6 7 8 9 10 / 10 09 08 07 06

FOR A FREE CATALOG OF NAVPRESS BOOKS & BIBLE STUDIES,
CALL 1-800-366-7788 (USA) OR 1-800-839-4769 (CANADA)

*To the bewildered ones under the tree limbs*

# Acknowledgments

THIS BOOK SPILLED OUT OF MY heart like a torrential river, in part because of my passion for the story. Any eternal impact it may have, though, rests on the shoulders of my prayer team. Thank you, Kevin and Renee Bailey, Gahlen and Lee Ann Crawford, Eric and Katy Gedney, Kim Griffith, Ed and Sue Harrell, Diane and Jessica Klapper, Susanne Maynes, Hud and Nancy McWilliams, Catalin and Shannon Popa, Tom and Holly Schmidt, J.R. and Ginger Vassar, Rod and Mary Vestal, Jodie Westfall, and Liz Wolf. You have all blessed me in ways I can't quantify in words.

Thank you, Sandra Glahn, for walking the writing path with me, but more than that, for journeying in friendship with me. Thanks, D'Ann Mateer, Suzanne Deschidn, and Leslie Wilson of my critique group, Life Sentence. Your words and encouragement helped me continue on. I can't wait to see your beautiful words in print.

Thank you, Chip MacGregor, for first believing in me as a novelist. Beth Jusino, you've taken his baton and sprinted. Thanks for finding homes for my stories, for working relentlessly on my behalf. Rachelle Gardner, I am so thankful the Lord prompted you to read my book, but more than that, it thrilled me that you *loved* it. Lissa Halls Johnson, you took my meandering words and deepened them in ways I didn't expect. The Lord used your keen eye not only to make the novel dance but also to show me where I needed to grieve and heal in my own journey.

To my children, Sophie, Aidan, and Julia, thank you for giving me constant and utter delight. I desperately love you! To

Patrick, my best friend and handsome husband, I couldn't have begun this endeavor called writing without your relentless cheerleading. I love you.

Jesus, You are the One I sing to. Thank You for rescuing me. I owe it all to You.

# One

FOLKS LIKE MY FRIEND CAMILLA HAVE lofty goals before they die, like stealing a kiss from a movie star or seeing the Sahara. Mine's quite simple. I want to tell my story unsevered, as if it was actually *me* walking the sweltering pavement of Burl, Texas. But the words never spill out that way. Not in the foothills of adolescence or adulthood or even today as I recount my life in retrospect.

My childhood flickers in front of me like a black-and-white movie. Used to be I couldn't watch more than five minutes of it, as the popcorn dropped kernel by kernel onto my tear-soaked lap. The weight of the story made me shut my eyes and clamp my hands over my ears until the memories faded in gray silence. But Jesus stayed with me, holding my hand while the images assaulted me. As He held me, I was able to watch through to the credits. Truth be told, there are still times I long for the projector to sputter so I can rewind, in vain hope that watching the tree limbs will be replaced with playing hopscotch or wearing Popsicle-stained smiles.

Someday I'll be able to admit I'm Mara.

Mara's world was quite small, as it should've been for a girl who'd barely trod nine years on the country roads of East Texas. New to town, her feet now explored the treed world called Burl, Texas—home of the Fighting Armadillos and the Stinging Scorpions. The Loop, a stoplight-dotted road that encircled the center of Burl, served as one of Mara's play boundaries. Even her house was small; its paint was sunshine yellow, and although it made her smile when she skipped by, it maddened her that the paint was flaking.

"It's the tyranny of the South," Aunt Elma would say nearly once a week. "Peeling paint. Bugs too big. Hotter 'an heck." Aunt Elma always wiped her brow with a red bandana when she complained of the merciless heat, and she did it with a dramatic flourish as if she might faint clear out.

Although Mara would never say it out loud, Aunt Elma was the ugliest beautician in Burl. She couldn't figure out *why* folks actually asked the woman to beautify them. It didn't make sense. The government gave Aunt Elma some money, so she only had to beautify folks twice a week. When that happened, Mara was supposed to stay inside the house; she had permission to go outside only if the house was burning clear to the ground—otherwise she had been told to stay put, a nearly impossible request when the adventure of living in a new town enticed her to walk its sidewalks, learn its secrets.

According to Aunt Elma, life had always been better "back there." She meant in Little Pine, where they'd lived before.

"Back there folks knew how to be friendly, how to give and give some more. If your neighbor shot him two possums, why, he'd give you one, sure as day," Aunt Elma would say. And then she'd fan herself again.

Truth was, Mara missed Little Pine too, but not because of the possum-giving neighbors. She missed friends, yes, but mostly she missed Nanny Lynn, Aunt Elma's mother. They'd lived on the family farm on the outskirts of Little Pine, an hour and a lifetime from Burl. There, Nanny Lynn taught Mara how to bait a hook, scrape and paint a fence, build a tree house, say simple prayers to God out in the fields, and swift-kick an angry rooster. "I knows you'll grow up to be someone amazing," Nanny Lynn would whisper over her as she tucked her between sunshine-smelling sheets. "God told me."

But Nanny Lynn couldn't live forever, no matter how much Mara prayed in the fields.

They buried her at Little Pine Cemetery next to her husband, Walter, the same day the For Sale sign marred the farm. It took near a year to sell the place—to some Dallas man who wanted to make it into a housing development called Pine Tree Estates.

Three months ago when the house was packed up and the man was ready to bulldoze, Mara moved to Burl with a few boxes and a nervous stomach—like June bugs were dancing a jig inside her. At least Aunt Elma didn't make her go to the last month in a new school.

While Nanny Lynn loved on her, she'd never really thought about who her parents were and why she didn't live with them. Nanny Lynn was big enough to fill her heart and quiet her questions. But when they buried Nanny Lynn next to Walter, Mara's heart emptied and her questions grew.

Now, whenever Mara asked Aunt Elma who her parents were, Aunt Elma repeated the same exact words—like when their Beatles record of "I Wanna Hold Your Hand" got stuck on "I think you'll understand." A large woman with blotchy skin, she pinched her face into a concerned look and said, "Now, don't you be asking things about them folks, you hear? Truth is, they don't exist. Your father is God, and He made it so me and Nanny Lynn was your mama. She ain't here anymore to answer you, rest her soul. And I don't know how to answer. Don't ask me again."

Every time Aunt Elma said those things, Mara replayed "I think you'll understand. I think you'll understand. I think you'll understand" in her head. And every week, she vowed to ask Aunt Elma the same question, hoping to jar the needle of her repetitions. Once, just maybe, Aunt Elma would skip over her usual words and give Mara a clue as to who or where her parents were.

She had one measly memory of what might have been her real home. She was two, or maybe three, and she sat on a green porch swing. A woman sang behind her, pushing her. Mara sometimes would lie in bed listening to the crickets chirrup, mulling over the memory and wishing she could remake it. She'd squint her eyes tight and tell herself, *Turn around and look at the singing lady. Turn around.* But her memory wouldn't obey her. And although Aunt Elma spouted all sorts of random, careless words about the glories of life "back there" in Little Pine, she never leaked one clue about the faceless lady.

It was that summer, the summer of 1979, that Mara took to watching the tree limbs waltz above her—the summer that snailed by. Aunt Elma seemed bothered nearly every day with Mara underfoot. "You need more tending to than a cow about to calve for the first time," she said. "I'm plain sick of your questions, child. Go talk to the rocks or the neighbor cats, you hear? I'm fixin' to take a nap on my day off. Skit scat, baby."

"Yes, ma'am," Mara said. Once Aunt Elma was in the

skit-scatting mood, she could not be reasoned with, and that's the truth. So Mara went looking for rocks or cats to entertain. One day she walked around the block looking for a friend—any friend in this new town—while sweat ran drippy races down her forehead.

"Hey, Beautiful," came a cracking voice behind her.

Mara jumped. "You scared me half to death," she said to the older freckled boy. He wore shorts, an old T-shirt, and a green John Deere baseball cap that had seen better days.

"My name's General."

"What kind of name is that? You an army brat?"

"Nah, my first name is Robert E. Lee."

"That's your first name?"

"Yep, my mama wanted it, but Daddy, he got tired of saying so much, so he shortened it to General. Folks who know me real well call me that. Only teachers call me Robert E. And folks at church. My daddy's a preacher, you know."

"Really?" Mara looked at General's feet. They looked like blocky two-by-fours.

"Well, he mainly repairs air conditioners, but on Sundays, he's a preacher. From the church down 'round the corner. He's the finest preacher this side of Louisiana. At least that's what I think."

"I haven't ever been to church, but I'd like to. My Nanny Lynn, she seemed like a church person on the inside, but she never went to one. Now she's in heaven singing in the angel choir. My aunt says churches are for buttoned-up hypocrites. What's a hypocrite, anyway?" Mara took out her handkerchief and mopped her forehead with a flourish, exactly like Aunt Elma.

"I have no idea. But I do know folks are buttoned up when they come to church. I even have to wears me a tie.

Makes me crazy." General sat down right there in the middle of the sidewalk. "C'mon, sit here a while. I haven't had company in a long time, 'specially not from a beautiful gal. Been on restriction."

There was something in the way he said "beautiful" that wasn't pretty. Her skin felt creepy-crawly while crickets did a hundred hiccups in her stomach.

He patted the cement. When he did, a red cloud of dust flew up and gritted her eyes. The summer sun had transformed spring's clinging red mud into a fine layer of dust. It was impossible to remove the red stuff from shoes or socks, so Mara had taken to wearing flip-flops.

Something told her to turn around and walk away, but her loneliness in a friendless town kept her stuck to the sidewalk.

"Restriction? Were you bad?" Mara tried to sit, but the cement was roasting so she stood back up.

"Yeah, I suppose. But my parents are strict—too strict." He took off his hat, ran his fingers through his red hair, and looked up at her. "Hey, you wanna go to Central Park? We could play. I like to play with beautiful gals."

The word danced awkwardly in her head. It didn't make sense. *Beautiful is for dogwoods in bloom or ladies in magazines. But me, beautiful? I'm only nine years old.*

He stood back up, and that's when Mara realized how tall he was—nearly two cats taller—and it made her uneasy in a way she couldn't put her finger on.

He grabbed Mara's hand—tight. At first she wanted to tell Aunt Elma where she was going, but then she remembered the lashing she got the last time she woke her. So even though she didn't want to go, as his bigger hand engulfed her own, she resigned herself to follow the capped boy toward the center of the sleepy railroad town.

And then she had a strange thought—*he doesn't even know my name.*

Good parks had swings where you could kiss the sky with your toes, but Central Park was not really a place for playing; it was more of a tree place. There were nearly forty varieties of trees, but mostly pine, pecan, and the well-loved Burl dogwood. In March, according to Aunt Elma, folks in big tour buses would drive through the park with its narrow roads and angular switchbacks and gawk at the dogwoods in full white bloom. Old people with cameras would step off the buses in a precarious sort of way and pose for pictures—something Aunt Elma thought ridiculous. "How many pictures does someone need in front of a silly tree?"

As General pulled Mara deeper into the woods and farther away from the park's winding path, her heart thumped a little harder and a little faster. She strung questions together like plastic beads on a string. "What's that tree over there? Does your daddy like air conditioners? I don't have a daddy, but I have an Aunt Elma. She's a beautician, but the government pays her too. How old are you? Do you think cats really have nine lives?"

General ignored her, his grip on her hand growing painful.

Mara remembered the words of Nanny Lynn while they poked holes in garden hoses for something Nanny called drip irrigation. "If a man ever makes you feel uncomfortable, you run, child. Run as fast as you can. And pray, pray, pray, you hear me?"

But he was a boy, his grip was too tight, and her prayers caught in her throat.

"Here. Sit down. Here's a nice place, Beautiful." His voice sounded different—less like a boy and more like a general.

*I want to go. I need to run.*

"Anyone ever told you how to make a baby?"

Mara shook her head, even though she knew perfectly well what went into baby making, thanks to Kristin Moeller, her world-savvy friend from Little Pine.

"You want to have babies someday?"

Mara nodded but then she wished she hadn't. Instead, she wished to rewind the last minutes. Wanted to choose a different street, a different sidewalk. She wanted to run from the moment she'd met General.

"Well, this is what you have to do." General tugged at his belt.

Mara squirmed, trying to free herself, but somehow he'd managed to remove his shorts while squeezing her arm.

She could not find her voice to pray.

Or scream.

Or cry.

The only thing she could find inside herself was a sickly feeling that something very bad was happening and she could do nothing about it unless she could find her voice. She took a deep breath and tried to talk, but no words came out. She closed her eyes, prayed, *Give me my voice*, and breathed again.

"Let go of me!" she hollered. "I want to go home! I'll scream! I can scream real loud!"

# Two

"GO AHEAD. AIN'T NOBODY HERE TO listen, missy. Now this won't take long, so you best lie back and let me do my business." He grinned.

He stole pieces of Mara in one vile act on a bed of Central Park's brambles. She vowed that she'd never be a mommy if this was how it felt to make babies. She'd stick with owning cats.

She curled into a ball as General stood above her to zip up his shorts. His menacing shadow blocked the sun. Her rocking body shuddered. Even when the sun fell again upon her face, she shook. She wished he would go away. Hoped he would leave. Prayed he'd turn around and walk away.

But he didn't. He stayed. Watching her.

Terror pumped through her from her heart to her still-tingling arm where his grip had made indentations matching the shape of his hand.

General, now fully clothed, dropped once again to the ground over her on all fours like an overgrown ape.

*No! Please, no! Not again!*

Her chest moved up and down fast. Though she tried to tell herself to breathe easier, slower, her lungs wouldn't listen; instead, they gasped for air.

He pulled her retreating face toward him and held her chin in a vise grip, his chewing-tobacco breath polluting the air her lungs screamed for. The bill of his John Deere cap shaded them both.

Mara's shivers hatched shivers.

"If you tell anyone, I'll kill you. And I'll kill that aunt of yours. I'll be back tomorrow at two thirty, and if you ain't out on the sidewalk where we met today, I'll hunt you down, you hear? My daddy's got a big gun."

Fear stole Mara's words.

He stood up, blocking the sun again, and kicked her, square in the back. Pain mingled with sheer terror exploded throughout every part of her. She gasped. She scrunched her eyes shut, waiting for the next blow.

"You hear me, Beautiful?"

She nodded. He stood, then walked away. He left her there, trembling, bleeding, and feeling that she knew far too much about life. One thing she did know—"beautiful" wasn't a pretty word. It meant trash.

She tried to push herself up only to see him standing under a long-armed tree, watching her. She willed the contents of her stomach to stay in place, but waves of nausea heaped upon her. *Don't do it. Keep it in.* Somehow she felt if she threw up, it would be some sort of strange gift of satisfaction to him. Mara swallowed. And swallowed again.

General's hands were folded across his chest, looking like he'd been impaling squirrels with a slingshot—as if nothing unusual had happened to him that afternoon. "Hello," he said. He sniffed and pulled his bare arm across his nose, catching snot. "Remember. Two thirty." He picked up an imaginary gun and cocked it, aiming it at her head.

Remembering his swift kick and feeling the weight of the air gun on her face, Mara nodded.

"And another thing—you're mine. You'll *forever* be mine." He tipped his cap in mocking salute and walked away through the brambles. The sunlight seemed to follow him.

It didn't fall on her. Maybe it never would.

Every part of her body hurt. Her insides felt like they were turning inside out and outside in. She sat there a long time, burning in places she didn't know could burn. She stood, feeling woozy. A nearby pecan tree became her support while she picked dead grass from her clothes. She pulled sticker-burrs from her hair, one by one, each one pricking her fingers. Blood usually freaked her out, but the blood she saw now hardly registered with her. In what seemed like hours, she made her way back down the winding path General had made. It felt spooky walking in his path, so she made a point not to step in his footprints. She worried he lurked in the shadows, watching her.

But he was nowhere. Though she looked up and down the empty, tree-lined streets of Burl, she was not comforted by its blankness. It made her feel more alone with thoughts that twirled in her head. Alone with heavy sunshine now burning her ivory arms. Alone with a secret she could never tell.

When Slack, the neighbor cat, rubbed up against her leg, she jumped. The peeling yellow paint on her home seemed menacing today, as if the house was shedding. Mara longed to shed the afternoon, to erase its memory forever, but somehow she knew that nothing could remove the pain of this day.

Once safely within the four walls of her home, she went into her room, removed all her clothes, hid her bloodstained underwear in the bottom of the trash can, and pulled on two pairs of underwear followed by a pair of shorts and a tank top.

She went to the bathroom and folded up toilet paper to place in her underwear in case the blood kept coming. Kristin Moeller had told her all about toilet-papering her underwear when she went into intricate detail about what to do when a girl gets her period. Mara looked at herself in the mirror. A fat tear slipped out of her left eye and dropped off her jaw onto her foot. Her face looked different somehow. Sad and old. Though she wore fresh clothes, she felt stained, marked. Aunt Elma was not exactly an observant woman, but Mara worried she'd see the mark.

Dinner came and went as it always had. Aunt Elma seemed preoccupied with whether her boyfriend, Gus, was coming over that night for a date. Why she pined for that man, Mara would never know.

"Do I look pretty, Mara?"

Mara pushed her cold, gray peas around her plate and didn't look up. Every few seconds, she'd tremble and shoot a worried glance at Aunt Elma, but Aunt Elma noticed nothing.

"Mara, I asked you a question, and I expect a prompt answer. Do I look pretty, child?"

"Of course, Aunt Elma. You always look pretty," Mara lied. Why didn't Aunt Elma notice that she shook? *It's probably 105 degrees today, for goodness' sake. Who shakes in weather like this?*

"I think my nap did me some good. Beauty sleep, they call it on those morning shows. I got me some. I do think it favors me. 'Course you wouldn't know nothing about that—you having a nose full of freckles and all." Aunt Elma prattled on about everything and nothing, filling the empty space with word upon word.

Mara shook again. She closed her eyes and tried to talk the shivers down in her head.

"Hello! Wake up! Clear the table, child, and do the dishes

too. I need to get gussied up for Gus. Get it? Gussied up! For Gus! I might could be a comic, I tell you what." She pushed her large frame from the table and went into the bathroom to perform an exercise in futility called putting on makeup.

Mara resigned to washing the dishes, which really weren't very many. Aunt Elma believed in cooking things right in their cans. She'd open the lid with a can opener she'd seen on TV for $5.99 plus tax and put the lid in the drawer to the left of the sink. That poor drawer had dozens of can lids, so when Mara pulled out the drawer, it sounded like a gypsy's shaking tambourine. It smelled of peas, carrots, rotten chili, and Chef Boyardee mini raviolis, Mara's favorite. The lids got to where they clung to each other, caked with mold. After Aunt Elma would toss the lid into the lid drawer, she'd put the can on the electric burner on the countertop. They had a nice gas range the previous owner installed himself right before they moved in, but Aunt Elma refused to use it.

"How am I supposed to cook on this? I'll burn the house down," she told Mara as they were unpacking boxes. So she heated the cans up on a single plugged-in burner. Sometimes the cans would get so hot the labels turned black and curled toward the ceiling, but never you mind—she was being safe, sparing lives by snubbing the demon gas.

It was when Mara wiped the last glass and emptied the sink of spent dishwater that she first noticed a girl outside her window. The brown-headed girl was bouncing one of those red gym balls down the alley back and forth along Mara's property line with a rhythmic *spank-spank-spank*. When the girl spanked the ball to the other end of Mara's property, she'd stop, turn, and go the other way. Mara thought it peculiar; the girl looked like one of those yellow ducks in a shooting gallery.

"Aunt Elma?"

"What is it now?" she barked from the bathroom.

"Can I go out and play? There's a girl out back."

"Suit yourself. Be in by dark."

"All right."

She dried her hands on the soiled kitchen towel, wiped her brow with her handkerchief, and went outside. Perhaps meeting someone new would help her forget what happened and stop the shaking. Before she could speak, the ball-spanking girl walked right up to her, nearly nose to nose. Mara took one baby step back.

"I was wondering how long it would take you to come outside. What's your name?"

"Mara. What's yours?"

"Camilla. Camilla Rose Salinger. Isn't that a pretty name? My mama calls it downright poetic, probably because her name's Rose. What's the rest of your name?"

"Just Mara. Mara Weatherall."

"Just-Mara-Mara-Weatherall. Interesting. You don't have a middle name?"

"No, folks just call me Mara."

"Didn't your mama give you a proper Christian name?"

"I don't have a mama."

"Don't have a mama? Everyone's got a mama. That's nature."

"Well, I don't, so will you please stop bugging me about it?" She regretted ever coming outside to meet this strange girl.

"Sure thing. I'm sorry. I didn't mean no harm, really."

"That's okay. It's been a long, hot day," Mara told her. She motioned for Camilla to follow her to the backyard.

"Why, what happened?" Camilla asked behind her.

Mara had no words to describe her day, so she kept silent. She was afraid if she said something, a scream would come out instead. They sat in the shade on two metal chairs with rusty springs that allowed them both to bend backward and forward like rocking chairs. They did that for some time, neither speaking, rocking under the sky's darkening canopy. Mara pinched her knee skin into a face with lips.

"I'm thirteen," Camilla said, breaking the spell of the comfortable silence.

"I'm nine," Mara made her knee say. "Where do you live?"

"I'm one block over past the crepe myrtles on Anderson Street."

"The old Murphy house? Aunt Elma says it's haunted."

"Yeah, that one. It's my grandmother's house, but she's dead, so we live there. Grandma doesn't haunt it, but there is a room under the stairs that's pretty creepy."

"You have a mom and a dad?"

Camilla laughed. "Of course I do. Mom stays at home, and Dad, well, he works—like other dads. Actually, he's my stepdad. No brothers or sisters—I'm an only. They say one is enough for them." Camilla pulled her brown hair back and looked at Mara. "Do you have any secrets?"

"Why?" *If I told you, you'd run away. Far away.*

"Because if we are going to be best friends, we have to tell each other something secretive that no one else in the world knows."

"I don't like secrets." Mara squirmed. Her chair creaked.

"No one likes secrets. Secrets are things that need to be told. If you keep one too long, you'll burst, sure enough. Or you'll turn into a cat."

"What?"

"A cat, silly. People who keep secrets to themselves, especially deep, dark secrets, turn into cats."

"No, they don't."

"How do you know? Have you ever looked a cat square in the face?"

Mara nodded.

"Well, then you know exactly what I'm talking about. Cats know things. If you keep secrets in too long, you'll turn into one of those cats with a knowing face. I've seen it all the time."

"Where? You're crazy."

Camilla sighed a dramatic sigh. "Crazy is as crazy does, I always say."

"Well, I don't share secrets and neither does Aunt Elma. I suppose you could say we're private folks."

"There's no such thing as private folks in Burl. You know as well as I do that anything whispered somehow makes its way to Denim's radio show. That man, Denim, he'll broadcast your secrets before you can wink your pretty blue eye," Camilla said with a wink.

"I can't wink anyway." Mara kicked at the red dirt with her left foot. Although she was a righty through and through, she prided herself in being what she called left-footed.

"I need to go in. It's getting dark." Her shaking had returned, and the night had nothing to blame for it. Burl nights weren't much cooler than the days, only darker. Mara was tired of stopping the shakes. All she wanted to do was crawl into bed and dream away the shivers.

"Plum tuckered out?" Camilla asked.

"Yeah. It's been a long day." *The longest of my life. Please let me go to bed.*

"Wanna tell me about it?"

"Why should I? You're a perfect stranger. Aunt Elma says I'm not supposed to trust strangers."

"Then why are you playing with me now?"

"Your bouncing ball took my mind off things, that's all.

Besides, how do I know you're not some turncoat Yankee who won't shout my secret to the society ladies sipping their sweet tea?"

"You *don't* know it. That's where the best friend thing comes in."

"And that's another thing. How come you think we're best friends when we've never met before tonight?" Mara pulled her right foot up to her lap and tried to brush off the red dirt, but it clung fast, especially between her toes.

Camilla answered her question with a question. "How do you know we've never met?"

"Don't be spooking me, Camilla Rose Salinger. I haven't ever seen hide nor hair of you until you spanked that ball back and forth in my alley, and that's the honest cross-my-heart-hope-to-die truth."

"What if I told you I've been looking for you my whole life?"

"I'd say you were crazy."

"Crazy is as crazy does." Camilla was good at circles. She made circles with her feet, each going the opposite way—something Mara couldn't duplicate, just like she couldn't pat her stomach and rub a circle on her head. Or was it pat her head and rub a circle on her stomach? No matter, she couldn't do either. Not only could Camilla make opposite circles with her feet dangling from the rusty metal chair, she could make circles with her words. They'd already been to "Crazy is as crazy does," and now they had circled back to it. Mara was beginning to feel crazy dizzy from all this spiraling talk.

"I'm going in," Mara said.

"What about your secret?" Camilla stood.

"I told you, I don't have secrets, and if I did, I'd keep them to myself, sure enough." Mara pulled the creaking screen door toward her and looked back to see Camilla walking away, head down. "Aw, now don't you be pouting. Friends don't pout." Mara let the screen door shut quietly on itself and followed Camilla.

"They do when other *best* friends keep stuff from them." Camilla seemed encouraged, even though her voice forced a pouting tone.

"Will you promise to stick a needle in your eye if you ever *ever* tell this secret to anyone except on your deathbed and then maybe you could tell a priest?"

Camilla nodded. Mara walked her to the rickety gate. She took a deep breath and wondered one more time if she should tell. Then she cupped her hands and whispered, "There's this bully. He chased me and pinned me to the ground, and I couldn't get up."

"I see," Camilla said, tears collecting in her eyes. "That's hard."

They stood there a long time, and Mara wished immediately that she hadn't told her new best friend. Could she be trusted? Or would General see her tomorrow and instantly know she'd told someone, even if it wasn't the whole story? Maybe tonight would be her last night on earth. She shivered.

Camilla didn't ask about the shivers. She put her arm around Mara until the shaking stopped.

After a longer silence, punctuated only by grasshopper symphonies, Camilla said, "You must've been awful scared when he pinned you down."

"Yes, sure as day."

"If it happens again, watch the tree limbs, Mara Weatherall. Watch the tree limbs." Camilla turned toward Mara, cheeks tear streaked. They exchanged something between them, little gifts of friendship through sad eyes. Camilla held Mara's shoulders as lightning bugs meandered in and around them. She blinked her eyes and said good-bye, releasing her light touch on Mara's trembling skin.

Camilla walked through their gate and let it close on itself.

Mara watched as Camilla walked down the darkened alley, her red ball held in front of her like a pregnant lady. When she got to the edge of the property line, Mara half expected her to turn like she had earlier. Instead, Camilla stopped and looked right at her.

"At least you won't turn into a cat."

# *Three*

THE NEXT DAY, SUNDAY, MARA STOOD on the scorching pavement. It was 2:25. She made sure she arrived early to avoid getting shot. Even though getting shot on TV didn't look so bad, the way General had said it made her think it would be a painful ordeal, much worse than drinking orange juice after brushing your teeth.

General sauntered down the road at three o'clock. Mara tried in vain to calm her trembling hands that were now slick with Texas sweat. Waiting had made her jumpy.

"The church's been having a revival. Some visiting prophet preached forever and two years. C'mon, let's go." He held her hand, not tenderly like she imagined a husband or a father would, but like a door slamming on a finger. He warned, "Don't be looking to the left or the right, missy. You walk straight ahead. Don't say hey to anyone. Pretend we're playing, like you're having fun with a friend."

She stared straight ahead at the grand sycamore whose spreading branches welcomed folks to Central Park.

General took her to the same place. At least this time the brambles and prickles were already matted down.

She pled, *Please, God—make him stop.* General's Sunday tie

tickled her nose like a taunting mosquito. She had to look beyond his piggish face to watch the tree limbs—limbs that played clashing sword fights when the wind blew.

Tangled with fears, she shivered. A lone tear tracked down her face, settling in her ear.

She spent the rest of her summer looking behind, beside, and in front of her while her stomach tied itself in knots. Wherever she went, she felt General's presence. His eyes seemed to peer from trees. He was the passenger in every car, the rider on every bike. Many days she stayed cocooned in the safety of the yellow house, closed behind her bedroom door where she could escape into books or drawing or make-believe with hand-me-down Barbies. But then Aunt Elma would shoo her out and she'd be scurrying here and there like a mouse being tracked by a hungry cat.

Sometimes the cat found the mouse and dragged her by the hand to the same park, under the same trees, while she watched the limbs sway under a hot breeze, fighting back tears and trying to talk sense to a stomach that never seemed happy with food in it.

Every time he caught her, the tree limbs did something unique, something that stirred vague longings inside her. If only she could fly above those limbs and look down on them like Nanny Lynn did from heaven. She asked Nanny Lynn to please tell God to make General stop, but somehow, He must've been too busy to listen to the likes of Nanny Lynn. If Nanny Lynn were God, she'd for sure make General stop.

The third time General found her, the limbs caressed each

other when the breeze lifted over their leafy tops. That night Mara held herself in a similar treelike embrace and cried into her pillow while Nanny Lynn listened from heaven.

The fifth time, thunder rumbled the earth, the limbs flashing silver like a flying bass. After that, Mara dreamt of flying away—up and up to heaven where Nanny Lynn danced on golden streets.

The eighth time, the storms twisted and swirled around her instead of blowing straight out, causing the clashing limbs to surrender their leaves.

Each time, she removed her underwear and hid it beneath papers in the trash can, as if shedding it would erase the mark she now wore. She feared someday Aunt Elma would discover her secret. Besides, her supply of underwear dwindled until she had only one pair left.

As General continually sought her out, Mara wished she hadn't told Camilla the secret—even if it wasn't the whole truth. Turning into a cat wouldn't be so bad; cats got fed and petted, sure enough. And they didn't get torn apart on the inside. At least if she had kept her flapping mouth shut, she'd be able to pretend it all away, to carefully tuck this summer of watching the limbs beneath papers in the trash can of her mind. Nothing doing, though. Camilla kept asking questions.

"Does he stink?" Camilla asked one lazy August day. They sat at Mara's dining table, sheltered from the heat by a window-unit air conditioner.

"Who?" Mara poured Camilla a tall glass of tropical punch Kool-Aid, trying to keep her shaky hand steady.

"That bully you told me about." She took a long drink. When she put the glass down, her upper lip was painted purple.

"Like a boy," Mara said. She folded her hands on her lap.

"He a liar?" Camilla licked her lips. "Or a thief?"

"Probably." Mara looked beyond Camilla, pretending interest in one of Aunt Elma's tall stacks of magazines on the counter.

"How do you know? Does he lie to you? Or take stuff from you?"

*If you only knew. Please don't keep asking these questions!* Mara held her stomach. "I just know, that's all. Can we please talk about something else?" Mara felt her stomach turn inside itself. She willed the rumbling thing to keep her breakfast down.

"Sure," Camilla said with an air of boredom. "Let's talk about Aunt Elma, shall we?"

Mara let out her breath and released her hold on her stomach. At least the topic of Aunt Elma was relatively safe. "What about her?" She poured Camilla another glass while hers remained untouched.

"Don't you believe anything that woman says, Mara. I'm sure your Nanny Lynn lady was a kind old woman, but this one? I can see into people, I can. And she is a fakery bakery. She cooks up lies, and makes them look right pretty too—like frosting on a brick."

Mara could tell Camilla was starting down another possum trail. She sat back. There was comfort in letting someone else field words, especially rhyming ones. "Why do you say that?" Mara said.

"It's not just her words; it's her goings on. You watch her, Mara. She's not one who loves the truth like I do. If she found truth, she'd hide it if it didn't flatter her. If it showed her in a happy light, she'd puff it up, sensationalize it."

"Nothing Aunt Elma says is sensational. It's plain and ordinary."

"That's because she's hiding something, covering up the real truth." Camilla pointed her finger at Mara. "She's being sly."

"Sly? About what?" Mara leaned forward.

"The tumor rumor, for instance."

"What do you mean?"

"The word around town is your aunt's been seeing an awful lot of that doctor on the Loop. Been seeing him steady since y'all moved here. The way I figure it—either she's in love or she has a tumor." She took another long drink.

"She's not in love with him. She likes that Gus man—the police officer. They've known each other for years. Says she met Gus when she used to live in Burl over five years ago. She was sad to leave Little Pine, but at least she had Gus to move here to." Mara made patterns on her sweating glass with her index finger: moons, stars, and circles.

"If that's true, then the tumor rumor is correct."

"No, of course not! She'd tell me if it was. She's a blabberer—can't even keep her age a secret, which, by the way, is twenty-nine."

Camilla jumped to her feet. "That's what I'm saying, Mara. Fakery bakery. Twenty-nine! You can't possibly believe that, can you?"

"That's what she said."

"Don't believe everything folks tell you. That's what my stepdad always says. And he knows a lot about what he calls human nature."

"When am I ever going to meet him?" Mara asked.

"I don't know. Sometime." Camilla squirmed, something Mara hadn't seen before.

"And why don't you invite me inside your house? Is it really haunted and you don't want me to know?"

"Nah, it's my mom, she . . . well, she's a little shy around folks."

Mara swallowed. Seeing Camilla stammer her words was new indeed. "I'm not scary."

"Anyone who's not kin is scary, Mara. Can we please drop the subject?"

Mara nodded. She'd have to settle for playing on the sidewalk in front of Camilla's big house, and that was that. For a moment she felt she should reach across the long table and grab Camilla's hand, but she couldn't seem to lift her own fingers.

Camilla stood. "Gotta go. Mom wants me to organize the kitchen—said she'd pay me. But I thought you needed to know about the tumor. Tumors are serious, you know." Camilla ran out the back door before she could say good-bye.

Mara's hands stayed lonely on her lap.

Mara mulled over Camilla's rhymed words: *tumor rumor.* Seems Camilla always told the truth even if it were tinged with horseradish. *Tumor rumor.* Mara decided she'd ask her aunt the next time they were together.

Mara remembered their many visits to the doctor— must've been six visits in the past two months. Aunt Elma made Mara sit in the waiting room on those awful chairs that made her legs dangle, cutting off blood to her feet. She'd wait there over an hour, reading every tired Dr. Seuss book over and over while her feet protested with tingles. She'd counted everything—the light fixtures, the stains on the ceiling (there were sixteen if you counted the smashed June bug), and the wooden animals for Noah's ark where two-by-two had been reduced to one-by-one most likely by thieving, sniffling toddlers.

One evening Aunt Elma took Mara shopping for school clothes. Her aunt seemed sweatier than normal—her armpit wells were larger, even in the air conditioning at the local Value Villa. Folks had very little to do in Burl when the mercury topped 110 degrees except shop at Value Villa. That's why everyone in Burl wore similar tired-looking clothes. Originality apparently was a shunned trait in this town with everyone donning identical Value Villa shorts and flip-flops. Even General wore shorts that looked like Mara's.

"Aunt Elma?"

"Yes, child, what is it now?"

Aunt Elma always said that, emphasizing the word *now* as if Mara had been some sort of constant nuisance. "Well, um, how're you feeling these days?"

"Why in heaven's name are you so interested in my health?"

"Don't know. You seem sick lately—like Nanny Lynn before she died."

"I've told you before. Don't mention her name, especially not in public. Makes me want to weep right here and now." She pulled out a bandana, held it to her nose, and blew.

"It's . . . well, I'm worried. About you."

"Mara, look!" Aunt Elma pointed to an end display. "It's the new foggers. Won't it be great to get one? Gus tells me they can kill every bug in your house like that." She snapped her fingers in a fumbling way; she never could snap—it sounded more like a muted *thwap*.

"Aunt Elma?"

"Yes? Here, take three foggers. Can you hold them?"

Mara nodded and juggled them loosely in her hands until she dropped them into the cart. For a while, she and Aunt Elma walked the aisles—every single aisle—neither of them speaking. Mara decided Aunt Elma was a touch shopper. Every time they walked past something soft, Aunt Elma seemed to have some primal urge to pet it.

Mara couldn't muster up the courage to ask her question again, at least not until they got to the meat section when her aunt tossed in a single serving of ground beef—the pink stuff with all the fat. "Why're you buying that small one? We usually buy the big pack."

"Don't be messing with me. I'm fixin' to go on a diet. All that meat's a temptation, so I'm buying little bits. I have to keep my twenty-nine-year-old shape." This she followed with a long discourse about how good she *did* look for her age, and by the way, Mara should be thankful she was born in 1970—that way she'd always know *her* age.

"Do you have a tumor?" Mara blurted.

The large woman either didn't hear or chose deafness. She began singing with Elvis, whose voice crooned constantly over the store's speakers. It was Value Villa's tribute to the King who died in Graceland two years ago today—August 16, 1977. To see Aunt Elma jiggle and croon to "Heartbreak Hotel" was an odd scene indeed, a scene Mara meant to interrupt.

Had it not been for a piercing voice, she would've had the courage to ask the tumor question again.

"Betty Mae! Git back in the cart, you hear me?" The demand came from the skinniest and greasiest woman Mara had ever seen. Her hair poked out from pink curlers in wild tendrils, and on her feet she wore dingy yellow house slippers. The lady grabbed Betty Mae by the scruff of her T-shirt and crashed her into the cart. Betty Mae, a dirty-looking waif, seemed to resign herself to her mother's treatment. She looked at Mara with pleading eyes.

Mara looked at her hands. She did that whenever her face reddened.

"Sammy! Stop sassing your sister!" Twelve Sammys and Betty Maes surrounded the woman, accompanied by an angry man wearing a baseball cap that read, "My other woman's a three-wheeler."

"Not our kind of people, Mara," Aunt Elma whispered, pulling Mara away from the menagerie, as if that was supposed to explain everything.

"But that woman—"

"Shush now. Time to go."

"But I need some new underwear." Mara's face reddened again, so she looked at her hands that she now tried to steady. She wished she could tell them to stop shaking, but they disobeyed.

"What in heaven's name are you talking about?"

"It's . . . well, you know. School's starting and I need new underwear—oh, and socks too. Besides, aren't you always saying I need to wear good underwear in case I'm in an accident?" *Does Aunt Elma notice my trembling? Does she know my secret?*

"Very well then, child. Let's get you some."

She let her pick out days-of-the-week underwear, something Mara had begged her for last year but Aunt Elma thought vanity. There was something in the way her aunt said, "You get whatever you want" that made Mara uncomfortable. She was well accustomed to being treated like an annoyance— in a way it was a reassurance to her, something she could always count on, like cold peas in a can. When Aunt Elma strained her voice to sound kind, it unsettled Mara's stomach.

They made it to the checkout line in time to see Betty Mae's mama unbutton her blouse, remove a sweaty twenty from her bra, and hand the wadded thing to the poor teenage clerk. The clerk reached out, forming her fingertips into hesitant tweezers, and took the very corner of the bill. When she handed back the change, the greasy woman nabbed it like she was worried the clerk was going to take it. She placed it all, coins included, back into her purse-bra.

"Those are the types that stew up squirrels and make blankets out of possum hides," Aunt Elma said as they hit the wall of muggy oven air outside. "Lord knows how many kids those kinds of people have, seems their families grow two to three kids a year. It's a mystery to me."

Apparently Aunt Elma had said all her words for the day because she turned the radio on high. It was her way of hushing Mara when she needed to think—as if any real thinking could happen when the music pounded in her ears.

Pretty much the only thing working in her Pinto was the radio, so she used it to its potential just because she could. That's the type of person Aunt Elma was. She wouldn't bother much with fixing things, but if things did their job, she used them until they limped and died. Then she'd curse.

The Pinto Aunt Elma drove proudly was a stick shift—a contraption she had yet to master. It was fixing to limp and die soon, Mara was sure of it. Every time Aunt Elma drove, she stalled the thing at least once.

The music stopped, and the radio announcer said, "Now, here's the man you love to hate. He tells the truth about our sorry fate—none other than Denim, the Radio Man on KBBQ."

"Here's that troublemaker again," Aunt Elma said as she turned the volume up a notch.

"Hello, fellow Burlites. Denim here. I speak for those who don't have a voice. Today's news is nothing new—we live in a corrupt little town, I'm telling you. Corrupt with a capital *C*. Seems the bank mafia's at it again, no thanks to the rich man's brother. That judge will do anything he can to crookify this town."

"He's so brash," Aunt Elma hollered at a decibel Mara didn't think possible.

"Let's turn our attention to Burl's finest, the ringleaders of the bank mafia—the police—"

Aunt Elma abruptly turned the radio all the way down.

"What's a mafia?" Mara yelled just as the radio quieted, her voice resounding through the car.

Aunt Elma shot *the* look at Mara—the look that said she was getting close to a licking. "Nothing. None of your business. Now shut your trap. I'm listening to the radio." This time she twisted the dial until country western music interrupted the static. She turned the poor radio to its highest setting. If the windows hadn't been rolled down, they would've shattered in protest.

Mara slunk down and held her ears, hoping her aunt would keep her scolding to herself. Although she was mildly interested in the word *mafia*, she grew weary of hearing more controversy. Her life contained enough. Besides, she hadn't asked Aunt Elma about her parents for nearly a week. It was time. She wanted to know who pushed the green porch swing.

What frustrated Mara more than the lurching and whiplash of the Pinto was that Aunt Elma didn't understand the beauty of driving from point A to point B. The direct route from Value Villa to their home was a straight shot right through downtown Burl, but Aunt Elma always went way around, saying that brazen criminals lived there and it was in their best interest to avoid that part of town forever and ever, amen. Whenever Mara asked about the criminal part of town, or even what the word *brazen* meant, Aunt Elma scolded her and said, "You mind me. Don't go over there. It's for your own good."

If her own "safe" neighborhood had the likes of General in

it, well then, she'd rather scat around the part where the real criminals lived.

After Aunt Elma drove around the town instead of through, they lurched toward the little yellow home; the Pinto's open windows allowed a song about someone's cheating heart to pollute the heavy evening air.

General stood in front of their house, baseball bat and ball in hand.

Mara's stomach curled inside out.

"I wonder what that boy wants. You suppose he's taken with you? Is he your *boy*friend?"

Mara wanted to speak, but her voice was caught down deep in her curling stomach. It was like the nightmares she'd been having where a giant shadow shot after her, chasing her up and down dark alleys. Every time Mara tried to scream, she couldn't. Every dream ended with the ghost-creature throwing her to the ground and slicing her in half with a kitchen knife.

"Cat got your tongue? It looks like he's waiting for you."

Aunt Elma jerked the Pinto into the gravel driveway and pulled the keys out of the ignition before taking it out of gear. As a result, Mara's head bonked on the hard headrest.

General approached Aunt Elma.

*Don't talk to him*, Mara's head screamed. *He's fixin' to kill you.* Fear snagged her stomach, squeezed tight, and wouldn't let go.

"Ma'am, I was wondering if you'd let Mara come play baseball with me?"

*Say no. Say no! Look at me. I need to tell you something!*

"I don't see why not. That's mighty good of you to include Mara. She doesn't have many friends. She's new in town, you know."

Aunt Elma pushed Mara toward General. In that instant, he grabbed Mara's hand—tight.

"Thank you, ma'am," General said in his best Eddie Haskell voice. He even tipped his baseball cap at the sweating lady.

"Be home before dark, Mara, you hear me?"

Mara nodded and looked up at the sycamore tree in her yard, memorizing it.

As soon as Aunt Elma lumbered to the front door, General spoke. "C'mon, girl. It's time for a little baseball."

# Four

GUS'S PATROL CAR WAS PARKED OUT front of the yellow U-shaped house. Before stars pocked the sky, Mara lit upon the porch. When she heard the animated voices of Gus and Aunt Elma filter through the front screens, she opted to slink to the back of the house by the kitchen and enter through its back door so she could slip unnoticed into her room, take off her clothes, and try to forget what had happened.

As she padded to her bed, the floors squeaked under her feet. Someone was coming. Her bed was near the window but not butted up against it, so there was a one-foot gap where Mara rolled quietly off her bed into hiding. She wished her house didn't have rooms all connected to each other like off-kilter train cars. Hers was connected to the only bathroom, followed by Aunt Elma's bedroom, so folks had to tramp through it to use the john.

"You may as well tell her," Gus yelled in response to something Aunt Elma had said. She heard her aunt's footsteps following his.

"Why? It'll only make her ask more questions. And that girl is chock-full of questions. Tires me out." Mara looked under the bed to see both sets of feet facing each other right outside the bathroom.

*Please go away.*

Aunt Elma sighed her sitting-down sigh and planted her fanny on Mara's bed, which squeaked back in complaint. Gus's plop followed, causing the springs to bend the mattress nearly to the floor, obscuring Mara's view of the bathroom's illuminated floor.

"Where is she, anyway?" Gus asked. Mara tried to quiet her breathing. Her insides ached from General's lesson about the four bases, and her neck was at such an angle that it took every bit of will within her to stay put while the crick worsened.

"Out playing. She's supposed to be home by now. I'll be giving her some choice words—you know what I'm saying?"

Gus laughed, if you could call it that. He had a permanent gurgle in his throat that came alive with laughter. "She been playing with that Camilla girl again?"

"Not this time. Seems she has two friends in the world now—Camilla and General."

*How does she know his name?*

"The preacher's son?"

"Yes, that's one and the same."

"Interesting."

"Why so?"

"No reason, really."

"If you ask me, *anyone* who gives me a break from the child is a welcomed friend."

"Suit yourself. Whatever makes you happy, darlin."

"You know exactly what makes me happy, Gus."

Mara held her stomach. She heard the two kiss—or slurp, really.

"Let's go get happy, you hear?"

Gus gurgled a reply Mara could not make out. He cleared his throat. "What about the girl?"

"She'll be home soon. I'll hear the front screen slam, yell at her from my room, and tell her to go to bed. The talking-to will come tomorrow."

Mara watched their feet hurry through the bathroom and heard the door to her aunt's room shut and lock. She pulled herself up from behind the bed and massaged her neck. Without a sound, she tiptoed back through the kitchen, out its back door, and around the house to the front. She sat on the porch a good ten minutes by counting to sixty in her head ten times.

She pulled back the whining screen door and let it slam on itself, shaking the porch.

"You'd best be getting to bed." Aunt Elma's voice carried from her bedroom's screened window to the opened window of the front room. "Expect punishment tomorrow."

Mara reentered her bedroom, put on her Holly Hobby nightgown, and curled up in a ball on her unmade bed. *God, say hi to Nanny Lynn, please. She's probably telling You things about this kid named General. Or maybe she's busy tending Your garden. Mind if I ask You to make General stop too? Nine times he's burned my insides. I suppose that's a naughty way to put it, but I don't know what else to say. I'm nine. And he stole me away nine times. I can't do it again. Can't feel any dirtier.*

Without thinking, Mara placed her thumb in her mouth and sucked. It had been her friend until she was five when Aunt Elma discovered the habit and put Tabasco on her thumb. "Thumb sucking's for babies," she'd said. But having something familiar like a thumb in her mouth calmed the part of her that wanted to cry and cry. Or maybe it simply plugged her up.

*Oh, and if You aren't too busy, can You please show me who the laughing lady was behind the green porch swing?* She twisted and turned in her sheets, entangling her sweaty self in them like a cocoon. She closed her eyes and longed for a hug—for a fond touching from her mama or daddy. For a moment, one tiny moment, she willed her parents alive—parents who would hold her like the sheets held her now. Instead of fighting against the bedding, she slowed her breathing and begged for sleep.

As she started to fall asleep, a tear trailed out of her eye. She wiped it, but another one came. Then another. Before she could wipe them all away, a sob burst from her chest. She smashed her pillow to her mouth, suffocating her wail. Heaving chest, watering eyes, aching heart—all these combined into a display of weepy helplessness. She ached for Nanny Lynn to come back from heaven, to swoop down like a cowbird to rescue her from General. But no matter how much she cried, nothing would change. And this made her weep all the more.

Aunt Elma appeared in her doorway. "You crying? What for?"

Mara heard a tinge of tenderness in her aunt's voice. For a moment, she wanted to spill everything out. "I'm sad."

"Mara, how many times have I told you that Nanny Lynn ain't coming back, no matter how much you boo-hoo?" Aunt Elma walked over to Mara's bed and bent low. In a rare show of motherly attention, she smoothed the covers over Mara and stood. She shook her head.

Mara could see her aunt's wet eyes. *She misses Nanny Lynn as much as I do. Maybe she'll understand if I tell her about General. Maybe that's love behind her eyes.* "I know, but—"

"No buts about it. Get over it. I want no more tears about her. She's gone. You should be over her by now." She turned abruptly and shut the door behind her.

Mara slipped her thumb in her mouth, thankful she hadn't spilled her words, worried if she didn't plug her mouth, she would.

The voices of Gus and Aunt Elma invaded her room. They were in the kitchen, clanking plates and talking. Mara smelled the familiar whiff of bacon, Gus-style—so black you could make charcoal out of it.

Mara put hands to her throbbing head and wiped the morning from her eyes. She took off her Sunday underwear and noticed blood—only a little, but enough to alert Aunt Elma that something was wrong with her. The last thing she wanted was to be carted off to the doctor and have to answer more questions with lies. She rolled her underwear into a ball and put it at the bottom of her hamper. She pulled on Monday's underwear, her blue Value Villa shorts, and a garage-sale striped T-shirt.

"Well, it's about time, lazyhead," Gus said. "You want some bacon?"

She shook her head.

"When Gus speaks to you, you answer—the way I told you to." Aunt Elma bored her words into Mara by pinching her shoulder.

"No, *Officer*, I want some cereal."

She went over to the lower cabinet that held the stale Cheerios and was surprised to see Froot Loops instead.

"What's this? You never buy me sugar cereal. When did you—"

"It was on sale, that's all. I got it when you weren't looking yesterday." Aunt Elma flushed and then turned away.

Mara didn't know what to make of her aunt's antics. Last night, when she and Gus sat heavily on her bed, she called Mara "the child"—as if she were some sort of unwanted doll. But she had bought her Froot Loops and days-of-the-week underwear. Something was fishy, wide-mouth-bass fishy.

"Aunt Elma, can I ask you something?"

"Another question? All you do is ask questions. Someday, I'd like to hear some answers fly out of your mouth."

"It's just that I'm getting older now, and you're awfully busy with stuff."

"You got that right."

"Well, um, I was wondering if you'd let me do the laundry. I think I'd be good at it. I've watched you. Can I?"

At this, Aunt Elma looked like her red face would birth tears. "Sure, child. You be my guest. And while you're at it, why don't you hang the laundry too? The dryer's been squeaking ever since I tumbled my bedspread in it—I'm afraid it's going to bust."

Mara nodded.

"You've got yourself a right nice little maid, Elma." Officer Gus stood stout on his lumber legs and asked Aunt Elma if she wanted a ride in the patrol car. Giggling, she freshened up in the bathroom, and the two left together, leaving Mara and the Pinto behind.

Mara finished her sugary cereal. She'd longed her whole life for Froot Loops, but now that she tasted them, they felt like a bowling ball in her stomach. Maybe sugar wasn't the cure for all her wants. It sure didn't remove the pain. Or the fear.

She put her dishes in the sink, clutched the hamper to her chest, and brought it into Aunt Elma's room where the washer and dryer lived. When the previous owner had made the garage a bedroom, he kept the hookups in the room so he wouldn't have to mess with plumbing.

Mara pulled back the curtains, letting in the hot sun. Dust danced in midair, circling and diving like a fairy dance. Piles of magazines stood propped in every corner. Aunt Elma never bothered to box them all when they moved from Little Pine to Burl; she put pile upon pile in her Pinto and repiled them on the yellow house's floors. Aunt Elma may not have been a learned woman, but she loved her magazines, especially *Good Housekeeping*—a strange thing indeed considering the moldy can-lid drawer and the toilet with a permanent brown-yellow ring.

Mara emptied her clothes into the washer, poured wash soap into its gaping mouth, and started it. Now her aunt wouldn't know her secret and Mara could pretend she was a maid, happily cleaning the house—with no mark, no stain, and no tree limbs.

As a maid, she certainly had to dust. She grabbed a stray sock from one of her aunt's piles and began wiping. There was something deeply satisfying about wiping dust away from things. In one blessed instant, the book or dresser or magazine or mirror or desk or basket was freed from its dusty cloak. For one moment, a dusted object shone, free of the layer that once robed it.

She dusted while the washer whirled and bumped. She dusted everything—the clock, the headboard, the lamp, even the floor. When she got on her hands and knees to hunt for dust bunnies under Aunt Elma's bed, she saw something peculiar—a file of papers under her bed that had no dust, not one speck. The dust bunnies rollicked and rolled over other piles of magazines beneath the bed as she swept her socked hand in their direction, but the papers were clean. She knew about the evils of snooping, but she couldn't help but peek. She pulled the short pile of papers toward her and rested against the mattress and box spring. The papers were housed in a manila folder, the kind Mara's teacher used when she took home math to correct. She felt the folder's top—no dust. Inside, on top of a neat pile of paper, sat a certificate.

Mara mouthed the words as she read, "Certificate of live birth. Burl, Texas. Johnson County. Maranatha Jo Winningham. Born April 12, 1970, to Zady and Jo Winningham." *This Maranatha person has my birthday.* It took a while for the dust bunnies in Mara's head to clear from her mind.

"Maranatha—that must be me!" She said it so loud, she peered behind her shoulder in fear that someone had heard. She mouthed the names of her parents over and over, caressing their names with her mind. A loud knock made her drop the papers, scattering them like wind over Aunt Elma's bedroom floor.

"Just a minute," she yelled. "I'm coming." She retrieved the littered papers and hoped she placed them back exactly as she had found them. The moment she put them back in the manila folder and set them under the dusty bed, she heard footsteps.

# Five

"MARA. MARA! WHERE ARE YOU? I know you're in here."

*Camilla.* Mara sighed, her heart returning to its rightful place.

Mara met her in the kitchen. "What're you doing here? You can't come running into people's houses!"

"I didn't *run*, I walked. And besides, why didn't you answer the door?"

"I was doing laundry in Aunt Elma's room."

"What *are* you—her slave?"

"No, I wanted to help her out, that's all."

"Oh, on account of the tumor?"

"Camilla, stop that. I asked her about it." Mara took some Kool-Aid out of the fridge and poured some.

"And what did she say?"

"Well, nothing, really. She sang Elvis songs."

"See," Camilla said as she took a big swallow of cherry drink, pinking her upper lip. "She's got a tumor, I tell you what. I checked the cheese curls today. Cheese curls don't lie."

"Cheese curls?"

Camilla rolled her eyes and changed her voice—like she

was a professor trying to educate an idiot. "When you grate cheese, you have to ask it a question, see?"

Mara looked at her, confused.

"Three or two grates will do it. You ask the cheese a question, and the cheese answers back with a *Y* or an *N*, for yes or no. It's amazing."

"I don't believe that."

"You have some cheese?"

"I think so," Mara said. She rummaged through the nearly empty fridge and found some greening cheese in the back, next to the neglected jar of kosher pickles.

"That'll do. It doesn't matter if it's moldy. Now, where's your grater?"

Mara found their box grater, hidden behind a pile of *Good Housekeeping*s. It used to be shiny silver when it was a young grater, but now it wore a coat of bronzy rust.

"Okay, now I will ask the cheese a question." Camilla cleared her throat. "Cheese, cheese, answer me please. Does Aunt Elma have a tumor?"

Camilla told her to grate, so Mara pulled the cheese across the grater's holes. *Maybe there'll be a message from God there. Maybe I should ask the cheese if it knows where Zady and Jo live.* Mara looked at the curly pile and didn't know what to think. It looked like a tangle of moldy cheese.

"It's usually in the center—yes, there it is. See the *Y*?"

Mara shook her head. The cheese still looked like a curly heap. She had always wished she owned an imagination, and now she longed for it.

"Right here. Look." Camilla traced a *Y* with her left index finger. "The tumor rumor's correct, Mara. It's as plain as cheese. You wanna go play?"

Mara nodded and followed Camilla to the alley where

they had safely hidden Camilla's red ball under their fort bush—a shrub that was hollowed out on the inside. Camilla named it the Shrub Club.

They hit the ball back and forth in a lethargic game of two square. The heat sucked the spontaneity out of them both.

Mara wondered why Camilla didn't say much, and she wished upon wish that she would. There was simply too much for Mara to think about, and she was accustomed to Camilla's chattering ramblings to fill the world inside her puzzled head. At least then she wouldn't have to think. Or feel.

"What're you thinking?" Mara finally asked. "You're awfully quiet."

"Well, with your aunt dying and all, I was wondering where you are going to live."

"She's not going to die."

"Yeah, but where will you live when she does?"

Mara could see that she was getting nowhere. "I'll live in the Shrub Club. There, does that satisfy you?"

"No—a person can't live in a bush. You'd have nothing to wear except shrubbery."

"Don't worry about me and Aunt Elma, okay? She does *not* have a tumor."

"Suit yourself, but don't say I didn't tell you." They passed the ball to each other like an egg toss. First they handed it to each other, toe to toe, and then each took a giant step back and tossed again. They did this until they were five giant steps back and Camilla missed the ball. She ran like a fool, arms flailing and feet kicking this way and that. Mara laughed—not a polite laugh, but an out-loud belly laugh. Her belly was so used to being angry at her food that laughing felt really good.

"It's nice to hear you laugh," Camilla said as she retrieved the runaway ball. "Here comes the heavy Chevy."

"The what?"

"You know, the heavy Chevy—Gus's patrol car. With him and your aunt in there, the poor Chevy's tummy nearly drags on the ground. Yep, that's one heavy Chevy." Camilla threw the ball to Mara. "You keep it again, okay? Put it in the Shrub Club." With that, Camilla walked toward the crepe myrtles and disappeared around the corner.

Mara hurried into the house.

Aunt Elma machine-gunned Mara with her words the moment Mara opened the back door.

"I don't see the laundry flapping on the line, young lady. Did you forget to do it already?"

"No, um, I was waiting for it to spin in the washer." She felt dizzy, and the sweat on her forehead that had felt hot and sticky now felt cold.

"The clothes have probably been waiting for you." Aunt Elma mopped her face with her wet bandana. Her eyes were red, and mucous ran out her left nostril. "Now get to it before another thunderstorm comes. Besides, I have to run the foggers today."

Mara followed Aunt Elma to her room, hoping she had put the papers back in the right spot. "What in land sakes have you done to my room?" she roared.

Mara backed up till she was framed by the doorjamb. "I thought it was awfully dusty, that's all. I wanted to surprise you."

"Don't you ever, *ever* do anything other than laundry in this room, you hear me?"

Mara nodded.

"Don't nod. What do you *say*?" She pounded over to Mara and grabbed the top of her head with one perspiring hand and her chin with the other, forcing her to nod again. "Say it."

"Yes."

She removed her hands and put them on her stout hips. "Yes, what?"

"Yes, ma'am."

"My piles—did you move them? Any of them?"

Mara started to shake her head, but then remembered she had to actually speak. "No, ma'am. I only dusted the tops."

"Very well then. I know where everything is. What's that saying? A place for everything and everything in its place? That's me." She handed Mara the plastic hamper. "Now, empty the washer and hang the laundry. Stay outside two hours, you hear? I'm setting the foggers, all three of them. If you come inside, you'll die of poison."

Mara emptied the washer and wished she had eyes in the back of her head. She heard the rustling of papers, but she didn't dare turn to see what Aunt Elma was doing. She lifted the heavy laundry basket from the washer and started to exit, turning sideways to fit through the doorjamb. That's when she saw her aunt fingering the manila file.

"What're you looking at?" Aunt Elma said, breathless.

"Nothing, ma'am. I'll stay outside for two hours. I've got my Mickey Mouse watch on." She hurried through the doorway, but Aunt Elma followed.

"Count two hours from the moment I leave."

"All right."

"That boy, General? I ran into him today while I was with Gus. He told me to remind you of your ballgame at two thirty. Best be quick and hang that laundry. He told me to tell you not to be late."

Mara's hands started shaking, so she twisted them around the basket. She knew the message meant she *had* to meet him or he'd kill her or Aunt Elma or maybe even Camilla. Perhaps being killed wouldn't be so bad. At least she'd be with Nanny Lynn. But then she remembered the pain in her heart from missing Nanny Lynn and realized folks would have those same feelings for Aunt Elma and Camilla if they were taken to heaven. She decided she must go today to protect others, even if it meant enduring a tenth time under the tree limbs. "What about lunch?" She tried to look at anything except the papers in her aunt's ham hands. *Does she know I've looked through them? Can she tell?*

"Fix yourself a peanut butter and banana sandwich and eat it outside. I've got foggers to set off. Those bugs don't stand a chance in hades after I get done with them."

"Yes, ma'am," Mara said. She toted the wet laundry through the bathroom and her room and then plopped the whole sorry mess down onto the kitchen table. While she made her sandwich, she could hear papers rustling in Aunt Elma's room. At once she wished two opposite things—one, that she had never disturbed the dustless papers under the bed, and the other, that she had read the papers underneath.

*Zady and Jo Winningham—my parents. God, help me find them. Get me out of here, please.* She'd never been one to pray much. She'd heard some about prayer on the TV when curly-haired preachers threw their arms in the air and shouted, but usually she felt they were a waste of her thoughts. Today, though, she'd try anything short of screaming like Preacher Bobby on channel 8.

Thankfully, Nanny Lynn had taught her the quiet ways of prayer. "Looking at the stars and smiling is prayer," she had said. "Taking a walk on a breezy day and saying thank you in your mind is prayer." Whenever Nanny Lynn spoke of prayer, her blue eyes seemed bluer—like a June sky after a blown-through storm—and Mara felt sure that every word she said was spoken from heaven. *Nanny Lynn, I miss you. Why'd you have to go?* Memories jumped in and out of her mind like popcorn—taking walks through corn fields, learning how to mend with needle and thread, seeing a campfire spark from a match, feeling Nanny Lynn's wrinkled hand wrapped around her own.

She looked at her own hands. So young. Skin like new. But she felt so old. And so alone. And so ugly. Hideous, really. She shook her hands to rid herself of all the memories and downed the sandwich, forgetting to take a drink. Her tongue stuck to the roof of her mouth. Wrestling her way through the back screen door, she set the heavy laundry basket with a thud next to the springy chairs.

Mara heard the familiar slam of the front door and the cough-rumble of the Pinto. Two hours.

She wished she could rewind her life back to before she and Camilla sat on the chairs bouncing back and forth—and even further back to before she met General. She longed for the rainy-day recesses at Little Pine Elementary in the days before this summer of watching the tree limbs. All the students would squirm for a small place on the library carpet to watch cartoons. If they were particularly good during the showing—no yelling, no poking—the librarian would rewind the movies and they'd get to see Bugs Bunny hop backward and Wile E. Coyote fly up from the bottoms of canyons to safety.

If only she could rewind this summer.

Hanging the laundry was harder than it looked. Of all the things Aunt Elma failed at, she did have some sort of knack for making laundry hanging look easy. Mara had to stand at the edge of a springy chair to reach the line, which had been suspended between two sycamore trees. The clothespins were gray-brown, aged by the sun and gully washers, and nearly each one held a small spider. It gave Mara the willies.

She hated hanging underwear before God and nosy neighbors. She was sure a parade of important folks would come driving through the alley as she was hanging skivvies— she flushed at the thought. But that all faded when she hung Aunt Elma's underthings. *Camilla and I could both fit in these.* She turned toward the back door, half-expecting a reprimand from her aunt who always seemed to be able to hear her thoughts. But she was gone.

No Aunt Elma. Only a shut back door—a door that kept her from a pile of papers and a flurry of foggers. She was hanging the last clothing item—Aunt Elma's flowered house-dress—when she first noticed the stain. Down the backside of the tentlike dress ran a dark brown bloodstain nearly one cat long. It made Mara's stomach churn and her teeth itch. *Maybe, just maybe, Camilla is right. Maybe Aunt Elma's got a tumor.*

And that's when she made the decision to leave the back-yard to go hunting for flowers for poor Aunt Elma.

She forgot to look at her watch.

# $Six$

MARA TRIED TO SKIP BACKWARD OUT of the yard. Sometimes she did things like that, backward and unique. As an only child being reared by a disinterested aunt, she found she had to make her world exciting by creating challenges and contests for herself. For the past two months, she'd wanted to back-skip the alleyway to the main street without once tripping or missing a beat. So far she had failed every time, usually because she was interrupted by Slack, the neighbor cat. She was a sucker for cats—especially him because he seemed dejected and needy most of the time. She had even snuck one of Aunt Elma's beautician brushes so she could brush out Slack's matted fur. She'd hid the brush in the hollowed-out shrub right next to the red playground ball. *Maybe living in the Shrub Club wouldn't be so bad.*

This afternoon, on her quest to find flowers, things seemed to be going her way. Slack did not perch like he normally did in the low-lying branch of the neighbor's pecan tree. So she skipped past in the cadence known only to jump ropers and hand slappers. She skipped to the beat of Camilla's oddly transformed rhyme:

*Hear, hear, dear Mara,*
*I want to play with you*
*And fling off all our shoes*
*Go tromping through the dew*
*Jump off a hay bale*
*Onto the field below*
*Avoiding scorpions, our only foe, foe, foe, foe, foe*

When the song finished, her feet met the sidewalk. Victory! *I must be the only person in Burl, Texas, to have ever skipped this alley backward.*

She turned left onto Moore Street, one of several one-way streets heading away from town. Aunt Elma had driven toward town on that street a dozen times. Oncoming drivers would shake their fists at her and she'd say, "Wonder what's wrong with them? Musta got bees in their bonnets." Mara would slump lower in the front seat, both out of fear for her life and sheer embarrassment.

So she walked against traffic toward the town's center, Aunt Elma's forbidden city, and chose to care less about the criminals that lurked there. Mara was on a mission—a flower mission—criminals or no criminals.

Aunt Elma said flowers were better than food, and once, when she was laid up for a day, Gus's handful of flowers made her get out of bed—a simply amazing recovery.

Yep, flowers might heal Aunt Elma's tumor, Mara was sure of it.

Her goal was the Baker House—Burl's history museum. It was open on Tuesdays for field trips, according to Camilla, who learned everything there was to know about Burl from her mama. Field-trip outings were slim pickings in Burl, apparently, so primary classes rotated between the Hasselhoff

Fruitcake Factory, the nearly defunct Dogwood Railroad Roundhouse, and the Baker House, which, Camilla had told her, was surrounded by a flower garden. If she could make her way there, she'd pick a perfect bouquet. Since the museum was closed today, she could forage undetected.

When she saw the Victorian mansions that lined Moore Street, she imagined herself living there like some sort of princess, waited on by white-gloved servants, drinking tea at precisely the right time, wearing a long, flowing gown, and being called "Miss" by British butlers. Fortunately for her, she had an imagination when it came to houses. These houses, although huge and some even stately looking, were mostly in disrepair. Porches tilted, windows were broken and taped, and paint peeled in sheets, revealing weathered wood. It rotted her sensibilities to see such diamonds turned to coal.

When she came to the corner of Main and Moore, Mara stopped. This is where Aunt Elma would turn left and take the Loop round about the town. Two or three times, Aunt Elma nearly drove into Burl's center, only to remember the criminals and do a screeching U-turn, stalling the Pinto right there in the middle of Moore and Main.

Once, Aunt Elma forgot her fear of criminals and nearly drove straight through. Mara remembered studying each house, each stray dog, straining her eyes for criminals. However, being in a Pinto and walking alone down a street were two different things altogether. In the car, metal protected her. On her feet, she was protected by nothing except flip-flops. As soon as she took her left foot and plunged it onto the Loop's crosswalk, she knew she was probably committing some sort of crime. She looked both ways, not for traffic but for criminals, or Officer Gus. No one, not even a car, populated the street. This journey she would have to make alone.

She pressed on toward the Baker House, which Camilla said was three-quarters of the way down the street. A few mosquitoes sang high-pitched melodies around her ears, and her feet started smarting. Flip-flops were poor walking shoes and she wished she could free herself from them at once, but the frying-pan heat of the sidewalk made her think otherwise.

At least the street was tree lined. She recognized the different trees now. When school started she would check out tree books from the library so she could put real names to them. She wanted to know what Droopy was, a tree that seemed to cry and touch the ground with its branches. She wanted to know what the green Wiffle-ball tree was called, whose green mottled fruit pelted her when the wind blew sideways. And Purpley—the tree who blushed a stinging violet every East Texas spring—it must have a name.

Fascinated by names, she had asked Aunt Elma what a roly-poly's real name was. "How am I supposed to know that, child? Its name is roly-poly, sure enough, because it rolls into a ball when you touch it." Mara turned to the school librarian in Little Pine to help her find its true name: *Armadillidium vulgare. He does look like a little armadillo, doesn't he?* she thought the next time she touched one. From that day forward, she never looked at a roly-poly the same. She pretended the poor things used to be armadillos, only to be shrunk by criminals. Every time she saw one, she picked it up, whispered, "Don't worry, little armadillo bug, I'll find a way to unshrink you," and set it back down so it could go on its roly-poly way.

In a baby-name book, she'd found her name's meaning— bitter. She didn't really like the sound of that. It reminded her of the face she made when she drank Aunt Elma's homemade lemonade. Bitter. *Why couldn't my name mean "pretty" or "queenly" or "smart"? And what does Maranatha mean?*

She had two more blocks to reach the Baker House. That's when she saw the house. Rising three stories and surrounded by a rusted iron fence stood the biggest house Mara had ever seen. This house *had* to be haunted. Its grounds took up the entire block, and the yard looked like an overgrown, tangled garden. Vines crept up over windows and doors. Wisteria knotted itself around the front porch, pulling down beams in its wretched grip. The grass was tall enough to tunnel through. To the left of the house stood a flagpole with a frayed and faded Confederate flag, hanging limp.

Even though the house was haunted, Mara knew she wanted to live here someday—maybe as an old maid with fifty cats. One thing for sure, she'd fix it up. She'd make it the prettiest mansion in Burl. Everyone would pass by and think a rich person lived there. And Mara would smile from the windows.

She stood a long time at the iron gate, staring straight ahead at the barely visible front door. *Someone lives here.* She looked left and right. No cars sped by. No bikes rattled and bumped on the sidewalk where she was planted. Even the mosquitoes seemed to have stopped their singing. A voice she couldn't hush up called Mara to come closer to the house.

She tested the gate. It opened, screeching in protest.

She took one step. And then another. And one more— until she stood on the decaying front porch under the canopy of one hundred wisteria vines. She wanted to go farther, but every step she took now came with a loud wood-bending creak. She stood still, afraid even her wispy weight would cause too many squeaks. To her right was a rusted bicycle, entangled in kudzu vine. To her left was a porch swing with only its right side tethered to the porch ceiling, the other end piercing the rotted porch floor.

Sweat burst from her face, more from worry than heat. She looked at the front door that guarded the entry like a silent soldier. She tried the door's rusted handle—locked. It was then that she noticed the unusually wide mail slot in the door's middle. She bent low, her knees pressing themselves into the decayed wood, and lifted the metal slot.

Because of the angle, all she saw was wood flooring and the lower half of the first floor. She scanned the cut-in-half rooms and saw headless paintings, coat trees without tops, and light switches without lights. She puzzled at the high sheen on the floors. Someone obviously lived here and kept a clean house. Everything hushed quiet, like a museum. Off to the left of the entryway she could see a room that held a large black piano; to the right was a dark-paneled room with red-brown chairs and a dining table. The legs of the chairs and table had feet that looked like claws clutching balls.

"Meow."

A tabby cat approached her, padding across the polished wood floor. Its tail stood straight up, but the end had a kink in it, like it had been broken. He stopped and sat, his crooked tail curling around him.

"Here, kitty, kitty," she said, forgetting she was crouched at the mail slot of a haunted house.

The cat stayed put, eyeing her.

"Here, kitty. Here, kitty."

She heard footsteps coming from the back of the house. She wanted to jump up and run away, but her body wouldn't leap. Anchored to the porch, she peered through the open mail slot. Finally, as black shoes and gray pants came into view, she willed herself to stand up, and as she did, she spied the name Winningham engraved above the mail slot. "Winningham," she whispered. She hadn't meant to say anything out loud; she had wanted to run. Instead, she stood there below the wisteria.

"Stupid kids," the black-shoed voice yelled. She could feel the stranger's footsteps vibrate under her feet. "I'm calling the PO-lice, you hear? I've had enough of your pranks."

The footsteps came nearer. Mara took a deep breath and backed away, hoping today's backward-skipping practice would come in handy. Finally, at the gate, she turned toward home just in time to see a pale-faced man in a proper suit standing on the porch, shaking his fist at her. "I'm calling the PO-lice."

Hearing the word *police* put magic tread on her flip-flops, and she ran toward her little yellow house, breathless and heaving. When she turned around the last time and saw an empty street behind her, she collapsed around herself like a roly-poly at her alley gate. *Winningham.* She wished she had a little more courage and had asked the pale man if he knew Jo or Zady, but she had failed.

She looked at her Mickey Mouse watch. His hands pointed to 3:45.

*I forgot about General! This time he will kill me!*

# $Seven$

MARA SPRANG CATLIKE TO HER FEET, running all the way to the meeting place. No General. She looked up and down the street, straining her eyes. Her lungs gulped air at the entrance to Central Park. She had memorized the trail General pulled her through, so she picked her way through it with sad ease. Standing at the spot where flattened brambles withered, she looked around, afraid General was lurking in the bushes to scare her.

But he didn't appear.

Instead, she noticed two haunting reminders in the matted grass where General stole her childhood: her red plastic flower barrette perched atop his John Deere hat. *Is this some sort of trap?* Her heart thumped so loud she thought the squirrels would turn from their nut gathering to see who was making such a racket.

When she didn't see General anywhere, she wondered if he was trying to tell her something. He never went anywhere without his cap—never. She picked it up, examined it like a clue, and put it back on the ground, hoping she hadn't moved it from its original place. She did pocket the red barrette. Aunt Elma was always scolding her about losing her barrettes, right along with scolding her for not curing her freckles with lemon juice.

Mara walked back through the park and then returned to the meeting place—no General.

*He said he'd kill me.* The thought bounced in her head like a wild Ping-Pong ball. She didn't doubt he could do it. She walked back home, thoughts twirling, worries mounting. An ambulance raced by, causing her to jump. It roared around the corner, its siren punctuating the heavy afternoon air.

She rounded the corner too, only much slower and much quieter than the ambulance, and sucked in her breath when she saw where the ambulance had stopped—in front of the yellow house. *Her* yellow house. Fear thundered through her. *Aunt Elma!*

Why she didn't run like a wild turkey to rescue her poor aunt, she didn't know. Instead, she hid behind the neighbor's pecan tree, sneaking long peeks around its girth. She let her hands trace over the rough surface of its skin. Touching something solid made her stomach stop flipping like a pancake.

Nothing much happened in Burl, so when a 911 call came in, all three fire trucks and the ambulance kicked up rocks onto dusty driveways. Red lights circled, sirens wailed, firemen looked painfully hot—all while Mara watched and hugged the tree bark. Whole families from the block, along with several passersby, stood in small, hushed circles, stroking their chins, wrapping their arms around themselves like hugs, or placing their hands on their hips.

Mara glanced at the looky-lous—searching to see if General was among them. When she didn't see him, she rested her eyes on the front door. If she and Camilla had a staring contest now, she'd have won hands down, so steady and wide-eyed was her gaze. More than anything, Mara willed her aunt to walk through the front door and say, "What in tarnation's going on here? You think I'm having a party? Is that it? Skit scat, all of you."

The door opened.

Out came hatted firemen, coughing, a faint blue haze trailing after them.

Behind them came a stretcher that barely fit through the front door. Mara tried to find handles in the tree's bark so she'd have something to hang on to. *She's sick, that's all.* The stretcher tipped left and right as strong men steadied it. It rattled and clanked over the rickety porch. She could hear it clear as day, but she couldn't see the whole scene very well since the porch was paneled halfway up. The men's faces purpled as they carried the stretcher down the three sagging stairs. They let the contraption down with a thud.

*Hey, watch it, you'll hurt her.*

On the stretcher's top was a starched white sheet, whiter than any sheet she'd ever seen, covering a large lump. The sun seemed to follow the lump as the firemen pushed the stretcher toward the ambulance's open mouth. They heaved it into the ambulance and shut the door. But the ambulance didn't come alive with noise and lights. It sat idling in the driveway.

Mara loosed herself from her fierce tree grip. *Maybe that's not her. Maybe it's Gus.* Again she ran, her body becoming sweat. So focused was she on reaching the ambulance that she ran right into a fireman.

"Easy there, little lady."

"My aunt. My aunt—she lives there. Someone's going to kill her." She put her hand to her mouth. She shouldn't say the word *kill*. *Maybe General is near and he can hear me. Maybe I'm next.*

The fireman bent low and looked right at Mara, a soft

look in his eyes. "'Fraid she's already gone," he said with such tenderness it pulled tears right up into Mara's eyes. "Can I call your mama and daddy?"

*Aunt Elma is gone? Dead?* Mara looked around, frantic. She remembered that General's hat rested in the park, blocks away, and that she'd have a hard time finding him without it. She scanned the crowd, looking for redheaded boys, but found none.

The fireman put a hand on her arm.

Mara jumped.

"Are you okay? Would you like me to call your parents?"

"Aunt Elma—she is my mama and daddy. I live here. This is my home." She wondered if the fireman had X-ray vision, if he could see into her thoughts. She tried not to, but she couldn't help but think, *General might have killed Aunt Elma, but it was* my *fault. I should've kept his appointment.* I *killed Aunt Elma.* The words tumbled through her chest at first in a jumble, but then with a rhythm that beat like her heart. *I killed Aunt Elma. I killed Aunt Elma.*

The fireman knelt again, sitting on his haunches, and pulled a loose hair from in front of Mara's face and tucked it behind her ear.

She looked away. *Does he know?*

*I killed Aunt Elma.*

He looked concerned.

Mara wanted to run. But if she did, General would find her.

Gus swaggered toward her.

"Mara, where've you been? I've been hollering for you ever since I found your aunt and called the ambulance."

She looked at her flip-flops, examining the dirty straps. *Why couldn't it be you under the sheet?*

"Answer me!" His anger seemed rattled a bit, like if he kept yelling, he'd cry like a baby.

The fireman stood, towering over thick-bellied Gus. "Give her some time, Gus. She lost her aunt, for goodness' sake."

"What does she know, really? I lost my woman. Ain't nothing worse than that." Gus looked at the ambulance and placed a thick hand over his mouth. He looked toward the sky and took a deep breath. As the sun kissed his face, Mara saw a small tear glisten under its heat. She almost felt sorry for him.

Gus pulled the firefighter a few steps away from Mara and whispered a few things. Mara inched closer. Now she could hear the rumble of Gus's voice.

"Elma's not her aunt—she's a kind soul who took the hungry orphan in. Do you know where I can take an orphan?" He turned to see Mara, caught her eye. "The farther away, the better."

Mara shivered. She wasn't sure what an orphan was, but the way he said it made her think it was a bad thing. Out of the corner of her vision, she saw red hair. Mara shuddered. She turned to look full on and saw a redheaded girl run behind a tree. *At least being an orphan is better than being dead.*

The sad-eyed fireman placed a large hand on Mara's shoulder. "Maybe to Dallas or Houston. I hear they have a large foster care system." He shook his head. "Surely she has some sort of kin."

Gus grabbed the firefighter's arm and took him aside again. They spoke in quiet voices—the kind of voices that grown-ups use when they hide Christmas presents or use words they don't want kids to know. Mara strained to hear, but only heard murmurings and uh-huhs.

She inched around them toward the house. Part of her

worried that General was inside, gun in hand. She could almost see him cocking it and aiming it at her left eye. But the curiosity part of her felt she must go inside and find out what happened. She knew little enough about her own life that she didn't want one more mystery. Not knowing who her parents were etched a large question mark–shaped scar across her heart; she couldn't live with another one.

Fear hiccupped in her stomach with each tentative step she took toward the house. Thankfully, no one seemed to notice her. The ambulance idled and people milled about in their little circles, casting glances at the ambulance, preoccupied with God knew what. She was able to get around them undetected, maybe because she was small, maybe because she was sneaky. Smoky haze greeted her when she opened the front door, stinging her eyes.

*The foggers!*

She backed out of the house, afraid the blue cloud would kill her, and sat on the front porch, shielded by its half wall. As fog seeped through the front door, a new thought came. *It could be as simple as the foggers. She said they'd kill me if I came inside. Maybe Aunt Elma forgot her own advice and stepped inside. Maybe the foggers killed her.*

"What in the world is going on here?" Camilla had discovered Mara's hiding place and sat down next to her, grabbing her knees and looking straight ahead.

"The fireman said Aunt Elma is gone. I suppose he means she's dead, right?" She hoped this was all a terrible mistake and that Camilla could tell her, "No, *gone* just meant she's taken a vacation." But Camilla sat silent.

Mara felt at once that she should cry, but her eyes were so dry they stung. *Aunt Elma is dead. And she's not even my aunt.*

"Grown-ups always use weird words to describe death.

Probably hope it will make us feel better somehow. When I saw Guppy lying belly up in my fishbowl, it didn't matter if my mama used 'passed on' or 'died.' It right near felt the same."

"Yeah," was all Mara said.

"Why aren't you going inside?"

"The foggers were set off. I could die."

"Really?"

"Yeah—you think maybe the foggers killed Aunt Elma?" She wondered why she called Elma her aunt now. Probably because she *had* to call her that. She *needed* to call her that. If Aunt Elma wasn't her aunt, then Nanny Lynn wasn't her blood relative either. Not calling her Aunt meant she was without relations, as Gus had said. One thing was for sure, she wasn't telling Camilla this news. She knew too much already. The less she knew, the safer she'd be. If General *had* killed Aunt Elma and he saw Camilla and Mara together, he might take off after Camilla and kill her too. No, it was time to break away from her. For Camilla's own good.

Camilla had that look in her eyes that said she knew Mara was up to something. She answered, "Hard to say what killed her, Mara. Hard to say. It was probably the tumor."

"What if it was something else altogether?" Mara chided herself for leaking even a little information. Camilla could see right through folks. Mara was glad they were both facing ahead so she could avoid Camilla's searching gaze.

"What do you mean?" Camilla straightened her legs and tried to touch her toes, but she couldn't. Her knees always bent.

"Nothing."

Camilla studied her for a moment. Mara hoped she wouldn't pry hard. Then Camilla asked, "Where are you going to live?"

"I don't know." She hadn't thought about it. Panic shivered through her. Where *would* she live? *Where* was home? *Who* was home? She steadied herself. "Here, I suppose. This is my home. I can make my own dinner. I can use a can opener, and I know how to do the laundry now."

"You can't live here. You're only nine. You don't have a job. Besides, they won't let you."

"Who's they?"

"The authorities, that's who. They're going to take you away. I know it." Camilla sighed one of her crazy sighs and wept—loud.

"Shh! *They'll* hear you."

"Who cares? My life is over. My best friend is leaving me FOR-ever," Camilla said as she pulled her knees up to her chest. "You and I? We're together-forevers, you hear me? You can't move away. You just can't. I'll boo-hoo." She took a deep, shrill inward breath and let out another cry.

Mara looked around, but of course she could see nothing, sheltered as they were on the porch. "Don't be crying. I'll be fine," she whispered. Mara wished things were going to be fine. Truth be told, her mind was a mess of tumbleweeds. She tried to pet Camilla's tangled hair in some sort of "together-forever" gesture, but Camilla brushed her hand away.

Camilla wiped her nose and sucked in her tears. "Well, what're you going to do, then?"

Mara fidgeted with her hands. "I could . . . live with you. In your house."

Camilla said nothing for a long time. It made Mara nervous since Camilla always had Kroger bags full of words for any situation.

Mara made her hands into a church and steeple without people.

Camilla sat herself straighter against the porch's half wall and turned toward Mara again. "I wish you could live with us. Cross my heart. It's just, well, my mama, she—"

"I'm living here and that's that. Don't you bother with me. I told you I'll be fine. And I will be." *I will be fine.* Mara wondered if by saying those words over and over again she'd really believe them.

Camilla slumped a little, supporting her back more by her hands behind her than by the porch wall. "You sure you're going to be fine? I don't think you're thinking straight. Tell me one thing you're going to do that will help your situation."

Mara looked straight ahead while her brain ran a panicky search. She blurted out her first thought. "The first thing I'm going to do is find that KBBQ man, Denim. He'll know how to fix this situation. He says he speaks for those who don't have a voice, and if I'm not one of those folks, I don't know who is."

Camilla scooted to face her. She crossed her legs and bent close to Mara's face. "You can't call him. He's a mystery—like Willy Wonka." Camilla's voice rose. "No one knows who he is or where he lives."

"Shh. I'll find Denim, sure enough. He's the only one who can help."

"I want to help." Camilla patted Mara's leg. "I do."

Mara pressed her hands together and kept looking straight ahead. All she wanted to do was cry a river, to collapse under the weight of Camilla's kind hand, but if she did that now, if she allowed a cry to escape, she'd surely endanger Camilla. Somehow General would find out they were friends, and he would kill Camilla straight out.

Mara placed a hand over Camilla's. "Yeah, I know. No adult wants to take care of me, Camilla, understand? I've

taken care of myself all these years. It's no problem. I will survive all by myself. Aunt Elma," Mara choked, "she never did
much for me anyway except make me do her chores and let
me know how much of a 'financial burden' I was."

"You're nine, Mara. N-I-N-E. No nine-year-old can take
care of herself. You'll become one bitter critter."

Usually Camilla's rhymes shocked Mara into laughter, but
not this time. She stood, looking at the top of Camilla's head,
fighting back tears. "I gotta go in. I'll see you tomorrow. Don't
worry about me, okay?"

"But what about the foggers? You said they'd kill you."

"There are worse things than foggers," Mara said as she
pushed open the front door and stood in its threshold. She
looked over her left shoulder, catching a glimpse of the ambulance where Aunt Elma reclined under a white sheet.

Camilla stood and walked right down the front steps as if
she didn't care if anyone saw her. Her walk was halted and her
shoulders hunched so that Mara thought she was pouting or
crying. *I'll probably never see her again.*

Mara turned and faced the doorway. The haze had lifted,
but its lingering smell stung her nostrils. She stepped into the
house, realizing that even though she wanted to stay, Camilla
was right. This might be her last time through. Even Aunt
Elma's piles made her sad. *I'll miss those piles.*

"Is anybody here?" she said, barely loud enough to hear
herself. When no one answered, she said it again, louder.

Silence. She realized if General had killed Aunt Elma, he'd
be like a criminal running from the likes of Starsky and
Hutch. He would probably not be here. *Yes, he's probably running right now.*

The dining room piles stood nearly to Mara's waist, covered in dust. *Maybe one will hold a message for me.* In childlike

hopefulness, she spun crazily on her right foot, eyes closed and left hand pointing. When she stopped, her finger pointed to one of Aunt Elma's *Good Housekeeping* piles. She picked up the top magazine. "Fifty Ways to Shed Fifty Pounds" graced its dusty cover.

"I suppose you won't have to worry about that in heaven," she said aloud. She gulped in a breath and told herself not to cry. She entered the kitchen. A fogger stood at the center of their table. Aunt Elma hadn't bothered to put her own half-eaten plate of sunny-side up eggs in the sink. Now the eggs were full of fogger juice—hardly appetizing. Mara took the plate, jiggled it over the garbage so the yolks and whites slid in, rinsed it, and placed it in the sink.

Mara's neat-as-a-pin room welcomed her. She sat on the sagging bed, hearing the familiar song from its creaky springs. Behind her was her pillow with Donny Osmond's perfect smile plastered on the pillowcase. Every night she kissed Donny smack on the lips, not because of puppy love, but really out of a vain hope that she'd have his perfect teeth someday. Posters of Olivia Newton-John and Leif Garrett covered her walls, along with four poster prints of children with big eyes. Her dolls sat in a corner. She had sparse furniture, so she had placed her dolls on a box covered with fabric she'd found in the trash can. All three dolls stared blankly at her as if to say, "What now, Mara?"

"I don't know," she answered back. "I just don't know."

She sat there a long time, probably five minutes, looking at her room. She ran her hands over the rough walls—evidence of layers of wallpaper and paint—and remembered the day Aunt Elma brought home butter-yellow paint. "I found this in the dumpster behind the beauty shop. Thought it might suit you," she said. Problem was, the gallon was half-empty.

Her room had been baby-boy blue, and the small amount of paint allowed for only one coat, making her room a hazy green color. She told herself it was the thought that counted. Aunt Elma, with all her sorry habits, at least occasionally thought of Mara, even if her thoughts were secondhand thoughts. No one else did. *Now who will think secondhand thoughts about me?*

Mara stood, letting her bed rise with her, and headed toward Aunt Elma's room. Her aunt had apparently let the sheets fall back over the windows, darkening the room. Mara blinked her eyes, trying to adjust to its dimness. A bloodstain, red and wet, colored the carpet in front of her aunt's bed. Was that proof that General had been there?

*What happened to you, Aunt Elma?*

Blood, in any form, made Mara's stomach ache, so she tried to avert her eyes—an impossibility considering her ingrained curiosity. She'd peek, hold her stomach, and look away, only to repeat the process. The stain was shaped like a pillow-sized kidney bean and shimmered in the dim light. She pushed her hands against her stomach, trying to force it to hold together, but it started to erupt anyway. She stood and ran toward the open washing machine, throwing up into its belly until her stomach emptied. When she finished, she closed the washer lid, grabbed a clean towel from atop the dryer, and wiped her mouth.

She slid down the front of the washing machine and held her face in her hands. Everything tangled from inside her unraveled in tears. She could speak no words but sat heaving and gasping. There on the floor where the smell of blood mixed with fogger chemicals, Mara was alone. With no one to help her. Except her crying self. And maybe God.

But God wasn't too easy to understand. Sure, Nanny Lynn

had happy things to say about Him, even told her a story about someone being angry about seeing only one set of footprints in the sand and God saying it was because He carried the person through his trial, but God didn't seem to be hefting *her* upon His shoulder and carrying her along. And He sure didn't seem to answer any of her prayers.

Mara wiped her tears from her face. No, if she was going to survive, she had only herself—her sad, broken self.

From this vantage point, she could see under the bed where so many dust bunnies had lived on and around piles of stuff. It was then that she remembered the manila folder with her parents' names. Was it still under the bed? She crawled around the bloodstain, looking away, and peered where it had been. No folder.

The front door opened and shut, hard. Mara stood, looking all around the room. *I have to find those files!*

"Mara, I know you're in here." Gus lumbered through the living room in metered *hut-two-three-four* steps.

*She couldn't have them with her. Come on. Think. Where would she hide something?*

Hidden in one of the piles!

*Hut-two-three-four* in the kitchen.

Like one of those Indian ladies with bobbling heads, Mara swiveled this way and that, trying to spot an out-of-place pile. *There, by the dresser.*

*Hut-two-three-four* through Mara's room.

She lunged toward the pile. *Good Housekeeping*s slipped off one another. In the heap, a hint of manila caught her eye.

Success!

Mara grabbed the manila file. She thrust it into the pages of the closest magazine and clutched it to her chest. She stood.

Gus opened the door.

"There you are. What do you think you're doing going through Elma's stuff?"

"I wanted to be near her things. . . . You know, her magazines." This seemed to soften Gus.

"Well, uh, yeah. She did love her magazines, didn't she?"

Mara nodded.

"Listen, you can't stay here. I've put a box in your room. You have ten minutes to put whatever you want in there."

"Where are you taking me?"

"None of your business. Let's just say I'm sick of bothering with you."

"What about this house?"

"What about it? It's mine now. She willed it to me—told me that the other day—and I don't need a skinny little snoop living with me." He backed away from the doorway and motioned for her to go to her room.

Aware that she was clutching the magazine to her chest, she casually moved it to her side, hoping Gus wouldn't notice, and walked by him.

"Mara?"

She jumped a bit. "Yes?"

"Ten minutes, you hear?"

"Yes, sir."

# Eight

THE BOX WAS SMALL. TOO SMALL. How could Mara pack what she *needed*, let alone what she *wanted*, in this whiskey box? It had a grid inside it to hold twelve bottles, so she took that part out, hoping to magically enlarge the thing.

It didn't help much.

She took the manila folder out of the magazine and placed it on the bottom. She'd need underwear and socks, so she pressed them on top of the folder. She didn't have a dress— never had any occasion to wear one—so at least that left more room. Her jeans, both pairs patched with hearts or squares, went in, followed by Value Villa shorts and five T-shirts. She'd need her tennis shoes too, but they took up the rest of the box. No more room.

Her dolls seemed to cry, "Take me, Mara." She shook her head and looked at her watch. Only three more minutes. When Gus said ten minutes, he meant it. He probably had a stopwatch timing her to the second. She looked at her clothes, then at her dolls. She didn't know why it hurt so much to leave them behind. She didn't even play with baby dolls anymore, and these were castoffs from the charity stores. Still—they were a part of her.

With two minutes to go, she got a sudden inspiration. She pulled out all the clothes and layered them on herself, sweating more with each addition. After that, she put her dolls, two 45s, her straight-teethed Donny Osmond pillowcase, a palomino horse statue, and her half pack of Bubble Yum into the box.

"What in the world?" Gus grunted from the doorway.

"You said one box. Here's my box."

He shook his head and swore under his breath. "Time to go."

"Where are you taking me? Dallas?"

"You'll see soon enough." Gus lifted his stare and looked through Mara's bedroom window to the alleyway. "Your friend is here. You wanna say good-bye?"

Mara started to turn, box in hand. *It would be good to say one last good-bye to Camilla.*

General stood in the alleyway. He was far away, but he looked bigger somehow, like a redheaded Jolly Green Giant. He wore a smirk—one corner of his mouth up and the other down. He leaned on his baseball bat and took off his retrieved John Deere cap as if he were paying Mara respect, but his eyes were narrow and she knew his thoughts. He wanted to kill her.

Mara put her hand in her pocket, feeling her red barrette. *He knows I went there. He knows.*

"Go ahead. Say good-bye to your *boy*friend." Gus took the box from her and kicked her on the backside just enough to put her off balance.

She stumbled forward. "That's okay, really. Let's go."

"No. I insist."

"I thought you were in a hurry. Didn't you say I only had ten minutes?"

Gus left her room, dropped her box of things on the kitchen floor with a clunk, and flung open the back door. "Hey, Robert E. Come on in."

Her hands trembled and her forehead leaked cold sweat. Her bedroom twirled crazily around her. She stared at Olivia Newton-John in an effort to stay steady on her feet, but even Olivia danced in ovals. The panorama of her room narrowed into a kaleidoscope, black all around with spinning colors in the middle. Far, far away she could hear a man and a boy laughing and maybe even backslapping. She so much wanted to know what they were saying, but their words became a roaring train in her ears as she whirled to the floor and her kaleidoscope turned black.

# Nine

"RIBS, CHILD. EAT."

Mara didn't know whose voice insisted on ribs. Wherever she was must've been a large place because the woman's voice echoed. She could smell sunshine—an odd sensation since wherever she was, it was a dark place. *It must be the sheets. Maybe the rib lady had hung the sheets in the hot Burl sun.*

The back of Mara's head throbbed, each throb intensifying the pain. *Open your eyes. Open your eyes.*

"C'mon, baby. Ribs will make anyone feel better, don't you know?"

Mara smelled smoke and ketchup and vinegar, and she felt the warmth of food right under her nose. She opened her eyes.

Standing above her was a dark-skinned woman waving a rib in wild circles.

"It always works, yes ma'am. Call it the rib-awakener. I swear I could revive the dead with one of these Red Heifer's ribs, bless Jesus."

Mara rubbed her eyes and tried to turn her head. Shards of pain stabbed her from both sides.

"You look straight up at me and heaven, all right? You've got yourself a goose egg. A real knocker."

"Where am I?"

"Home, child."

"Where's Aunt Elma?"

"Gone to be with the Lord, little lady. Probably soaring above the thunderheads right now, bless the good Lord."

Mara rubbed her eyes and tried to adjust to the dim room. It was darker than Aunt Elma's cavelike bedroom. "Why's it so dark?"

"To help your concussion. Doc says we needs to keep you in the dark till the swelling goes down." The woman with pecan-colored eyes pulled a rag from her button-popping bosom, dipped it in some water, and cooled Mara's forehead. "There now, baby. Close your eyes and rest. You let those blue eyes roll right back in your head and dream of Hershey bars and kittens."

Mara's eyes seemed to understand the woman's words; in obedience, they rolled backward. The room blurred, but Mara squeezed her rolling eyes together and made herself look at this stranger in an apron.

"What's your name?"

"Zady, child. My name's Zady."

"Mama?" Mara said weakly. The kaleidoscope of her vision narrowed again with darkness haloing the room. "I . . . you . . . are my—"

"You gone color blind? I can't be your mama." She wiped Mara's forehead again. "Look at you—pasty and pale with that paper skin. You make me laugh, Maranatha. That's what you do."

"What'd you call me?" Mara tried to pull herself up but in the effort felt her stomach juices rush up and singe her throat. She settled back down onto her wet pillow.

"Your name, child. Maranatha. I swear! Kids these days don't know nothing—not even their own names."

Something slammed shut in the house, like a door or a cupboard. Where Zady had stooped over Mara, she now stood erect as a porch pillar, as if the slamming was an unwritten command.

"What was that?" Mara asked.

"Hush, child. Pretend you're asleep, you hear?"

Mara hushed. In the quiet, she could hear faint footsteps. They got louder like a piano crescendo in Miss Peavey's music class. Then nothing.

Zady whispered, "He's outside the door. Shut your eyes."

The door opened and Mara tried to keep her eyes shut. She hoped she wasn't trying too hard or she'd look all scrunchy instead of sleepy. *Relax!*

"This her, Zady?"

*A man's voice. Was it Gus?*

"Yes sir, Mr. Winningham. The policeman brought her over this evening. Said she fell and hit her head."

*Did she say Mr. Winningham? My daddy?* Mara tried to keep her eyes closed.

"She going to be okay?"

"Yes, sir. Doc said it's a concussion. We need to wake her every hour, even at night, but once she makes it through the night, she should be fine other than a screaming headache."

"Don't use the word 'we,' Zady. She is not my responsibility. You will stay the night and wake her."

"But, sir, my family—"

"Call them. Tell them Mr. Winningham needs you overnight. That should be enough of a reason for anyone in this godforsaken town."

"Yes sir, Mr. Winningham."

Mara could hear a resigned sadness in Zady's voice. She felt bad that she was such a burden to the rib-waving lady.

"Oh, and Zady?"

"Yes, sir?"

"Did she come with anything? Clothes?"

"Well, sir, she was wearing layers and layers of clothes when she came here. I had to take 'em off, she was sweating so much."

"That it? Nothing else?"

*Please let my box be here. My toys, my pillowcase, the file . . .*

"Only this liquor box, sir—crammed full of little girl things, toys and such."

"Burn it all, Zady. Every last bit. You never can tell where lice live. You know how I hate those vermin. Burn it all."

"But, sir, these are her toys. The only thing Maranatha has this side of heaven."

Mara could hear his steps come closer. "Zady, I don't ever want to hear that name again in this house, understand?"

"Yes, sir."

Mara could feel Mr. Winningham's hand on her forehead. More than anything she wanted to jump up and run into the corner—far away from any man's touch, but she had to keep playing the sleeping charade.

His was not a tender nurse touch like Zady's, but a doctor's medical touch. Mara hoped he'd pull his arm away—she even asked God to move it. Mr. Winningham lifted his arm, as if he were promptly obeying God.

"She is filthy. Scrub her."

The footsteps faded away, perhaps down a hallway or corridor, followed by another door slam. *Could this man be my daddy?*

"You awake, Maranatha?"

Mara opened her eyes and nodded. The payment for nodding was pain that whipped from the top of her head to the middle of her back. She tried to stop herself from crying, but a few straggling tears wet her cheeks.

"Don't you worry too much about Mr. Winningham. He's an old man whose bark's louder than his bite. You want a rib?"

Learning from her nod, Mara spoke. "No. I'm not hungry."

"But, child, these are Red Heifer's ribs—the best ribs you ever did eat. Trust me, you'll love them ribs. They'll put some meat on your skinny bones. Really, they will."

"I can't. Too sick." Mara had so much more to say, but her words swirled like tornados in her hazy head. *Where am I? Please don't burn my box. Where's General? Does he know where I am? My toes hurt. How did I get here? Aunt Elma's dead. Gone. She's not my aunt. Is that man my daddy? Zady is short. Why does my tongue feel so big? This room is big.*

"You'd best rest," Zady said. She mopped Mara's forehead again and left the room.

Hearing "best rest" strung together like that in a rhyme made Mara long for Camilla. She'd be good company tonight, on a night when her thoughts were so knotted. Yes, it would do her some good to hear Camilla blab on and on. Mara disliked silence; maybe that's why she liked Camilla so much. She filled Mara's life with so many noises and songs and words that Mara had less time to think about worrisome things. Now she was imprisoned by silence—a silence that forced her to think about making babies under General's lanky body; a silence that led to dreams where she could neither run nor scream; a silence that showed movies in her head, movies of Aunt Elma's lump under the white sheet. *Silence.*

In that silence, pictures of her ride over to this room flashed in her mind like a rapid slide show. She rubbed her eyes, afraid of remembering, wondering if she was remembering what happened that day or if her head was dreaming up things.

Picture one: Gus's squad car—she was lying down in the front seat next to him. The smell of sweat mingled with Old Spice wakened her. The buckles poked into her back, but she was too weak to move away from them. Then, blackness.

Picture two: She sat up and looked at Gus, who was smiling. Why was he smiling?

"Bet you're wondering where I'm taking you. To the other side of town where your kind live. It's good riddance, if you ask me."

But she wasn't asking.

Her mind couldn't form words, let alone string them together to ask a question. She tried to find a word. Something like "where . . ." formed behind her front teeth, but before she could speak, blackness overcame her again.

Picture three: She awoke but pretended to sleep, her left ear listening to the hum of the car that never stalled. Gus spoke in an angry voice on the radio, "I already called him. He's expecting her, sir."

A gruff voice hollered from the radio, "I knew I shouldn't have trusted you, Gus. That house is the last place I want her, you hear me?"

That was it. The slideshow ended. Three snapshots—none of which helped her figure out what was going on.

She could make out a faint outline of a tall window opposite her bed, covered in a sheet. Dusk was settling in because the outline was getting less and less clear, the whole dark wall absorbing what little light came through the shrouded window.

She could hear birds, and for one crazy moment she wished she could talk to one.

"Bird," she'd say. "Please tell me where I am."

The mockingbird would cock its curious head to the left and then to the right. It would then go into a long chirping discourse not only telling Mara where she was but why she was there and where Camilla was and whether she'd be okay.

"Thank you, Mr. Bird. You are very kind and also chock-full of information," she'd say.

"Well, I never!" the lady-bird would say. "I am certainly not a man-bird! The nerve!" And with a proud flip of her tail feathers, the lady-bird would fly away, never to return.

The darkness settled in at last, inking the corners of the large echoing room. Darkness settled into Mara's heart too—a helpless, crying sort of darkness that felt like Aunt Elma was sitting squarely on her chest. Fitful, she drifted in and out of sleep, where dreams swirled in her lumped head. One dream kept weaving its way through—the dream where the dark shadow was chasing her, yelling at her, quickly gaining on her. Again, she couldn't scream, and her usually agile legs turned to JELL-O. She awakened, sweat wetting her pillow, and tried to look around. Darkness. Even the birds had stopped their singing. She fell asleep again and dreamed of the singing lady behind her on the green porch swing. *Turn around,* she told herself, but as she started to turn, Zady came in, woke her up, and took her temperature after removing Mara's thumb from her mouth. She didn't scold her about it either.

All night it went like that: Chasing dream. Camilla dream. Zady nearly carrying her to a bathroom. Chasing dream. General dream. Aunt Elma dream. Zady putting a cool cloth to her head. Gus dream. Cat dream. Zady pulling the covers off and leaving the sheet. Chasing dream. Then sunlight. Thumb in mouth. Morning.

Zady came in, pulled a chair to Mara's bedside, and looked

at her. She held a bowl of yellowish mush, its steam reaching fingers toward the ceiling. Zady had a broad white smile; it seemed to illuminate the gray room like the Cheshire cat's. Her teeth would've been like Donny Osmond's had she had every last one of them. But Zady's remaining teeth were whiter than a picket fence—a picket fence with a few boards missing.

"How you feeling, child?"

"Tired."

"You got tired of me poking you all night, didn't you?"

"No. My head's tired, that's all." Mara tried to pull herself up, and again she felt woozy. This time, Zady pulled a pillow from behind her and set it under Mara's head. Now she could see the room. Her stomach settled back down.

"You need to eat. Or at least drink a little something."

"I don't know." And she really didn't know. She felt as though she never wanted to eat food again, even if it was a forbidden Pop-Tart. Food didn't sound good. Why a headache could be so connected to her stomach, she'd never know.

"I got you some grits. Grits are gentle on a stomach— that's what my sweet grandma always told me. And she was right, Jesus rest her soul." She circled a spoon around and around the grits and finally swabbed up a spoonful and pressed it to Mara's lips.

"I'm not a baby."

"Then don't act like one and take the spoon. I'm not your nurse-lady." Zady's serious voice had a playfulness about it— the kind that corrected and calmed in the same breath.

"You remind me of someone." Mara took the spoon and swallowed some warm grits.

"Who could that be?" Zady stirred the grits again and handed her another spoonful.

"My Nanny Lynn. You have her eyes."

"Maybe she has *my* eyes. Where does Nanny Lynn live?"

Mara swallowed another bite. "In heaven."

"I see. I'm sorry."

A door slammed.

"Mr. Winningham's here. Now, don't you be fretting. Act natural."

From down the hall came, "Zady, you in here?"

"Yes, sir. Same place as last night."

Now that Mara was propped up, it was easier for her to turn her head ever so slightly to the right. There, framed by the doorway, stood an old, pale man—the man from the white house! *Am I in the big white house? Is this man my daddy? My grandfather?*

He wore a hat, the kind she'd seen men wear in black-and-white movies, a dark three-piece suit, a white shirt, a bow tie, and dark shoes. He seemed smaller than his voice.

"Well, there she is. She wakes. Best get to feeding her."

"I am, sir—some grits."

"You burn her belongings yet?"

"Haven't had the chance yet, sir. Don't you worry, though. I'll get to it today, sure as peach cobbler on a summer's day."

Mara tried to memorize Mr. Winningham's face. Did he look like her? They had the same long, narrow face, but his was wrinkled and he wore a permanent frown—like his face would fuss if he dared to smile. No facial hair. He was thin and shortish, but Mara surmised he must've been wiry—one of those men who was feared not for his muscles but for his scrappy fighting. His suit was pressed and clean. She tried to catch his blue eyes, but they stared above her head, never lowering to hers.

She would've thought he was a hollow man had he kept

his hat untipped when he left. It made her mad when he did it. She had him all figured out—a mean old coot, and then he tipped his hat. Hat tippers were good honest folks—well, at least if their names weren't General. *Who is this man?*

Mr. Winningham left as he came, black shoes clipping down the hallway and out the door.

Mara examined Zady's shiny face. She must've been old— over thirty at least—but she had few wrinkles and mahogany skin that shone when light hit it. "You look like Aunt Jemima," Mara said.

"Mm-mm." She laughed and shook her head, back and forth, back and forth. "Girl, you're possessed of the Devil! I'm not that pretty, leastwise not pretty enough to pose for a syrup bottle."

Mara leaned toward her. Zady smiled her picket-fence smile and wagged her head.

"You going to burn my things?" Mara asked while Zady smiled.

"That depends on if you can keep secrets."

"I've learned my lesson about secrets. Poke hot needles in my eyes, and I won't tell any more secrets."

"You let some secrets fly?"

Mara cleared her throat and coughed, the kind that brings parts of lungs up—the kind Aunt Elma used to cough when she had bronchitis. She missed Aunt Elma, missed her ways.

"Here, little lady," Zady said, handing Mara a tissue. "Spit in this."

Mara obeyed. She spit, pressed the tissue together, and then pulled it apart to examine it, just like Aunt Elma. There was something sad and happy about remembering her aunt— sad because Aunt Elma was dead under a white sheet, but happy because she wasn't coughing up blood-tinged phlegm anymore.

"What *are* you doing, Maranatha? You want double germs? Spit's for spitting, not for examining." Zady's smile turned to a gaping cavern.

Mara flushed. "I . . . well, never mind." It was too hard to explain things. She was guilty of mimicking the habits of some strange grown-ups. *I must be the sorriest child in Burl.* She handed the germy tissue to Zady, who pinched it between two brown fingers and threw it away.

"Zady?"

"Mm-hmm?"

"I'll keep a secret, really. Please don't burn my things."

"Enough said. When you're walking around again, I'll let you in on our secret."

Mara sighed a thankful sigh. Everything was unfamiliar to her in this new place. She felt like she was a stranger in her own life. Having her dolls and pillowcase meant everything to her now—they were like an unbroken thread that wove itself through her old limb-watching life to her new hat-tipping life.

Zady picked the box up with a comfortable ease and turned to leave the room. "Don't you worry none, Maranatha. Your box is safe."

Mara watched her box leave the room with Aunt Jemima and felt the weight of Aunt Elma's death in her ribcage. She turned toward the wall, buried her nose in the sunny-smelling pillowcase, and cried like a hyena—loud, high-pitched, and barky until she plugged her crying with a familiar thumb.

# Ten

NOW THAT MARA KNEW WHERE SHE was, she wished her rubber legs would let her explore the big white mansion. But they wouldn't budge, at least unless Zady helped her. A faint whiff of acrid smoke confused her. *Why a fire on another one-hundred-degree day?* Nothing really made sense to her anyway; her life had become kitty-corner.

She pulled herself farther up on the pillow that Zady had propped under her and studied the room. She'd become a good student of details since General had rooted himself in her life, so she contented herself with counting the cracks in the ceiling plaster. Seventy-two, to be exact.

That accomplished, she puzzled at the starkness of the room—white walls, white ceiling, and a wood floor painted gray. She reclined in a twin bed, one of those heavy iron beds that looked more like it should be in a hospital than a Victorian mansion. To her left was a single wooden peach box with a white pillowcase thrown over it in some haphazard attempt to accessorize the room. On top of that was a shadeless lamp with a dusty white bulb.

*Where's the color?* There were no paintings, no mirrors, no draperies except for white sheets thumbtacked to the windows, no other furniture, no toys, no nothing—only a huge echoing room with white everywhere. Even her bedspread was downy white. Her surroundings seemed to poke fun at her—telling her she was like a coloring book uncolored.

She lifted the pillowcase on the crate next to her bed. Hidden under it, in the peach crate's gaping mouth, were some books and a portable radio. She pulled the books out one by one, setting them on the bed next to her lap. *The Black Stallion. The Lion, the Witch and the Wardrobe. Pilgrim's Progress. The Holy Bible. The Little Princess.* None of them were like the flashy paperbacks with bosomed ladies that Aunt Elma had piled next to her *Good Housekeeping*s around the house. No, these were hardcover books, some with ragged-edged pages, others edged with faded gold.

Mara blew the dust off each book. Then she opened each cover as if it were a beautifully wrapped package. She frowned. Every book had a scar. The first blank page where a friend might write a friendly note was torn out—even in the Bible.

She leafed through every page looking for any identifying marks, but there were none—simply old books without clues to the owner. She stacked them one on top of the other on her bed. *Where to start?*

Camilla's wisdom came back to her. Whenever they couldn't decide what to do or when to do it, Camilla would say, "Don't forget to use the eenie-meanies!"

Mara eenie-meanied the books, starting with *The Holy Bible*, figuring that was the correct book to begin with. "Eenie meanie miney moe. Catch a book by its toe. If it hollers make it pay fifty dollars every day. My aunty told me to pick the very best one, and you are not it." Her finger slammed down on the leather Bible. She felt somehow that she was wicked for eliminating the holy book first, but she pushed that thought way down deep and eenie-meanied until she finally selected *The Lion, The Witch and the Wardrobe* by C. S. Lewis, copyright 1950.

Her head throbbed a little less today; its pounding was insistent but seemed farther away like the drumbeats of a distant tribe or a less-than-zealous marching band. Even so, she could only read thirty minutes at a time or the pounding would roar.

Mara was thankful she'd learned to read when she was four. Even Aunt Elma, who was thrifty in her praise of Mara, told everyone that her niece was a genius, a bona fide smartypants. "Read something," she'd say, handing Mara a *Good Housekeeping*. On the one hand, Mara needed and loved the attention she received from being clever; on the other, she felt as if she were a circus act in the tent of Aunt Elma's dreary beautician's life. But Mara's craving for attention would win out and she would read to folks about how to keep a man, what colors are in this spring, how to do one hundred things at once, what an assertive woman does when her boss overlooks her performance, why it's important not to mix bleach and ammonia—interesting, life-changing things like that. Whoever listened to Mara read ten-dollar words would slap Aunt Elma alongside her wide back and say something like, "You got yourself community college material, Elma. That you do."

Mara read C. S. Lewis's dedication page first. "To Lucy Barfield." It was signed, "Your affectionate Godfather, C. S. Lewis." Mara wished she had an affectionate godfather, whatever that was—and that someone would love her enough to dedicate a book to her.

She thought of Mr. Winningham, the pale man who never

said her name. No, he was not the kindly godfather type, she decided—more someone to endure than endear. Fortunately she didn't think he was prone to touch her like General did. The thought of any boy or man touching her, even an accidental brush on the arm, made burning vomit rise to her throat. She would be a feline-loving spinster, that's the truth. Maybe God did want her to live in the big white house—she had sensed as much when she looked through the mail slot. She decided that at nine her life was already laid out before her. *Grow up with an angry old man. He dies. I buy the big white house, fix it up for the world to see, and open the door to homeless cats—a good life, all in all.*

The next days went faster, thanks to Godfather C. S. Lewis, who opened her eyes to the world of Narnia with its fauns, dryads, a great Lion, giants, Turkish Delight, and an evil White Witch. Daily she updated Zady on Aslan's feats and the wickedness of Edmund. Zady, meanwhile, helped Mara get to the bathroom. She brought Burl Delight, in the form of Red Heifer's ribs, every time her stomach rumbled. One thing about Zady—she knew Mara's hunger better than Mara did.

Three days had come and gone now—just like that. In some ways, she felt protected by the dark, enclosed room, but as each day passed, the tension in her gut grew. Once she left her safe room, that day could be her last. General would see to that. It could come when she walked to school. Or when she played outside with a cat. Or when she was eating a Popsicle. Anytime. *Who knows? If General knows where I am, even today could be my last day on earth.*

After three days in a row of the same routine—reading, going to the bathroom, and eating—Mara's fears gave way to boredom. The sun beckoned her, and the birds sang rollicking songs—the sorts of songs that made her long to fly.

Zady must've noticed her wistfulness. She made Mara sit up while she fluffed her pillows. "It's high time you got out of bed more, child."

"Really?"

"Yes, little ma'am."

Zady flung the tangled covers off Mara, revealing her pale ostrich legs underneath. "Girl, look at those pasty white sticks." She flailed her arms like she did the first day with the rib. "C'mon, child. I can tell you's an explorer. Probably hoping you'll find Narnia in this old house. Pull yourself up. That's it."

Mara turned on her side and let her legs dangle over the bed's edge.

"That's it. Now when you feel woozy, pray to Jesus."

Mara stood. The room seemed tilted and twirly. She knew a little about prayer, thanks to Nanny Lynn, but she'd never heard of saying woozy-preventing prayers. She sat back down, bowing the bedsprings.

"I told you to pray."

Mara felt like if she cut apart her brain, she'd find Swiss cheese—full of holes and gaps. She opened her mouth, but her tongue glued itself to the back of her teeth, like it had fallen asleep.

"Haven't you ever prayed before?" Zady softened her voice to the point that Mara thought it held a ladleful of pity. She hated pity.

Mara stood again, this time determined to walk, but her feet felt like cement blocks.

"Pray to Jesus. Say His name, child."

"I thought praying was silent. You know, like in your head."

"No, it's all things. And I happen to think it's best done *loud.*"

"Jesus," Mara shouted, willing her feet to walk. They didn't.

"And?" Zady tapped her foot.

Mara's Swiss cheese couldn't think of a prayer, but she knew she had to say something to stop Zady's foot-tapping impatience. The only thing that rang in her mind was a melody—which she hummed. It took her a few seconds to realize she was humming the ABC song. Opening her mouth, her tongue awoke. She sang mousy at first, but by the time she ended with *W, X, Y,* and *Z,* she was practically hollering.

"That ain't no prayer."

Mara planted her left foot in front of her. "Maybe not. The way I figure it, God can put the letters together any way He wants. Besides, I'm walking, aren't I?" She smiled when she touched the glass doorknob.

"You sure are, baby. C'mon back, will you?"

Mara sang the ABCs again, this time with a little bounce in her step.

Zady grinned. "There you go, beautiful girl. There you go."

Mara frowned. "I'm not *beautiful.* You take that back." Mara's eyes narrowed.

"What on earth, child? What's got in your head? All God makes is beautiful. The trees, the animals, His children."

"There are some children who don't want to be beautiful. Please, don't call me *that.*"

"Sure enough, princess pie." Zady crooked her arm around Mara's shoulder, but Mara recoiled and plunged back into bed, pulling the covers over her.

"I'm tired, Zady. Please leave me alone." She peeked out from her cave.

Zady shook her head, slow and deliberate. Her brown eyes, normally full of life and sparkle, cast themselves downward. "I'll leave you to your books."

Mara's face pinked with shame. *What did Zady do except take care of me? Why'd I have to go and say all that for? I was mean to Camilla the last time I saw her too.*

She thought for a long time why it was that she pushed away the people who weren't mean to her and attracted the ones who were. Maybe she was crazy. "Crazy is as crazy does," Camilla used to say.

Mara's head pounded again, so much that the light hurt her eyes. Reading was out of the question. She took her pillow and put it over her head, darkening her view. She tried to remember every detail of her visit to the big white house only days ago. There was the iron gate, rusted and squeaky, the rotting porch, the door, the mail slot, the piano, the cat, the skinny man. She pulled off the pillow and sat up. *The cat! If this is the big white house, it has a cat.*

She decided it was time to discover at least a little truth. She swung her legs over the side of the bed, where they hung like two knotty twigs, rodlike and cylindrical from the ankle to the hip with huge burled knots in the middle. She hated her knees, even though she could scrunch the loose skin on them to make a face.

Mara hobbled like a wounded possum across the room— she'd forgotten to sing her ABC prayer. The room felt bigger now, the door farther away—like one of her chasing dreams where she could see safety but the faster she ran, the quicker safety ran from her. She reached the glass doorknob, leaning on the doorjamb, panting. Sweat dappled her forehead. She wiped it with her nightgown. But she was determined. If she couldn't figure out life, surely she could count on a cat to be her friend. Cats always loved her, and yet they were independent enough not to need her.

"Here, kitty, kitty. Here, kitty," she called. "Meow. Meow."

She could make a cat's meow like no one else. Sometimes, to irritate Aunt Elma, Mara would meow from her bedroom. Aunt Elma would pound toward her room, screaming, "A cat! A cat! Get it out of here, Mara!" Aunt Elma thought if they looked at you sideways, they'd steal your soul. Mara would answer back, "Don't worry, Auntie. I'll get rid of it for you," which she would by ad-libbing screeching and clawing noises. It was great fun, probably the best acting Mara ever did. And besides, she'd get a Reese's Peanut Butter Cup every time she scared away a demon cat—a fitting reward.

The tabby cat didn't come. Mara's hand clenched the glass doorknob. The farthest she had walked was beyond the door directly across the hall to the bathroom. It had one of those toilets from the pioneer days with a tank way up high toward the ceiling and a handle on a chain you pulled down. That's it. That's as far as she'd been allowed to go.

"Here, kitty. Here, kitty." She took a deep breath and walked down the hall. Each footstep made a creak. There was a door to her left, so she opened it—another empty room, like her own, with a mahogany wardrobe in it. Tall, uncovered windows beckoned her, so she hobbled over to them and peered out. She *was* in the big white house. Her heart did a happy tap dance at the thought. She could see the Baker House museum to her left, the roof of the porch below her, Moore Street in front of her, and the flagpole to her right. She was eye-level with the poor Confederate flag.

"So here I am. Mara Weatherall in the Winningham mansion. What *will* Camilla think?" she said out loud. As an only child she did that sometimes, often without realizing it. She'd be in the middle of what in her mind was a long, drawn-out *thought* about turning roly-polies into armadillos when Aunt Elma would appear in her doorway and say, "Who on earth are you talking to?" It always startled her and, of course, broke the spell of her think-talking.

And then she thought of the wardrobe. *Wouldn't it be wonderful if there were such a place as Narnia?* She had to know if the wardrobe led to Narnia.

She turned.

Standing in the doorway of the nearly empty room was Mr. Winningham—in the same suit and tie as before.

Mara jumped.

He stood there with neither a scowl nor a look of delight on his face. His lips, neither upturned nor in their usual frowning position, were pressed into a thin, almost green line.

"Hi, Mr. Winningham." Mara looked at her long feet, wishing she had more than a nightgown on.

"I brought you something."

*He spoke!*

"What?"

"School clothes. School starts soon. They're on your bed." All these words seemed painful for him to say, as if he was one who measured his words and allowed only twenty or so to be said in an entire day, or he would be consumed by some awful fate, like spontaneous combustion.

"Thanks, Mr. Winningham." She started to walk toward him, but for each step she took forward, he took one backward, like they were walking on some sort of parallel path, always an equal distance between them.

He tipped his hat. "There's something else on your bed too."

"What?" She took another step forward. He stepped back, turned, and clipped down the hall.

When she heard the door close behind Mr. Winningham, she tiptoed to the wardrobe and opened its reddish doors. The scent of mothballs stung her nose, reminding her of Aunt Elma's shoes. "You never know when a moth could build a nest in your shoes," she'd tell Mara. "Best keep three mothballs in the toe of each shoe, I always say."

In the mahogany closet-box were dresses, beautiful flowing dresses, all zipped in hazy plastic bags. Mara unzipped the plastic off one. She'd never really seen a dress close up, at least not like this. Nanny Lynn always wore long shorts and T-shirts, and Aunt Elma wore those snap-down-the-front dresses with loud Hawaiian prints from Value Villa. These dresses were delicate and lacy. With great care, Mara removed each dress from its plastic prison. She caressed the fabrics between her thumb and forefinger like she'd seen Aunt Elma do and wondered why Mr. Winningham had pretty dresses in an empty room. *Who could these belong to? Mr. Winningham's dead mother? No, too modern for that. Maybe he has a sister or a daughter.*

Camilla and Mara had always loved mysteries. After they playacted their way through *Little House on the Prairie*, Mara being Mary and Camilla insisting on being Laura, they traded in their bonnets for magnifying glasses. They'd had an argument about who got to be Nancy Drew, neither one liking to play second fiddle, until they decided that the world was big enough for two Nancys. Nancy Camilla would have loved to solve "The Mystery of the Pretty Dresses" with Nancy Mara.

She missed Camilla all over again and wondered if she'd ever see her best friend again. She wished they were the exact same age—at least then they'd go to the same school. Maybe she'd see Camilla anyway. The schools were next to each other. At least there was that. Mara realized, all at once, that if she went to school, General would be sure to find her. Camilla said you could throw a Super Ball from Howard Elementary and bounce it off Coppler Middle School's roof if you were a good enough thrower. Beyond Coppler was the high school—General's domain—behind a low chain-link fence. *He'll find me.*

For once, she wished she were God Almighty. According to Zady, He knew everything—like Santa knowing when you've been good or bad. She wondered if God got bored since He knew all the mysteries. She wondered if He got His kicks creating mysteries for people to solve, planting clues and leading folks down wrong paths, only to laugh and finally bring them down the correct path where the mystery was solved. She pictured God above a giant maze, prodding some folks like Mara down thorny paths and others—those who had perfect lives—down well-groomed and flowery paths. None of it made sense to her. Although she figured she'd ask God to help keep her safe at school and solve this mystery of the dresses, she didn't really think He'd hear her on either count, even if she sung Him the ABCs.

Besides, He'd probably say she was beautiful.

# Eleven

WHAT MARA WOULDN'T GIVE FOR A rerun of *Gilligan's Island*, or any TV show for that matter. TV was the one comfort she'd had in Aunt Elma's house. It made blessed noise when the house was empty; it drowned out Aunt Elma's Elvis singing; it made Mara laugh when laughter seemed far away.

On the television screen of her mind, Mr. C. S. Lewis had presented his imaginary land of Narnia, which she had unfortunately discovered did not exist through the back of the wardrobe. She had knocked. Solid wood. Though Narnia intrigued her, she longed for the antics of Gilligan, the Skipper too, the millionaire and his wife, the movie star, the professor, and Mary Ann here on Gilligan's Isle. Channel 33. Being nearly alone in this big house with no TV to speak of— at least she hadn't *heard* one—made her feel she was on her own deserted isle.

Mara hummed the *Gilligan's Island* tune while she made her way back to the white room with its seventy-two cracks. She could smell burning rubber, like Little Pine's tire-burning dump—not strong, but enough to make her look out a window. No, no fire.

On the bed, which Mr. Winningham had apparently

tucked in like a straightjacket, was a set of clothes underneath a newspaper—well, not an entire newspaper, just one page. She gave a cursory glance at the clothes—only one set—a white, frilly blouse and a pair of very short Wrangler jeans. *Great, I'll look like Elly May Clampett expecting a flood.*

She picked up the page of the *Burl Atlas.* The headline "Passages" caught her attention. PFC Dogan Phelps was headed to Fort Hood to learn the ins and outs of Jeep repair. Billie Flay had passed her beauty school entrance test. "I am hoping to major in permanent waves," she was quoted as saying. Lillian Buck was promoted from counter girl to pizza engineer at Sam Doodle's Pizzeria and Lube Shop. In the accompanying photo, Lillian Buck smiled from one side of her headgear to the other. Elmore Linbeck was once again "Teller of the Month," which didn't mean much since there were only two tellers at Burl Oil Savings and Loan and the other one—Myra Manowski, the owner's sister—was a bit slow according to Camilla, who learned it all from her mama.

*Why would Mr. Winningham give me this?* She scanned the page twice, top to bottom. On her third look she spied it. In small type in the bottom left corner, under the Hasselhoff's "Buy One Fruitcake, Get One Free" coupon, were the words,

ELMA LOUISE WEATHERALL. BORN SEPTEMBER 2, 1937. DIED AUGUST 20, 1979. BELOVED FRIEND AND RELATIVE. LEAVES BEHIND SEVEN COUSINS, ONE UNCLE, TWO AUNTS, AND FRIEND GUS. MEMORIALS CAN BE MADE AT BURL OIL SAVINGS AND LOAN.

Mara read the obituary several times, hoping she was missing something. Thirty-six words—and no mention of her. *Why? What was so wrong with a thirty-seventh word?* Mara sat on her tightly tucked bed and turned the paper over, hoping there'd be more—maybe a story of Elma's life—but the other side happened to be the Opinion page. *I'm not important enough to be mentioned in Aunt Elma's obituary. Maybe the newspaper knows Aunt Elma's death is my fault. I wandered off, missed General, and now she's dead.*

She sat on her bed beneath the seventy-two cracks and hugged her knees—tight. Her swirl of thoughts filled the quiet room.

*I'm not worth mentioning.*

*I'm an orphan.*

*I should've met General. If I had, Aunt Elma'd be alive.*

*So maybe I'm a criminal.*

*Will Zady find out about me?*

*Does General know where I am?*

*Maybe General will do Burl a favor and kill me too.*

What did it matter? She'd die soon enough.

She would've stayed in that "dump slump," as Camilla was fond of saying when Mara was crabby for too long, had it not been for the radio. She'd been so captured by the books that she had completely forgotten about it. It was about the size of a shoebox and shiny black; it smelled like grease, as though its previous life had been in an auto shop. Its cord was just long enough to plug into the wall beside the lamp.

The buzzing static startled her when she plugged it in. She found the volume, turned it down, and tuned it back and forth until she heard KBBQ 1550 AM. She knew it would come in clear because it was the only local station. Burl was in the middle of small hills, hills that made it hard to receive signals from Constance or even Ellery. Certainly not Little Pine.

She listened as Esther Hasselhoff sang, "I'm a little fruitcake, short and moist. . . ." *This town's sure in love with its fruitcake factory.* Esther finished her cake ballad, followed by static and silence. A man's voice flustered a few words, like "technical difficulties" and "stay tuned." Five more seconds of silence.

Mara put her hand on the dial, intending to turn the radio off. A man's voice, familiar, stopped her. "Denim here on KBBQ. I speak for those who don't have a voice. If you're voiceless, you've come to the right place. I've got a burr in my bustle, and this time it's about a beautician dying. Anybody see that in the *Atlas*? Turns out Elma was the girlfriend of you know who. It's pure speculation on my part, but my thought is it seems a bit odd that Mr. Policeman's gal dies right when—"

"What's all the commotion in here, child?"

Mara turned down the radio like she had been caught with her hands in the Little Debbie package. "I was listening to the radio—filling the quiet."

"Keep it down. Mr. Winningham—he don't like noise of any kind. He's one of those strong, silent types you see in the movies. Don't say much, but when he does, you better be listening."

"Zady?"

"Mm-hmm."

"Why am I here?"

"Because the Good Lord wanted you here. Besides, you belong here."

"Is Mr. Winningham my daddy?"

Zady didn't laugh; she didn't look angry either. Just neutral. "He's a part of you, that's for sure."

"But is he my daddy?"

"There are some questions that can't be answered so easy. That'd be one of them."

Mara sat back on the bed. "Did you know my Aunt Elma?"

"Only from a distance." Zady sat next to her, bowing the bedsprings. "Do you miss her?" She tried to put her arm around Mara, but Mara inched away.

"Yes." She felt guilty then and there because the truth was she missed Nanny Lynn far more than Aunt Elma. All at once she felt she must cry, but she was too weak to endure the tears, so she changed the subject. "Where are my clothes? The ones I had on when I came?"

"He made me burn them. Thought they had bugs in them. I meant to hide them where I hid the other stuff, but while you were snoozing he picked them up off the floor and brought them to me. Told me to throw them in the fireplace. 'It's the only way to kill the vermin,' he said."

"Even my shoes?" She remembered the burning-tire smell.

"Sorry." Zady put her smooth black hand toward Mara, but pulled it back.

"He says I'm supposed to go to school—in these." Mara pointed to the out-of-date blouse and the too-small jeans.

"I'm afraid it's been a long time since Mr. Winningham's had a gal-lady around. That's just his way, and there's no arguing otherwise."

"What about shoes? All I have are flip-flops now."

"I'll see what I can find, okay?"

"Do I really have to wear these clothes?"

"'Fraid so. You'll have to wear them to Jenkins when school starts next week."

"Jenkins? I'm not supposed to go to *that* school. That's for blacks—" She regretted saying it the moment *blacks* left her mouth. Even though Zady's brown skin didn't register anger, she could see red erupt in Zady's brown eyes, or at least she thought so.

"You've crossed the line, child."

"I know. I'm sorry."

"No, you don't understand. This house you live in is across the district line, the line that separates Craigmont ISD and Burl ISD. You live in Craigmont ISD now. You'll be going to Jenkins."

"But Aunt Elma said ruffians go there." Mara folded her school clothes and placed them inside the peach crate. "What's a ruffian, Zady?"

"In her language, I'm supposing it meant black."

"But Camilla—"

"Camilla?"

"My best friend. Or at least she was. I'll never see her now."

"She goes to Howard?"

"Naw, she's thirteen. She'll go to Coppler."

"You know where she lives, don't you?" Zady asked.

"Of course, about seven blocks from here."

"Well, then. Go visit her."

"Really? What about Mr. Winningham?"

"As long as you aren't in his gray hair, he won't care. Be sure you are home for supper, which is every day at six o'clock sharp."

Mara had thought she was a prisoner in the Winningham house, so this news was as good as black-eyed peas with ranch dressing. Once she felt up to it, she'd walk the seven blocks to see Camilla. What a reunion they'd have! She could almost hear Camilla's yakking—and rhyming, of course. Maybe Camilla would know something about what Denim said on the radio—she always knew the buzz around Burl, that's for sure.

Mara picked up her froufrou blouse, remembering that

she'd have to go to a different school than she thought. Something needled her. "This isn't a big town. Why are there two districts anyway, Zady?"

"Good question, darling." She sat next to Mara and smoothed her paisley skirt. "Many years ago when we black folks came to Burl to work the oil rigs on the outskirts of town, the white ladies couldn't stomach their prim and propers supping and learning 'rithmatic with little black heathens. So they got together one day and stormed the mayor's office—apparently had signs and petitions and everything—and demanded he make two districts. One for 'Burl' children, the other one for everyone else. They named this district Craigmont for Elijah Craigmont, the first black farmer in the area."

"Yeah, but what about equal rights?"

"There's no such thing as equal rights in this little town. None 't all."

"You go to Jenkins?"

"Yeah, forever and a year ago. It was a good school back then. It's good today. My Charlie, he goes there."

"He does?"

"Yep. He'll be in fifth grade this year."

"I'll be in fourth." She wrung her hands on her lap, over and over again without even knowing she was doing it.

"You nervous?"

"Yes." Mara stopped fidgeting.

"How 'bout if I have my Charlie boy walk you to school? He'll take you to your class. How'd that suit you?"

Mara brightened. "That'd be great. Thanks." She remembered General. "Zady? Is Charlie big?"

"Biggest in his class." She seemed to sense Mara's fear. "Don't you worry. He can protect anyone, you hear?" Zady rose and started toward the doorway. "You able to walk that far to school in a few days? It's about two blocks away, you know."

"I think so. I made it down the hall."

Zady turned and looked at Mara. "Don't be snooping too much. Mr. Winningham doesn't keep normal hours. He could catch you any old time, and believe you me, he doesn't take fondly to snoops."

Mara nodded. "Zady?"

"Mm-hmm?"

"I, well, I'm sorry—about the 'beautiful' thing."

"Don't you say a thing more, darling." Zady put her hands on her stout hips. She did that when she was about to say more than ten words. "Some folks go entire lifetimes thinking they's trash. Even though you've been treated like a nobody, I see a spark in you. Jesus and the angels smile on you, don't you forget it. Someday—and it may be a long time from now—you'll believe that you is beautiful, and later—you'll think beautiful's a good thing."

"Zady?"

"Mm-hmm?"

Mara looked at her feet, white and thin. "I'm sorry about the 'black' thing too."

"Enough said, little gal. It's gonna take a heap of years to undo prejudice—a huge heap. You know what?"

"What?"

"It starts one person at a time. One person realizing that skin is skin and the heart's what matters. You and me—we both have hearts, right?"

Mara nodded.

"God made these hearts burstin' with beauty, child." Zady patted Mara's chest and hers at the same time. "Mm-mm-mm. Beautiful."

Mara grabbed her folded hobo clothes from the peach crate. "How can I be beautiful when I have to wear these?"

"It's not what you wear, Maranatha. Beauty comes from deep inside."

Mara couldn't imagine a hole that deep.

# Twelve

MARA SPENT A FEW DAYS EXPLORING the house and dreading school. She desperately wanted to see Camilla but was afraid of running into General, so she stayed inside the big house.

Zady brought several pairs of shoes, none of which fit. Mara felt like a wicked stepsister every time she tried one on—either too big or too small, never just right. She'd have to wear flip-flops.

On the morning of the big day, Mara wrestled with her clothes. The pants Mr. Winningham had given Mara were so tight she had to lie back on her bed to zip them. She sucked in as much breath as she could and pulled the tab, letting out a raspy cry when the metal teeth bit a small pinch of her belly skin on its way toward the button. She unzipped her purpled skin, fighting tears. Again she zipped—this time successful. Unfortunately, there was no room for the blouse to get tucked in, so she looked like some sort of pale swashbuckler with a flowing white top and knickerlike pants. Gauchos had been in style two years back, but knickers were never in style. Never would be.

It was six thirty, and she was trying to get ready in a hurry.

It would be her first day of school in Burl. The tight Wranglers didn't help the nervous rumblings of her stomach. What if she was the only white face in her class? Did kids really flush new-comers down toilets? Did the cafeteria really have possum stew on Mondays, squirrel kabobs on Tuesdays, wild hog pie on Wednesdays, armadillo pancakes on Thursdays, and calf fries on Fridays as Camilla had said? She couldn't imagine eating baby calf testicles every Friday.

She was used to having subsidized lunches in Little Pine—something akin to being held prisoner by starch- and goop-wielding cafeteria ladies adorned with hairnets and scowls. On the few days she had been required to bring a sack lunch for field trips, she had to make it herself. Kids had teased her about her aluminum-foiled sandwiches; pickles thrown in, soaking the bag with wet dill smell; a can of peas with a can opener; and no drink. She had never gotten used to teasing. Never. And now there'd sure to be more.

Although the sun was up, it hid behind the overgrown trees in the yard. School started early—at 7:15. A knock at the front door made her look at her watch—6:38. Seeing Mickey Mouse smile back at her made her worry. The last time she wore the watch was the day she missed her appointment with General. At least he didn't go to school in her district. If the worlds really were separate, as Aunt Elma had said, maybe, just maybe, General would forget about her. If she never went to Value Villa or rode in a car, and if she could make sneaky visits to Camilla, then maybe she'd never cross his path again.

Mara waited for Mr. Winningham to answer the door, but the knock was as insistent as a woodpecker. She made her way down the stairs. She still had a headache, and all that looking down at the stairs made her woozy. At the downstairs landing, she took a deep breath, walked to the door, and opened it. A very tall black boy stood in front of her—two cats taller, exactly like General. Her hands began to shake.

"My mama said you needed a walk to school. That right?"

Mara nodded.

"I'm Charlie." He stuck out his hand—brown like Zady's—and waited for her to shake it. "C'mon, I don't bite."

Mara shook his hand but quickly took it back again. "I'm Mara."

"I thought your name was longer, like Marionette or something."

"Nah, just Mara—plain as paper."

Charlie opened the front door wider and motioned for her to come out. "We don't want to be late—not on the first day of school. Here." He handed her a brown sack, its top folded over neatly.

"What's this?"

"Lunch. Mama made it for you. She makes the best lunches. Besides, you can't eat that cafeteria food anyway—Mama says it's not fit for wild hogs."

"Thanks." Mara held it loosely in her left hand, slightly away from her body like it was full of breakables. She looked at it in awe. "No one's ever made me a lunch before."

"You kidding?"

He said it in a way that embarrassed her. She was accustomed to secondhand gifts, secondhand attention, secondhand conversations; she did not know how to respond to this neat brown bag. It was the best thing she had ever received—a totally undeserved gift.

"Please tell your mama thanks, okay?"

"You can tell her sure enough. She practically lives at your house anyway. Now, let's be getting. We've got a few blocks to go. You get breakfast?"

"No. I'm not hungry anyway," Mara said.

They must've looked like an odd duo, more Tom and Jerry than Batman and Robin. Charlie didn't say much. It made her nervous. Used to be she'd talk and talk to silence all the nonsense in her head until Aunt Elma told her to shut up. But now when her thoughts tap-danced in her head, it calmed her more when someone else filled the world with talk—someone like Camilla, who went on and on like a chattering squirrel.

"How old are you?" Mara finally asked, interrupting the silence.

"Almost eleven. Why?"

"Just wondering. You look older."

"Everyone says that, especially Mama when she has to cut the toes off my shoes 'cause I grew another size." He cleared his throat, way down deep, and spit clear across the sidewalk.

"How'd you do that?" Mara asked.

"Simple. You round up all the spit you can like this." Charlie cleared his throat again. "And then you spit." His voice marbled with all that saliva near his tongue. His spit flew again, arcing through the air like a wet, colorless rainbow. "Okay, you try."

"Me? But I'm a girl. I'm not supposed to—"

"Don't be a pansy. How're you going to know if you can do it unless you give it a good try? I'll do it with you."

They leaned their heads back—pale and blonde, brown and black—and cleared their throats in unison. Charlie motioned one-two-three with his fingers and they both let it fly—Charlie's four feet ahead and Mara's one inch. Spit dribbled piteously down her lip, some landing on her white swashbuckler blouse. Charlie laughed, pulled out a pressed hankie, and handed it to her. "You'll get better with practice. I guarantee it. My father always says nothing's worth getting without hard work and practice."

Mara wiped her chin and blouse and absentmindedly handed the hankie back to Charlie. He apparently tried to hand it back to her, but she stood on the sidewalk in front of Jenkins Elementary School, silent and motionless, and ignored the hankie that Charlie waved like a penalty flag in front of her staring eyes. If only she tanned well. Then maybe she wouldn't stand out in the sea of brown faces milling into Jenkins' entrance. *I'll be the only white girl.*

"We're here." Charlie brushed her face with the hankie.

She stared, saying nothing.

"Yoo-hoo. Mara!" He waved the spit-filled hankie once again, finally catching her gaze.

"Oh, sorry. Thanks. I'll be sure to get it back to you."

"You okay?"

"Yeah, I'm fine. You don't reckon I could turn around and run back to the house, do you?"

Charlie laughed a chest-ribbing laugh—like his mama's. It had some sort of magical power; it broke the tension in Mara's throat. She took a breath. She couldn't remember the last time she'd sucked it in and let it out—must've been minutes ago because the new breath felt sweet and needed.

"Over this way, to the left side of the building. I'll take you to the office first." He put his hand on her shoulder.

Mara inhaled sharply and jumped away.

"Sorry about that. I didn't mean to startle you."

"It's okay," she said. But her stomach protested. Charlie was the same height as General. Something about that made Mara want to run away.

The closer she got to the building, the more breath she sipped in. She needed Charlie to laugh again or her face would turn blue. At least her skin would have some color. She searched to find even one pale-faced student, but amid the sea of faces, hers was almost the only white one. She felt sure that everyone, even the shy kindergarteners, stared at her, pointed to her hair, laughed at her lack of color. She looked down at her pink toes wiggling at the tip of her flip-flops.

"No flip-flops at school, young lady," came a voice from behind the front office desk. The voice was attached to a very wide lady with piggish eyes and a wide, thin mouth. Mara looked again at her pink toes and forbidden footwear.

"This is her first time coming here, Mrs. Walker. She doesn't have a rule sheet," Charlie said. "Mama said she's supposed to be in Mrs. Truett's class. Should I take her down myself, or do you need to?"

"Child, I have phones to answer. You think I look like an escort service?"

Charlie smiled.

*How could he smile when this woman was being so loud and angry?*

"I'll take her down and save you the trip, Mrs. Walker." He bowed before her, then stood erect and saluted her.

She stood up and pointed her stout finger in Mara and Charlie's direction. "Charlie! I'll have your hide. Don't you be all high and mighty, you hear me, boy?"

Charlie laughed again and grabbed Mara's elbow.

She let out a quick, "Hey!"

Charlie pulled his hand away. "All right. I get the hint. No touching. Follow me, okay?" He walked down a long outdoor corridor. Before Mara could ask, Charlie said, "She's my aunt. We always give each other ribbings. It's our way. Don't you worry a stitch about her. She's got a huge heart to match her voice—at least that's what Mama says."

Mara held her lunch bag in one hand and realized that she had no pencil, pen, paper, or any school supplies at all. She'd completely forgotten she'd need them. It didn't matter anyway since she had no idea how to get to Value Villa to buy supplies or how to ask Mr. Winningham for them. Sometimes she thought Mr. Winningham must've been a ghost. She hardly ever saw him even though Zady assured her that he *did* sleep there at night and not to be afraid.

"Here we are. Mrs. Truett's class. She's pretty tough, but a good teacher." He patted her on the back, and she jumped away from his touch—again.

"My mistake, sorry." He wore a look of mild amusement and then turned and walked away, leaving her alone in front of her new fourth grade class.

Before she could muster the courage to go in, a tightly braided girl scooted in before her, the braids swaying back and forth in a happy dance. The door now stood ajar, welcoming her to a world she'd never been in—a classroom inside the district chock-full of criminals. Mara inched through the opening, keeping quiet and hoping that no one would notice her.

Everyone looked up—about twenty pairs of eyes boring into her. She hurried to the back of the class and sat in the very last seat, placing her lunch bag carefully below her desk.

"Good morning, class," Mrs. Truett said, rising. "We have a new friend joining us this year. Her name is Miss Weatherall. Everyone say hello properly."

"Hello, Miss Weatherall," everyone said. The girl with the braids was sitting in front of Mara. She turned around and smiled, a toothy glad-to-see-you smile, and then faced forward again.

Mara waved a sheepish wave to the class, her face reddening.

Mrs. Truett stood at her desk, cleared her throat, and

motioned for everyone to stand. They said the Pledge of Allegiance like Mara had at Little Pine Elementary.

Then, as Mrs. Truett called roll, Mara scanned the classroom. The posters were faded but were all aligned perfectly with thumbtacks in each corner. Mara didn't like it when three thumbtacks held something down, allowing one poster corner to curl to the ceiling, so she appreciated the care someone took to keep all corners tacked. Four wide windows looked out to the playground. The equipment was old—the kind her former school had replaced years ago.

Mara was accustomed to waiting for her name to be called, seeing as how she was a *W*. She was always in the back of the line or the last to get her lunch or the last to check out a library book. A name like Weatherall did that for her. Many times she wished she was an Anderson or even a Colby.

"Thomas, Antoine."

"Here."

"Timmons, Chantall."

"Here."

"Weatherall, Maranatha."

Silence.

Mrs. Truett said it again, this time looking right at Mara. "Weatherall, Maranatha."

"Here," Mara said to a classroom of snickering children. She'd never heard a teacher call her Maranatha before. Zady'd called her Maranatha. That manila folder called her that. And it also called her a Winningham.

*Who am I? Am I really a Winningham?* Zady hadn't given her any clues—yet. She knew this: Zady wasn't her mama; that was for sure. Her identity seemed like one of Aunt Elma's one-thousand-piece puzzles of flowers or castles. She'd get real gung ho on one, framing the edge pieces, but the middle would stay hopelessly empty with scattered bits of flower or castle brick speckled across the table in a random mosaic.

In her life puzzle, Mr. Winningham had a few scattered pieces on one side of the boundary. Zady's name belonged to another boundary. Mara's name being Maranatha created the third side, and for some reason she couldn't put her finger on, she felt sure the house framed the fourth side. But there was nothing inside those broken boundaries, only scattered pieces that never seemed to connect and a vague feeling that Aunt Elma's death had something to do with everything—like the one piece that made it all fit.

Things had happened too fast. She'd gone from Burl white girl to Craigmont criminal. From a niece to a nobody. From Mara to Maranatha. From comfortable clothes to clothes that cut off blood to her toes. From being lost in a crowd of white faces to a pale face among a sea of brown.

That day she'd looked through the mail slot of the white mansion, she thought her life would be perfect if she lived there.

It wasn't.

But at least General couldn't find her on this side of town.

# Thirteen

MRS. TRUETT GAVE MARA A NOTEBOOK full of blank pages and a school-bus yellow number-two pencil. The teacher had kind eyes and a full, red-lipped mouth, and she wore the most beautiful flowered dress Mara had ever seen—one that flowed in ripples when she walked.

The braided girl in front of Mara's seat was Vonda Rae Groveland. Vonda Rae showed Mara where the bathroom was, how to line up for recess, and which kids were trouble. Mara thanked her right before lunch. Vonda Rae said, "Ah, shucks, it's nothing, Maranatha. I'm glad to have a new friend." She wasn't a rhyming friend like Camilla, but she was nice enough—that is until she complimented Mara.

"I like your frecks." Vonda Rae pointed her brown index finger right at Mara's nose so close it crossed Mara's eyes to look at it.

"You mean my freckles?"

"Yeah, your frecks. I wish I had me some frecks."

Mara let the comment hang in midair. For a good twelve minutes she felt sour inside. She could hear Aunt Elma's scolding voice telling her she hadn't done enough to get rid of them. It turned the corners of her mouth down. When the lunch bell rang, Vonda Rae skipped cheerfully to get her lunch sack from the cloakroom, oblivious to Mara's frown.

At lunchtime it almost felt like Christmas, and her frown melted away. Sure, Mara was surrounded by darker faces, and the cafeteria rules were stricter—no getting up, for one—but she had a real homemade lunch. She opened the mysterious present's neatly folded top, peering inside. She pulled out an egg salad sandwich, then a baggie full of cheese puffs—the kind that painted her fingers orange. Next was a Dr Pepper wrapped in tinfoil. She didn't know Zady's saving rules, so she carefully unwrapped the Dr Pepper, flattened out the tinfoil, and folded it into fourths—just in case. Popping the soda's top was a thrill for her. Other kids had the cafeteria ladies pull the tabs off their Cokes, but Gus had taught her how to open a beer can in one smooth motion so as to keep her fingers slice free. *This'll impress them.* Mara pulled back the tab in one fluid motion, but she had to jump back when gas and Dr Pepper erupted. Thankfully, Zady'd put a yellow paper napkin in her lunch, so she used it to mop up. She looked up to see a boy across from her, smiling. Mara dropped the soda tab into the can like Gus always did.

"You can't do that. You'll die," said the boy.

"What?"

"My mama says you'll choke and die if you put the tab in the hole. You'd better pull it out."

Mara tried, but her fingers were too big. "I can't."

"Best sip, then," he said.

She nodded and took mini sips, hoping she wouldn't choke and die in the Jenkins Elementary School cafeteria.

The best part of the lunch was last—a fried cherry pie. Aunt Elma always talked about fried pies, that they were heaven's food next to chicken fried steak, but she never let

Mara have one. One day she brought a dozen home and kept them all to herself, saying they'd upset Mara's tender stomach. Well, this fried pie did *not* upset her stomach; in fact, she was sure her stomach was smiling from rib to rib.

Mara didn't know if she should be Maranatha or Mara. To Charlie she was Mara, but to everyone in her class she was Maranatha. Part of her didn't mind much; if she mustered up enough gumption she might be able to set Mrs. Truett straight about her name, but the sticky heat and her own lethargic will melted away with the afternoon. Maranatha was a fine enough name. She hated to admit it, but she liked the way Vonda Rae said it with an emphasis on nath—MaraNATHa.

After school Charlie walked Mara back to the Winningham house. They walked side by side on the root-bumped sidewalk. Tree roots buckled nearly every sidewalk on this side of town, so they both had to watch their step. Charlie knew every bump and walked with his head proudly held high. Mara picked at the ground with her feet, afraid if she looked up she'd trip sure as pie.

Charlie spied the capped boy first. "Looks like there's someone standing under the big pecan. You expecting anyone?"

Even though they were a block away, Mara knew who it was. Her tormentor, wearing his John Deere cap, kicked at the sidewalk. Mara stopped dead. She knew she should move as though nothing were wrong. An actress at heart, plotting never-told stories in her head and casting herself as the heroine, she knew she should walk on by and get inside the house, playacting like she wasn't so afraid she would throw up. But she couldn't. Her hands were already shaking.

"You okay?" Charlie asked.

Mara nodded and tried to make herself walk. At the moment she thought one of her flip-flopped feet might finally move, she heard a door slam. Mr. Winningham stepped down the creaky front steps and opened the gate. He stood as tall as General, his black shoes toe to toe with General's sneakers.

"You want something?" he bellowed.

General mumbled. From a block away, she couldn't make out what he said.

Charlie extended his arm across Mara's chest, the way Aunt Elma would do when she stalled her Pinto and Mara lurched forward. "Stay put," he whispered.

"Mara? I don't know who you're talking about, young man. No Mara lives here. If I ever see you here again, I'll use this."

Mara saw Mr. Winningham pull a long, dark rod from his side. He held it in front of him, caressing its top.

"It's a gun," Charlie whispered.

"You and I, we have an understanding, don't we?"

General must've said something that riled Mr. Winningham. His voice intensified. "Don't we, boy?"

"Yeah," General said in the smallest voice she'd ever heard him speak.

"Take that hat off when you address an adult, son."

General obeyed. He pulled the green hat off, leaving him with matted-down hair. Some of his power left him, like Aslan being sheared hairless by the White Witch.

Mr. Winningham let his gun drop to his side, paralleling his leg. He grabbed the green hat from General's hand and flung it down the sidewalk toward Mara's old neighborhood. "How do you address the richest man in town, son?" He paused, but General said nothing. "What? Cat got your tongue?"

General backed up. The old man matched him step for step and kept his gaze leveled right on General. "You use a small word, only three little letters. S-I-R. Now, before you go scampering off to retrieve your lice-infested hat, what do you *say*?"

"I won't be coming around here, sir."

"Very good. What's your name? I want the full name. If I find you're lying to me, boy, I'll find you." Mara didn't think he could step any closer to General, but he did. "Cough it up."

"Robert E. Lee Townsend, sir."

"Preacher's son, eh? I know your daddy. Know him all too well. Suppose I told your daddy about you hanging around my gate when you should be in school. Would he take kindly to that?"

General shook his head.

"Would he?"

"No, sir."

Mr. Winningham turned on his heel. Mara wanted him to look down the block at her so she could thank him with her eyes, but he walked up the stairs and slammed the door.

General headed toward his hat, not looking back. His usually erect back looked stooped like an old man's. Funny how Mr. Winningham could reduce the most awful kid in Mara's life to a slumping rodent. She wished she could hug the man who flung the hat, but she knew better. He may have defended her, probably without even knowing he was doing her a heroic favor, but he *was* the man who slammed doors. Best to remember that.

General picked up his hat, settled it on his head, and stood straight again. He turned around now, the hat giving him renewed bravery, and walked toward Mara.

She trembled. She swallowed her unruly stomach back.

Charlie tried to step in front of her, but General pushed past him. He leaned in so she could smell his breath and whispered, "You're mine, Beautiful."

He tipped his hat at her and went his way, back toward his side of town.

Mara didn't know whether she should laugh or cry. Instead, she tripped on a protruding sidewalk root and fell end over teakettle. Charlie grabbed her arm right before her head was about to say hello to the sidewalk.

"Whoa, there. You okay?"

Mara nodded. "Thanks." She dusted off her knees and retrieved her school papers.

"What did that boy say?"

Mara ignored the question. "Tell your mama thanks for the lunch."

"Tell her yourself. She's in there—in your home."

"It's not my home. It's just a big white house." The gate squeaked a greeting and the flagpole clanked a hello—a fitting welcome at the end of her day. The porch swing hung askew. Nothing had changed. Except one very important thing.

*General knows where I live.*

# Fourteen

ZADY TRIED TO PRY HER DAY out of her. After Mara thanked her for her lunch, she only gave Zady basic nuggets, shrugged at her persistent questions, and then went upstairs to her room. She'd had a lingering headache all day, and now it pulsated through her temples to the back of her head all the way down her spine. All she wanted to do was sleep. She didn't care if Mr. Winningham caught her walking down the wrong hallway. She didn't wonder about the clothes in the wardrobe. She didn't even want to lurk around like Nancy Drew. She flattened herself on her white bed, school clothes and all, and unzipped. Relief.

Sleep met her in the next instant, thrusting her into a realistic nightmare of General and swaying tree limbs. Mara tried to pull herself out of the dream, even told herself to wake up, but the magnet of her dream world trapped her. The farther she ran from General, the closer he got. Every place she hid, even in the tops of the trees, he found her. Even though the big white house with the angry man seemed to shield her from General, no one could protect her from his advances when her eyes shut. No one.

"Maranatha. Maranatha. Wake up!"

Zady was shaking her shoulder. At first her words seemed distant, like Aunt Elma yelling for her to come home when she'd wandered off. So far away. With the shaking, the voice got closer and General's face, under the shadow of the John Deere cap, faded away like a disappearing mist.

"Maranatha!"

Mara opened her eyes. Zady looked at her with a concern she'd never seen before. It was a mixture of anger and something she couldn't put her finger on.

"Wake up, child. It's nearly six o'clock. Mr. Winningham is a scheduled man when it comes to meals. Come on."

Mara stood, the white room whirling around her.

"I thought you'd never wake up. Your head okay?"

"Feels like it's swimming in a fish bowl. I'm fine though." She smoothed her blouse and looked down at her flip-flops. She had forgotten to take them off before she napped.

"You crinkle my worry lines, baby." She patted Mara on the back and ran her hand around Mara's shoulders in a side embrace.

Mara inched away. "Sorry. I didn't mean to worry you— really."

"No harm done. Now let's get you some dinner. You're a birdie, Maranatha—tiny bones and no fat. You need to eat."

They walked in silence side by side down the wide stairs. Mara watched each foot land on a step—she didn't trust them. That's when she noticed her open fly. She sucked in her breath and zipped it up, her face flushing.

Zady seemed to know her embarrassment. "I have some girl clothes from when Della was your age. If Mr. Winningham will allow it, I'll bring them over. They aren't much, but at least they'll fit."

Mara sat down at the claw-footed dining table she had

first seen through the mail slot—she on one end, Mr. Winningham on the other. He wore the same suit, but his hat lay on the table near his tea glass. Zady brought in plates of steaming food: corn bread, mashed potatoes, black-eyed peas, and cold milk. She'd brought the same food to Mara on a tray the previous week, but it looked and smelled different in the dining room.

"Here's your ribs, Mr. Winningham." With silver tongs, she placed a heap right on top of his helping of potatoes. To Mara, she said, "Mr. Winningham, he likes his ribs. Red Heifer's ribs—the best ribs you ever did eat. It says so on Red's sign."

She dropped a pile of ribs onto Mara's plate and nudged her. "Eat now."

The first time she'd eaten Red's ribs in her white room, she thought heaven lived in her mouth. Juicy, tangy, sweet, with strings of meat falling off the bone—yep, these were the best ribs you ever did eat. She'd never liked ribs before, probably because Aunt Elma's version was dry and tough as nails and tasted like charcoal and sugar. These Red Heifers were like Turkish Delight—they made you hungrier after you ate one. She devoured the ribs, picking them clean to the bone. She attacked the creamy mashed potatoes with similar vigor. "What's in these potatoes? They taste different."

Mr. Winningham cleared his throat, wiped his tangy face on a white napkin, and gave her the don't-talk-at-the-dinner-table lecture without uttering a word. His eyes were full of lectures, full of noes.

"Only potatoes, Maranatha," Zady said quiet and fast. "Butter, cream, salt, and pepper." She walked into the kitchen, humming the kind of tune that makes you want to dance or flat out cry.

Aunt Elma had always made potatoes from a box called

"Tasty Tater Flakes." She added water and stirred them over their plugged-in burner. Sometimes it was all they ate for dinner, with ketchup of course, and maybe some peas heated to lukewarm in their can.

Mr. Winningham ate quickly and efficiently like he was being timed for competition. After wiping his hands finger by finger, he folded his napkin, stood, put on his hat, and walked away, leaving his plate on the table. He had bunched his silverware diagonally on his plate like they were clock hands making 1:35. That was it. He was gone. Mara decided she probably wouldn't see him for another twenty-four hours, until the shadow of the house moved from the front yard to the backyard.

"Nice dining with you, Mr. Winningham," she said, when she was sure he was gone.

Zady came back in and cleared his plate, humming. "I forgot to tell you to be silent. I'm sorry."

"That's okay. Does he always eat so fast?"

"Every night."

"Thanks for dinner. It was delicious."

"Best get used to it, dear. He orders the same dinner every night—like the Israelites and manna."

"Every night?"

"Yeah. Every night I make the potatoes, corn bread, and black-eyed peas from scratch. While things are cooking, I run down to Red Heifer's and pick up a white sack. It used to be they'd put Winningham on the bag, but they don't bother any longer. It's the same order every night, except lately it's been a double order. Proves Mr. Winningham *can* change." She walked over to Mara's side of the table and patted her head. "You're good for him."

"Zady?"

"What is it?"

"Can you tell me now if Mr. Winningham is my daddy?"

"There are things I can say like a free bird—words that fly wild and free like a dove on a breeze—but about Mr. Winningham, I'm caged. I can't say. Sweet Jesus knows I'd like to. I just can't."

"Then he is my daddy?" Mara looked into Zady's brown eyes. Zady was no fakery bakery.

Zady turned as Mara's eyes met hers, a quick pivoting turn like a ballerina on one foot. "A caged bird, Maranatha. Zipped, my lips be." She spoke in heavy tones—the kind adults use when someone's died and they don't want to burden children with the details, the kind Aunt Elma used when Mara asked about the tumor rumor. Zady disappeared into the kitchen, leaving Mara confused.

*My parents are Jo and Zady Winningham. Am I a Winningham? Since this Zady couldn't be my mama, then maybe Jo isn't my daddy either. Why doesn't Jo's name have an e, anyway?* The thought of trying to crack the mystery of Mr. Winningham made her tired. Her only hope was getting under Zady's skin. Surely Zady would offer up some information if she prayed for it.

God had answered a prayer. In a strange way, He had protected her through Mr. Winningham, who certainly wouldn't win any trophies for personality. But now she was walled inside the big white house—sheltered from General, yes, but lonelier than she'd ever been, sharing a house with a housekeeper who kept secrets and a man who ate rib dinners.

Mara stood and called for Zady.

"Yes? You need something?"

"I need to know where my box is." She hoped her eyes showed Zady how important it was to her.

"Follow me," Zady said as she mounted the stairs.

They reached the landing to the second floor right down the hall from Mara's room. Mara expected Zady to turn right but instead she jiggled the doorknob of a small door in front of the landing. It looked like the door to Aunt Elma's hot water heater, so Mara had thought nothing of it before. Zady swung it open, revealing a narrow staircase.

"Careful," she said.

Mara placed each foot on the risers, only a foot and a half wide and very steep—more like climbing a ladder than a stairway, especially considering all the other stairways in the house could hold four people side by side with elbow room.

The ladder stairway ended in a musty, overheated attic. Small windows, one on either side of the eaves, shot light back and forth—light that made the dust Mara and Zady stirred up dance disco.

Zady wasn't a tall woman, but she couldn't stand upright in the attic's center. Instead, she crouched Alice-in-Wonderland-like. In the stifling heat, Mara's pants felt even tighter, glued on with sweat. She wished she had a bandana to mop her forehead and then remembered Charlie's hankie crammed into her pocket. It took some effort but she wrestled it free and tried to wipe the drips from her eyebrows. Instead, the damp hankie only smoothed the droplets around her brow. At least she wasn't dripping anymore.

"We're going to bake up here. Take me out in an hour, and I'll be a fully cooked sweet potato pie. Only I won't smell as sweet." As Zady smiled, her cheeks lifted.

Zady's words had an easygoing way of slicing through the tension of Mara's hard day. As it was, Zady had made Mara a sack lunch, something that brought added sunshine to the school day. Maybe someday she'd let Zady hug her. Not today, but maybe in a week. Or a year.

Mara handed her the wet hankie. "Here. This is Charlie's. He lent it to me today."

"If I hang the moppy thing from one of these rafters, it'd dry clear out." She shook her head and smiled. She turned left and stooped her way down the center of the attic. Mara followed. On both sides of them were relics of another time— old suitcases, dusty furniture, a large instrument that appeared to be a violin for a giant, and boxes from floor to ceiling. The boxes weren't liquor boxes; they weren't even cardboard. Burl Peaches said one. Hanker Plums said another.

"Here. Right here. Halfway down, turn to the left and look between the boxes."

Mara shut her eyes tight and opened them again, trying to adjust to the dark spot behind the boxes. "My box!" She shimmied through the narrow slit between two towers of peach boxes, which opened barely wide enough for her to go through sideways. She sat down and pulled each doll out, smelled their plastic heads, and remembered a few good things about her old life. She looked up to see Zady bent over and sweating. "Thanks."

"Nothing to it, child. Anytime you want, you can come up here and remember. Half our problems in life come from forgetting. You need to remember. Spend enough time in the past and you'll be able to live happy in the present. That's the secret to life."

Mara tucked Zady's words away for another day. Right now she wanted to hold her dolls and tell them they'd be okay. When she looked up again, Zady was gone. The side windows let in less and less light until Mara could not make out the knuckles on her hands anymore. She repacked her box, making sure the dolls could see out, and scooted through the box towers. She'd look at the manila envelope another day when the heat of the day hadn't baked her brain in the attic.

She slept hard that night—dreamless as if her mind were a deep boiling pot full of nothingness. But uneasiness was ladled into that dark pot, uneasiness that Mr. Winningham was watching her. He'd watched her some other nights. When the moon rose above the trees, angling its pale light into her white room, he stood in the shadows beyond her door and watched her while she shivered and hoped he'd walk away. Even when charcoal clouds hid the moon, when it longed to shine on her upturned face but couldn't, he watched her. She knew because her eyelashes concealed the frantic back and forth of her pupils that searched the same shadow beyond her door. Nearly every night, at twelve thirty, she woke up and looked through her eyelashes and saw his shadow move.

When the shadow shrunk away tonight, it was replaced by a cat whom she immediately named Stripes. When he sauntered over to her bed and jumped a tentative leap up onto it, his white stripes glowed in the moonlight like Cheshire's smile.

"Hello, Stripes," Mara whispered. "Nice to finally meet you."

Stripes' purring calmed her heart and made her eyelids flutter. He snuggled next to her, and his peace flooded through her.

Why couldn't the world just have cats?

# Fifteen

WHEN MARA FINALLY REUNITED WITH CAMILLA, even Camilla was rendered rhymeless, for at least five minutes anyway. It was the weekend after Mara met Stripes. Mr. Winningham was eating his poached egg—as he did every morning at six o'clock sharp—with two pieces of burnt Wonder Bread and a grapefruit half, the folded paper sitting like a napkin to the left of his silverware. Mara dared to walk into the kitchen and sit across from the frowning man and his idle newspaper.

"You going anywhere? It's Saturday." She tried to sound matter-of-fact, like a bank teller or a green grocer, but her voice wavered on the word *Saturday*.

Mr. Winningham peaked one eyebrow, picked up the newspaper, and looked above Mara. He nodded. That was it.

She waited an hour before she dared to open the front door. She ran full out toward Camilla's house. The sun tagged along behind Mara, spotlighting her shadow forward, creating a shadow giant. A few blocks from Camilla's door, Mara realized she didn't know where General lived. He could be behind any door, around any corner, hiding in any alley. Her running became darting—she flitted from one tree to the next, looking left and right and even up into the trees to make sure no capped redhead lurked nearby. Almost to Camilla's, and out of breath, she wished she could be as menacing as her shadow giant.

Camilla was playing out front when Mara ran square into her.

"Hey," Camilla yelled in a huffy voice—miffed until she realized it was her long-lost friend. Camilla hugged her so tight, Mara thought her eyes would pop out of her face. "It's you!"

"Yep. It's me," Mara said.

"Where have you been? I checked the Shrub Club that night after the ambulance. You weren't there. You weren't any-where."

"Gus took me away."

"Why'd he do that?"

"Said since Aunt Elma was dead, he needed to get rid of me."

"So the tumor rumor was right," Camilla said. "The tumor killed her."

At first Mara wanted to put up a fight and tell Camilla she was wrong for once, but then she realized life would be easier if the tumor rumor was true. "Yes, you were right."

"Are you okay? Where did the kindly officer take you?"

Mara wanted to go inside, to feel air conditioning against her warm face, but she knew there was an imaginary line around Camilla's house, one she couldn't cross. She took shel-ter under the giant live oak that kissed the sidewalk in front of their gate.

Camilla followed. "Well?"

"He drove me to a house inside the Loop."

"Inside the Loop? Really?"

"Yeah. It's not as bad as Aunt Elma made it out to be. Haven't met any criminals yet."

"What about that kid that pinned you down? You see him?"

Mara looked up at the live oak's leaves. She grabbed her stomach. She pretended she didn't hear Camilla's terrible question. "And you'll never guess exactly where I live."

"With Red Heifer?" Camilla twirled a piece of hair between her thumb and forefinger.

"Don't be silly." Mara watched as Camilla sucked the cord of twirled hair. "I live in the Winningham house."

Camilla pulled the hair out of her mouth. "With the richest man in town?"

"I guess I never thought of him that way. He's just Mr. Winningham." Mara twirled her hair now.

"There's no such thing as 'just Mr. Winningham.' I can't believe you live in the Winningham mansion!" Camilla stood to punctuate her point.

Mara'd never heard it put quite that way. *The Winningham mansion.* Made her sound almost proper. Or at least acceptable. "Yeah, I live there." She stood.

"Why?"

She wanted to yell, "Quit your questions!" but instead said, "I think I'm a Winningham, that's all. Gus dropped me off, though I'm not sure he was supposed to, and that was it. I haven't seen him since."

Mara and Camilla walked down the block, away from her house. Steam rose from the street where a street cleaner had been, curling toward the hot canopy of trees. For a moment, they walked and said nothing.

Camilla interrupted the comfortable silence. "Well, that's good news at least. Where're you going to school? Jenkins?"

"Yeah."

"I heard it was scary."

"No. Not scary. But a little uncomfortable sometimes."

They spent a good half hour walking and catching up.

They circled back around and stood under the live oak again. Camilla sat on the ground and poked sugar ants with a stick while Mara told all. Camilla had to continue moving to keep the busy ants from tickling her flesh.

"Sounds like that Mr. Winningham's had a difficult life. I bet he was someone altogether different before he became barky. Bet he was a singer."

"I don't think so. He's not one for singing—hates it, in fact. At the dinner table he told me I couldn't sing in the house."

"It makes perfect sense to me. Folks who sing can't stand to hear others croon. It's part of their artistic nature."

"I doubt Mr. Winningham has an artistic bone in his skinny body."

"I'm sure he has several. And I'm convinced his first name must be Sam."

*What in the world is she getting at?* "No, it's not. It must be Jo. That is practically the only thing I do know about him. At least, I think so."

"You're wrong," she said as she moved again, brushing off another ant. "He's Sam. Singing Sam Winningham."

Mara laughed a wide-toothed laugh and realized a bit of Zady had rubbed off on her. She had Zady's laugh now.

"Yep," Camilla said. "SSW."

Camilla and Mara met once a week that autumn. Those weekend meetings kept Mara's mind away from the thoughts that spun like hives of released angry bees stinging her during the week.

Mara hated that she was nine, desperately wanting to be ten. She knew that all she needed to do was turn ten, and then she could erase the number nine from her life forever. Nine years. Nine forced visits with General. But she was still nine, feeling awkward in a school where her face stood out like a white Tic Tac on a heap of chocolate ice cream.

Thankfully the school had books. Hundreds of old, dusty books. They were unlike the shiny covered books at Little Pine Elementary. The poor old books wafted mold when she opened them. When Mara told Camilla about them, she quipped, "Sounds like Jenkins has a case of the dusty-musties," and she was right.

But every Saturday, after SSW dissected and ate his poached eggs, burnt toast, and grapefruit half, he was out the door and into his white Cadillac by 6:20. Mara and Camilla took advantage of his absence by trading meeting places. When it was Camilla's turn, they met inside the Shrub Club behind Aunt Elma's (now Gus's) house. "It makes for an exciting rendezvous," Camilla said, although Mara got tired of having bits of shrubbery in her hair. When it was Mara's turn, Camilla came to her back door.

Camilla especially loved the attic. They'd already gone through Mara's box. They made a house for Mara's dolls out of a huge empty crate and decorated it with scraps of wallpaper, pieces of carpeting, and little boxes made into beds. Mara's favorite doll, Holly Hobby, got the Donny Osmond pillowcase for a bedspread and the Breyer horse statue to use for transportation to the other corners of the attic. They set the 45s on top of blocks of wood, making two dining tables, one formal, one informal. They chewed the Bubble Yum, even though it was a bit melted and stuck fast to the paper. "Chew the paper," Camilla had said. "Paper won't kill you."

They discovered there wasn't much to the papers in the manila folder. The birth certificate was the only document they understood. The others had words like *guardianship*, *residuary estate*, *executor*, and *beneficiary disputes*. The last document Mara looked at had something to do with the Burl Oil Savings and Loan, something about dividends to share-holders and short-term borrowings. It may as well have been written in French. Mara stashed the file in the Johnnie Walker box, behind the towers of boxes.

Camilla called the attic the "Dare-it Garret" precisely because she could make Mara snoop up there by using the word *dare*, and *garret* was a much more interesting name than *attic*. "I dare you to go through that trunk," she'd say, and Mara, who understood the competitive sensibilities of Camilla, always said yes, albeit with reluctance at times. On one such occasion, before the trees shed their leaves and read-ied themselves for Burl's two-week winter, Camilla said, "I dare you to go through the big crate."

The crate, probably four feet tall, was shaped like a giant Starburst candy, square on the front, but rectangular on the sides. It had stars and a moon painted on its front. It spooked Mara—she imagined it was some sort of gypsy box full of dark arts and wizardry, the kind Zady would say, "is from the Devil himself."

"Why me? Why don't *you* open it?" Mara asked her.

"Well, because this is the Dare-it Garret, and I thought of the dare before you did. Them's the rules." Camilla stood even taller when convinced of her own rightness.

"You always think of scary dares before I do. I don't think that way." She tried to stand tall too, but Camilla had higher tiptoes than she did—plus she was taller to begin with.

"I *am* blessed with a clever imagination, aren't I?" Camilla smiled and folded her arms across her chest as if to say, *Well, I'm waiting.* She tapped her toes on the plank floor.

Mara pulled a dusty stool over to the giant Starburst crate. She was thankful the weather had chilled to a bearable seventy degrees, so now the Dare-it Garret was merely ninety. The girls had tried to open the windows for air, but they were painted shut.

Mara blew off the thick dust covering the crate, making her sputter and cough. "It *does* say something."

"What does it say? Tell me!"

"I can't tell. It's in some other language. '*Pour les étoiles,*' whatever that means."

"I think it's Spanish, or maybe German. Yeah, it's German, sure enough," Camilla added. She knew so much more than Mara.

"There are hinges and a latch." Mara pulled at the latch and opened the box. It squeaked as the rusted hinges worked for the first time since the days of the gypsies. "Oh, look at this! It's a telescope." Camilla helped her tilt the box until it lay on the floor of the attic. With both of them pulling, they eased the device out of the box.

The rest of that October Saturday they set up the telescope as best they could, considering how the instructions were in a foreign language. They wobbled it over to the window that faced toward Gus's house and took turns looking. The day was peppered with, "I see Slack the cat," or "There's Pop Calverley walking his hot-dog dog," or "Look at that bird nest."

A whole new world of Nancy Drew detective work sprouted from the foreign seeing-eye contraption. Every unsuspecting person minding his own business on a Burl street became a notorious bank robber or a widow with a jaded past or a mysterious librarian who held the key to the library's rumored back room. Camilla and Mara spun outrageous stories that Mara would later write down in a journal.

But the pretending took a different twist altogether when Mara said, "Let's find Denim."

"Like I said, he's like Willy Wonka. Not a soul's seen him. Best leave that alone." Camilla picked at a scab on her hand.

"Oh, ye of little faith," Mara swooned, pulling the back of her hand across her forehead. "We're Nancy Drew, you and I. If Denim's in this town, we'll find him."

"Well, we might could find him if we had his address, but we don't," Camilla said.

"Address schmaddress," Mara rhymed, smiling to herself. "Detectives don't need silly things like addresses. We need good extinct."

"Are you sure you got the right word? Why would we want to be extinct? Doesn't that mean we are dead forever?" Camilla flicked the scab across the attic and wiped the blood it left behind with her sleeve. "I think the word you want is *instinct*, you know, like a sixth sense. Like cats, silly. We're fixin' to have instinct like cats. Got it?"

Mara nodded. She wished Camilla had left her scab alone. She didn't want to think about the blood. Her stomach tightened.

"You have a Band-Aid?" Blood trickled down Camilla's skin.

Mara looked away. Her mind flashed to a picture of a kidney bean–shaped pool of blood. She grabbed a piece of fabric they'd set aside for a future project. "Here. Use this."

Camilla took it, and the blood disappeared. Mara took a deep breath and forced her mind to other things. "Let's investigate." It was a strange reversal for Mara to be the initiator.

On one hand, she felt a surge of power, but on the other, she felt ill at ease.

Eventually, though, Camilla came around. "Well, if your mind is set on finding Willy Wonka, I may as well help you. Who knows? Maybe we'll find the Wonka bar with the golden ticket."

"Don't be silly," Mara said.

The rest of the day, they used the telescope to map out as many Burl streets as they could see. It was Mara's *instinctive* idea to draw on one side of the telescope crate, making a giant map of Burl. They drew streets as best they could and then drew a square for each house they could see. They'd write the owners' last names on the houses Camilla knew. Mara didn't know Gus's last name, so that house was labeled "Officer Gus." By day's end, they'd figured out twenty-seven houses.

"Someday, we'll come across a house that we can't label," Mara said. "And that, my dear Camilla, will be Denim's."

"That doesn't make any sense. We can't see all the houses in Burl. The sign outside the feed store says Burl has 23,489 folks in it. How can you possibly think we'll find Denim by labeling houses in town?"

"Instinct," Mara said.

A door slammed downstairs. Mara looked at Mickey's hands: 5:55. "Camilla! Quick! I have to eat dinner at six o'clock sharp, and you can't be here."

"How come?" Camilla examined her nails with furrowed brow, like there was something compelling about them.

"Because I'll get in trouble."

"Trouble is as trouble does, I always say."

# $S$ixteen

THE ATTIC STAIRS WERE DIFFICULT TO climb down in a hurry. Camilla managed fine, but when Mara descended, she missed a step and tumbled toward the second floor landing, causing a ruckus. She had the scrap of mind to say, "Go on, Camilla, I'll be fine." Camilla shot back an are-you-sure look.

Mara whispered, "Yes, now go, but quietly. SSW might find you. Use the back stairs."

The footsteps grew louder—she could hear them echoing from the bottom step, ascending higher and higher. She turned her torso enough to see the open attic door. Straining, she pulled herself up and shut the door, being careful to latch it without making noise. The steps grew nearer, noisier.

"What in heaven's name are you doing, child?"

*Zady.*

"I fell coming down the stairs. What're you doing here on a Saturday? I thought you had the weekends off." Mara had grown accustomed to TV-dinner weekends. Monday through Friday, she ate ribs—ribs that on day thirty-something now tasted like stale feet. Saturday and Sunday were for TV dinners.

"Sweet Jesus told me to come, and now I see why. Don't you see what time it is?"

"I know. Camilla and I got caught up trying to find Denim with a telescope we found in the attic."

"You been snooping and spying with that Camilla girl? Maybe Denim's a mystery because he wants to be. Ever think of that? Ever think that if you got caught by Mr. Winningham in the attic that I'd be blamed?" Zady's face never reddened, but Mara knew that underneath her brown face, red flared hot.

"I'm sorry."

"You say sorry a lot, Mara. Good thing God's after confessors."

"What do you mean?"

"He doesn't ask us to be perfect, just honest." Zady shook her head. "Look at yourself." She took Mara by the hand and led her to the bathroom. Mara had scraped her back on the rough-hewn stairs so that each bony knob of her backbone stung. "It's the mercy of Jesus that you didn't bonk your head again. Mm-mm-mm. Now this might sting."

Mara had lived long enough to know that when a grown-up said, "might," it meant "will." Whatever liquid Zady mopped on her felt like a range fire searing up her back.

"Ouch!"

"Shush your face. It's only Mercurochrome. Quit your boo-hooing, child. You're late for dinner."

Zady slipped out, leaving Mara to face Mr. Winningham alone. At the dining table, his hat was off, his head down. Heat radiated from the Salisbury steak, but he held his face in its steamy path. Mara looked at her place—it was empty.

"Sit."

"But there's no—"

He concentrated on his food as if he were on an archeological dig, steam heating his pale face. "You will sit while I eat my dinner. I threw yours away. Don't be late again."

It was the most he'd said to her in the past month, and although she felt silly sitting while Mr. Winningham ate, she was thankful he at least acknowledged that she lived in his house. But this quiet delight evaporated when he spent an entire hour eating. He cut the steak into pill-sized pieces and chewed each one twenty times—Mara counted. When he dipped into the mashed potatoes, he did it with his fork, letting the four tines barely scrape the white stuff. He cut the green beans into fourths. Between each bite of blueberry cobbler, he touched the corners of his lips with a white napkin. His milk was untouched until his entire aluminum tray was practically spot-polish cleaned. Then, head bowed, he brought the glass to his thin lips and sipped. When he finished, he stood, grabbed his dinner "dish," and left Mara feeling like she'd been his prisoner.

No more spoken words, just footsteps and a slammed door.

# Seventeen

THE DOOR SLAMMED A LOT THAT school year. Mara was lucky to hear so much as a grunt from Mr. Winningham. To humor Camilla, she referred to Mr. Winningham as SSW. But, try as she might, she couldn't picture Mr. Winningham—the slamming, silent man—as Singing Sam Winningham. So she decided to rename him—Slamming Sam Winningham.

Mara's only companions after school were Zady and books. When Mr. Winningham was gone, Zady filled Mara's afternoons with singing at the top of her lungs about deliverance and redemption, whatever that meant, "Come, sweet Jesus's," and "do your homework's." Zady went home to her family at seven o'clock—as soon as Red Heifer's ribs had been eaten and the last dish washed. Mara wasn't for dishwashing any more than she was for lima beans, but she took to helping Zady for the company.

"Tell me about church," Mara asked one evening while they washed rib bits from white plates. "My Nanny Lynn never went, but I keep thinking she would've liked it."

"Church? Well, it's a beautiful thing, Maranatha. A beautiful thing." Zady scrubbed the plates even after the barbecue sauce that once clung to it was a distant memory. "Folks go to church to get cleaned up, kind of like we clean up these here plates."

"I'm not dirty." *At least not on the outside.* "Why would I need cleaning?"

"Everyone needs cleaning, child. You ever so angry you want to scream? You ever think bad thoughts about folks? You ever cheat?"

Mara nodded. Zady had a way of asking questions that made Mara shift her weight from one foot to the other. With each shift, she hoped the shame rising to her face would fade, that it wouldn't be noticeable to Zady. If only she had a nice brown face so she could hide all her shame—especially the nine times General had tried to make babies with her. No church could hide that.

"Church is where you hug Jesus, child. You meet Him in lots of places, to be sure. Sunsets. Family. Babies. Maybe those are the places where your Nanny Lynn met Jesus. But there's something about being with other Jesus-loving folks that makes Him seem more real. More *with* you. And then there's the singing. Child! You ain't heard nothing until you sung your lungs out for Jesus with a herd of God-lovers. There ain't nothing more beautiful this side of heaven."

Mara wiped the last dish. She held it to her face and could see her reflection. She saw no celebration resting on the corner of her lips. Only sadness. Maybe church was the thing she needed to become happy. To take her mind off how dirty she felt. Sometimes she could still feel the brambles in her backside. But then she remembered General—a church-going boy with a pastor for a daddy. "I don't think I'm ready for church," she said.

"I won't force you. All in good time," Zady said.

As Zady clanked the plates above the sink, uneasiness settled into the place beneath Mara's ribcage. She couldn't put words to the feeling, but it was there nonetheless—leaden and ominous.

Mara climbed the stairs, placing one heavy foot above another. She hoped somehow that the uneasiness would lift with each step, that by the time she reached the top step, she'd feel safe. Even so, when she stood at the top, worry wormed its way from her chest to her throat.

It only left when she discovered a new book on her nightstand. Mara smiled and dusted off another volume. *Where do these books come from? Zady?* In her room, she had made friends with all of the Boxcar Children, Peter Pan, Scout Finch, Black Beauty, and Anne of Green Gables. She longed for Anne's carrot hair and wild imagination. As a tribute to Anne with an *E,* Mara with an *A* imagined this white house with cheerful green gables.

The clothes Zady gave Mara weren't beautiful like the mysterious dresses in the wardrobe, but at least they fit. Mr. Winningham didn't seem to notice her "new" clothes. In her other school, she'd have been teased about the wide collars and flared pants, but at this school no one seemed to care much. Hand-me-downs were a staple at Jenkins, and pride was stitched more to courtesy than fashion.

Vonda Rae turned out to be a fun friend. School sped by, mainly because Vonda Rae always turned around, braids flying, and made jokes. After winter break, Mara even cracked a smile at one of Vonda Rae's endless silly stories. When the smile came, it was as unexpected as snow flurries in Burl.

"That's one pretty smile you have there," Vonda Rae said. She bent forward to say something more, but then settled back and grinned at Mara.

By springtime, Mara smiled nearly every day, and she had

relieved Charlie of his walking duties. The afraid-of-General part of her wanted Charlie to walk her to and from school forever, but another part hated that she needed Charlie. She wanted to take care of herself. So she said thank you very much but she'd be fine alone, while knots twisted in her stomach. Her feet memorized the bumpy sidewalk, so now she walked back to the big white house with her head held high, though she shot nervous looks back and forth. Mr. Winningham's warnings had kept General away, but life was never safe until she closed the Winningham gate behind her.

Every time she walked by the trash can in her room she was thankful she didn't have to hide her underwear anymore. She hoped soon she'd be able to take her thumb out of her mouth at nighttime.

But nights were different. Once her eyes shut, shadowy creatures found her—in her bedroom, in the bathroom, under the pecan tree. No matter how much she ran, they'd chase her. She'd breathe silent screams and then trip on sidewalk roots. Every dream ended with whispers of the word *beautiful.* Mara's sleep came in fits after the dream whispers. Stripes understood this. Whenever Mara sat straight up in bed after another dream, Stripes would jump up and curl onto Mara's belly and purr. Sometimes when she woke up, Mr. Winningham's shadow stood near her doorway, as if he were protecting her once again from the monsters in her dreams. But mostly, it was Stripes who watched over her. And maybe God—or Nanny Lynn.

The novelty of attempting to find Denim wore thin for Camilla, but Mara's staid enthusiasm kept her at the task. Denim's program aired on KBBQ at 2:00 every weekday, so they both missed his show. On occasion, at 10:00 p.m., they'd re-air the program, so Mara tried to stay up late to catch it. He always started his show saying, "Denim, here. I speak for those who don't have a voice—those who can't afford a lawyer from the back of a phone book." Mostly he talked on and on about the bank mafia and some corrupt judge who had a rich brother. He used words like *secrets* and *lies*. The police, Denim said, were in on some sort of scandal, tangled with money and politics and what he referred to as "The Burl Cover-up." When he'd say that, Mara would picture the whole town of Burl wearing a Value Villa swimming cover-up. *That Denim, he's a funny one.*

Camilla and Mara had named and numbered every house they could see from the Dare-it Garret's telescope, and by April Fool's Day only two homes in that swath had yet to be identified.

"I bet it's the green house with pink trim," Camilla said. "Better yet, I'm sure it's probably one of the thousands of houses we *can't* see."

Mara rolled her eyes. "His name's Denim. A Denim is *not* going to live in a pink and green house, silly. No, he lives in the blue house. It makes perfect sense. Denim and blue. Get it?"

"Only one way to find out I'm right, and I know I am." Camilla headed toward the attic's steep stairs. "Let's go knock on some doors. That'll stop this wild goose chase and we can get on with other things."

Until now, their detective work had been undercover. There was little risk in investigating from an attic. Venturing door-to-door was something completely different. "It's April Fool's, you know," Mara said. "You sure this is such a good idea? People might think we're pranking them."

"You a 'fraidy cat?"

"Why do you always answer a question with a question?"

"Why do you always answer a question with a question with a question?" Camilla laughed. "Come on, Mara Nancy Drew, it's an adventure."

Mara sighed. Maybe she could use her reluctance to her advantage. "On one condition—I'll be the *only* Nancy Drew. You be Bess."

Camilla shrugged. "All right. Now come on, Nancy."

"Sure thing, Bess."

Camilla grimaced like Bess was a bad word, but her mood lightened as soon as they were outside. "We're going to the house I chose first."

The green house with pink trim certainly stood out from the weathered homes surrounding it. Mara's bravery came from having Camilla by her side—the kind of bravery that comes in twos and shrinks away when two becomes one. Camilla pressed her forward, making her feel alone.

"Knock."

"Why me?"

"Why *not* you?"

"There you go again—a question with a question."

"I triple-hog-dare you."

Mara looked at her toes and wiggled them. Camilla had her; she knew from experience Mara's weakness for dares and always managed to dare before Mara even thought along those lines. Those four extra years made Camilla a downright genius.

"All right, but stay right by me. Don't go running off. The criminals—" *Or General.*

"We're on the safe side of town, silly. Ain't any criminals here. You're fixin' to wet your panties with all those nerves of yours. Relax!"

"Easy for you to say." Mara pressed the doorbell. It answered back with a clanking ding-dong. Mara counted to one hundred as fast as she could. "It's time to go. No one's here."

"Ring it again. I bet Denim didn't hear you."

Mara shot a red-faced glance at Camilla and was about

to run off the porch when the door opened out, nearly hitting her.

A thin woman stood behind the door. "Sorry 'bout the door. My man, he don't knows how to fix things. Told 'im the door was off-kilter, and he fixed it, made it swung to the yard. Don't even get me started about the A/C. Works in the winter, but dies in the summer. Makes me nutty."

The bony, tired lady looked young and old at the same time, and she ran her speech together, barely taking breaths between words. She wore tight jeans, like a teenager, and a Dallas Cowboys half shirt, revealing a thin, pale belly. Half moons darkened her darting eyes, and her lips had wrinkle-creases, like she had pursed them too much. "You gal-ladies selling cookies, or what?" she rasped.

"No, ma'am. Just looking for someone," Camilla said.

"You lose someone?" A smile crept to her lips, and that's when Mara noticed the gold tooth with a diamond imbedded in it near the back of her mouth. "Like my dia-mel? Can't afford no diamonds, but my man—he takes care of me. Got me this genuine dia-mel *and* the golden crown."

"It's . . . um . . . lovely," Mara said. She cleared her throat. "Do you mind if I ask you your husband's name?"

"Is this some kind of an April Fool's joke? What kind of Girl Scout *are* you?" She brushed her hair out of her eyes. "More like a Nosy Scout, if you ask me." She grabbed a half-smoked cigarette from the window ledge and lit it, her eyes looking back and forth down the road. "Mind if I smoke?"

Mara shook her head. She didn't know what to say and hoped Camilla would pipe up, but apparently her pipes were clogged.

"You writin' a news story or something? The *Burl Atlas* did a spread on my husband once—'bout his jobs. Name's J.T."

"Does he go by any other name?"

"No, little Miss Nosy, just J.T. I suppose you want to know what the letters stand for?"

"No, ma'am. Thanks anyhow."

"Hey—where's that gal that was with you? I spied you both coming here."

Mara looked behind her. No Camilla. "Must've run off, I guess."

"You sure you're not selling me cookies?"

"No. I'm investigating," Mara said.

The smoking lady tapped her left hand on her jeans like a snare drum. She craned her long neck toward town as if something menacing were coming from there. She lowered her voice and bent close to Mara. "Investigating? You like Scooby-Doo? I always love the part where the bad guy says, 'Yeah and I would've gotten away with it too, if it weren't for those meddling kids.' You a meddling kid?" She looked right through Mara.

"No. I'm a plain old kid."

"Who you investigating?" She sucked down the cigarette all the way to the filter, flung it on the porch, and grabbed another half-smoked one from the ledge in one smooth motion as if she'd done that same repetitive action her whole life. The woman kept looking toward town, then to her watch.

"Well, no one really. Gotta go." Mara backed off the porch and turned. Camilla was gone.

The lady in the pink and green house called after her. "You'll come back, won't you? My boy and my man aren't around much on the weekends. Used to be home weekend mornings, but now they's busy working every weekend. After a whole week alone, I get lonely. You'll come back, right?"

There was such desperation in her raspy voice that Mara

felt pity deep in her stomach. Pity had been a me-only emotion for Mara. Ever since she had the word on a second grade vocabulary test, she'd taken to pitying herself, but never someone else. Well, maybe Zady when Mr. Winningham barked at her, but other than that, nobody.

"Yeah, sure," Mara heard her voice say, full of pity.

"M'name's Belinda. Lindy for short. You come by anytime, okay?"

"Sure." Mara walked out to the sidewalk and peered up and down it. No Camilla. She walked in the direction of the blue house, hoping to catch up with her. Still no Camilla. *I'm going to run home. Fast.*

"Up here," came a voice above her. Bradford pear blossoms snowflaked down on her from a shaking branch above. "In the tree."

"Why'd you leave me? You sore that you lost? There's no Denim there, only a scared lady."

Camilla jumped clear down, landing on the sidewalk in front of Mara. "Nope, I'm not sore—just shy."

"You? Shy?"

"Yeah, I'm fine with you or my friends at school, but I don't like to meet strangers. Makes me edgy."

"Edgy? What does that mean? Besides, you met me when I was a stranger, and you were a regular chatterbox."

"Yeah, but that was different. I was meeting my best friend."

They walked past the dividing line between Craigmont ISD and Burl ISD toward the blue house. Mara was sure Denim lived there, so sure she felt lucky. "I bet you a beauty parlor hour Denim lives in the blue house."

"What's a beauty parlor hour?"

"You know—whoever loses has to wash the other person's hair, dry it, curl it, and put on toenail and fingernail polish."

"You're on," Camilla said. "My toes could use some spit and polish."

Camilla made another excuse why she simply could *not* be expected to knock on the blue house's door.

The familiar fear Mara had walking any street in Burl roared in her ears. Any house could be General's. He could be lurking behind any tree. "Please come with me. I can't do it alone. We're a team, remember?"

"Nothing doing. You either knock or you don't. But I can't."

Mara sighed. "Okay, promise me one thing, then. That you'll stay at the gate and not climb a tree. I need you nearby."

Camilla picked up a red rock and threw it at a tree. "It's the bully you're afraid of, isn't it?"

"So what if I am?"

"All right then, but I'm not knocking."

"You are Bess through and through. Only Nancy would dare to approach the door. I'm glad I'm Nancy. I deserve it," Mara said, a bit triumphant.

"Well, aren't you a prideful eyeful?"

Mara laughed. "You're going to be a poet—I hope I live to see the day."

"You'll certainly be old and gray," Camilla rhymed.

The shuttered house had a white picket fence out front bursting with spring flowers in neat rows. Mara opened the latched gate—it opened without a sound. Camilla stood there as Mara walked up the flower-lined path to the pale blue house, painted perfectly. The green grass sported a flawless crew cut—no termite mounds—and on the porch sat two white planters full of purple pansies.

Before Mara could knock, the door opened. A tidy old man, short and stocky, stood behind the screen door and smiled. "What can I do for you, little ma'am?" When he said it, his voice quavered—certainly *not* the voice of Denim.

The screen door opened and the man stepped out onto the small landing where Mara stood. He walked with a gnarled cane, all hand whittled and shiny, and sat down on the top step.

"Not often I get company anymore." He rubbed his hands and grimaced. "You alone?"

"Sort of. My friend's at the gate; she's a bit shy. I can only stay a moment."

"Why don't you invite her in?"

Mara looked up and beckoned Camilla with her eyes, but Camilla shook her head. "She'd rather wait there, sir." She looked around. "I like your flowers. Does your wife garden?"

"Wife? No, little ma'am. She's gardening in Eden now." He looked beyond Camilla and rubbed his forehead. "Been four years now since she went to heaven."

"I'm sorry."

"No need. It was her time, sure enough. The cancer ate her insides—took her pretty fast."

"She have a tumor?"

"How does a little girl like you know about tumors? Nah, it was a spreading thing, like a monster. Took her stomach first, was mighty hungry, and took to eating the rest of her up."

Mara sat down on the step. The man, like his lawn, had a silvered crew cut. Maybe he was Denim's father. "You have any children?"

"My Millicent couldn't have babies, a crying shame since children practically followed after her like the Pied Piper. No, she taught kindergarten thirty-eight years. How old are you?"

"Nine."

"Nine, huh? What's a nine-year-old doing knocking on doors on this side of town? Your mama not teach you any sense?"

"Don't have a mama."

"Now I'm the sorry one. What's your name, child?"

"Mara."

"Unusual name, Mara. Short for something?"

"I guess Maranatha, but folks mostly call me Mara."

"Well then, Mara, I'm Eliot. Eliot Campbell." He thrust his left hand toward her, and she shook it, even though it felt strange to shake a left hand. His right hand, she noticed, turned on itself, curling toward his stomach. "Got me a withered hand. Millicent, she didn't mind none. Said she wouldn't have me any different. Said when I was in my mama that God spun me up perfect, then turned my hand in and said, 'I'm done.' No use in messing with the hand of God. He may've curled my hand, but he also gave me a beautiful wife."

Mara thought it strange that the man had answered all the questions she would have asked him.

"I like your freckles." Eliot foraged around the pansy container, pulling up little weeds. He set them in a small pile between them.

"I wish they'd go away. I wish I had a normal face. My aunt used to tell me to put lemon juice on them—to make them disappear." Mara looked up toward the sun, letting it kiss her nose.

"If God painted little brown dots on your face, best wear 'em proud-like." Eliot picked a purple and yellow pansy from his weeded pot and handed it to Mara. "Now, Sephie, tell me why you're here. You selling something?"

*Sephie? Who's Sephie?* "No, sir. Not selling anything. I'm trying to find someone." She didn't think it polite to tell the old man he'd renamed her, so she kept quiet and hoped he'd remember the next time the conversation hopped back to him.

"Your mama?"

"No. A man named Denim."

"The radio guy?"

"Yeah. My friend and I think he knows everything about this town, and we have some questions we need answered."

"So you went door-to-door looking for him?"

"No, we narrowed it down, going only to the houses we didn't know."

"Sephie, I'm sorry to say, I can't help you. Denim's a truth-teller, you know. He speaks for those who don't think they can speak, but he's smart enough to know that if you tell the truth in Burl, you're a target. He's hiding for a reason."

"Sir, my name's *Mara*." It took every bit of her to say it, and even at that she whispered it.

"Mara? Name's Mara?"

Mara nodded.

He put his hand to his chin, his faced scrunched as if considering. "You're the spitting image of Sephie—look like her twin."

"Is she nine?" Mara often imagined that somewhere she had a secret twin sister living in some exotic locale like Dallas or Timbuktu. She'd made movies in her head—touching movies—about her reuniting with her twin in sobbing embraces.

"Nine? Heavens, no. Was near twenty-three when she died, at least that's what the paper said. Lost track of her after she turned twenty. Beautiful gal. Used to be a student in Millicent's class way back when. They were pretty close. Broke Millicent's heart when she stopped coming around."

"That's sad."

"Yep, it was."

Mara felt her time was up. She could feel Camilla's impatience. A light spring breeze, the kind that brings hints of honeysuckle on its breath, bent the flowers gently to the left. Mara twirled the pansy in her hand round and round. She stood.

"Mr. Eliot, sir—I have to go. Didn't mean to take all your time." *Camilla's going to kill me for all this yakking—without clues or evidence, no less.*

"You can take my time whenever the wind brings you, little ma'am. Time is something I have a lot of." Eliot stood, leaning on his cane with his left hand.

"Thank you. Oh, and thanks for the flower."

Camilla opened the quiet gate for her.

Mara turned. "Good-bye."

Leaning on his cane, he waved with his withered hand. "Good-bye, Sephie."

Camilla and Mara walked in quiet a long time, Mara wondering who this Sephie was, while her worried eyes looked beyond each block.

"Let's do a grace erase," Camilla finally said. "Neither of us found Denim, so we'll call off the beauty hour, okay?"

Mara liked grace that could erase—especially considering Mr. Winningham had no stash of nail polish anywhere. She'd looked before.

Camilla left Mara at her gate under the shadow of the great pecan tree. She opened the gate, climbed the crooked stairs, and sat between two columns, staring at the tree. *I wonder if grace could erase the dirtiness I feel inside. Could stop me sucking my thumb like a baby. Could make me whole again.*

# Eighteen

MARA WOKE UP ONE DAY—APRIL 12—with the persistent feeling that there was something special about the day, but she couldn't think what it could be. A flash of a thought would singe her eyelids for one hundredth of a second, only to disappear as quickly. *What was it about this day?*

She ate her Frankenberry cereal that morning and looked for the Booberry spyglass, but it was gone. Mr. Winningham, serious as he was, had some sort of crazy desire for cereal toys. Someday she wanted to beat him to it. Not today.

She left her house, stood for a moment under the large pecan tree, and looked up. The sky was crayon blue, and she loved the contrast of the new green leaves against the bright blue puzzle-shaped sky that peeked through—something about it made her happy she was alive. She heard Zady talk about God most every day, but God, whoever He was, was clearest to her when she stood under the pecan's shadow, the sky peek-a-booing through its swaying leaves. She wondered if God would show Himself to her this Sunday. Zady's gentle persistence made her say she'd go to church.

Even Eliot's pansy made her think there must be a God. She had loved the purple gift to wilted death, or at least she thought so until she gave it a cool drink of water in a juice glass and it perked back to life. If only her life would perk up by merely adding water.

Vonda Rae didn't tell Mara jokes today; in fact, she never turned around. She spent half the day with her head down, moaning about her brother George and how he was a soldier headed to South Carolina. Mara tried to calm her braided friend, but Vonda Rae would not be comforted; she moped instead, and when she moped, she cleaned. Some folks got lazy when sadness came knocking. Not Vonda Rae. She erased the chalkboard, leaving Mara to swing alone at morning recess. Vonda Rae washed all the desks during lunch, forcing Mara to eat her lunch with Lou Ann Scroggins, the *Brady Bunch* know-it-all.

"Tell me this," Lou Ann quizzed. "Who broke the vase when someone said, 'Mom always said, don't play ball in the house'?" Then, she'd answer the question before Mara's mouth, full of peanut butter and jelly, emptied. "Peter, silly. Don't you know nothing?" Before taking a breath, she continued, "How about this one? What amusement park did the Brady kids go to where they lost Dad's plans? King's Island. It's in Cincinnati, Ohio. How can you *not* know that?" On and on it went—from Jan's glasses to the Silver Platters to Marsha's broken nose—until the bell rang, relieving Mara from Lou Ann's endless stream of Brady know-it-all.

Vonda Rae scrubbed the floors on her hands and knees during afternoon recess, but this time Mara joined her, wetting the knees of her jeans and callusing her hands. Jokeless, Vonda Rae moped. And scrubbed. But she did mutter a "thank you" when they finished.

Vonda Rae's sour mood rubbed off on Mara. So on her

way back to the big white house, Mara stopped at a vacant lot, finding shade under the weeping willow.

Mrs. Dobson, Jenkins' part-time librarian, had helped Mara give Droopy its proper name. "It's right here in *Deciduous Trees of North America*," she had said, handing the unopened book to Mara. Mrs. Dobson was one of those librarians who didn't believe in spoon-feeding information; she'd hand you a book and expect you to find the facts for yourself. The Wiffle-ball tree became the more poetic *bois d'arc*; Purpley became redbud. In her quest for names, she leafed through Jenkins' baby-name book only to find Mara and Marcia—no Maranatha sandwiched between them.

When Mara discovered Droopy's real name was weeping willow, it made her sad to think a tree would cry. But today there was comfort in it. She held her knees and let her back rest against the weeping tree. The vacant lot was flowerless and grassless. Only red dirt, garbage, some tangled weeds, and a few overgrown bushes at one edge populated it. As she sat there, Mara rethought her day—no cereal prize, no fun at recess, no playful conversation, no jokes. All in all, a crummy day. Nothing special about it.

She stood, wiping off bark bits from her backside. It was then that she noticed a pink fuzzy ear poking out from behind some trash. On closer inspection, the ear belonged to a shabby stuffed rabbit. She picked her up and dusted her off, much like she had done to herself. "Well, hello there, Mrs. Bunny. You okay?"

Pity came to her again when she noticed the bunny had no nose, only a thick piece of black thread that used to hold her nose in place. Her eyes were scuffed, like they had seen the tread of too many tricycle tires. She was more brownish than pink, but if you lifted her arms or opened the insides of her ears, the brightest, happiest pink popped through.

Mara looked around. The lot remained vacant, so she tucked the bunny under her arm and headed toward the big white house.

Zady greeted her at the door. "You stay clear of the kitchen, young lady. You hear me?"

Her voice had a playful sternness about it, and the way she shook her finger right in Mara's face made Mara laugh in spite of herself. "Why? You cooking up some ribs?"

"No time for sassing—you git." She patted Mara through the doorway and pointed her upstairs. "Do your homework, and don't come down till six."

Mara didn't spend the rest of the afternoon scoping out the neighborhood with the telescope or doing her homework, but making life better for the stuffed bunny, who she'd named Nose Bunny. She bathed Nose Bunny in the bathroom sink and rubbed Nose Bunny's dirty fur back and forth with Ivory soap until she pinked. Mara rinsed her over and over again, remembering that no one likes a hide full of itchy soap scum.

"Please forgive me, Nose Bunny, but I have to wring you." As she twisted the bunny's torso, water emptied into the sink, first in rushes, later in drops, until Nose Bunny was simply damp and no longer waterlogged.

In the attic Mara clipped Nose Bunny's ears with two faded clothespins to a clothesline that must've once held old-fashioned clothes. Nose Bunny seemed to smile as she dangled from the line.

She wanted to make Nose Bunny's world the best it could be. She crawled on her knees through towers of boxes way in the back of the attic. There hadn't been a need for her to go back there yet. It was too dark, too dusty, and too cramped.

But now, her new friend needed more than what she'd been able to scrounge from the front part of the attic.

She crawled and sneezed through the smallest of spaces and then she found it. Not only did she find some old curtains that would make a perfect bedspread for Nose Bunny, and a small wood shoebox that would make a wonderful bed for her, but she found a small black-and-white television set! Now she could study *The Brady Bunch* for herself and show up Miss Fancy-Pants Lou Ann.

Mara backed out and started moving boxes in order to rid that TV of its hiding place. Once she freed the black-and-white miracle, she finished creating Nose Bunny's cozy bedroom, complete with boxed nightstand, a cotton-ball-filled pillow on top of a shoebox bed, a tapestry rug (taken from the seat of an old chair), three cardboard walls with pictures from the peach boxes as wall hangings, and a stolen nightgown from Chrissy the doll.

"No one should be homeless," Mara said, half to Nose Bunny, half to herself. As Nose Bunny hung by her ears, Mara saw herself there and let pity take over. Like Nose Bunny, she dangled in midair. She never quite felt safe, never quite felt loved, never quite felt tethered to anything secure. No, she floated above security like an errant balloon waiting for someone to grab her flapping ribbon and pull her to earth, anchoring her to a huge rock or a rooted tree or a real home.

She forced the thought from her mind and contented herself with being the rescuer today. Nose Bunny was lost, scared, and dirty—and Mara saved her. Today, that was enough. It felt good to be needed.

She wished she could tuck Nose Bunny in for the night, but she was damp. "You'll have to stay up there until you're dry. I'll tuck you in tomorrow, okay?"

She crept down the attic stairs and sat at the claw-foot dining table, waiting for Red Heifer's ribs. Mr. Winningham took his hat off and sat, like always, at precisely six o'clock. As usual, he stared at his plate.

"Dinner is served!" Zady hummed and smiled as she served the familiar fare, like she had some secret delight she couldn't tell anybody about.

Mara picked at her food, feigning interest in her boring dinner. During the months of menu repetition, she had mastered the fine art of food pushing. First, she spread the mashed potatoes thin around the plate, coating its bottom, and then she rolled the black-eyed peas to the plate's outer edges. After she did that, she resmoothed the potato bottom with the back of her spoon. She did eat her cornbread and tried to make teeth marks on the ribs for good measure. It never fooled Zady, but she did it anyway.

"Dessert time!" Zady called. They'd ended the meal the same way for so long, Mara had forgotten there was such a thing as dessert after dinner. Something must've jarred Zady out of the rib rut—something important, something Mr. Winningham would approve of. Mara looked at the man and watched his face redden.

"Happy birthday to you," Zady sang. She carried a small, round two-layer cake with pink frosting and one candle. Icing roses wreathed the cake.

Mara joined in. *Mr. Winningham's birthday?* "Happy birthday to you."

"Happy birthday, dear Maranatha," Zady sang at the same time as Mara was singing, "Mr. Winningham."

"Happy birthday to you." Zady placed the pink cake squarely in front of Mara and smiled.

*April 12! I can't believe I forgot my own birthday!* She had a hard time recalling the last time anyone remembered her birthday and did something special about it. Seemed to be around the time the laughing lady pushed her on the porch swing.

"Aren't you going to make a wish?"

Mara looked across to Mr. Winningham, but in the hoopla, he must've left. His plate, cup, and silverware were gone, leaving no trace.

"Where's Mr. Winningham? Is he mad?"

"Oh, he's mad all right—mad in the sense of not enough hamsters running on the exercise wheel, if you know what I mean."

Mara looked up at Zady and started to speak.

"Hush, child. I told you, you're good for him. He needs to jump out of his routine now and again. Make a wish—the wax is dripping."

Mara took a deep breath and blew. As she did, her far-fetched wishes drifted to the sky where she hoped someone— *God? Nanny Lynn?*—would see them. She wished she could find Denim, her mama, and her daddy. She wished being ten would break General's spell of nine times in the brambles. She wished for some decent clothes.

"What'd you wish for?"

"You know I can't tell. It'll poof the wish."

"You deserve every wish. It's a miracle you're even here, you know?"

"Really?" Mara leaned forward as Zady pulled up a chair.

"I was there the day you were born."

"You were?"

"Yep, the day was a pretty one, sun high in the blue sky. When your mama was pregnant, she carried you right straight out in front, like a gym ball under her shirt. She'd sing to you and talk to you near every day."

*Please keep talking, Zady. Don't stop.*

"Zady—please tell me who she is."

"Wish I could, honey. Wish I could." Instead of catching Mara's gaze, Zady looked straight ahead into the house's entryway. "She loved you, Mara. I can tell you that. And when you finally came out, you screamed and screamed. She held you tight like she was never going to let you go and whispered all sorts of things to you until you stopped your hollering and looked into her eyes. April 12 was the happiest day in your mama's life. I can tell you that."

For a moment Mara was silent with delight. *My mama loves me. I gave her the happiest day of her life. Today. Ten years ago.* But something bothered her about what Zady had said. "Wasn't it meeting my daddy?"

"What do you mean?"

"Wouldn't that be the happiest day of her life—meeting my daddy?"

Zady shook her head and then settled her chin on her fist. "Some stories don't end up happily ever after. Your mama's happiest beginning and ending were you, child." She looked at Mara and touched her cheek. "You."

Zady pushed herself up, wiping away tears. "I have something for you." She opened the china cabinet and reached way behind the silver vases, pulling out a wrapped rectangular box. "Here. I only wish it could be more."

"For me?"

Zady nodded.

Mara looked at the ribbon and the paper—yellow curly ribbon atop balloon wrapping paper. She caressed the paper, tracing one balloon after another with her finger. She twirled an end of curly ribbon around her pinky.

"For heaven's sake, child. Open it!" Zady scolded, wearing

the same smile she had when she'd banished Mara from the kitchen. Zady must've had that uncanny ability to know when Mara was feeling insecure because she tempered her strong words with laughter or smiles.

Mara pulled the ribbon to the corner of the box and worked it free.

Zady grabbed the ribbon from her, laughed again, and wreathed Mara's head with it.

Mara could see Zady's impatience as she pried the ends of the paper, being careful to keep the balloon patterns from sticking to the tape. Zady tapped her fingers. Mara turned the box over and slid her finger under the last tape stronghold. She folded the paper into fourths and opened the white box.

"Oh, Zady!"

Inside were a brand-new pair of jeans, a red cotton top, five pairs of bobby socks, days-of-the-week underwear, some Bonne Bell lip balm, a cross necklace, and a yellow sparkled T-shirt.

One wish down, many to go.

# Nineteen

SCHOOL WAS NEARLY OUT NOW, AND uneasiness had settled into Mara that even at ten she couldn't explain. Maybe it was the whole turning-ten thing. Maybe it was the memory of General's chest blocking out the sun above her nine times. Maybe it was the fear that life with new clothes was too perfect, that the spell of her happiness would be broken somehow.

Mara wore her new clothes almost every day that week, washing them every three days. She even wore them visiting, first to Lindy's house, then to Eliot's. Lindy's eyes always darted back and forth. Mara never made it past her porch, but she felt happy that she brought company to such a scattered and afraid woman. Eliot had invited her inside. The interior of the blue house was as neat as the gardens surrounding it. The furniture sat in square formation around a square table. Pictures hung perfectly. He even served sweet tea, the best she'd ever tasted, in square glasses.

Even so, she didn't find so much as a clue as to where Denim lived. Camilla tired of Mara's investigations. She quizzed her when she'd return from a visit. "You find anything out?" Camilla almost seemed happy when Mara reported she had found out nothing new.

Today she'd learn something new. She was going to church! As the sun danced through tree leaves, Zady opened the front door of the big house, humming. When Mara greeted her, Zady handed Mara a dress—frilly with lace and tucks. "You'll need this for church, child."

"Why?"

"Folks in our church dress up for Jesus, like He's their best date. I can't be taking you to church wearing a nightgown, can I?"

"I guess not."

"I'll let you dress. Let me know when you're ready."

Mara fumbled to get the dress on, but she couldn't reach the zipper. "Zady?"

Zady entered. "Well, aren't you a pretty sight?"

Mara took a deep breath as Zady zipped her up and fussed over the lacy dress.

When she finished, Mara turned to face her. "I need to ask you something. Don't take it the wrong way, okay?"

"Anything, child."

"Are there any white folks at your church?"

"What kind of question is that? You afraid?"

Mara nodded. It was an honest nod. She was afraid—not of being the only white face in a pew full of black folks—but of running into General. The only church in Burl she'd heard much about was General's. For all she knew, there was only one church in town, and Zady was leading her right to it.

"No need to be afraid. We don't bite. Sing real loud and say a lot of 'amens,' but we's not scary."

"So, there's no white folks?"

"Not a one, baby. You'll be it. But don't be afraid. I'll take care of you."

Mara let out a sigh in spite of herself.

"Let's git to gitting. We're fixin' to be late."

"Zady?"

"Yes, child."

"Those dresses—in the wardrobe next to my room—who do they belong to?"

"Your mama."

*I knew it!* Mara'd been thinking on them since Zady said she knew her mama. Ever since, she'd gone into that room and touched the dresses. The faint scent of rose petals lingered on every garment. Sometimes Mara went in there just to smell the fabric.

Mara tried to sound matter of fact, as if this were stale news. "You think I'll ever get to wear her dresses?"

"M'not sure. They're put away for a reason." Zady turned from Mara and sniffed. She pulled a white hankie from her pocket and blew her nose into it. She stuffed it back in her pocket and faced Mara again. "Best be going."

A horn out front spurred Zady to fussing. "Raymond's getting impatient. Time to go." She spit on her fingers and smoothed the hair away from Mara's eyes, tucking it behind her ears. She smoothed out Mara's skirt. "Turn around."

Mara obeyed.

"Beautiful."

The word shot an arrow of fear into Mara's heart. She trembled, thankful her face was turned away from Zady's knowing gaze.

"Let's go."

Mara had always wanted to ride in a station wagon. Lou Ann Scroggins's *Brady Bunch* kick had rubbed off on her, and ever since, she longed for everything Brady, including a station wagon with fake wood sides. Raymond and Zady's station wagon was beige with brown siding. Although the seats were ripped in places, the car was shiny clean inside and out.

Raymond limped to the other side of the car, dragging one foot. Mara tried not to stare, but she couldn't help it. He held the door for Zady, "Be careful, Precious," he said.

Zady waved her hands, a gesture that said, *Now don't you be fussing with me, Raymond.*

He dragged his foot toward the back door, opened it, and bowed. "You noticing my limp, sweet Maranatha?"

"Sorry, sir."

"No need to be sorry. Had me an accident at the poultry plant. Got my foot caught in some machinery. They fired me."

Mara slid into the seat next to Charlie. She waved a shy hand at Zady's other children—two girls, one older, one younger, in the way back of the station wagon. "Hi."

Raymond shut the door gently behind her, a feat in itself with such heavy doors, settled behind the wheel, and finished his comments to Mara. "The Good Lord, He takes care of us. Thanks to Zady's job and the little bit from the government, we get along fine."

"No thanks to the banks in this town." Zady turned around to face Mara. "My Raymond, he's really a carpenter. Makes us the finest furniture. Once the chicken factory ate his leg, he decided he'd start himself up a business. No bank would loan him money. Not one."

"Mama, she don't want to know all that business," Raymond said as he turned the key. Silence. He turned it again. The engine sputtered. The third time he turned the key, the engine percolated to life, loud and rumbling.

Zady turned to look at Mara. "In the way back is Della, my oldest, and Sadie, my youngest. Say hello to Maranatha, girls."

"Hello, Maranatha," they said in unison.

After a long silence, Mara said "Nice car." She caught Raymond's gaze in the rearview mirror.

"This'd be a Dodge Aspen."

Charlie nudged her and rolled his eyes.

Mara let out a startled gasp and recoiled.

"Oops," Charlie said, throwing up his hands in apology. "I forgot about you being jumpy. It's . . . well . . . you mentioned *the car*. Now we'll never hear the end of this."

"The finest car you'll ever find," Raymond said. "Slant six. Genuine veneer wood paneling. Manual three-speed transmission with overdrive."

As he said it, Charlie mouthed the words in unison, then his voice joined his father's: "Yessiree, the most powerful station wagon on the planet," they said.

Raymond revved the engine as if he was putting his own exclamation point on his admiration and looked at Mara again through the rearview mirror. "Church is a speck far. You get carsick?"

"No, sir."

"Good. We've got a good thirty minutes on rolling roads till we get there. Up and down. Up and down. But these Aspen shocks, they absorb it all."

What geographers call the East Texas Piney Woods surrounded Burl. Mara had gotten that question right on her last Texas state history test. She hadn't ventured much beyond Burl's Loop, so she took to gazing out the window at rolling hills and the stands of pine trees. Every once in a while, they'd pass a cow pasture full of shiny black cows and their babies. The sky seemed bigger when the pastures stretched between the pine trees. The farther they got from Burl, the more pastures they passed and the bigger the sky stretched.

"What's that?" Mara asked Charlie, pointing to giant round rolls of something dotting a pasture.

"Hay, silly. That's how the farmer bales his hay, round and round and round until it gets to be that big. Then he cuts another bale."

"I've only seen rectangular bales before," she said.

One field had the giant marshmallow-shaped hay bales lying end to end, making one long roll. "Looks like a package of Rolos," Mara said.

Charlie laughed. "Never thought of it that way."

"All y'all cool enough back there?" Zady asked.

The four children said yes.

"We don't have air-con, so Mama worries that we'll get overheated," Charlie explained.

Mara nodded and took to looking out the window again, this time at the road. Dotting the wide shoulder were huge shreds of tires. Every mile or so, a dead animal bloodied the road. She'd seen an upturned armadillo, three possums, one particularly smelly skunk, one crow, and half of some poor critter. The sky, wider and wider, held circling vultures.

Every so often Raymond drove on the shoulder to let faster cars pass. Mara must've looked confused enough for Raymond to notice her expression in the rearview mirror.

"It's courtesy. Folks are trained around here that if they're motoring too slow they use the shoulder. Comes from all the John Deeres on the road, I suppose."

Normally, God had been kind enough to lock Mara's mind shut. Some rare days she forgot about General, that is, until a boy would touch her, or something like John Deere was mentioned. Then, the memories rushed into her head. Every time they did, her stomach galloped.

"You all right?" Charlie asked. "Getting carsick?"

Mara held her stomach.

"Mama says we're supposed to look at the horizon."

"Thanks," Mara said. "I'll be all right."

She watched the telephone wires scallop up and down, up and down between crooked poles for the last ten minutes of the drive.

To her surprise, the long country road abruptly ended. A small one-story building stood on one side, surrounded by a pasture and a garden. A hand-painted sign read, "Mt. Moriah Church—God's home, God's family." Right before they entered the drive, Charlie, by some sort of unspoken command, rolled up his window. A split second later, dust flew into Mara's. She cranked the handle to close hers so fast her arm cramped.

"Burl won't let us build a church in town. Too many taxes and restrictions," Raymond explained. "This here's the only place we could find. Someday, we'll build us a real nice house for God."

"I think it's lovely," Mara assured him. She liked Zady's husband.

"Mighty kind, young lady. Mighty kind."

The May heat swirled with the kicked-up dust, making it seem even hotter outside. When they entered the church's back door, someone handed Mara a funeral fan and a hymnal. Three ceiling fans spun so wildly from the rafters Mara thought the blades would wobble off and fly right at her. Zady took her elbow.

"We're in pew four, left side."

The words were like a foreign language to Mara, so she allowed herself to be led.

As soon as they sat, the organ piped up. The music rollicked and jumped—much different than Mara imagined it would sound. She thought church music meant stained glass windows and dignity. Must've been TV that made her think that since Nanny Lynn's idea of church was nature, plain and simple.

A smiling, dark-skinned Jesus, framed in gold above the pulpit, seemed to welcome Mara. He looked so happy to see her she almost waved.

"All y'all stand up," Zady motioned to her children. "It's time to praise God Almighty. Look alive!"

Alive, they looked. Electricity seemed to jolt them all—even calm-mannered Charlie. Mara tried to clap in rhythm but kept clapping in the blank spaces. No matter, though—the music was so loud she didn't think anyone would notice. A man stood on the platform, five women flanking him. They sang with big, gulping, deep-down breaths that fueled large melodic voices. Miss Peavey'd be impressed, that's for sure. At Mara's old school in Little Pine, Miss Peavey could barely get them all to sing one part. Two parts were a disaster, and three parts nearly killed the poor lady. Jenkins had no such music program—a fact Mara lamented until this day. The music embedded itself into her this Sunday morning, lifting her eyes and heart.

"God have mercy," they sang, waving their funeral fans.

"Bless sweet Jesus," they shouted, arms raised to heaven.

"I need You," they prayed, knees buckled under.

Mara looked at her Mickey Mouse watch. His hands told her she'd been there three hours, but it felt like only a few minutes. For one moment of time Mara felt she had found home.

# Twenty

BISHOP RENNY, TALL AND PROUD, APPROACHED Mara. He petted her hair and looked into her eyes. "You're the spittin' image of your mama," he said.

*My mama? He knows my mama? And I look like her?* A part of Mara's heart, the part that had been longing for her parents, leapt for joy. She looked up at Bishop Renny. "Really? What do you mean?"

Zady stepped between them just as Bishop Renny opened his mouth to answer. "May I have a word with you, *Reverend*? Over there?"

Zady pulled Bishop Renny away from Mara. He looked back at her, an apology in his eyes.

*Why can't I know about my mama? What's Zady so afraid of?*

"You hungry?" Charlie asked.

"Yeah, a little," Mara said.

"You're probably not used to such a long service. White folks have such short ones. Not us. To get the Devil out and Jesus in, we need time. And we need food." Charlie showed Mara the back entry of the church, which had been transformed into a feasting spot.

Plates and dishes of piled food sat on bright yellow table-cloths. "What's that?" she whispered.

"Okra, silly. Haven't you ever eaten it?"

"No. What about that green stuff?"

"Greens? Girl, that's God's food right there. You haven't ever lived until you ate greens." He slopped a big steaming pile onto Mara's Dixie plate.

The rest of the spread looked familiar—corn, beans, black-eyed peas, cornbread, sweet potatoes, and pumpkin pies—nearly ten of them.

"I love pumpkin pie," she told Charlie.

"Pumpkin pie? What're you talking about? This here's sweet potato pie—a little slice of heaven's what I call it."

She saved her sweet potato pie until the end, although Charlie ate his first. He was right; it was heaven—creamy, custardy, puddinglike, but smooth and sweet. Sure beat Aunt Elma's pumpkin pie from a Libby's can hands down.

An elderly lady wrestling a walker creaked and pushed her way toward Mara. "Hello, little lady. M'name's Mama Frankie. Yours?"

"Mara. Mara Weatherall."

"You seem a little hesitant. Don't know your own name, child? There was a time when I didn't know my name either. My daddy, he loved Spanish names. Named me Francesca. Ooooh, did I get teased, 'specially when I started developing. 'Nice chesta, Francesca,' they'd say and laugh. I turned myself into a Frankie on my eighteenth birthday. Daddy, he was a stubborn one. Called me Francesca anyway, and I let him out of respect. But t'everyone else, I'm Frankie."

"My name's also Maranatha."

"Come, Lord Jesus," Frankie said, lifting her cataract cloudy-day eyes to Mara's. Her gray hair frizzed and skewed in crazy directions. She lifted her right arm into the air, her palm facing heaven. "Come, Lord Jesus," she shouted.

Mara stepped back.

"Yes, come, Lord Jesus. Today. Come into this child's weary heart. Come, Lord Jesus. Spit-shine her soul. Clothe her in righteous clothes. Oh, sweet Jesus. Come!"

Frankie raised her voice, ambled her walker closer. She lowered her arm and took Mara's hand. "The sweet Lord Jesus says to you, Maranatha, 'You are beautiful. You are Mine. You'll forever be Mine.' "

*General's words!*

Mara yanked her shaking hand from the old woman's grip and ran out the back door into the hot rush of air.

"Hey!" Charlie called.

Mara kept running into the church garden, where Charlie caught her. "Don't worry none about Mama Frankie. She's old and losing her hearing. She always yells. Used to frighten me to death. Used to hide in the corner, hoping she wouldn't walk her walker over to me and tell me the words of God."

"She had no right to say those things to me."

"Old folks have rights to say anything. They've earned it. 'Sides, she's harmless. Some of the things out of her mouth are purer than truth. Best take to pondering her words. Usually I shrug 'em off, but then, when I'm in bed at night, Mama Frankie's words play over and over in my head like a—"

"Broken record?"

"Yeah, how'd you know?"

"Ah, nothing." Mara kicked the dry, red dirt with her sandal, reddening her toes. She looked at the neat rows of tallish green plants, climbing up lines of string that had been pulled between two rotting posts. "What plant is this?"

"I can't believe you really live in Burl and don't know that."

"My Nanny Lynn, she was a farmer, but I don't remember ever seeing plants quite like this." Kicking the dirt, she blushed this time.

"Purple-hulled peas. There's nothing finer. Makes the poor black-eyed pea look like plain ol' grits." He bent low to the ground and pulled a green tendril from its twining place. "See here?"

Mara nodded.

"What do you see?"

"A purple flower."

"That's right. That little flower will grow up and turn into a huge purple pod with eight or ten peas inside. We have us a shelling party when they're ripe and ready. Can't wait for you to come." Charlie laughed.

"What's so funny?"

"White folks, they get the purplest hands when they hull the peas. Bright purple. And you can't wash it off. It dyes your hands until the skin flakes off. Not even bleach will unpurple it."

"What about you? Don't you get purple hands?"

He laughed again. "Look here at my hands, Mara. What do you see?"

She smiled. His hands, at least on top, were a rich, dark brown. His palms, pink. "I see what you mean."

When the tree shadows lengthened and the afternoon ended, Della and Sadie fought about who would sit in which seat in the sweltering Dodge Aspen. It made no sense to Mara since both seats looked the same to her. She wanted to scold the sisters and tell them they should be eternally grateful that they even have a sister. If Mara had a sister she'd never fight with her. No way.

When Zady's family and Mara rode back toward Burl's

center—windows open—the hot air blew through Mara like an overactive hair dryer, causing beads of sweat to burst from nearly every pore of her body. Mara took to farm gazing as the wind whipped her hair into a hot, stringy mess. Farms made her ache for Nanny Lynn, for lazy days in the hammock, for a piece of time when she was cherished. She wanted to memorize every farm, every trailer home, every hay bale, every cowbird, everything. The country beckoned her. When she once dreamed of living in the stately white house with English butlers and envious neighbors, she had forgotten one thing—it could never be in the country. The house was permanently planted on city soil.

A sign greeted them on the Loop: "Burl—National Historical Treasure." Mara wondered where on earth they had put Burl's historical treasures. Burl and treasure mixed about as well as Aunt Elma and beauty school.

That night, in the silence of her room, the moon shone through the window, casting pale light on the foot of her bed. Mr. Winningham's shadow had not yet haunted the corridor, and Stripes had yet to curl onto her stomach.

Charlie was right. Mama Frankie's words settled into Mara at first in a whisper, then in a shout. "The sweet Lord Jesus says to you, Maranatha, 'You are beautiful. You are Mine. You'll forever be Mine.'"

# Twenty-One

THE UNEASINESS SHE FELT ABOUT SUMMER'S dawning gnawed at her stomach. With school a fading memory, Mara filled lonesome days by playing with Nose Bunny in her room when the attic got too hot. Camilla took to visiting her whenever she could. She said it was more exciting than her boring old yard, and she was probably right. Camilla's mom hardly ever let her inside unless a tornado warning came over the airwaves. She said Camilla should be outside "to get her stink blown off," so their adventuring was limited to Burl's hot-as-a-griddle sidewalks or the Shrub Club behind Gus's house. However, Camilla's mom was wrong: In Burl's heat, their stink never did blow off.

After "decorating" the Shrub Club with a wooden stool, a remnant of stained carpet from someone's alley trash, an old cracked mirror, a paisley curtain they tied to the upper branches to make two tiny rooms, and a set of plastic plates and tumblers, its novelty had worn off.

It was in the Shrub Club that Camilla said, "This summer's a butter cutter, sure enough." Camilla wiped her forehead with the bottom of her T-shirt, leaving a smudge of dirty sweat.

"What?"

"A butter cutter—you know, like a hot knife."

Mara shook her head. She wished she could rhyme like that.

"Anyway, I'll be coming to the Dare-it Garret from now on. You game?"

"Sure. It can't be much hotter than this. Zady gave me an old fan, besides."

"Great."

"We're bound to find Denim's house someday. We've got more of a chance from my house than yours." Mara was careful to never use the word *home* when she referred to the big white house. It was simply a building with tall windowed walls and a shale roof. *Home* meant someone living there loved you. *Home* meant at least a little secondhand attention. Peeling away the layers of *home*, like peeling away layers of nail polish, was something tedious and painful. *Home*, at least in the *Brady Bunch* sense of the word, did not exist.

"Can we leave the Shrub Club? I'm getting hot." Mara mopped her forehead with her bandana.

"Shh! I hear something."

Footsteps—not pavement-smacking footsteps, but dust-splaying thuds—intensified. Mara wrapped her arms around herself and squeezed her eyes tight. The familiar creak of the back gate caused her to push her eyelids tighter. *Why I let Camilla talk me into this Shrub Club, I'll never know.*

"Ahem!" Gus's voice boomed.

Mara heard rustling. She opened her eyes. The shrub's limbs moved violently until daylight shot through to Mara's face.

"Well, well, well. Lookie here." Gus grabbed for Mara. She pressed her back against the shrub.

"Run, Camilla!"

Camilla inched through their back tunneled entrance, escaping. Mara turned to follow her when a thick hand grabbed her ankle.

"Now, let's see here. Got me a runaway. The law don't look kindly on runaways. No sir."

Gus dragged her toward the widening daylight, her skin chafing along the dirt and gravel. She kicked at him with her strong left leg and threw red dust at his eyes, but his grip held steady.

"What's wrong?" Gus curled his lip in a sneer. "Mr. Winningham ain't taking right good care of you? You miss ol' Gus?"

"No," Mara gritted.

He dragged her into the backyard, knocking Mara's head on the gatepost. Gus grabbed Mara's kicking leg. He shoved her ankles together in a painful crack, taking them both in one hand. He kept the other hand free. "You've caused me a lot of heartache, child. Got me in a heap of trouble. Just what *do* you know about Mr. Winningham, huh?"

"I'll scream! I can scream real loud!"

His wide hand closed over her mouth, muffling her.

"I'm sure you can. Yes, I'm sure of it." Gus settled his wide behind on her legs. Mara winced from the pressure. "Now, let's see. Trespassing. Destruction of property. These are some serious crimes, little lady. Serious, indeed. I could press a few charges, you know. Or, if you choose to keep your hollering mouth shut, I'd be willing to overlook your trespassing."

Mara muffled a reply, but Gus's sweaty hand erased her words.

"Being tricky, eh? All I want is you to keep quiet, understand?"

Mara squirmed. *Keep quiet about what?* She could see Gus's face above her, but if she cricked her neck and looked beyond her shoulder, she could see the sycamore's tree limbs swaying under the clouds. She closed her eyes, trying to blot out Gus's face, and opened them again, memorizing the waltz of the tree limbs.

"Look at me!" Gus's voice gurgled. He cleared his throat. Hocked spit flew by her left ear. Gus took Mara's chin in his other hand and forced her head downward till her chin hit her chest.

She strained to see one limb. Her eyes ached, but she rolled them backward, straining to see even one fluttery leaf.

"I said, look at me!"

Mara closed her eyes. Gus's weight on her legs had made them tingle and fall asleep. *Where is Camilla? Did she go for help?* She couldn't fetch her mom because her wacky fear of the outdoors kept her inside the house. Camilla's stepdad was always busy working on this and that. Calling the police wouldn't help, being as how one of Burl's finest was sitting on Mara's legs. No, Camilla was right to run away.

*Think, Mara, think.*

"Must be mighty awful living in that big ol' house in the black part of town, you being milky white and all." Gus looked around, a hint of fear glazing his eyes. "I don't know why he's giving me grief about putting you there. Seems like the perfect place for the likes of you."

She wanted to yell, *Who's giving you grief? What do you mean?* But her questions stayed muffled beneath Gus's hand.

Gus shook his head. "I don't know what Elma, rest her soul, ever saw in you. Her big heart felt sorry for you bein' all alone. She took you in—out of pity."

Mara kept her eyes mostly closed, but squinted so she could see a little. She could make out Gus's face, red and wet, his eyes darting left and right, nervous-like.

Mara tried to convulse her body. Since her arms were free, she jerked them back and forth. She moaned and pushed all the saliva she could to her lips, dribbling a pool into Gus's hand.

"What the—" He yanked his hand away.

Mara screamed, or at least she tried to, but nothing came out—just useless air. She forgot to keep flailing her arms.

"Trying to fake a seizure, huh? The druggies, they try that. Never works on wise ol' Gus. There's more to me than these good looks, you know."

Mara squirmed under Gus's torso, but his weight kept her pinned.

"What do you say we go inside for a little while? I think you'll like the way I fixed up the place."

"Take your hands off her, Gus," boomed a strong male voice. "Now!"

Gus stood quickly—in spite of his ample size—and backed away. Mara turned and sat up, rubbing her aching legs. Next to Camilla was a tall black man, thin and serious. "Come here, Mara."

Mara struggled to stand and stamped her feet toward the gate. When she opened it, the man held his hand to her, gently pulling her away from the yard. Camilla hugged her.

"What're you doing on *this* side of town, Markus?" Gus sneered. "Your kind don't belong here. You're lucky I don't have my gun."

The man named Markus didn't flinch; he kept looking right at Gus, unafraid. "You'll be hearing about this," he said.

Gus laughed. "Oh, that's a good one, Markus. You could shout it to a thousand pecan trees, and even they wouldn't listen. Not in this here town. You black Yanks think you have power, think you have a voice. You don't know much about the workings of Burl."

"I know enough to know a corrupt police officer when I see one," Markus said.

Camilla pulled at Markus's sleeve and pled with him with her eyes.

"What's that?" Gus bellowed.

Camilla yanked at Markus now, but he wouldn't budge.

" 'Corrupt police officer,' I said. And you are wrong. Everyone has a voice in this town, *Officer*, even this black man."

Gus shot a glare at Markus and ran his fingers through his thinning, greasy hair. He turned and lumbered back to Aunt Elma's house, most likely to get his gun.

Camilla was crying now, playing a desperate tug-of-war with the firmly planted Markus.

Before Gus opened the back door, he looked back at the three of them. "You're crazy, Markus."

"Crazy is as crazy does, *Officer*."

Gus slammed the door—a noise that finally made Markus give in to Camilla's pulling and pleading.

"Dad, *please*. Let's get home."

*Dad? He's her dad?*

After they had walked a few paces, Camilla interrupted Mara's spinning thoughts. "Mara, meet my stepdad."

Markus extended a dark hand to Mara and shook her hand vigorously. "Pleased to finally meet you, Mara. Camilla's told me all about you."

Something in Markus's voice changed once he extended his hand and spoke to her. When he talked to Gus, Camilla's stepdad sounded like most of the kids in Mara's school, like he really was from that side of town. Now, when he spoke to her eye to eye, his voice lost its drawl. In one moment he had gone from Sanford and Son to Mr. Rogers.

"You sound different," Mara said.

Camilla shook her head. For the first time in their friendship, Mara saw what fear looked like on Camilla. Like a pair of pants from charity, it didn't fit well.

"We need to get home, Dad. He's going to come back. You *know* what he's like," Camilla said.

They started walking down the alley. It looked different now that Mara knew one of Camilla's secrets. She felt a bit betrayed—Mara had told Camilla her secret, but Camilla apparently had some secrets of her own.

"He was wrong," Markus said to no one in particular. "I do have a voice. I speak for those who can't speak for themselves."

# Twenty-Two

DOWN THE ALLEY FROM THE SHRUB Club under the shadow of a slender black man, Mara felt as if she were the guest of honor at a surprise party.

"Denim?" she asked.

"Surprised?" He let out a wide laugh, kicking back his head like he was laughing at the sun itself.

"Mm-hmm," Mara said. She looked over at Camilla, whose face registered both fear and relief.

"Best be getting to our house before ol' Officer Gus decides to arrest us." Denim extended his arm to shelter Mara under it, but she trotted away. His right arm remained outstretched so that he looked like an *F* without its top. Instead of standing there like a topless *F*, he extended his other hand, making himself a small *T*, and stretched a yawn.

Mara allowed Camilla a spot of affection. Her friend's loose arm curled around her neck. "My dad wouldn't hurt a fly," she whispered. "No need to be afraid."

She hadn't given much thought to her reflex before. Usually she'd pull away from someone, tuck their hurt expression in some sort of emotionless box in her head, and go on—oblivious. This time she lingered. *Why do I pull away from*

*Zady? Charlie? Why pull away from the man who saved my hide?*

They made an interesting trio—a tall black man daring to walk proud in the good part of Burl, his teenage white daughter, and an orphan.

"You mind if I ask you something?" Mara asked Denim.

"Sure, fire away."

"Well, you and Zady don't sound the same—at least not right now."

"Who's Zady?"

"Our housekeeper. She's black too. Your voice—it doesn't sound like hers." Mara flipped her arms in front of her, tangling her forearms in a brief instant and then snapping them back to her side.

Denim laughed again, head back, teeth bared. "You mean I don't sound black, is that it?"

"Yeah, I guess. On the radio, you sound like a regular white guy." Mara blushed. She knew enough about racism to know there were words and phrases you shouldn't use, but she was never quite sure which ones she could use and which would offend.

"I'm not sure if that's a compliment or an insult," he said, smiling. "Gus *was* right about one thing—I am a Yankee. From Illinois. Went to college. Got a decent job at a radio station. Met Camilla's pretty mama there. You know she worked at a radio station?"

Mara shook her head.

"Yep, there she was, all blonde and shiny under those fluorescent lights. I thought I'd died and gone to heaven the first time I met her. Called her Daisy."

"But, her name's Rose," Mara said.

"She had such a happy, upturned face, I couldn't call her

Rose. Besides, calling her Daisy made her laugh. She was the front-desk secretary at the radio station—wide-eyed and afraid of the big city, so anytime I could make her smile or laugh, I did."

"Mama's from Burl—was born here," Camilla added.

"Sooner than later I asked Ms. Rose Salinger for her hand, even though I thought she'd say no, being a proper southern white gal and all."

"What happened?" Mara asked.

Denim stepped in front of them and got on his knee before Mara. "Well, I did what any black knight should do when courting a princess. I got on my knee, opened a velvet box, and said, 'Will you?' She stood there, like she was hammered to the floor. Didn't move. Didn't speak. But I knew I had her when I saw one tear slide down her flaxen face. She brushed it away, nearly knocked me over while throwing her arms around my neck, and yelled, 'Yes!' The happiest moment of my life, that's the truth." He stood and walked ahead of them.

"They got married a few weeks later," Camilla said. "I was the flower girl. I was only four then. I threw petals pell-mell at the poor audience—even managed to hit Aunt Patty in the eye. She had contacts. I ain't never heard the end of that."

"Was it a big wedding?"

"No," Denim said. "We got married at my church, a Methodist church downtown. Most of my side came, some didn't—on account of me marrying a white gal and all. My great-grandmother refused to come, said I sold out to the slavery establishment. She's still sore at me."

"Did Rose's family come up for the wedding?"

Camilla grabbed Mara's arm and shook her head—a sure sign to shush.

"That's okay, Camilla. No, Mara. None came. Said it was too expensive. We pretended that was the reason too, since the real reason hurt too much."

Camilla chimed in. "After he lost his job, he and mama decided to come down here and live in grandma's vacant house. It was free, and we could grow lots of food out back."

When they reached Camilla's house, Denim opened the door with a key—a strange thing indeed. No one locked doors in Burl, not even where the criminals lived. His nervous eyes seemed to be watching a tennis match—looking back and forth.

"C'mon, Dad. There's no one around. Let us in. It's hot."

Although Mara had been in the yard on many occasions, today everything looked different, what with Denim there. He opened the door, letting Mara and Camilla inside.

A proper parlor with high-sheen antique furniture, tall ceilings, and a rotating ceiling fan greeted Mara. No pictures adorned the green wallpapered walls. And there was no sign of Camilla's afraid mama.

According to Camilla, Rose started being scared to leave the house about a month after they moved in. Something happened to her at Value Villa that made her speechless for nearly a week.

Mara's legs twitched nervy once she sat down, still smarting from Gus's rear-end planting. She hadn't even noticed that Camilla and Denim were on the stairs.

"Come upstairs. I want to show you something," Camilla said.

Mara rubbed her thighs, hoping that would ease the deep muscle pain, and followed Camilla up the wide staircase.

"I'm working on the house bit by bit. Been stripping the staircase, but it's slow going." Denim caressed a section of stripped banister. "Camilla will have grandbabies by the time I finish remodeling."

So much of Burl was blanketed in peeling, neglected paint that it swelled Mara's heart to hear someone speak fondly of a home's restoration. Even her own white mansion was falling apart—something that apparently didn't bother Mr. Winningham but nagged at Mara nearly every time the sun coursed the sky.

"Here we are—my room," Camilla said. She opened a tall eight-paneled door, rattling the transom on top. "Voila! My paradise!"

The walls were purple and pink and blue and sea green, all at once. It looked like an ocean explosion, or seven puzzles crammed together all kitty-corner and wild. "Amazing," was all Mara could say. She'd thought herself progressive with greenish-yellow walls at Aunt Elma's, but this, *this* was pure art—swirling and dancing on the canvas of walls.

"You paint this yourself?"

"Yessirree. Call it my crush-smush technique. I grab a paintbrush, douse it with some leftover paint my dad finds for me, and crush and smush it on the wall, however I want to."

Mara's white-walled room became stifling in the face of this. *How can I live one more day surrounded by white?* She was forever ruined for the ordinary. From now on, she'd live life with a paintbrush in her hand.

# Twenty-Three

MARA HADN'T THANKED DENIM FOR RESCUING her from Officer Gus. She turned away from Camilla's wild walls to do just that, but Denim was gone.

"Where's your dad?"

"Up in the recording studio, probably," Camilla said.

"Really? You have one here?"

"Yep. Dad got stuff together and wired one. Used those foam mattress pad thingies to make the walls soundproof. Got radio equipment from an estate sale up the road a piece and built it himself."

"You mean he doesn't go to KBBQ's studio on Perry Street?"

"He's never been there." Camilla sat with a plop on a yellow beanbag chair. Against the backdrop of the purplish walls, it looked like a glowing sun about to set for the evening.

Mara sat on Camilla's huge bed—tall and high, so high you could easily crawl underneath. "Never been there? I don't get it."

"He tried to get a job first thing after he moved here. He called KBBQ, gave them his qualifications, and asked if they were hiring. Brad, the station manager, sounded real interested too, until he told him his name—Markus Jackson."

"But I thought—"

"Don't get your panties in a wad. Let me tell my story. See, everyone knew that Markus Jackson was the black man who married Rose Salinger. She'd been the town beauty—homecoming queen and the Dogwood princess. Douglas Salinger snatched her up early. Douglas is my real dad."

"But you call Denim Dad."

"You call a person by how they act, not by who they are related to. At least, that's my explanation. Markus is my dad. Douglas was a bad man who nearly killed my mother. No one who nearly kills can be called Father. Fathers, according to Denim, are supposed to give life, not take it, and I agree."

Mara sat on the tall bed, pulling her knees to her chest and holding her ankles. Camilla had never said much before about her family, and Mara hadn't asked. She knew her own pain was tangled up with the word *family*—she figured Camilla was the same. "I'm sorry I never asked you about your family before," she said.

"No matter. Wouldn't have told you anyway. I promised Dad I'd keep his secret. Even made up an acrostic. S-E-C-R-E-T. Silence Elbows Crime, Ruins-it Every Time," Camilla said.

"So how come he's on the radio?"

"Changed his name to Denim—thought it sounded white—and called the station again. Said he'd dig up dirt on Burl politics and that he'd have to stay in hiding to do that. Made it sound really intriguing—even used the word *clandestine*."

"What's that mean?"

"Undercover and secret. Hush-hush."

"And they hired him?"

"Right then. The manager was looking for something spectacular, he told Dad, and this was it. They mail his check to a post-office box, and we pay someone to pick it up and remail it to us in an envelope we provide so the postman won't snoop. Return address is always Hollywood, California. That was my idea. May as well dream big, I always say."

"How's he get his words to the station?"

"Big antenna. Our attic is blessed with a very steep roof. Inside is a huge antenna that Dad uses to beam his program to the station every day."

"How does he keep from being discovered? I mean, your mom—she doesn't shop or run errands, does she?"

"Dad drives at night mostly and does his shopping inside the Loop, where his black face is one of many. Sometimes he goes to Value Villa to get stuff for the house. He buys stamps through the mail—did you know you could do that?"

Mara shook her head.

"Well, you can do lots of stuff through the mail. And, if anyone comes over, he's rigged the doorbell so that it rings all over the house. That's his cue to go to his studio. I'm the only one who answers the door."

"Is that why I've never seen inside your house?"

"Yep. It's our cruel rule. No one's allowed to come inside—not even you, until you got captured by Officer Gus."

"Hey, thanks for rescuing me."

"No problem." Camilla said it so matter-of-fact, like she had done something as nonheroic as making a peanut butter and jelly sandwich.

"You *saved* me. You risked *everything*. How can I repay you?"

"You want to see the studio?"

"I'll never understand why you always answer my questions with your own questions." Mara laughed and jumped off the high bed and yelped out in pain, forgetting that the wide man had nearly crushed her thighs.

"You okay?"

"Yeah—it smarts though."

Camilla led her to the end of the hall and knocked a furtive and gentle knock.

"Come in," came a voice that sounded far away and muffled.

Surprises came in all sorts of packages today—first Denim's appearance wrapped in black skin, then Camilla's room shrouded in purple ocean fantasy, and now the studio decked out with padding and wires and *Burl Atlas* clippings attached to the walls with duct tape.

"Shut the door, I want to show you gals something."

Mara did. It thwammed shut. Then silence.

"Hear that?" Denim wheeled around in his office chair, expecting an answer.

Camilla shrugged. The taller she got, the shruggier she became, as if height was a thing to be ashamed of like a wart or head lice.

"That, ladies, is the sound of nothing. *Nada. Ne rien.* Nothing. It's what all Burl's afraid of—silence. See, if folks would be quiet and think real hard about the issues in this town, they'd probably start thinking for themselves. Hey, they might even demand some change."

"Here he goes." Camilla rolled her eyes, but in a playful way.

"What this town needs are some thinkers—folks who take to logic like a hog to some grubs. So, what do I do? I tell 'em stuff to think about when they're on their beds at night. I raise questions. I—"

The padded door swung open. Rose stood there, quiet with pursed lips, looking terribly distant and frightened—like she'd seen one too many Hitchcock movies. "The door—"

Denim stopped his speech. Mara expected him to yell. Whenever she'd interrupted Aunt Elma, she got a word licking—stinging and serrated. But instead of yelling, Denim stayed quiet, like the room had sedated his voice. He walked over to the quavering Rose and hung his long, dark arm over her small shoulder. "What's the matter, Daisy?"

Mara swore she saw the sad woman press a half smile to her thin lips. "The door. Someone's here—knocking." Rose took a deep breath, like she was ready to dive under water. "White Cadillac."

Mara's face mimicked Rose's. In one second of time, she had changed from fascinated explorer to frightened deer—big-eyed and frozen to the soundproofed floor.

"C'mon, Mara. Best be going," Camilla said, grabbing Mara's hand. Mara followed begrudgingly like one of Red Heifer's doomed cows on its long walk to the slaughterhouse.

"You won't tell SSW about my dad, will you?" she whispered.

"'Course not. I don't talk to him anyway. I'll keep your S-E-C-R-E-T." Mara felt like she was almost floating above her body. She could hear herself say the words calmly, but somehow she was removed, hoping that removal would lessen the shock that was about to come. Aunt Elma's verbal wrath she had learned to bear. Not Mr. Winningham's silent rage.

*Pound, pound, pound.* The front door shook with Mr. Winningham's fists.

"Knocking is as knocking does," Camilla said. She opened the door in the midst of the pounds, throwing Mr. Winningham off-kilter. He stumbled forward, nearly losing his hat.

He straightened it. "I am here for the girl," he said in a monotone, his lips stretched back toward his ears, like he was trying to keep from roaring. "Got a call from the Po-lice, saying she'd been loitering. She's late for dinner."

Mara looked at her watch—6:16.

"It's my fault," Camilla said.

Mr. Winningham swept past Camilla, grabbed Mara, and

pulled her through the door in one smooth motion. His clenched grip pressed into her bony elbow. He pushed her forward toward the white Cadillac, its back door open like a hungry mouth. He shoved her in, slammed the door, and took his time walking around to the driver's side. He took slow steps; she could hear them—like his slow dinner eating the other night. Mara counted to twenty-three by the time he opened and shut the door and settled in behind the steering wheel.

She lay in the back, afraid to sit up. She hesitated to even look up, worried she'd catch his brooding gaze in the rearview mirror. Staying low—something she'd mastered in her decade of life—had been her salvation in the past. But tonight, she was pretty sure it caused the man's white neck to turn red.

# Twenty-Four

MARA DIDN'T REALIZE BURL'S ROADS WERE so bumpy, but in her curled position on the backseat, she felt every road rut on her sore hips and legs. Mr. Winningham's silence seemed to compound the jostling, although she didn't know quite how. Maybe if he'd turn on the radio, she'd be able to think away the bumps.

Mr. Winningham drove as if he had a Crock-Pot of soup on the floor of the Cadillac, ready to spill over. Despite this, the bumps would have splashed the broth all over his shiny floor mats.

The car stopped, jarring her body again. "We're here. Dinner's cold." He opened and slammed his own door, leaving Mara in the Cadillac's backseat.

She sat up. The back of the white house looked angry tonight. The sun beat on this side of the house, obliterating its long-ago paint job. It screamed neglect.

Mara wasn't the type of girl who gained attention from her disobedience, but tonight something bubbled up in her—something called rage. She opened the car door and slammed it—hard.

She opened and slammed the back door. Slammed it so

hard the glasses on the shelves next to the door clinked. She was hoping that slamming was some magic pill that would instantly make her feel better when she did it. But as everything in her life, her expectations and reality were worlds apart. Slamming didn't take away her helplessness, Mr. Winningham's silence, or her desire for love. No, it made her feel sorry for the poor door.

She stomped through the kitchen, past the dining room. Mr. Winningham's hat was to the right of his TV dinner—it was Saturday, after all—and he sat there erect, not speaking. At her usual place, opposite Mr. Winningham, was the same tired placemat, the usual properly placed silverware, a glass, and an empty spot where her own TV dinner should have been.

Maybe it was the slamming that made her do it. Maybe it was her weariness over having to watch the silent man eat while her stomach gnawed at her. Maybe it was plain foolishness. Whatever the reason, Mara stomped right past him, right past the table, right past her place. She turned and looked at Mr. Winningham square on.

"Enjoy your dinner, Mr. Winningham. Alone." She said it without so much as a quiver in her voice, turned on her dusty flip-flops, and walked upstairs.

Alone.

# Twenty-Five

IN THE NEXT DAY'S PALE SUNDAY morning light, Mara jumped when the doorbell buzzed. She thought of poor Denim having to hide every time he heard his own doorbell ring.

Zady's habit was to buzz and then walk into the kitchen. Mara put her dress on. She hadn't hung it up last Sunday, so it was a little frumpy. She tried to smooth her skirt, but eventually gave up and met Zady in the kitchen.

"He left a note, child." Zady handed Mara a neatly penned note—the kind where someone used a ruler under the cursive, making it look like lined paper even when it wasn't.

"Why?"

Zady shook her head. "Don't know, baby. Why don't you stick it in this Bible and read it on your way to church?" Zady handed her a red-covered Bible. "It's for you."

"But—" Mara puzzled over the beautiful red Bible. Why would Zady give her a Bible when she already had one? Didn't she give her all those books—including the Bible?

"Don't be 'butting' me. You're the worst child at receiving. Try living in our house with three kids romping around. You get real good at receiving, and if you're too slow, you'll get good at stealing too." She laughed.

Mara's stomach grumbled.

"You hungry?"

Mara didn't know what to say. Zady was hopping mad the last time she found out Mr. Winningham hadn't fed her supper, and Mara was too weary to think about how to explain why he took her dinner away from her last night. Too many words to say. She was afraid that if she told Zady one small piece of her story the rest would leak out of her mouth, putting Denim in jeopardy.

"Well, are you or aren't you?"

Mara didn't answer.

"Look at your dress, child! First things first. Grab me that box of Cheerios, will you?" Zady took the box and poured a fair bit into an empty Cool Whip container, snapping the lid shut. "Eat this in the car on the way to church," she said. "Hurry, follow me."

Mara followed her into the downstairs bathroom and pointed to the bathtub's edge. "Now stand right here."

"In the tub?"

"No, near the edge—quick-like." She turned on the shower until the hottest water steamed the room. "The steam, baby. It'll straighten out the wrinkles. Wait right here and let the dress iron itself." When she returned, she had a rubber band. She pulled Mara's hair back tight, making her yelp.

"That hurts!"

"Beauty hurts sometimes, child. Gotta wrestle this rat's nest into a ponytail." With a twist of her wrist, Zady finished the ponytail. Mara was sure that if her hair were alive it would scream bloody murder.

"Time to go. Hop into the Aspen and let's git to gitting."

Charlie bugged her all the way to church, asking her to solve impossible riddles—something about being on an elevator with lots of floors. There were times that simple company salved the loneliness in Mara's short life—this was not one of them. Today she wanted solitude and nature, not chattering about riddles.

"Leave her be, Charlie boy. I think she's sick." Zady pulled down her visor and applied wet red lipstick to her full lips. "You kids cool enough back there?"

"Yes'm," came the girls' replies.

Mara turned so that her back was facing Charlie. She could see the Burl countryside better this way. The hills ran slow races up and down, up and down, almost lulling her to sleep. The ache in her thighs kept her alert, though, and her head was sore again—probably from what Camilla called SMF. So many facts. She wondered if Denim went to church. She remembered his nervous glances when he unlocked his front door yesterday. On the radio he ranted fearlessly about Burl's politicians and police, but when she met Denim—blue eyes to brown eyes—she realized he was just a man, a scared man trying to do right. She hoped she would do right some-day, even if she was scared silly.

Mara managed to avoid Mama Frankie during the singing, mostly because she was sandwiched between Charlie and Zady. The music, although many folks sang to it, had a solitude that calmed Mara's nerves. She didn't sing this time. Instead, she let the words mingle and harmonize above her head and sink down to her toes. She took a deep breath in the midst of "His Eye Is on the Sparrow."

*I sing because I'm happy,*
*I sing because I'm free,*
*For His eye is on the sparrow,*
*And I know He watches me.*

*He watches me? He saw me under the tree limbs? He saw me struggle under General?* Her momentary calm changed to anger. *What kind of God watches helpless little girls and doesn't help them?* She didn't sing before because listening to the music soothed her, but now she deliberately chose *not* to sing. *I am not happy. I am not free. I will not sing a lie.*

Last week the sermon reached into Mara's heart. Every time Bishop Renny spoke about Jesus, Mara's heart galloped, scrambling to hear more about the Man who welcomed unruly kids on His lap, who put the know-it-alls in their place, who healed blind folks, who gave that thing called grace. This week—nothing. If Bishop Renny was right, and Jesus is God, then Jesus saw her too. And did nothing.

Out of respect for Zady, she had to fake her listening. She did this by watching the birds outside twirl midair, by counting the pews front to back, by trying to figure out if an "amen" came from a man or a woman. All this was interesting, so her fakery bakery was complete. Only one problem though—it felt a lot like slamming doors. Satisfying for the moment, but painful in the long run. She felt bad that she was pretending in church under God and Jesus' apparent gaze.

Mama Frankie clacked behind her in line for food. "Well, if it ain't the 'Come, Lord Jesus' gal."

Mara didn't turn around. She pretended she was picking through the peas, eliminating the bad ones from the good ones.

Mama Frankie tapped her on the shoulder. "Hey, girl. You hear me? I'm a talking 'bout you!" She barked it so loud, people turned around. On noticing it was Mama Frankie, they went back to piling food on their plates.

Mara turned and faced the tapping woman. "What do you need?" Mara asked, hoping she'd think Mara was offering her a spoonful of handpicked peas.

"I need to see you smile, little girl. You used to smile all the time. C'mon, now. Show me those white teeth." Mama Frankie grabbed Mara's chin and squeezed. "One smile. C'mon now, sugar. Life ain't that bad, now is it?"

Mara tried to look around, tried to find Zady, but Mama Frankie's firm grip kept her from looking too far. Mara clenched, "Don't know what you're talking about, ma'am. I've only been here one week. I don't remember smiling last week."

"It's not right to tell lies in God's house," she said, removing her molasses-brown hands from Mara's chin. "I remember when you was as high as this walker."

Zady came from the back of the room and put her arm around Mama Frankie. "Now, don't be scaring my Maranatha, you hear me? You know for a fact she's only been here once. I swear, Mama Frankie, you've got one wild imagination."

Mama Frankie coughed into a white hankie and waved it at Zady. "It's not right to tell lies in God's house. You, for one, should know that better than the child here."

Mara looked at Zady, whose mouth was open, eyes wide. Zady said nothing to Mama Frankie, who pushed herself farther down the potluck line, balancing a sturdy paper plate on the corner of her walker.

"Don't you worry yourself about Mama Frankie's words, Maranatha," Zady whispered. "She's a little crazy."

"I heard that!" came Mama Frankie's loud reply.

Zady left Mara standing there with a plate full of peas and a head full of wondering thoughts. Three people had sworn they'd seen her, or someone like her—Bishop Renny, Mama Frankie, and Eliot, the man with the flowery yard. And Zady was acting funny. Her eyes hinted that she held a terrible secret. Used to be Mara could pester Aunt Elma to near death in hopes of getting a scrap of information. No longer. When she was really quiet inside she missed Aunt Elma, not for the secrets she held, but for her *being*.

Mara sighed. It only reasoned that she'd have to stick to live folks to uncover the mystery of her own family. Zady had already pulled aside the kindly bishop, so he was probably tight-lipped now. Mara decided she'd swallow her fear and talk to Mama Frankie someday, that is, if she was ever in the same room without Zady nosing around. She could ask Eliot straight out who this Sephie person was, but he might ramble on and on about hollyhocks or furniture repair. Funny how both Mama Frankie and Eliot were old and a little crazy—how Mara's fate was mixed up with nutty old folks. *The key to unlocking the mystery of my life is hidden in two gray heads.*

The ride home was slow going, what with Zady talking on and on about the price of gas while Raymond said, "uh-huh" and "yes, dear," and Charlie wanting to teach Mara all the rules of football.

After she shushed Charlie, Mara took to watching the swaying trees—an attempt at giving her mind a break from too much thinking. She spotted two weeping willows, several redbuds already greened, a few stately live oaks, and a million or so pines.

When they arrived at the big white house, Raymond opened the car door for her. "See you next week, ma'am."

"You're wasting gas, Raymond. Stop your chattering," Zady called from the passenger seat.

Mara accompanied her half wave with a lukewarm smile and walked up the house's porch stairs.

It wasn't until well after supper with the mute man and the steaming TV dinner that she remembered Mr. Winningham's note crammed into her red-coated Bible. In the quietness of her bedroom, she opened the folded letter and smoothed it out on her bed.

*To Miss Maranatha,*

*No more leaving the house to go to that crazy girl's house. No more visits from the crazy girl. No more wandering the neighborhood knocking on folks' doors. No more telephone. No more mail. I am getting myself a post-office box and canceling our mail service. No more nothing, unless you're with Zady.*

*Mr. Winningham*

The "no mores" of Mr. Winningham shut down the rest of Mara's summer. No more nothing. That meant no more investigating—no asking Denim what he knew about scandal or her mama. No more listening to rhyming Camilla. No more visiting Lindy with the darting eyes. No more chance to ask Eliot about Sephie. No more life. All she had was church, *Brady Bunch* reruns on the small black-and-white TV, and the books that kept appearing in her room.

There was only one gray head that could help her now—Mama Frankie's.

# Twenty-Six

THUS IT BECAME THE SUMMER OF Nose Bunny adventures. Although Mara was glad the big white house protected her from the likes of General and Gus, she felt a sinking loneliness settle into her that even Nose Bunny couldn't shoulder. Sure, Nose Bunny listened quite well with her shabby ears, but she never rhymed back. Even Zady seemed too busy for her; they hardly ever crossed paths, and when they did, Zady would change the subject if Mara peppered her with questions. It was as if Mara's questions wearied Zady.

Summer TV lost its fascination. She'd memorized every *Brady Bunch* rerun and actually looked forward to school and silencing Lou Ann Scroggins' know-it-all talk. A few new books appeared in her peach crate—enough to keep her reading. Currently, Mara was crying her way through *Little Women*. She longed for sisters, and her longing seemed emptier now that Mr. Winningham had plucked Camilla from her life. Life had become so silent that Mara had taken to talking to herself. She begged Nose Bunny or Chrissy the doll to talk back to her, but both remained mute.

Every day she sat on her bed at 2:00 and listened to Denim. At least *he* talked to her. He spoke of politics, whatever that was, and how if he could, he'd personally oust the judge. Today, he spoke of the bank mafia, how if someone went against the will of the city council, they'd be squeezed out of things like loans or land.

"Seems all the banks are in cahoots with each other, each scratching each other's back. They've got the same phone line, I'm convinced. Just try to get a loan if you are on their blacklist. Why, in the course of one day, I was turned down flat by all three banks. I'm sure they called each other, saying, 'Some guy is coming over. Seems like trouble. Don't loan to him.' Of course, they didn't know it was Denim the Radio Man, otherwise they'd treat me to a nice police escort."

Mara laughed. She loved knowing the deepest secret of Burl. *Denim is a black man!*

Usually, right at the end of his broadcast, Denim would sneak in a message to Mara in the form of a fake commercial for Mars Bars. "This show has been brought to you by KBBQ and Mars Bars, the sweetest treat you love to eat. My daughter begs me for a Mars Bar every day and wonders how they are doing all lonely on the store shelf. I swear that girl would eat ten a day if she could. Today she cried about Mars Bars. Hopefully someday soon we'll get to Value Villa and get her one, so she'll stop her boo-hooing."

Smiling, Mara turned off the radio. *At least Camilla misses me.*

Mara divided her days between the hot attic, the room with the beautiful dresses, and closet exploration. Just like she didn't believe in Santa Claus, she didn't truly believe in Narnia, but she secretly hoped to discover a faun in the back of an unorganized closet. Mostly, though, she was hunting for clues. She was rummaging through a downstairs hall closet when Zady caught her.

"What are you doing, child?"

"Exploring," Mara said. "There's nothing better to do." She stood and dusted her hands on her shorts.

"Closets are off limits—strict orders from Mr. Winningham."

"Why are you so scared of him? You could probably beat him up, Zady."

"Hush, child. Some people's strength is not as it seems. Mr. Winningham is a powerful man. He could run my family out of town if I so much as gave him a cross look."

"Why? He's just a strange man. Why's he so powerful?"

"One word, little lady. Money."

Mara shook her head. Zady motioned for her to close the closet, so she did. "Now, that's what I don't get. If he's so rich, why doesn't he dress rich? Why do I have to wear your family's hand-me-downs? Why is this beautiful house falling down? Why can't he hire someone to paint and fix it? Nothing makes any sense, especially why I'm living here. Why *am* I here?"

Zady sighed. "You're here because God wants you here."

"How did Mr. Winningham know my mama?"

"Complicated," Zady said. "Very complicated. Much too complicated for a ten-year-old. Besides, I'd lose my job if I told you. You don't want that, do you?"

"No, I guess not."

"You guess not?" Zady said, laughing. It was the first time she had laughed one of her jaunty laughs since Mama Frankie had rebuked her. Zady tousled Mara's already messy hair and looked straight at her. "I'm not one for apologizing, child. Mm-mm-mm. But I got to give you what I owe. I'm sorry for treating you like a bad cousin. Sorry right down to my black toes. I'm forgetful, that's what the Good Lord says. I forget that you're only a child—that you did nothing to get this life you have. Forgive me for treatin' you wrong?" Zady's dark eyes rimmed with eye-water, nearly spilling out.

"What does *forgive* mean?"

"That's a lifelong lesson, child. For me, I guess it means that you are willing to let me off the hook for treating you distant. You willing to do that?"

"Of course I can do that, Zady. Of course I forgive you." Standing in the hallway, her back to the closed closet door, Mara wrapped her skinny white arms around the stout black woman, inhaling her scent—a mixture of bleach and perfume and sweat. Mara's sudden burst of affection must have startled Zady at first, but soon she wrapped her arms around Mara, squeezing her.

"Your hug's a gift to me. I know how scared you are of folks touching you—of loving on you." Zady kissed the top of Mara's head and let her go. "You're going to make my eyes into a spring."

"Zady?"

"Mm-hmm?"

"It's not so hard to forgive you. I mean, you asked for it, and you were sorry. What about forgiving folks who aren't sorry for what they done?"

"That's the hardest question in the world, it is. Bishop Renny says something every once in a while that might help you. He says forgiveness is giving up all hope of having a different past."

"I don't know what that means. What do you think that means? That I should be happy I'm an orphan?"

*Happy that ol' General did awful things under the tree limbs? Never!*

Zady shook her head. "C'mon outside with me."

"But I'm not supposed to go anywhere."

"You can if you're with me, now come on."

Mara followed Zady to the front porch. "See that swing?" Zady asked.

"Yeah. I wish Mr. Winningham would fix it. I like porch swings."

"So did your mama."

Zady said nothing more, but she met Mara's eyes. "So did your mama," she repeated and then lifted her gaze from Mara to the swing and back to Mara again.

Mara looked again at the swing. One end tethered itself to the bead-board ceiling, the other end plunged its corner into the rotting deck. Its green paint was peeling. *Green paint.* Mara gasped. "Green paint," she said out loud.

"Your mama liked to swing," Zady said again.

In the pale light of the porch, a light went on for Mara— all at once like a flicked switch. "I used to live here! This was the porch swing my mama pushed me on. This swing right here!" She wanted to sit on the crooked swing, but thought the better of it; she'd had splinters before. "Did my mama like to sing?"

"All the time, child. All the time. Sang like a songbird from sunup to sundown."

"What happened to her, Zady? Where is she?"

"Mm-mm-mm. I can't say. But I can tells you this. At least one time in your life, you had a mama, and you were loved. You had a home. So don't go worrying about needing a differ-ent past. Part of it was beautiful. A dream. And someday, God will make your life beautiful again."

Mara dropped her gaze. "I'm not sure I want a *beautiful* life," she said quietly.

"There's a whole world of hurt in those words, child— hurt I can't understand. Only Jesus can bear those hurts."

"He seems far away—in heaven with Nanny Lynn and Aunt Elma, in the stars, in the flowers. If He really wanted to help me, why did He take Nanny Lynn? Or kill Aunt Elma? Or let Gen—" Mara put her hand to her mouth and looked under the large pecan tree, half-expecting to see General's grimace. He wasn't there, but his haunting remained.

"Jesus doesn't take and kill, He gives life," Zady said. She reached out to touch Mara's shoulder, but Mara recoiled. "All right, child. All right. I won't touch you and I won't preach to you. That's the sweet Holy Spirit's job, anyway. There'll be a day when Jesus will become clear to you. Until then, don't give up hope."

Zady went back into the house, leaving Mara with her thoughts.

Mara sank to the rotted floorboards. She touched the green swing's arm and turned around, hoping to see the singing lady behind her.

All she saw was peeling white paint.

# Twenty-Seven

IF MARA EVER MET RED HEIFER, she'd smack him. Not that she was prone to violence, but after eating countless helpings of his sweet ribs, she couldn't help herself. Every night was the same except that each time the summer sun coursed the sky, the days grew both hotter and shorter, a sure indication that school was coming. Mama Frankie had taken ill, so Mara knew nothing more about her parents except that her mama used to push her on the green porch swing.

Exploring forbidden closets, reading dusty books, and playing in the sweaty attic all lost excitement, so Mara spent the remaining part of the summer doing what she should've been doing all along—fixing the house. Doing things with her hands connected her to Nanny Lynn somehow, as if she could hear the dear woman's voice talking to her through each repair.

She begged Zady for some of Raymond's old tools, something to which Zady reluctantly obliged. First thing Mara did was reattach the porch swing to the eyehook on the porch's roof. It took a lot of hefting, but she did it. That accomplished, she sanded the swing right down to the raw wood, like she had done with Nanny Lynn's fences, until she'd ousted all the splinters. Zady found some primer in the cellar and an old horsehair brush. Mara primed the swing. It soothed her to cover over the bare wood completely, like every brush stroke erased its fatigue, its decay.

Nanny Lynn's voice coaxed from what seemed like years ago, "You have to prime, Mara girl."

"Why?" Mara had asked, the wind whipping her hair in a tangle on the hills of their Little Pine farm.

"Because nothing worth doing should be done halfway. If you don't prime the wood, you'll have to do this job again next year. And the next. Best prime it now."

Mara obeyed, pulling the paintbrush across and under fence boards.

"It's a lot like hurts, Mara girl. If you don't get them out, don't share them when they happen, they come back. And you have to attend to them again. Best get them out when they happen."

Mara pulled the last bit of primer over the porch swing's arm. *You're wrong, Nanny Lynn. Some things are best kept inside.*

Zady couldn't find any green paint, so Mara spent the next few weeks scraping the front of the house under the porch eaves. With each curl of paint that floated to the porch's deck, Mara felt a weight lift. It was hard work to fix things, but just like she felt when she cleaned up Nose Bunny, she felt happier when she was doing something outside herself, something for something else's good. She wanted the house to smile, and in wanting that, she smiled.

Mr. Winningham didn't notice her hard work. Secretly, she hoped he would reward her for her labor by maybe letting her go see Camilla, but nothing like that ever happened. He was as crabby and stern as ever, especially at dinnertime.

One evening Mr. Winningham counted out two hundred dollars to Zady right after she placed a heaping platter of ribs on the lonely table—two crisp bills.

"What's this for?" Zady asked.

"Buy the girl some clothes. She'll need some for school," he said as he pressed the bills into Zady's outstretched hand. Zady shot a look at Mara, who looked equally surprised.

"Pencils!" Mr. Winningham shouted from his chair, making Zady jump.

"Pencils?"

"She will need pencils."

Mara flip-flopped over to Mr. Winningham. The *thwap, thwap, thwap* of her rubbery shoes was the only noise in the echoing dining room. She stood over him, examined his neatly combed silvery hair, and put a tentative hand on his shoulder. He stared straight ahead, ignoring her sweaty palm.

"Thanks, Mr. Winningham—for the money."

Mr. Winningham nodded. Mara removed her hand.

Zady's eyes widened. She winked at Mara and motioned for her to return to her seat.

Mr. Winningham's nod—a small victory—made Mara think that perhaps a man lived beneath the proper hat, and that maybe someday, he'd have the wind in his lungs to tell her his secrets.

# Twenty-Eight

THAT EVENING, VALUE VILLA'S AISLES BUSTLED with possibilities for Mara. She fingered the smooth lingerie while Zady looked for sensible underwear. Touching the fabric like that made her ache for Aunt Elma.

"What're you doing?" Zady asked.

"It's soft—feel." Mara extended a silky nightie arm toward Zady.

"Girl, we don't have time for touching. We's got to shop." Zady took the extended nightgown arm. Instead of letting it fall back on itself, she held it a moment. "Mm-mm-mm. You're right. It's awful silky."

"Then, let's get it—for you."

"This money is for you, child. Mr. Winningham would birth a Red Heifer rib if he knew you didn't spend it how he meant it."

"Well, *I* mean to buy you something pretty and soft. What's your size?"

Zady laughed. "Extra large, child. Can't you see that?"

Mara found an XL and placed it in their shopping cart. "Now for the paint aisle."

"What?"

"The paint aisle. I need some green paint for the swing and a new brush—oh, and a lot of white paint for the front porch."

"That ain't clothes."

"No, but you said yourself that Value Villa has the best deals around when it comes to clothing. I'll be sure to get good deals."

Zady shook her head, her hands resting firmly on her wide hips.

"Please? It's not like I'm buying candy." Mara pushed the cart away from Zady, hoping she'd give up and follow behind.

Zady did, but that didn't stop the words spilling from her red mouth. "You'll be the death of me, Miss Maranatha. The death of me."

The paint aisle was really three aisles with paint stacked from floor to ceiling. At first, Mara pushed the cart back and forth, trying to figure out how someone chose the correct paint. Zady was little help. She rambled on and on about Mr. Winningham not liking paint buying one bit.

"You gotta choose a color first," came a man's voice behind her.

"De—" Before she could say his radio name, Denim shushed her with his finger.

"Choose a color. Over here." Denim led her to a bright display of hundreds of colors.

Zady noticed Denim's interest in Mara and made a beeline for the color display.

"I'm Markus Jackson," Denim said, extending his hand to Zady. "The girl looked lost—thought I'd help her out a bit."

"You work here?" Zady asked, eyeing him up and down.

"No, come here a lot, though. Fixin' to shine up an old house." Denim's voice sounded like Zady's—thick-accented and slow. If Mara closed her eyes, she'd swear she was hearing

Bishop Renny preach or Raymond talk on and on about his prized Dodge Aspen.

"Now, what color're y'all looking for?" he asked.

"Green." Mara slid her fingers down the green section, stopping at a grassy green color. "This one here—Emerald Isle. And some plain white."

"No need to mix white. What're you wanting to paint white?"

"A house."

"Inside or outside?"

"Outside."

Denim left momentarily and came back with three gallons of Value Villa Basic Outdoor White, placing them in her cart. "Five dollars each. That should start you out."

Mara looked again at the paint swatches. "These free?"

"Of course they's free," Zady said.

Mara didn't care what she bought with the two hundred dollars as long as she could have as many paint cards as she wanted. She chose Purple Passion, Flaming Pink, Amber Sunrise, Butter Yellow, Orange Daiquiri, Azure Sea, and Watermelon Patch.

Denim rang a small buzzer at the paint counter. "For mixing," he said, as if that was explanation enough.

He drummed his fingers on the counter and looked at Mara. "You look about my girl's age. She's awful lonely without no friends. I bet she'd like you very much. She likes to paint."

"But De—"

"Don't be 'butting' Markus Jackson. I'm telling you if you was my girl's best friend, she'd think about you every day and every night. She'd even try to write you letters if she knew they would get to you."

Mara smiled. *Camilla's thinking on me.* "Well, you can tell your daughter that I would write her too if I were allowed, I mean, if she was my friend."

"Little lady, I'll tell her that."

Zady looked at them. "What in tarnation are you gabbing on and on about?"

"Oh, nothing, I'm always looking out for my girl. She's an only child and she needs friends," Denim said. He winked at Mara.

A tired elderly man ambled to the counter. "What color?" he asked, leaning on his thin elbows.

"Emerald Isle," Denim said, handing the man Mara's paint card.

"How much?"

Mara shook her head. She really had no idea how much.

The old man cleared his throat. "What are you painting?"

"A porch swing," Mara said.

"One gallon should be plenty," the paint man said, yawning.

Mara watched in rapt attention as he grabbed a gallon from a high shelf, brought it to a machine, and pulled levers down, letting streams of deep colors flow into the white paint. She covered her ears when the paint shaker shook the paint wildly for several minutes. When he finished, he opened the paint can, revealing the perfect green.

"Thank you, sir." Mara lugged the can to her cart and set it inside. By the time she looked up, both the tired man and Denim were gone.

"I've got $170.00 left for clothes. We've paid twenty for the paint and ten for your pretty pajamas. You think I can get a lot with that?"

"Mm-hmm. Let's not forget one important thing." Zady looked at Mara so serious-like, Mara expected a stern lecture.

"Pencils!"

# Twenty-Nine

VONDA RAE WAS NOT A PAINTER, didn't like paint at all. When the fifth grade teacher, Mrs. Armitage, greeted Mara and Vonda Rae the first day of school, she greeted them with paintbrushes. "Paint," she said, "is the essence of life. Art," and here she paused, motioning with her paintbrush like a conductor, "is the window to the soul."

Vonda Rae looked at Mara and shook her head. Mara had heard rumors about Mrs. Armitage—that her head was always in the clouds and she made you paint your book reports. Mara felt at once that to appease Vonda Rae she had to pretend that painting was for babies, but secretly she thrilled at the thought of all that paint and all those colors and all that white paper. Painting the porch swing had its satisfaction, but Mara grew tired of the same old Emerald Isle green. And finishing the clapboards of the front porch in plain old white lacked imagination. Coloring her world, that's what Mara longed to do.

"I hate paint," Vonda Rae whispered as she blobbed some brownish green on a piece of construction paper.

Mara rolled her eyes for maximum effect. "I *know* what you mean. I'd hate to get my new clothes all paintish." She smoothed her shirt, one of the many shirts she had bought at

Value Villa. The night she and Zady shopped, she hid the paint cans under the stairway and laid out her outfits all over her room like flattened ten-year-olds without heads. Mara walked around each outfit, exchanging a T-shirt with cords with a blouse and jeans, trying to combine as many outfits as she could. She could go to school twenty-six times without wearing the same thing twice. Truly miraculous.

"Paint what you feel!" Mrs. Armitage said without embarrassment. Her long brown hair was parted right down the middle until you got to the back of her head where her part jutted to the left like a fork in the road. She was freckled, something Mara admired since she didn't think grown-ups could have freckles.

Clarence Baker laughed as he doused his page with black tempera paint.

"Beautiful, Clarence. Capture your first day of fifth grade. Be free!"

"She's crazy, that's what," Vonda Rae whispered. She had painted a crude tree. It looked more like a spider web with green-black smudges around it, but Mara'd never criticize.

Mrs. Armitage bent low by Vonda Rae's desk. "Crazy is as crazy does, I always say."

Mara laughed. And then she felt a tear singe her eyelid. It had been two months since she'd last seen Camilla, but it seemed more like a year.

Mara picked up an empty paintbrush and painted a creamy white oval. While that dried, she painted brown hair, exactly like Camilla's—parted on the side and a little stringy. Mara closed her eyes and remembered Camilla's teasing face. She painted almond-shaped eyes. Halfway down the oval she made rounded humps for the bottom of her nose. For her mouth, she chose a pale pink. Because she didn't think she could paint teeth, and because Camilla was sometimes very serious, she painted her lips straight across, neither smiling nor pouting, firmly closed.

She looked at her painting again. Yep, it was Camilla. Painting her made Mara feel particularly lonely on her first day of fifth grade, and somehow Mrs. Armitage could tell.

"Having a rough first day, Maranatha?"

Maybe Mrs. Armitage was right. Maybe art was a window into her soul. She felt a little helpless and exposed by Mrs. Armitage's art insights, and she worried that if she kept painting, all her secrets would come blazing out from the page. She set her paintbrush down, put the painting under her desk, and pulled out a math book. At least math wouldn't tell her secrets to a crooked-parted teacher.

Mara's other great disappointment the first day of school was learning the *Brady Bunch*–loving Lou Ann Scroggins had moved to Fort Worth to live with her aunt. Mara had devised a whole series of Scroggins-stumping questions; she'd even written them down and had them memorized, so she'd appear to be a *Brady Bunch* wiz. During lunch, she asked everyone at her table, "What name did Sam the butcher call Bobby in the episode where Bobby is worried about being short?"

No one knew the answer, so Vonda Rae unofficially crowned Mara the *Brady Bunch* queen in Lou Ann Scroggins' place. There was little glory in that, though, since Mara was pretty sure Lou Ann would've yelled out "Shrimpo" if she'd been there.

Charlie had graduated Jenkins and gone on to Beauregard Middle School, so Mara had to walk home from school alone now, whether she liked it or not—something that made her uneasy. It seemed different, somehow, now that she didn't have a choice. He still dropped off her lunch in the mornings—set it right on the porch swing.

Walking alone didn't bother her much, at least that's what she tried to tell herself over and over again. But no matter how much she tried to believe walking alone was a piece of cake, it never felt that way, unless the piece of cake was mud pie topped with ants and worms.

Her life as an only child had its maddening moments, those deeply lonely times when only Nose Bunny heard her cry, but it also had its upside. Mara had learned the art of being alone and quiet with herself. Since she had no siblings, she learned she could be her own best friend.

With Camilla out of the picture and Vonda Rae lacking imagination, all she had was herself. Besides, she shouldn't have trusted Camilla with her secrets anyway. She had a nagging itch that Camilla had told Denim her bully secret. Why else would he have showed up when Officer Gus was crushing her? No, the only ones she could trust to keep her secrets were herself and Nose Bunny—whose mouth was conveniently stitched shut.

Of course Zady was there, but she was a grown-up—at times moody, at times gushy. There were moments when Mara swore she should let the cat out of the bag and tell Zady everything, from Aunt Elma to General in one long, scary sentence. She always thought the better of it, and every time she did, she was glad for it. No sense in bringing Zady into the mess.

Although she knew it wasn't logical, she'd assigned General a place near God—that he knew everything Mara was thinking and exactly who knew what. In her chasing dreams, sometimes General would list people: Zady, Mr. Winningham, Camilla, Eliot, the darting-eyed Lindy, and Denim. Each name he'd spit out right after he said, "I'll kill 'em."

The hot sun followed Mara all the way home, making her hair drip sweat. Jenkins had a makeshift weather station on the playground. At recess the thermometer read 107. Dull-headed and slow, that's how she felt. She plodded toward the big white house like a tired Clydesdale. Clop. Clop. Clop. In her head, she rambled the tortoise's words: *Slow and steady wins the race. Slow and steady wins the race.*

Near the vacant lot, she picked her way over the roots that buckled the sidewalk and admired her new Famolare look-alike shoes. They had a four-humped rubber sole so that when she put her heel down, it rocked forward. They were all the rage last year at Jenkins, so she felt a sweet vindication when she bought them. The advertisement was right. They put a spring in your step.

Mara heard rustling, but kept moving.

"Whatcha doing, Beautiful?"

*General!*

Mara's voice caught in her throat. Her hands trembled. Her heart pounded so loud she thought she'd scare the mock-ingbirds away.

"Cat got your tongue?"

She could hear General's breath rasp in and out, like he'd been running. He smelled like sweat—grimy, pitted sweat. Mara stopped. General faced her.

"You're mine, remember? You didn't think a little thing like living in a different part of town would change that, did you? Besides, we're friends, right? I miss my friend." He touched the back of her neck, softly at first. Then he pinched—hard. Pulling on her pinched skin, he directed her away from the bumpy sidewalk toward the vacant lot where she found Nose Bunny.

Mara meant to scream—really she did, but just like in her dreams, she couldn't. He pushed her now toward some over-grown bushes. "Why aren't you talking to me, Beautiful?"

She didn't answer.

He closed his fist until his knuckles turned white. General hit her cheek below her left eye with his terrible fist. White-hot pain splintered her vision. He shoved her and she fell into the brambles. Red dirt gritted the back of her new jeans. "It's okay if you don't want to talk. I don't mean to talk anymore." The bill of his John Deere darkened his face.

Mara put her hand up to her throbbing cheekbone and looked beyond General's face. A gigantic live oak swayed gently above her.

General began to unbuckle his belt. At that moment Mara snapped. She rolled onto her side and scrambled to her feet. He grabbed her arm to yank her back down. Mara resisted. With her free hand she smacked his hat off his red head. Her left foot connected imitation Famolare to real flesh with a swift kick that landed right below his belt.

He buckled under, groaning.

She ran through the brambles, high-legged and wild, and didn't look back.

She heard his tortured voice moan, "I'll kill you. As sure as day. I'll . . . kill . . . you."

# Thirty

"GOODNESS' SAKE, CHILD, WHAT IN THE world?" Zady said as Mara raced through the front hall and up the stairs.

Mara ran all the way up to her room and slammed the door.

She sat on her bed and touched her throbbing cheek. At least today General lost. At least today she didn't have to watch the tree limbs.

A tentative knock came to her door.

Mara wiped her face with her sleeve. "Come in."

"You have a bad day at school, child? What on earth?"

Zady looked at Mara. Mara couldn't decipher whether Zady's eyes showed anger or pity, neither of which made Mara feel good. She decided Zady was mad at her for soiling her clothes.

"I'm sorry I got my clothes all messy. I fell. In the vacant lot. It's dusty and I was sweating and—"

"Hush, baby, hush." Zady sat down next to Mara and was about to put her arm around her when Mara scooted out of reach.

"It's called comfort, child. When something bad's happened, folks want to love on you, that's all." She moved next to

Mara and put her arm around her again—not heavy and hot, but light and tender.

Mara cried—hard, so hard she thought her lungs would burst or all the water in her body would drain out of her eyes. Big, gulpy sobs combined with can't-catch-your-breath bellows. Long and hard and deep she wept; she cried so long she couldn't remember ever smiling.

Eventually the ocean of tears stopped, leaving Mara feeling puffy-eyed and exhausted.

"Care to let me in on what *really* happened, child?" Zady removed her arm from Mara's shoulders, backed away a little bit, and looked at her. "When you came in like you did, you looked like the Devil himself was chasing you. Fear—that's what I saw. Falling can't draw the face you wore."

Zady was serious, more serious than when she shooed Bishop Renny away. Mara squirmed. She knew she had to tell Zady something, or she'd have to face her concerned and serious gaze for days on end. She remembered Camilla and how she had kept Denim's secret in such a way that she rarely ever lied. If only she was as smart.

The only thing she could think of was Aunt Elma's sheeted body on the gurney. If she told Zady the truth, there'd be another gurney. Charlie and his sisters would have no mama. Raymond would have no wife. She would have no one to talk to.

Mara took a breath. And then another. Each breath bought time—time to think of something to tell Zady.

"Well, what scared you?"

"A bully," Mara said.

"At Jenkins? What bully?"

"I don't know her name. She goes to Beauregard, I think. She's tall and mean."

"Well, what does she look like?"

Mara looked at the white ceiling with seventy-two cracks, hoping for inspiration. "Tall. Black girl. Mean."

"That's all you know? Why did the tall-black-mean girl put the fear of God in you? What in the world did you do?"

"Nothing. I was walking home and I saw this girl out of the corner of my eye—out by the vacant lot. By the time I turned back to the sidewalk, she was right beside me, pulling me toward the lot by all the underbrush."

"Why on earth?"

Mara looked right at Zady, holding her gaze. More lies leapt from her tongue so easily she worried that maybe she was what Bishop Renny called a reprobate. "Said, 'White girl, I don't like you,' and then she pushed me down."

"Because you're white?"

"I guess so." Mara stood and walked over to the window and looked at the big pecan tree, centered within the top windowpane. "I didn't stop to ask why because she kept pushing me. I lost my balance and fell down. She came after me. I rolled away, but she grabbed my right leg. She didn't know I could kick so hard with my left leg, I guess. She looked real surprised when I kicked her knee. That's when I stood up and ran here."

"Did she hurt you?"

"Nah, I was too fast. I didn't let her lay a hand on me. You'd a been proud." The pecan tree swayed gently enough to reveal green-brown nuts under the leaves, but not enough to convince the tree to release them to the ground.

Zady joined her at the window and stood there with her a long time.

"There're only two problems with your story, Maranatha. Someone hit you in the face—hard. And Beauregard students aren't out of school for another fifteen minutes." Zady patted Mara's back. "When you're ready, you can trust me. The truth has a way of setting you free, Maranatha. Think on that."

With that, Zady padded to the door and shut it gently, leaving Mara alone with her lies, a bruised face, and a comforting thumb in her wet mouth.

# *Thirty-One*

BY THE TIME MARA'S BRUISE CHANGED from green to purple to bronze, she'd pushed the memory of General down deep. She used her story about the mean-tall-black girl all around school. Thankfully, Beauregard Middle School had plenty of tall black girls, and apparently by the nods she got when she told the story, there were plenty of mean ones too. Mara had almost convinced herself that she was telling the truth. Didn't matter, though. She took to running all the way home, trotting briskly on the other side of the street opposite the vacant lot. But she couldn't get General out of her dreams.

Mara spent the week avoiding Zady. "Homework," she'd bark, panting when she got in the door. "That Mrs. Armitage is a killer." Then, winded, she'd run up the stairs and shut her door.

If she ran fast enough she was able to catch the last fifteen minutes of Denim's radio program. He'd continued his chatting about how his daughter loved and missed Mars Bars. Lately, though, he'd been giving what he called "the word of the day" right after his Mars Bars commercial.

"Write this down," Denim's smooth voice said today.

"*Harm* is the word of the day. Keep each word of the day written down and see if you can figure out the connection. In a month or so, I'll tie them all together in one neat knot. If anyone is smart enough to unlock the mystery, please call KBBQ. If you're right, you'll get a free KBBQ mug and a gift certificate to Red Heifer's Ribs—the best ribs you ever did eat."

Mara wrote *harm* right next to *officer, judge, silence, politics,* and *evil*. She didn't have any inclination to win a mug or, heaven forbid, more ribs, but the words intrigued her. What did a judge have to do with evil? And how were silence and officer connected? She ripped off another sheet of paper and tried to rearrange the words into some sort of sentence.

"Evil politics silence a judge and harm an officer."

*No.*

"The officer and judge harms evil, silent politics."

*Can't be.*

"The silent officer harms the evil politics judge." No matter how she jumbled the words they made no sense. She'd never been good at the word scramble on the *Burl Atlas*'s Funnies page. If only she was as clever as Camilla, she'd have the mystery solved for sure. Truth be told, Camilla was the better Nancy Drew. Mara was simply a Bess—a follower with scant imagination. Besides that, Camilla could ask her daddy.

When Denim added *indigent* the next day, Mara had to ask Mrs. Dobson, Jenkins' librarian, for a dictionary. *Indigent* meant needy or poor. She had no idea how that mixed with judges and officers and politics, but she wrote it down anyway.

*Nepotism*, Denim's next word, meant favoritism shown to relatives. Now Mara was completely confused. Nothing seemed to match; the more words he added the more ridiculous the sentence sounded. The last word he announced was *entangle*—at least a word she understood.

While Mara wrote *entangle* down, Denim finished his show. "That's it, folks. Officer. Judge. Silence. Politics. Evil. Harm. Indigent. Nepotism. Entangle. I've gotten a few calls at the station, but so far, no one's come close. Eat some Mars Bars and noodle on it a while. You've got three more weeks to win the mug and ribs. Who knows? You figure this out, you might untangle the mystery of this entangled town. Let me say this too, as a matter of note—my daughter has a little friend who's smart enough to figure this out, so there's hope for you old folks out there. Don't give up."

# *Thirty-Two*

BUT MARA DID GIVE UP. NONE of the jumbles of words made any sense, and she was back to feeling like her life was an edged but unfilled puzzle. She'd spied a bill this week with Mr. Winningham's initials: J. Z. Winningham. *Maybe he is my daddy. Jo-without-the-e Winningham, father of one lonely girl. Maybe he put Zady on the birth certificate so I couldn't find out my mama's name.* But what J. Z. Winningham had to do with words like *judge* and *nepotism*, she didn't know. None of it helped her untangle the gnarled mess of her life, even though Denim had hinted at that.

The ride to church that week was quiet, at least between her and Zady. Charlie argued with his sisters about the greatness of the Cowboys and why they'd win it all this year even without Staubach. Raymond said, "Amen" every time Charlie spoke the retired quarterback's name.

Mara kept silent about what really happened in the vacant lot. According to Zady, withholding that information was some sort of sin. So, to get along, they plain didn't talk. "I need to take you to God's house," Zady had said as she straightened Mara's dress collar. "Maybe then some truth will rub off on you." Zady had looked beyond Mara, never into her eyes—a sure sign she was hopping mad.

Bishop Renny preached long and windy—something about Jesus being the truth and the truth setting folks free. *Did Zady tell him to preach that? Does he know my secrets?* Mara feigned interest, even shouting a few well-placed "amens" here and there for good measure. She had no idea what "amen" *really* meant, or "glory, hallelujah" for that matter, but she didn't want to feel more out of place than she already did, so she copied the crowd.

Their fall fellowship banquet was that day, so Mara had to wait with the other children in the hot sanctuary while the adults scurried around making table decorations out of cornucopias and plastic fruit. A renegade banana had made its way into the hands of the bishop's son, Jamal, who now used it to play keep-away from the girls. The banana had great flying capability, soaring from one end of the sanctuary to the other, curving almost like a boomerang.

"It's a bananarang," Jamal said as he held it high above his head. Minnie, his younger sister, jumped up and down trying to grab it from him, but she was too short. His arms were even longer than Charlie's, so the bananarang stayed safely in the boys' possession.

With Minnie clamoring at his waist, and other girls tickling his sides, Jamal flung the bananarang wildly. It soared high, almost intercepting a flailing ceiling fan, and then hit the window that flanked pew four. The window cracked. In a wink, the bananarang dropped right at Mara's feet.

Bishop Renny, followed by several wooden spoon–shaking ladies, ran into the sanctuary, saw the mayhem, and stood right in front of Mara, frowning.

"Care to tell me what happened, Miss Maranatha?"

At her feet lay the bananarang on top of a pile of colored glass shards. She looked up and caught Jamal's gaze. Although no words passed between them, she knew enough to take the blame for this one.

"I thought it would be fun to play catch with this banana." Mara looked back at her feet. She was awful at deception, a fact that Zady confirmed this week, so she didn't trust her eyes. Bishop Renny had a way about him, both strong and kind, so she couldn't bear looking into his eyes. She'd burst into tears, sure enough.

"Come into my office, young lady." He didn't beckon her. He walked to the front of the sanctuary and opened a door to the left of the pulpit.

Mara followed.

The room was so small that the desk ate up practically the whole space. Bishop Renny had to squeeze himself around one side of the desk to get behind it to his chair. A small window let in light. There were two folding chairs on the door side. He motioned for Mara to sit in one.

"Used to be a closet. I needed a place to think and write my sermons, so I cleaned out this here closet and made myself a study." Behind him were books from floor to ceiling, some dusty, some new. "You like books?"

Mara nodded, looking at her hands.

"No need to be afraid, sweetie." His voice was molasses smooth, something Mara didn't expect. She was used to impassioned or intense, but not molasses smooth. He straightened some papers on his desk—papers that were spotlighted by the sun shining through the little window. "I know that Jamal threw that crazy banana. Saw it in his eyes. He'll be punished. Don't you worry your pretty little head. I have to put on a show by taking you in here. Kids can't think I'm soft or anything. Tootsie Roll?"

He pushed a glass bowl full of Tootsie Rolls toward her. She looked up and caught his gaze. His eyes smiled. She took a Tootsie Roll, untwisted its ends, and popped it in her mouth.

"Didn't you listen to the sermon today? About truth?"

Mara nodded.

"Well, what did I say, child?"

Mara chewed her gooey candy and tried to swallow, but it stayed like a hard lump in her mouth. She pushed it to the side of her cheek with her tongue and tried to talk. "Jesus wants us to tell the truth?"

"Well, of course He does, but that's not what I said. Remember the Scripture?"

Mara was finally able to swallow the brown wad. "Something about John?"

Bishop Renny leaned back in his chair and clasped his hands behind his head. "I hope my other parishioners remember more than you." He smiled when he said it. "Jesus is talking to us all in John 8:31-32. He says, 'If ye continue in my word, then are ye my disciples indeed; And ye shall know the truth, and the truth shall make you free.' Later on Jesus says in John 14:6, 'I am the way, the truth, and the life.' Let's do some thinking on this, Miss Maranatha. What will make you free?"

"Truth," Mara said.

"Right, now what did Jesus say? He was the way, the life, and what else?"

"The truth."

"Right!" He hit the desk with his hand, smiling. "So *who* will make you free?"

"Jesus?"

"Don't say His name like you're afraid. Say it like you mean it!"

"Jesus!"

"That's right. Truth is a person. *Jesus* will set you free."

"What does free mean?" She looked right at the bishop. She really had no idea what freedom was or why it was so important that Jesus made her free.

"Free? Free means telling the truth about bananas breaking windows. Free means not having to worry about going to hell. Free means being the same person on the inside as you are on the outside." His voice rose with each sentence. He was preaching. "Free means Jesus paid for your sins and you don't have to."

Mara raised her hand.

"You have a question?"

"What about if it's someone else doing the sinning? To you? Can Jesus set you free from someone who's hurting you?"

*Watch it. Don't say too much.*

Bishop Renny sat forward and massaged his head with his hands. "You know, sometimes Jesus sends us people we can trust, and they protect us."

"What's trust?"

"That's when you can tell your secrets to someone and they will keep them. The only time they tell them is if they need to protect you. You always have to be careful about who you tell things to, especially in this town."

Mara remembered Aunt Elma under the white sheet. If General could do that to big Aunt Elma, then he could do that to anyone. Mara decided telling the truth was a deadly thing. "I don't need Jesus right now, Bishop Renny. He's got too much to do to bother with me anyway."

"That's where you're wrong. Jesus had a plan for your life

since the moment you came screeching into this world. I know. I was there. It was like Jesus willed you to be born."

"*You* were there—when I was born?"

The man with the steady gaze looked away from Mara and stared out the small window. "There are many things you need to know, Maranatha—like the truth about your beginnings. But right now is not the time. When you're old enough, I'll tell you."

"When will that be?"

"When Zady tells me you are ready." He stood. From where she sat, he looked like a basketball player—tall and handsome. "Best be getting to the fellowship hall. Don't want to keep the ladies waiting. No need to mention our talk with anyone. For all they know, I gave you a good talking to, all right?" He winked.

"Sure."

They exited his office together. Twenty pairs of curious eyes bored into Mara. She tried to look forlorn, like she had gotten a talking-to, and apparently she was convincing because the eyes looked elsewhere. Where the shards of colored glass had been was a neatly swept floor. After the bishop went to the fellowship hall to bless the food, Jamal approached Mara.

"I cleaned it up for you," he said.

"Thanks." She smiled. She wondered if she should warn him about his daddy knowing what he'd done, but decided against it. Life *was* more interesting with surprises anyway.

She walked into the fall fellowship banquet alone, wondering how many people knew the secret of her beginnings.

# Thirty-Three

"SURE ARE THE SPITTING IMAGE OF your mama." Mama Frankie balanced her paper plate of fall fellowship banquet food on the corner of her walker. "Follow me, child, so we's can talk."

Mama Frankie led Mara to a quiet corner inside the sanctuary. Mara knew it was against church rules to eat in there, but curiosity won her inner battle. The stilled fans allowed hot air to pour unhindered through the broken window. Mara didn't mind. She'd endure anything to find out the truth.

"Help me here, child."

Mara helped Mama Frankie settle into a back pew and moved her walker to the aisle. Mara placed the paper plate on her flower-dress lap.

"I needs me my hankie," she barked.

Mama Frankie's voice echoed off the walls. Mara looked around, expecting the back doors to fling open. Zady had a radar way about her. She always knew precisely where Mara was, and like a haunting shadow, followed her everywhere—especially at church.

"In the walker. In that blue pocket."

The walker had rainbow pockets sewn to its top, in the right order: red, orange, yellow, green, blue, indigo, violet—indigo and violet represented by one purple pocket. Mara reached into the blue pocket, and sure enough, there was a hankie residing there, crisp and clean.

"Beautiful hankie, Mama Frankie." *Hey, I rhymed! Like Camilla.* Mara smiled. She took a bite of purple-hulled peas drenched in ranch dressing.

"I knows it. My own grandmother, she stitched this hankie for me. Used my favorite colors—blue and green. Blue for the Burl sky and green for live oak leaves. I used to stare at the sky through the live oak in my front yard. I'd put my thin legs through the tire swing my daddy strung me and I'd look straight up through the tree's green leaves. I liked the way the blue sky blinked at me, especially when I was twirling in the wound-up swing. Nothing better, child. Nothing better."

"I look at the sky through trees too." Mara covered her mouth with her hand, not sure if peas were stuck in her teeth. Her heart tapped a faster rhythm in her chest as if she was revealing too much and Mama Frankie might figure out her secret.

Mama Frankie placed the folded hankie near her knife and picked up a plastic fork. "Mm-mm, I love them greens." Piled high on her plate, directly in the center, stood a hill of greens. Other food in insignificant piles surrounded the greens, playing second fiddle. Mama Frankie plunged her fork into the green, slimy things and ate, green tendrils hanging from her mouth. "That's the best part about being an old lady, Maranatha," she said as greens danced below her lips. "You's can dribble greens down your chin, and no one troubles you about it. Food tastes better when you're dribbling."

Mara's pile of greens could fill a tablespoon. She hesitantly lifted a few strands to her mouth, letting a few leaves hang from her bottom lip. Nope, they felt slimy and tasted like the earth. She slurped the renegade leaves like they were spaghetti and winced, hoping no greens painted her teeth.

Mama Frankie laughed. "Child, I'd think you were a Yankee with that sour face."

"I don't think I am." Mara didn't want to ask the old lady directly about where she came from, but she hoped the conversation was heading that way.

"Oh, yes, I was telling you about your mama, wasn't I?" Mama Frankie shoveled another forkful of greens in her mouth, this time leaving none on her chin.

"Was she pretty?"

"Was she *pretty*? What a question, child. Prettiest white gal I ever laid eyes on. Your mama was Cinderella. Only she never did find her handsome prince."

"My daddy, he wasn't handsome?"

"Oh, he was handsome on the outside, sure enough. Made the gal-ladies faint with longing when he walked in the room, at least that's what I've been told. But he wasn't handsome on the inside, in here." Mama Frankie patted Mara's chest. Her wrinkled brown hand had a few strings of greens on it so that one remained on Mara's shirt when she took her hand away.

Mara peeled it off. It left a green line on her white blouse. "What was his name?" After she asked it, Mara glanced toward the back doors.

"Let's see here." Mama Frankie squinted her eyes shut and rested her head on the back of the pew, her neck crooked to the ceiling. "Let me see."

"Was it Jo—without an *e*?"

"Joe? No, I don't think so. I have me a good memory 'bout most things, Maranatha. I remembered the tire swing, after all. But sometimes the memories get locked behind a heavy door and I can't seem to get at them. I remembers my childhood like it was a movie playing before me, but more recent history I can't seem to get at. Your daddy, he was handsome. He was charming. But, Joe? I don't think he was a Joe."

Mara sighed and picked at her baked beans. *Hopeless. Absolutely hopeless. The only one who is willing to talk can't remember a thing.*

"But your mama, child—she's one I can't forget. Long blonde hair that shone in the sun like a pretty penny. Clear green eyes. Your daddy, he could have any gal he wanted, but he wanted her. 'Cept that your mama turned her head when he came a calling. Said he was a wicked man. Wanted nothing to do with him."

"Her name—my mama's name—what was it?"

"Hasn't anyone told you that, child?"

Mara shook her head while her heart galloped in her chest. *Finally!* "Was it Zady?"

Mama Frankie laughed. Greens clung to her teeth.

The back doors swung open, and the real Zady walked toward Mara. "You call me?"

"No." Mara let out her breath.

"You know Bishop Renny doesn't allow victuals in the sanctuary."

Mama Frankie lifted her hand. "Now, Zady, don't be angry. I asked her to come in here so we's could talk. She helped me sit down—even got me my hankie."

"Talk about what?" Zady stood above them both now, in the pew in front of them. Her hands rested on her hips.

"Greens," Mama Frankie said, plain as day.

# Thirty-Four

FALL WAS HERE, ALTHOUGH DENIM SAID there was no fall in the South—just hot summer days until December when the leaves suddenly turned brown and dropped in a week. Just once, Mara would like to see a real autumn with turned leaves in bright colors. Fall's only indication was that the days were getting shorter and sometimes at night, a crisp breeze would shudder through the Burl trees. The pecan leaves clung stubbornly to their branches even though the tree had surrendered its brown nuts. Green the leaves stayed, and every time Mara looked at the blue sky through the pecan in their front yard she thought of Mama Frankie's words. Her daddy was handsome; her mama was pretty. But something didn't connect. If her mama didn't like her daddy, how was it that he became her daddy?

Mr. Winningham was gone more and more now, which really didn't make much of a difference to Mara since he was gone most of the time anyway. He still avoided her eyes, but there was an almost imperceptible softening about him. Instead of eating and looking at his food, he looked above Mara's head and to her side. One day he even asked her if she liked school. She prattled on and on about school, about Mrs.

Armitage's art projects, about recess and lunch, but before she could finish, he excused himself, hat and all. Well, at least he'd asked.

Denim gave up on the word contest. He said twenty-eight callers tried to guess what the words meant but none even came close. He kept insisting that his daughter's friend could solve the mystery if she kept first things first. She kept the list in the peach crate next to her bed, tucked inside a dusty book. Every once in a while she'd pull it out but couldn't figure out the mystery.

She wondered how Eliot was doing, whether he was putting his garden to bed for the winter and whether he knew something about Mara's mama. She thought about the scared Lindy lady and wanted to comfort her. She worried about how Camilla was getting along without her Mars Bars.

One crisp November Saturday after Mr. Winningham drove the Cadillac away, Mara decided to pay a visit to Eliot, Lindy, and Camilla. She knew it would be risky, but what else could Mr. Winningham do to her? Stay silent? She'd grown accustomed to that. Keep her chained to the big white house? She'd been its prisoner nearly six months now.

She pulled on a pair of jeans, a T-shirt, and a hooded zip-up sweatshirt. She trotted downstairs, skipping every other stair in a contest she made for herself. She could do it in thirty-five seconds flat, but she wanted to beat her record. With the anticipation of doing something spylike, her feet flew faster. When she landed in a huff at the bottom she looked at Mickey Mouse's second hand: thirty-two seconds. *Yes!*

She double-checked out the back kitchen window. No white Cadillac. She opened the front door and stepped out onto the porch. Its clean white paint gave the illusion that the house was fixed up. The green porch swing swayed to and fro with the gentle, cool air. Mara smiled. At least for the parts she could reach, she had made the diamond in the rough shine. Pushing through the gate though, she felt the familiar pang of disappointment. The rest of the gigantic house was peeling like a sunburned redhead. Paint from the upper dormers flaked onto the porch roof like dandruff.

In an instant, she felt a kinship to the old house. On the outside she was fine. She finally fit in at Jenkins and looked presentable with her new Value Villa clothes. But there were eaves and dormers in her life with peeling paint. And sometimes, if she was honest with herself—and this honesty usually came as she stared at the cracks in her moonlit room—she'd resign herself to the fact that the house of her life was crumbling beneath her. No rock to settle on. She was crumbling from the inside out, so much so that she was willing to risk her freedom to find out whose child she was.

She looked up through the pecan tree to see the blue sky jigsawed through it. One leaf flittered and floated toward her, brushed her cheek gently, and settled at her feet.

She filled her lungs with the humidless air and headed toward Eliot's tidy blue house. Weeds shot through the sidewalk cracks, erecting little grass walls every three feet or so. Mara took to hurdling them—a somewhat tricky endeavor since Burl's pecan branches had recently dismissed their nuts. If she leapt over a grass wall and landed on a pecan, she'd fall flat on her backside with a spank.

Truth be told, she managed two full blocks before the sidewalk spanked her.

Eliot's gate was cracked open. It squeaked when Mara pushed it inward. The yard, flushing with Indian summer color, looked different. Where neat rows had been, flowers had extended beyond their boundaries in wild hairdos. Where the crew-cut lawn once stood proud, bending grass tall as her knees now tickled her legs when the autumn wind blew. Where neatly planted pots of flowers used to greet visitors on the front porch, brown sticks said a neglected hello.

Mara bent low to the pots and touched the angled sticks. Dry brown leaves fell the moment she touched the stalks. Dead flower heads populated the pot's dirt. *How sad.*

She knocked a tentative knock on the once cheerful door. Where she knocked, skiffs of paint flaked beneath her knuckles. She pressed her ear to the door, but heard nothing. That's when she noticed the phone book. A small Burl book propped itself against the door, waiting for someone to open the door so it could fall inside and be protected from the elements. The elements, though, had gotten the best of it, bending pages this way and that, yellowing its white pages.

She knocked again, this time louder. "Mr. Eliot, sir. Are you in there?"

Nothing.

She turned the door handle to see if it was locked. The knob gave way and the door opened, letting the phone book fall and rest inside the door's threshold.

"Mr. Eliot?"

The house was dark, the curtains drawn. It took a while to let her eyes adjust.

"Anyone home?" Even though the house was small it seemed to absorb Mara's voice as if it were a mansion, sending it echoing off every wall. She worried again that General knew her thoughts, that perhaps he knew about her friend Eliot, even though she hadn't uttered a word about General to anyone. *Oh no, not you too, Eliot. Did General get to you?*

The phone rang. Mara jumped, tripping backward over the phone book, falling again on her behind. One ring. Two.

Three. Four. *Should I answer that?* Five. Six. Seven. As she reached for the phone, it quieted.

She'd have given up and left, surmising Eliot was on vacation, had the phone stayed silent.

It didn't.

*Ring. Ring. Ring.*

"Hello, Mr. Eliot's, I mean, Eliot's house."

"Baby, who are *you*?"

"Mara—a friend of Eliot's."

"Thank Jesus. Can I speak to Eliot? He hasn't been answering his phone the past two days. I'm scared sick." .

"Are you a friend of his?" Mara asked.

"No, his sister, Eugenia. Can I please speak to him?"

"Well, um, I came in looking for him. I don't think he's here. His yard's all messy."

"So he's been telling me. He'd been pestering me to come out and help clean it up a bit. Couldn't stand that he felt too sick to work in the yard, but you know how life is. Busy, busy, busy. He can't expect me to drive on over whenever a weed pops up, right?"

"Uh, yeah, I suppose."

"Can you do me a favor and look in his bedroom for me?"

"I don't know where that is."

"Down the hall, last door on the left. Let the phone dangle and tell me if he's in his room."

"Okay." Mara set the phone on the coffee table and tiptoed down the hall. She didn't know why she tiptoed, but the quiet hush of the house seemed to advise her to do so. When she got to the last door on the left she smelled urine.

"Mr. Eliot?" The room was dark, so she flicked on the light, but it didn't work. It took her more time to adjust to the dark room—more than when she entered the house. She could make out something on the floor, something long and gnarled. His cane. She squeezed her eyes tight and opened them again, hoping this time things would seem brighter. She picked up the cane and inched her eyes up from the floor to the bed's top. Lying on the bed was a lump under the covers.

"Sir?"

The lump moved.

Mara stumbled backward, her back hitting mirrored closet doors.

The lump issued a moan, low and deep.

"Mr. Eliot? Are you okay?"

Another moan.

She crept toward the lump, her hands shaking. She touched the top of the gray covers—it was only later that she realized everything in that bedroom seemed gray because of the lack of lighting. Even her hands looked gray. She pulled back the covers, revealing Eliot's contorted face.

The stench of urine, vomit, and sweat intermingled; Mara's stomach juices catapulted up her throat, burning the back of her tongue.

"Help," he said.

"Yes, help," she said.

Mara ran back to the phone, nearly tripping over her spindly legs.

"Ma'am, Mr. Eliot—he's sick, real sick."

"Hang up and dial 911. I'm two hours away. I'll be there as soon as I can." With that, the line went dead. From the hallway, Mara heard Eliot's faint groans.

She dialed 911. "Come right away. Please!" she heard herself say.

She ran back down the dark hallway. The stench hit her at his room, but she told herself to pretend it wasn't there.

"Don't worry, Mr. Eliot. Help's on the way." She opened the curtains and propped open the window, bringing light and air into the stuffy room.

Eliot's face, contorted, gazed blankly at Mara.

Mara smoothed Eliot's covers and touched his forehead—cool and wet.

"Sephie, help," he quavered.

"Help's coming. Hold on a little longer." Sirens, a long way off, whirred in the distance. "Hear that? They're coming. Coming to help you."

"Millicent? Is that you?" Eliot looked above Mara to the window.

She turned around, half-expecting to see Eliot's dead wife standing behind her.

Eliot coughed, shallow and raspy. The sirens screamed louder.

"First Sephie, now you, darling. Now you," he muttered, barely above a whisper.

Mara smoothed back his hair. Sweat plastered his grown-out crew cut to his forehead.

Sirens nearly shook the house, and a circling red light flashed on and off in the small bedroom. Eliot breathed in again, this time more labored like he was bobbing above water and pulling at the air before he went under again. His eyes widened. He lifted his withered hand, thrust it across his chest, and grabbed Mara's forearm. She examined his curled hand and remembered Eliot telling her that God turned it that way. Mara touched the bridge of her nose where her freckles lived and hoped that the God who painted them there would keep Eliot alive.

Footsteps pounded down the hall.

"Good-bye, Sephie." His withered hand nearly crushed

her forearm, and then slowly, nearly imperceptibly, he let go of his grasp, the shriveled hand falling to rest on his chest that no longer rose and fell.

Firefighters rushed in. One, tall and insistent, pushed her aside. "Get out of the way."

From then on it was all yelling and counting. "One, two, three . . . " At fifteen they yelled, "Breathe. Breathe." Although Eliot's chest rose with each breath, he didn't breathe again on his own. Mara crouched in the corner watching the firemen pound on Eliot's chest and blow in his mouth. She cringed when they pulled his urine-soaked sheet over his head. *Did General do this to you?*

Hoping no one would notice her, Mara escaped down the hallway, her hands trembling. In the living room, through the front door's opening, she could see two squad cars, one of them Gus's. She looked to the right. Gus stood in the flowerbeds, crushing dead flowers under his feet. Mara's stomach knotted.

He was looking down, but it would be a matter of moments before he looked up and caught her. She moved out of his line of sight, which took her into Eliot's narrow kitchen. At its end near the refrigerator was a door—hopefully her escape route. As she reached it, a familiar *hut-two-three-four* creaked the floorboards.

As she neared the fridge, she stopped. A picture of her smiled from underneath a butterfly magnet. *What am I doing on his fridge?*

*Hut-two-three-four.*

Mara grabbed the photo. The magnet fell to the floor. She opened the door and stepped inside the garage, clutching her picture.

*Hut-two-three-four.*

She looked around the garage, frantic. *There must be another door besides the big one.* She could see a slim line of light underlining the garage door. She looked for similar light—anywhere.

*Hut-two-three-four.*

To her left, Mara saw a small rectangle of similar light. *A dog door!* She scrambled through it like poor Peter Rabbit under Mr. McGregor's fence, scraping her hips as she pulled herself toward the light. A picket fence surrounded Eliot's backyard. Hurdling the gate, she ran down the alleyway so fast, she thought Peter Rabbit would be proud.

Mara ran all the way to the big white house, darting down alleyways and hiding behind trees. The house seemed to both beckon and welcome her. She ran upstairs and collapsed on her bed, breathless.

It took Mara a few minutes to gather herself. Counting the cracks helped. At crack sixty-eight, she remembered the photo in her hand.

She sat up and propped her back against the wall. The photo, black and white with a white edge all around, stared at her. If it hadn't been black and white, Mara would've sworn she was looking in a mirror. A girl, maybe a little older than Mara, smiled at her from the photo. She was wearing a dress—a really pretty dress—but her hands stuck straight down at her side, as though dresses made her uncomfortable. Even so, the girl smiled Mara's smile. Her eyes winked of Mara's—almond shaped and light in color—and her same knobby knees peeked at her from beneath the short dress. *My knees.*

Mara turned the photo over. The writing could have been hers—straight up and down with loopy *Y*s—but she didn't remember having her picture taken, never even owned a dress like that.

Dear Mrs. Campbell,
Thank you for being the best kindergarten
teacher ever. I'll be thinking about you every day
this summer. I hope we can visit each other
because I'll miss you something fierce.
Love, Sephie, age 10

Mara turned the picture over and looked deep into Sephie's eyes—her eyes. For a moment, she wanted to slip her thumb into her mouth—to do something familiar in this unfamiliar situation. But Sephie's eyes seemed to say no. Not this time.

"Nice to meet you, Sephie." She dropped her thumb to her side.

# Thirty-Five

"THIS HER?" MARA SHOVED THE BLACK-and-white photo toward Zady's face that Sunday after church in the parking lot. She'd kept it pressed and flat in her Bible since the day before, the day Eliot died.

"Goodness' sake, child. I can't see a thing that close. Let me have it." Zady grabbed the photo and moved it away from her face. "Sweet Jesus."

"Is that my mama?"

Zady nodded. "Where on earth did you get this picture?" Her voice was thin, angry.

"From a friend."

"A friend? What friend?"

"Just a friend." Mara looked at the gravel driveway and shifted her weight. The rocks underfoot crunched with each shift. She hoped she could crunch forever, anything to avoid Zady's penetrating look. She remembered Eliot, gasping for breath like a drowning man, and wondered why she hadn't cried. He was a good man. Some folks spent their lives pretending they were good. Not Eliot. He was good through and through like a tall sweating glass of sweet tea. She'd miss him. But she didn't cry.

"I'm talking to you, Maranatha!" Zady's voice pitched higher, a sure indication she was snippy. "Did you hear me?"

"No, ma'am, I didn't."

"A daydreaming fool—that's what you are. I asked you, how is it that a *friend* gave you this picture? You can't even leave the house, thanks to Mr. Winningham. Did a friend at school give you this?"

Lying was a sin; she knew it now that she'd heard a sermon or two from the lips of Bishop Renny about cheating and bearing false witness. If she said a friend at school gave it to her, she'd be lying. If she said someone else gave it to her, she'd get herself in trouble. Neither choice sounded good to her. Being like Jesus was hard—especially the black smiling Jesus that looked at her every time she sat in Zady's pew.

"Well, who gave it to you?" The *tap-tap-tapping* of her foot on the gravel sounded like sheets of paper being wadded and crinkled.

Mara replayed Eliot's last breath like a movie in her head. *He's dead. And it's probably all my fault.* Mara felt a tear trail down her cheek, followed by another, then another. She shifted her weight again.

The gravel crackled louder than Zady's *tap-tap-tapping*. Puzzled, Mara looked up, tear-stained face and all, and saw Raymond shuffling toward them, dragging his foot along the ground, making a trail in the gravel.

"Zady? You making the child cry? What's with you today? I'd swear a scorpion'd gotten to your temper."

"The child is lying, Raymond. Best be letting me have my way." Zady angled a glare at Raymond, who normally shrunk back.

He stood tall. "Law *and* grace, remember? Sometimes you focus so much on dos and don'ts that you forget Maranatha's just a little girl trying to find her way in this world. Cut her some grace, will you?"

"I'll cut her some grace when she tells me the truth."

Raymond scraped the ground with his bad foot and put a thin arm around Mara's shoulder. She shuddered, but let it rest there.

"Cut her some grace, Zady-Lou. A big slice, please. For me?"

Mara looked from Raymond to Zady; she tried to see if they were going to hit each other or hug. She wasn't sure which way the argument would go. Their laughter burst forth and Mara joined them. Her upturned mouth caught the rest of her tears. She lifted her mama's picture. Raymond looked at it.

"She was a beautiful lady, your mama. Her heart was also pretty. Like yours." He lifted his arm from around her shoulders and touched her nose. "Just like yours," he said again.

# Thirty-Six

MARA SMILED. THEY'D DONE IT AGAIN—gotten Mrs. Armitage to make them put their books away. Whenever she did that, Mara knew the class was in for a treat.

It started innocently enough.

Well, not really.

On the playground, Mrs. Armitage's students plotted how they could get her riled about a textbook. Every time they riled her, they'd succeed in lessening their workload because she'd ramble on and on about nothing in particular or assign another art project.

Today at recess J.R. Turnbull decided he didn't want to do history. "I bet I can get her to stop our history lesson," he bragged to Vonda Rae.

"I bet you can't. I think she's on to us." Vonda Rae folded her arms and leaned toward J.R.

"Nope, I'm going to win this one. What you want to bet?"

"I bet Mara's fried pie."

"What?" Mara said. "Why *my* fried pie?"

"Because I only have graham crackers. It ain't no bet unless you have a fried pie, right, J.R.?"

"Right! Mara's fried pie or my Coke. Deal?"

"Deal." Vonda Rae grasped his hand in five different hand-shakes.

When class started again, J.R. raised his hand. "Mrs. Armitage?"

"Yes, J.R.?"

"Sputnik being new and all, can we see it from the sky tonight? It says here on page 178 that the Russians just launched it. I'd sure like to see it."

"That's it, class. I've *had* it. Put your history books under your desks."

Vonda Rae shook her head. Mara put her hands to her forehead. J.R. mimed placing a fried pie in his mouth. That J.R. was pretty smart—for a boy.

"I've been wanting to teach something else for a while now anyway. Thanks, J.R., for once again pointing out how antiquated our textbooks are." She cleared her throat. Mara reached down to grab her paintbrush.

"Holocaust. Say it, class."

"Holocaust," the class said.

Mara put her paintbrush away. Time for Mrs. Armitage's ramblings.

"Anyone know what it means?"

Vonda Rae raised her hand. "My daddy says there's a worm holocaust on our sidewalk after it rains—dead worms everywhere."

"Although the Holocaust *does* have to do with dying, there's more to it than that. It took place during World War II. Anybody remember who Hitler was?"

Mara nodded, along with several others. Mrs. Armitage went on and on about Hitler wanting to get rid of folks called Jews. Mara didn't know what a Jew was, but she sure felt sorry for them. Jews couldn't buy things at their local Value Villa.

Eventually Hitler rounded them up and sent them to camp, only his idea of camp was to burn people up in furnaces. Again, Mara felt pity. She'd felt it for Lindy. She'd felt it for herself. And now she felt it for the poor Jews.

"Hitler thought some folks weren't as important as others. Understand?"

"Yeah," J.R. said. "You mean like when our school district has crummy books and the white district has brand spankin' new ones?"

Mara looked at her plaster-colored hands. White. The only white pair in the entire class. *Am I like Hitler?*

"Discrimination comes in a hundred forms, some as horrible as the Holocaust." Mrs. Armitage walked the aisles of the classroom. She always picked up her pace when she was impassioned, and today she practically sprinted between the desk rows. "And J.R.'s right. Having crummy textbooks can be a subtle form of discrimination. What I want you to think about today is not whether folks have discriminated against you, but whether you've discriminated against other folks. Tomorrow I'll expect a full page of writing about this."

"Can't we paint a picture or make a collage?" J.R. asked.

"Not this time. I want to read what you have to say."

Mara smiled. Maybe this meant she wouldn't have to give up her fried pie after all.

When she lifted J.R.'s Coke can to her thirsty lips during lunch, she felt sweet vindication. Vonda Rae had insisted that he give it to Mara, and Mara was happy to oblige since she had to make due with water from the fountain this week. "Doctor bills," Zady told her, "are sucking up our money. Will you be okay with water this week?" Of course, Mara had said that would be fine. They had made an unspoken truce, she and Zady. Zady stopped asking about the picture, and Mara didn't ask about Zady's money problems—at least not after she'd suggested they try to get a loan.

"Ha!" Zady had said. "Loans? From who? This town's banks don't loan to injured men, especially ones injured at the rendering plant. Too much at stake."

None of this made sense to Mara. She didn't even know what a rendering plant was.

After the cool Coke slid down her throat in delicious sips, Mara looked forward to the last subject of the day: English. She dreaded afternoon classes in the fall because the school's old air conditioners gave out at the end of the day and they all sweltered in the heat. But now that Thanksgiving was near, the crisp air made the afternoon at least bearable. Comfort had a brief window at Jenkins—the month of November when the summer heat finally surrendered, and the month of April when the winter's frost gave way to wisteria's purple fragrance. Neither air conditioner nor heater worked well. Like obsolete textbooks, the school's HVAC system tried to do its job, but failed miserably.

J.R., who had been smart during history, lost any shred of intelligence in English.

"Mrs. Armitage?" he said.

"Mr. Turnbull," she said. "I hope you have something of import to say."

"Yes, ma'am. Says here that an adverb modifies a verb. Isn't that outdated? Shouldn't we put our English books under our desks?"

"Some things are universal, J.R.," she said. "Like parts of speech. Nice try, though." She secured a loose strand of hair behind her ear. "Class, turn to page 459," she said with a wry smile.

Mara raised her hand. "But, there *is* no page 459."

"Precisely. I'd like to teach you something your parents might not know." The students in the room murmured approval. "Write this down. A-N-A-G-R-A-M." With a flourish, she squeaked it onto the chalkboard. "Anyone know what this word means?"

Mara's head hurt. Mrs. Armitage's word-of-the-day kick wore thin, even if the room temperature was fine and she might learn something Mr. Winningham didn't know.

"An anagram is a word whose letters you can rearrange to make other words. Here's an example. Write down *Elvis*. By using the letters in his name, can you come up with another word?"

Mara crossed out letters until she came up with something. "Evils?"

"Yes, that's right. There's another one too."

Vonda Rae blurted out, "Lives! Elvis lives! Hey, that's funny."

"For the rest of the period, I want you to figure on your own first names and see if there's an anagram there. If you get one, raise your hand. For the sake of starting you off, Armitage can be 'a ragtime.'"

"What about me? I'm J.R. That only changes to R.J." J.R. sat back in his chair and drummed his fingers together in mock victory.

"James Rodwin, I am sure you can work with your entire name."

Snickers filled the room. James Rodwin would *not* hear the end of that for many recesses.

Mara knew she'd have to use her long name. One thing was for sure—she had a lot of *a*'s packed in there.

Mrs. Armitage sat at her desk, grading papers in silence for a good fifteen minutes. *Smart move, Mrs. A Ragtime.*

Vonda Rae was the first to uncover her personal anagram. " 'Rode a van.' That's mine."

"Great." Mrs. A Ragtime wrote it on the board. "Anyone else?"

"Oh, man." James Rodwin said.

"What is it, J.R.?"

"The only one I could figure is 'major swined.' "

Mara laughed. "Mine could be 'Ha! A rat man!' "

On the way home, Mara looked at a list of anagrams Mrs. A Ragtime had given her. She was careful to avoid tripping over roots as she read the favorites on her list. *Decimal point*'s anagram was "I'm a dot in place." *Eleven plus two*'s was "twelve plus one."

So engrossed that *dormitory* turned into "dirty room" and *The United States Bureau of Fisheries* became "I raise the bass to feed us in the future," she forgot to steer clear of the vacant lot. When she finally looked up, she saw someone leaning against a tree—someone tall wearing a hat.

Mara's hand fluttered the anagram paper. The capped boy stopped his leaning and started toward her. She cut across the street, trying to remain calm. In her haste, she loosened her grip on the paper and it floated away in the November breeze. The boy crossed the street when she did and followed closely behind her.

She started running. The footsteps behind her matched her stride for stride. When she lifted her knees and sprinted, running straight through the grass hurdles instead of over them, the footsteps behind her quickened. Now aligned with the big white house, she knew she couldn't dart across the street to safety without the fast runner catching her, so she kept running toward Lindy's house. If she could reach the pink and green house, she'd be safe.

Huffing, her lungs screamed for more air. Her ribcage burned. Lindy's house in view, she scurried across the street and ran right to the front door. The footsteps behind her slowed. *I'm safe.* Mara pounded on the door with both fists. Lindy opened the door swinging out, nearly toppling Mara.

Lindy stood there, a cigarette dangling off her lip. "What the—?"

"Please, can I come in? Right now?"

"Why, sure you can. Sure you can." Lindy motioned for her to sit in the front room. "Don't mind the mess. I'm in the middle of organizing."

*Please shut the door.*

Lindy lingered at the opened door. "Hold on a second. My boy's coming in from school. Robert E., come on in, boy. I'd like you to meet a friend of mine."

*General!*

General took off his green cap at the door, not even winded. He winked at Mara when Lindy looked away.

Mara's stomach twisted.

"Robert E., this here's Mara. Mara, this is my boy, Robert E."

# Thirty-Seven

"NICE TO MEET YOU, MARA." GENERAL wiped his hand on his jeans and extended it politely to Mara.

There were no tree limbs to watch, no Denim to rescue her, no voice to scream in protest. With Lindy looking on, Mara lifted her hand to his. He squeezed. Tight.

"Mama's told me a lot about you, Mara. I look forward to knowing more about you. You'll have to come over for dinner sometime." He looked up and down her body, repulsing her insides. Her hands started shaking.

"I . . . I have to get back. They'll be worried."

"We can call 'em. Come on, sit down and visit a while. Mama really likes you, don't you, Mama?"

The room, darkened by drawn curtains, magnified the glowing tip of Lindy's dangling cigarette. She sucked the cigarette in, making the red ember race up its shaft. "She's a real sweetheart, she is. Comes and visits me when you and Daddy ain't here. You'll stay, won't you?"

Mara's pity for Lindy exchanged itself for fear. "No, I can't. I'm expected. Thank you for the invitation."

General stood between Mara and the door. The room's only light came through the door's upper window, making

General appear darker. When she looked at him, all she could see was a dark shadow outlined by sunlight. She squinted, took a deep breath, and walked around him.

"Good-bye," she said weakly.

"Wait just a minute." General wheeled around and took hold of the door handle. "It ain't proper for a lady to open the door for herself, now is it?" He turned the handle, opened the door out toward the street, and beckoned her. "Not proper at all."

When she scooted around him, he caught her wrist.

"You come back, now. Mama, she needs her a friend." He pressed his fingers deep into her wrist and smiled sickly sweet. "Promise?"

She worried that he'd never let her go unless she lied. *Forgive me for bearing false witness.* "Yeah, sure."

General's grip relaxed, but his painted-on smile stayed the same. "Good. We'll look for you tomorrow, then."

*Don't count on it. Nine times—no more.*

Mara backed down the stairs. The doorjamb framed Lindy's scrawny body while General held the door open with his wide shoulders. Lindy put a new cigarette to her mouth, pursed her lips, and sucked in, long and steady. She waved her bony hand to Mara, who by now was at the gate, waving as if this were a friendly neighborhood visit. Truth be told, she wanted to run. Fast.

Mara walked back toward Burl's center, back to Zady and the safety of the criminals. Every three seconds, she looked behind her for the boy in the green hat. When she reached the Loop that divided Burl's white and black population, she broke into a run and didn't look back until she opened the one-hinged gate. The Confederate flag, flapping in the breeze, clanking against the pole, welcomed her. The big white house was no home, but at least it was safe.

# Thirty-Eight

A *BURL ATLAS* SAT ON MARA'S bed, opened to the Obituary page. *Who put this here? Zady? Mr. Winningham?* Mr. Winningham had already given her Aunt Elma's obituary, so it made sense that he probably did it. But Zady wore fake smiles lately, like she knew a secret. No matter. Seemed everyone knew Mara's business and no one talked about it. For a short-lived moment, Mara worried that General's secret was common knowledge too. But instead of letting her heart fret about it, she scanned the *Atlas.*

Eliot's picture—of him as a smiling young man—looked at her from halfway down the page.

"Eliot, I'm so sorry. So sorry." She sat on the bed next to the *Atlas* and held her knees to her chest. Mara rocked back and forth, trying to control the rivers of tears that threatened to burst clear out of her. She opened her Bible, not for comfort, but for her mama's picture. *Sephie, why do I have to rock myself? Why aren't you here to rock me on the porch swing? Why am I alone? Why did you leave me? Where are you?*

Sephie smiled back at her, as if in mockery.

Mara stared at Sephie's happy eyes—her eyes, with only one difference. Mara's would never be happy. *Never.*

Mara took one last look at Sephie. She held the top of the photo and ripped Sephie in two, then in fourths, then once more.

"Good-bye, Sephie."

She let the pieces scatter from her hands onto the hard-wood floor below her bed. Never to be whole. The fragmented picture teased her sad life. Mara realized that unlike Sephie's, her picture had never been whole. She'd always been bits and pieces, scattered to the wind, never to be joined together, no matter how much tape and glue and staples she used.

She'd tried her Nancy Drew hardest to solve the mystery of her beginnings; instead, she was left with shards of memories. Every time she discovered a memory shard, it pierced her heart. With each piercing, the life drained out of her until only a meager portion of will and hope remained. Maybe there was no more hope. Maybe she'd give up trying and settle down for a life of shards and fragments and questions. Maybe she'd be like her mama—beautiful but absent from the world.

*Would anyone miss me if I were gone?* Surely not Mr. Winningham—the man who strung barely ten words together. Probably not Zady. Every time Mara uncovered something new about her mama, the discovery afflicted Zady. Mara could see it in her pained eyes. Eliot's dead, so he's not in the place to be missing folks. Nanny Lynn's probably chatting with Eliot right now. Aunt Elma—well, she had viewed Mara more like a water bug to be swept away. Camilla? She'd probably care, but after six months without Mara, she probably had new friends. Denim concerned himself with the problems of the entire world as if his broad shoulders were built for holding poor folks' pain. Most likely, Mara was one insignificant person amid a sea of injustice for Denim. Vonda Rae was a friend, sure, but one of those skate-on-the-surface friends. Nothing deep, just jokes and laughter and an occasional cheering-up session. Mama Frankie wouldn't even remember her, being as how Mara existed in Mama Frankie's less-than-reliable short-term memory. Folks at church gave Mara a pained look whenever she came, but that didn't mean they'd miss her. Gus, well, he'd be thankful Mara was out of the way. He pretty much said so when she lived under Aunt Elma's roof. Even Stripes the cat had his own independence. If Mara were gone, Stripes would curl up on top of the warm dryer, content.

Only one person on this spot of earth would miss her: General. He chased her around as it was—demanding parts of her that she was forced to give like a 7-Eleven clerk giving money to a gun-toting robber.

So, that was it. The only person who'd miss her was a stealer.

Mara scarcely remembered her tears for Eliot moments before. She gathered Sephie's ripped-up bits and threw them like confetti into her trash can.

*God, I'm tired. Tired of Burl. Tired of mystery. I thought You knew everything. Nanny Lynn and Bishop Renny said so, but I think they must be mistaken. Maybe You do know everything, but You enjoy keeping me in the dark. Why'd You put me here, anyway?*

Resolute, she laid on her bed counting the seventy-two cracks over and over while she sucked her thumb, making fun of her baby ways in her head. Dinner meant nothing to her, and she no longer feared Mr. Winningham's silent wrath. Instead, she counted cracks until her eyelids flickered and fluttered shut.

At least she didn't have to eat ribs.

# Thirty-Nine

BY CHRISTMASTIME MARA HAD LEARNED OBSCURE things about the English language from the paintbrush-waving Mrs. Armitage. After anagrams, there were palindromes, mnemonics, malapropisms, and J.R.'s favorite—oxymorons. More days than not Mrs. Armitage—or Mrs. A Ragtime as she sometimes liked to be called—made the class bury their outdated textbooks under their desks. In history she made the class write essays about words like *injustice, peace,* and *carpe diem.* Although most of the students moaned when she assigned a one-page piece, everyone looked forward to the next day when they'd spend a good hour or even two discussing each other's work.

Mara's favorite lesson, though, was learning nouns, verbs, adverbs, and adjectives through Mrs. A Ragtime's crazy made-up Mad Libs during English.

She held her sides when the teacher read, "A Vonda Rae is a purplish hog used to demolish stinky teenagers."

Vonda Rae didn't laugh. She'd been in another scowling mood since her pet squirrel, Jiminy, ran away. Vonda Rae kept the chalkboards clean for a week after Jiminy's disappearance and grimaced her way through lunch.

The last day before Christmas break, Mrs. Armitage showed the class all sorts of blurred paintings—mostly white folks with umbrellas on beaches—and told them to create their own pointillism masterpieces with tempera paint and a pencil's round eraser. For an hour, the noise coming from room 109 sounded more like twenty-six dull-beaked woodpeckers than painting children. Mrs. Armitage purchased a frame for everyone, on sale from Value Villa, and helped each student frame the dotted masterpieces once they were dry. "I want you to think of your very favorite person—and give this painting to him or her as a Christmas present."

This announcement made Mara's heart hurt. Not too long ago she'd have given it to the rhyming Camilla. Or maybe the kind-eyed Eliot. Out of pity she'd have given it to Lindy, but not now. Zady would qualify, but she had her own family.

After the class made potato-print wrapping paper to cover their pictures, Mara still hadn't decided. On her way back to the big white house, it came to her. *Nose Bunny could use a picture in her attic room*, she thought. *Yes, Nose Bunny. That's who I'll give it to.*

By that time Mara had stopped listening to Denim, even though her days were excruciatingly lonely and she could've used his friendly voice. His ranting about judges, officers, and mafias tired her, and he never said anything further about the word puzzle. She pulled out the words again. *Officer. Judge. Silence. Politics. Evil. Harm. Indigent. Nepotism. Entangle.* She about crumpled them up and fed them to the trash can, but thought the better of it. *Maybe someday I'll figure it out. Or maybe I never will if God has anything to do with it.*

She rested her back against the wall and looked out her window at the bare naked pecan tree. While she traced the tree from trunk to highest limb with her eyes, she remembered that the best advice Camilla ever gave her was to watch the tree limbs. Mara made it her eyes' mission to caress every tree limb she met. At any place, during any season, she watched tree limbs to remind herself that somewhere, sometime, she had a best friend.

Like Denim had said, the tree's happy green leaves turned brown on fall's first cold day. Not one of them turned yellow. Or red. Or orange. The next day, many dusted the tree's roots a good seven inches thick—just like that. Mara had secretly hoped the brown leaves were cocoons, ready to birth orange monarchs in the spring, but her silly hopes died when the leaves dropped to the cold, red earth and crunched beneath her feet.

She loved the pecan's winter silhouette though. Liked the way it stood in dark, twiggy contrast to the brisk blue sky. She wished she could sketch like Mrs. Armitage and capture that tree the way it deserved, but her renditions came out either looking flat or like a kindergartener had drawn them.

Mara spent the first few days of her Christmas break watching the small black-and-white TV and avoiding Zady. When Zady spoke, Mara grunted replies and avoided her caramel eyes. After the fourth day of this nonsense, she realized she was becoming like Mr. Winningham—never talking, never meeting people's gaze, never engaging.

"Nose Bunny," she said one day in the attic, "am I becoming like Mr. Winningham?"

Nose Bunny uttered no response—didn't even twitch her ears. Mara peered through the telescope toward Camilla's house and wondered what she was doing. *Will I ever see Camilla again? Will Rose ever leave the house? Will Burl find out who the real Denim is?* She panned the telescope's lens until she found Lindy's house. Even though Mara knew she was safe from General's hands, her own hands trembled. She panned again, settling on Eliot's house. A For Sale sign stood in front of the weedy yard.

"Merry Christmas, Eliot." Mara's voice echoed through the attic. Not a soul heard her. Not even Nose Bunny.

# Forty

"COME ON, CHILD. CHURCH."

Mornings were darker—especially today, the shortest day of the year. Mara did not like waking in the dark. She pinched her eyes together and then opened them, hoping some light would filter in. "Ah, Zady, it's dark."

"The Lord Jesus came as a tiny baby into this dark world. The least you could do is wake up for Him. It's nearly His birthday." Zady swept Mara's covers off her bed, leaving her with no option but to get up and put warm clothes on.

"Do I *have* to wear my dress?" Mara rubbed her face. Bits of sleepy sand gritted her eyes.

"Child, what's wrong with you? We's going to church, and when we goes to church, we dress up. It's like we's on a date with God. We gotta look our prettiest for the Lord." When she said Lord, it came out more like Low-add.

Zady pushed her dress and stockings in her face. "Hurry, child. You're making us late. If the Aspen has to sit idling in the cold too long, it will quit clear out. I don't know 'bout you, but I for one do not want to push-start that car. C'mon!"

Mara shivered when the cold air met her dress's thin fabric.

"Where's your coat?" Zady was halfway to the sputtering Aspen when she barked at Mara.

"Too small. My arms have grown since last year. And I forgot to buy one at Value Villa." Mara stood midyard, hugging herself, unsure if she was supposed to go back inside and get her small coat or run and get into the Aspen.

"I told you you shouldn't have bought me that froufrou nightgown!" Zady walked a determined line right back to Mara. Mara flinched when Zady came toe to toe with her, expecting a scolding. Instead, Zady pulled off her own Naugahyde coat with the fake-fur collar and hugged it around Mara's trembling shoulders. "For goodness' sake, Maranatha. Why didn't you tell me? You poor thing."

Mara liked to pity herself. She had spots of her heart that pitied the few folks who were less fortunate than her. But she did not like pity from someone else. "Keep your coat. I'll be fine."

But she wasn't fine. The Aspen's heat worked as well as its air conditioning, which meant it merely blew air—hot blasts in the summer, icy chills in the winter. Raymond tried to defend his noble Aspen, saying it had its seasons confused.

Mara told her skin not to hatch goose bumps, but it disobeyed her. She told herself to please stop shivering, but her shakes kept shaking. The only time they stopped was out of sheer defiance when Zady peered at her through the make-up mirror, pity mirrored in her brown face. Mara would not be pitied. Even if it meant she froze to icy death at the whim of the mixed-season Aspen.

Mt. Moriah's garden had been laid to rest. Huge black tarps blanketed the garden, held down by red rocks, bricks, and pieces of metal. The sun had risen barely above the tree line. Now that leaves covered the ground, the sun cast its cold light through the barren trees, creating tree-shadow monsters on the dead grass. As Mara walked to the church's double doors, she was careful to avoid each limb shadow. She remembered the schoolyard admonitions of Vonda Rae: "Step on a crack, you'll break your mother's back." Somehow if she stepped on a limb shadow she knew something worse would happen. Not to her mama, though. For all she knew, her mama's back *was* broken. No, if she dared step into the tree's shadows, General was sure to make another entrance into her life and she'd have to watch the tree limbs—not in tribute to Camilla, but out of the necessity that accompanied horror and fear.

Her dark heart lifted when she entered the warmth of the church. Space heaters had warmed the place and the entire church was decked with greenery. Burl pine trees gave up their branches to celebrate Jesus. Mistletoe, the plague that sucked life out of Burl's trees, adorned every doorway, held on with a thumbtack and red curly ribbon. Mara wished someone would teach her how to curl ribbon; then she could make Nose Bunny's present just so.

Mama Frankie broke rank and sat with Zady's family. Heads turned when she sang since most folks had grown used to her wild vibrato crowing from the rear of the sanctuary, not from pew four, left side. Change was in the air, a fact confirmed by Mama Frankie sitting proud in a new pew, her walker decorating the aisle.

She squeezed Mara's thin hand three times in a row and then looked at Mara. "Each squeeze means something. I." *Squeeze.* "Love." *Squeeze.* "You." *Squeeze.* "Get it?"

Mara nodded. She'd never been squeezed an "I love you" before.

Mama Frankie rattled when she breathed—a strange thing indeed since when she sang, the rattle went clear away.

Mama Frankie bellowed "Joy to the World." She barked "Silent Night." She hooted "Away in a Manger." When the "amens" ceased, Mama Frankie started rasping again. In and out. *Rasp.* In and out. *Rasp.*

Through it all, Mara smiled and held the old lady's hand, squeezing it three times in a row.

The annual Mt. Moriah Christmas banquet and talent show followed the service. Boss Taylor shot a wild turkey—Gobbling George—who sat basted and baked on a small card table whose middle bent under George's weight.

Bishop Renny clanked two knives together to rouse everyone's attention. "It is my honor to dice up Gobbling George before he breaks this table." Boss Taylor smiled. "Let's thank the good Lord for Gobbling George, for friends, for family, for the sweet baby Jesus, and for life." Everyone except Mara bowed their heads. She sometimes forgot that when someone said, "Let's thank the Lord," it meant you should shut your eyes and point your nose toward the floor. She was always five seconds late.

Mama Frankie's cataract eyes caught Mara's tardiness. "S'all right, Sephie," she whispered. "Ain't you the one who said you didn't like to pray with your eyes shut? Said you liked to look at what God made—people, trees, flowers. I understand, Sephie. You don't have to bow."

Mara meant to correct Mama Frankie right after the "amen," but decided not to. Maybe Mama Frankie would let something slip about the mysteries surrounding her beginnings.

The talent show was like nothing Mara had ever seen. For two hours she allowed herself to be carried along by a crowd of black folks who gave standing ovations to chicken tamers and two-orange jugglers alike.

Raymond's kind eyes winked at Mara, who remained sitting at the first ovation. Above the ruckus he shouted, "We stand, child, and cheer forever and another forever. That's our tradition. Folks get so used to being beaten down during the year, so here at our talent show, they's gets a chance to be appreciated." Raymond grabbed Mara's hand and pulled her to her feet. "Cheer, child! Everyone here needs some cheer."

Before Mara could ask what in the world these folks needed cheering for, she started clapping and hollering. Something about all that whooping erased some of the dark whispers idling around in her head. For those two hours, she felt as if the worries that plagued her were gone, as if she had been thrust into a different world, like Willy Wonka's Chocolate Factory. But her world was real. Instead of chocolate, there was sweet potato pie.

Mama Frankie called her Sephie all afternoon and Mara learned a lot about her mama. She was more than pretty, she was kind. She took to injured creatures and spent hours trying to fix the poor things. She cried a river when a baby mockingbird she had fed with an eyedropper died. She mourned roadkill. Nearly got herself killed darting in front of a passing car to save a turtle ambling across Pleasant Street.

"Sephie, it's amazing you lived through your childhood, it is." Mama Frankie touched Mara's hair and pulled a loose strand behind her ear. "You mind if I hug your neck?"

Mara shook her head. She really didn't mind. Mama Frankie pushed her body around the walker and squeezed Mara in a neck-and-shoulder embrace, so hard she thought her head would pop off her body like a rocket.

"Merry Christmas, Sephie. Merry Christmas."

# Forty-One

MARA WASN'T SURE WHAT A MERRY Christmas was. Nanny Lynn had always brought the same potted tree into the farmhouse for just two days so as not to kill a tree for the sake of tradition. At least Aunt Elma had a Charlie Brown Christmas tree two years ago that she'd uprooted from the side of a Little Pine road. Poor thing sagged within a few days and then dropped all its brown needles. Last year Mr. Winningham scarcely said a thing to her, not a "Merry Christmas" or a "Happy New Year." They certainly didn't have a tree. Zady's family had been in Louisiana.

This year hadn't given her any clues either. The only evidence of Christmas in the drafty house was that Mr. Winningham allowed mail delivery. Nothing ever came for Mara through the metal slot in the front door, but she enjoyed watching slick sales ads spit through right around eleven thirty. She'd always yell a thank-you and watch the postman wave as he walked beneath the pecan tree.

Mr. Winningham apparently had a softer heart these days because he told Zady she could arrive late on Christmas day and leave early too. She had just enough time to clean the already clean toilets and make a proper dinner.

She'd stood up to Mr. Winningham yesterday, a sight that sent Mara hiding behind a doorjamb. "Red Heifer's isn't even open on Christmas, sir. I'm making y'all a brisket, some mashed potatoes, a heap of cornbread stuffing, some greens, biscuits, and some sweet potato pie. If the Lord were here today in Burl, Texas, He most certainly would eat my sweet potato pie."

Mr. Winningham had raised his hand to shush her, but Zady kept at him. "You even think about buying Maranatha a gift? What about a tree? Poor thing's gonna think Christmas is like Groundhog Day. I'll be coming tomorrow, thank you very much, and I'll be bringing Christmas."

Before Mr. Winningham could raise his hand again, she huffed out. Mara remained behind the doorjamb and worried that Zady would lose her job.

But no matter. Zady was here today, on Christmas, with Value Villa bags that smelled like a combination of roast beef, cinnamon, and perfume. She wondered if the "We Three Kings of Orient Are" smelled like this when they brought the baby Jesus their gifts from afar.

Raymond was parked out front, idling the Aspen in hopes of keeping it alive for another few minutes. Mara pulled on her too-short coat.

"Well, if it isn't my Maranatha." Raymond had rolled down his window and let his elbow rest on the window's opening, like he was taking a summer ride.

"Where're the kids?"

"Back home. Playing. We's already sung happy birthday to Jesus. Even made Him a right nice cake. You ever do that?"

"What for?" Mara pulled the coat around her, but it didn't quite meet in the front.

"It's His birthday, child. You of all people should know that."

"What do you mean?"

"Your name." Raymond took a toothpick out of his pants and started picking holy birthday cake out of his teeth.

"I don't understand."

"Your name. It means, 'Come, Lord Jesus.' Maranatha. 'Come, Lord Jesus.' 'Course it's something we utter oftentimes now, especially when life's been knocking us upside the head. We want Him to come back to earth and make things right. But it works for Christmas too. 'Come, Lord Jesus.' It's a prayer God answered when He put Himself in skin-clothes on Christmas, and it's a prayer God'll answer again when He comes back to make everything beautiful."

Although her skin pocked itself into goose bumps, her eyes lit up. "Mama Frankie. She kept shouting, 'Come, Lord Jesus,' when she saw me. Is that why?"

Raymond nodded. "I am sure it is, Maranatha. Yours is the prettiest name I've ever heard. Your mama, she knew what was what when she named you. It was her prayer over your life."

Zady came outside, apron on, wielding a wooden spoon like a weapon. "Raymond, you going to help me with the presents or not?"

"Sure thing, honey. I was making sure the Aspen kept itself warm. It's mighty cold today." He turned off the car. Instead of shutting off, it rumbled and coughed until it finally died. "I sure hope it starts up again."

Zady shook her head, like she'd heard those words before. She looked at Mara. "Get your skinny self inside," she said, frowning. "You'll likely catch your death out here."

Mara ran up to her room and shut the door. *Presents? Oh no! What can I give them?* She scolded herself for not thinking about others, especially not Zady's family. She looked around her room. There was nothing of value except her hardbound books. *The attic!*

She darted up the steep stairs and scanned the musty room. Light filtered in dust particles through the window and settled on the telescope. *Yes!*

Her excitement turned sour when she knew she couldn't give it away without permission. A knot settled behind her ribcage. She looked out the window to see the white Cadillac parked in the back and wondered where Mr. Winningham could be. She found him in the downstairs study, in the part of the house she rarely visited. She knocked and he said, "Come in," so now she stood feeling small while he sat behind a large desk, drumming his fingers.

"Mr. Winningham. Zady's brought presents."

"So?"

"So, I'd like to give her family a present."

"It's hardly a day to go shopping."

"I know. It's just—there's this telescope I found in the attic. I was wondering if I could give it to Zady's family. Today. For Christmas."

She expected silence, but instead she got two words.

"You may."

"Really?"

"Yes. Now let me be."

"Thanks, Mr. Winningham." Mara forgot herself, forgot her fear of the silent man, forgot her wits. She ran around the imposing desk, wrapped her arms around the stiff man, and squeezed Mama Frankie–style, hugging his thin neck. He sat in the same position he was in when she walked into the room. Then he reached his hand out as if to stop her. Instead, he placed it on her arm. Though his hand looked white and cold, she could feel its heat through her blouse.

Mara released her hug. Mr. Winningham pulled his hand back. Mara left. She examined the spot where he touched her, half-expecting a handprint to be there, but he left no impression, no mark—only the memory of his touch.

She ran upstairs to the attic and wondered if she should wrap the telescope. Its crate seemed too heavy and awkward to lug down the narrow steps, so she decided to leave it unboxed and unwrapped and tie a ribbon around it. She located the abandoned rag bin, found a silky scarf in shades of green and red, and tied it loosely around the telescope's midsection.

She looked again at her unstained arm, remembering Mr. Winningham's touch. *I should give him something too.* She scanned the attic looking for something he'd like, but there was nothing. It was all his stuff to begin with. She sat next to the little bedroom she created for Nose Bunny. Her eyes fell on the present she meant to give Nose Bunny, all covered in potato-print wrapping paper and placed under a cardboard Christmas tree. She held the present and looked from it to Nose Bunny.

"You won't mind, will you?"

Nose Bunny didn't seem to mind.

"I'll find you another present. Really."

Mara brought the present to her room and then retrieved the telescope from its place near the attic window. From far downstairs, she heard Zady's familiar dinner yell.

"Time for dinner, Maranatha."

She stashed the telescope in her closet and came downstairs. Raymond had apparently brought the Aspen back to life and had gone home. Zady had decked the dining room table with greens and red curly ribbon from the church. On Mara's plate was a helping of heaven—of course, anything that didn't smack of Red Heifer would be heaven.

"Merry Christmas, Mr. Winningham. Merry Christmas, Maranatha." Zady lit two red candles in the center of the table and left the room, humming "Hark the Herald Angels Sing." Although dinner was a silent affair as it always was, the previously existing tension had been pierced through. She wasn't sure if it was because she had hugged Mr. Winningham's neck or if it was his quick touch. After he finished his last bite, Mr. Winningham made his usual exit, leaving Mara all the sweet potato pie for herself.

"Zady, please come back."

"What's it you need?"

"I need your company."

Zady smiled her broad, broken smile and sat herself next to Mara. "I thought you'd never ask."

They supped on sweet potato pie until Mara's stomach protested.

"I think you were right," Mara said.

"I ain't seldom right. What is it?"

"When you said Jesus would've eaten sweet potato pie. I think He'd eat it to remind Himself of heaven."

Zady laughed from her stout belly. "Come into the parlor, child."

Stacked neatly on the coffee table were three presents.

"Hold on a minute," Mara said. "I'll be right back."

Mara left Zady sitting alone in the parlor with a confused look on her face. She ran up the stairs again, this time a little slower now that brisket lined her stomach. Smiling, she tugged the telescope down the stairs, trying not to thud it on each step.

"What in heaven's name?" Zady asked.

Mara set the telescope square in front of Zady. "For you and your family. Merry Christmas."

"Maranatha," was all Zady said.

Mara examined Zady's face for any clues. *Does she like it?*

*Maybe a telescope is a dumb present for an old woman and her family.*

*Maybe she hates it.*

*I want to hide.*

"How did you *know?*" Zady stood and crushed Mara to her bosom—no neck hugging here—a full-body squeeze. "We sit on our porch at night, Raymond and me, and we count the stars. He shows me the Big Dipper and Orion's Belt and we choose stars for our kids. Just for them. I've never dreamed we'd have ourselves a microscope."

"A telescope," Mara muffled from between the folds of Zady's dress.

"Silly me. Yes, a telescope." She relaxed her hugging, letting Mara breathe again. "Thank you, Maranatha."

"Zady?"

"Mm-hmm?"

"Does my name *really* mean 'Come, Lord Jesus,' or was Raymond making that up?"

"My Raymond doesn't make up a thing, child. He's as practical as rain boots in Seattle, he is. And he's right. Maranatha does mean 'Come, Lord Jesus.'"

"Why'd my mom name me that? Was it really her prayer for me?"

"Certainly was. She felt like you were her future, her ambassador to a world she'd never see. She hoped so many things for you, child. Mostly she begged God to not let you go through what she did."

"My mama. Sephie. She's dead, isn't she?"

"I hate to tell you that, especially since I can't say no more. Saying she's dead is a small part of the awful story. I promised Sephie I'd keep you from the truth until you were safe."

*Safe? What does that mean?* Mara looked at her shoes and

closed her eyes even though she was not praying. Although she pressed her eyelids together, she could not lock out the tears that pushed at them like a river pressures a dam. One by one, tears leaked out of her eyes and dropped on her shoes until the dam burst and all heaving broke loose.

"There, there, sweet Maranatha. I'm so sorry." Zady sat next to Mara and pulled her closer. Mara did not resist. "So much for only ten years old. Too much."

This made Mara cry more. She'd been carrying far too many things—tree limbs, General, Camilla's lost friendship, Eliot's death, Nanny Lynn's death, Aunt Elma's death, Gus's hatred—everything. And now, her mama's death.

"It's not your fault, Maranatha. Nothing is your fault. Sometimes grown-ups do things and kids get tangled up in their messes. Sometimes kids have to pick up the pieces of the mistakes adults make. If I could change things, I would. But I wouldn't change the fact that you were born into this world, Maranatha."

Zady produced a hankie from the folds of her dress. "Here. Blow."

Mara obliged, blowing like a Burl train whistle into the poor white hankie.

"Now, open your presents. This one first."

The rectangular box was wrapped in Christmas tree paper. Curly ribbon shivered on top when she shook it. Mara pulled the ribbon off and tried not to rip the paper. She could tell by Zady's tapping foot that she was taking too long, but she couldn't help it. Presents amazed her, and she wanted to revel in each one. Opening the box, she smiled. A winter coat. Brand-new. Naugahyde leather with a fake-fur collar. Like Zady's.

"I bought this one a little big, so maybe you can wear it two years."

Mara hugged Zady, this time pressing her thin body to Zady's fleshy one.

"Thanks, Zady. It's beautiful."

"Here. This one next."

The box, shaped like a shoebox, rattled when Mara shook it. She opened it more carelessly this time, ripping one corner. Yep, a shoebox. Mara lifted its lid and looked at Zady, confused.

"Stationery and stamps. To write your friend Camilla. I don't know how long Mr. Winningham will let the mail keep coming, but if you'd like, I can send it to her from my mailbox. She can write to my house and you can write back."

Mara traced her finger along the edge of the rose-covered paper and examined the flag stamps. She turned an envelope over in her hand and caught Zady's eye. Mara thought all her tears were spilled out, but one more ran down her cheek and dotted her jeans. Before she could say thank you, Zady handed her a small package.

This one had no ribbon. She slid her finger under the paper, revealing the back of a picture frame. When she turned it over, black-and-white Sephie stared back at her—whole.

"Housekeepers are good for something, child—like snooping and fixing."

"I don't know what to say." Mara's hoarse voice, a remnant of crying, squeaked.

"Nothing to say, child. It wasn't no trouble putting Sephie back together. I'll remember her dear sweet face for the rest of my days."

Mara examined Sephie up close. If she held the frame

right next to her nose, she could see tiny lines where she had ripped Sephie. "Thanks for putting her back together."

"Wasn't nothing putting Sephie back. I only wish I could be Jesus and put you back together. I'm afraid folks have ripped you up one side and down the other, Maranatha. Only Jesus can glue someone like you back together. Only Jesus."

# Forty-Two

AFTER ZADY WENT HOME, MARA HANDED Mr. Winningham her pointillism gift. He looked at her like she was a ghost.

"Open it," Mara said.

Mr. Winningham obeyed, being careful not to rip the potato-print wrapping paper. Mara tapped her foot. His eyes widened when he saw the painting. She could swear she saw a hint of a smile trying to form in the corner of his thin lips.

"Thanks."

"Merry Christmas, Mr. Winningham." Mara turned to leave the room.

Mr. Winningham cleared his throat. "Maranatha?"

"Yes, sir."

"There's something for you—in the wardrobe."

"Thank you, sir."

*What would Mr. Winningham give me?* Climbing the stairs seemed easier now that a present awaited her upstairs. She flung the doors open. There, at the bottom below the dresses, sat a plain brown box. Mara pulled it out and sat it on her lap in one smooth motion, like she was made to open presents. She lifted the brown lid and gasped. A dress. A beautiful Jessica McClintock Gunne Sax dress in pink and blue calico. She pulled it out of the box and held it up to herself. A perfect length.

Without thinking, she put the dress back in the box and ran downstairs to Mr. Winningham's study.

But he was gone.

# Forty-Three

*GONE* WAS THE WORD THAT BEST described Mr. Winningham that next week. He'd taken to generosity and given Zady the week off to be with her family. Mara was glad, of course, but it made for lonely days. Most days she wrote letters to Camilla. She wrote about her mama being Sephie and about the bully's mom being Lindy. Eliot's death and the bully's pushing her down in the vacant lot took a few lines. Sometimes writing about stuff that hurt made the pain seem more real. Mostly she prattled on and on about school, Mrs. Armitage, and how great her Christmas was. She asked Camilla lots of questions too. Mara could hardly wait until Zady came on Monday when she could give her the Camilla letters for mailing.

Her loneliness and boredom enticed her to listen to Denim's KBBQ talk show. She turned her dial from KARB, the county's best country, to KBBQ in time for Denim.

"Hello, fellow Burlites. Denim here. I speak for those who don't have a voice."

"Like me," Mara said.

She leaned against her headboard and glanced at Sephie, who smiled at her from atop the peach crate. While Denim went on and on about the judge with the rich brother, Mara drew a picture of Denim. She took extra care to make his eyes look right through her. When she finished drawing his wide nose and his open, smiling mouth, she wasn't sure how to color him in. If she used her #2 pencil, he'd look gray. She remembered her crayon box and was about to retrieve a warm brown when Denim's voice changed.

"Mars Bars—if you like Mars Bars, you best listen."

Mara went back to her bed and turned up the radio.

"The judge is afraid of Mars Bars. Thinks Mars Bars threaten his way of life. My daughter is worried that there won't be Mars Bars in this town anymore after he sends them all away. If you're a Mars Bar, you best be watching all around you. Trouble's a brewing. No Mars Bar is safe in this town, especially now. The judge is fixing to ship them all far away."

Mara stared at her drawing of Denim—looked right into his penciled eyes. "Am I in danger?" Denim's one-dimensional eyes seemed to scream, "Yes!"

# Forty-Four

MARA LOOKED ALL AROUND WHILE SHE walked to school. Even though the Naugahyde coat kept the winter wind away from her pale skin, it could not calm the shivers that came from the place of fear deep inside her. She took to running. She arrived at school early and breathless. Vonda Rae was an early bird too. She was cleaning the chalkboards.

"Jiminy still missing?"

Vonda Rae nodded without turning around. She could not be interrupted when she did the horizontals. Mara had made the mistake once of trying to talk to her while she did the horizontals.

"Shh," Vonda Rae had said. "I'm doing the horizontals."

"What?"

"The horizontals, silly. I drag the eraser straight across, and then I move up. I go all the way across and work my way up to the top. Then I do the verticals."

So, on the Monday when danger lurked behind every shrub, Mara waited while Vonda Rae did the horizontals. She hung up her coat and took out her markers. On the back of an old handout about palindromes, she drew the classroom from the vantage point of her desk—everything but Vonda Rae whose preoccupation with Jiminy's disappearance bothered Mara. No, she'd take her out of the picture.

Mara wanted the day to meander at a turtle's pace, but instead it hopped like a hare. Mrs. Armitage had spent Christmas break thinking of creative ways to teach, so she spun the day with games and riddles and charades. When time for English came, Mrs. Armitage decided to do a review.

"Who remembers what an anagram is? There will be a prize for each correct answer."

Every hand shot up. Whenever she said "prize" she meant candy bars.

"Maranatha?"

"An anagram is a word that you mix up to make into another word or sentence."

"Example?"

"Your name—Armitage—can be worded 'A ragtime.'"

"Correct. One Mars Bar heading your way." Mrs. Armitage threw a Mars Bar at Mara. It fell at her feet. The rest of the day whizzed by, thanks to the teacher's candy-throwing quiz game. Mara didn't raise her hand again; instead, she examined the Mars Bar and worried about her run home.

Mara tripped over roots three times in an attempt to run forward and look backward. She dusted off her gritted palms, jumped to her feet, and ran as fast as she could. She remembered what Eliot had said about Denim, that he was a truth-teller. Mara hoped that this time Denim was not telling the truth. *Will I be looking around me the rest of my life?*

Safe behind her front door and then her bedroom door, Mara took out her Mars Bar and examined it. She'd never actually had one. She turned it over and was thankful she remembered what an anagram was. She wondered what other words she could create by jumbling up their letters. She turned the candy back to the front. Mars Bar. Ram's bra. Mara laughed. She decided to write down "ram's bra" for Camilla before she signed her letter and gave it to Zady to mail. Instead of the stationery, she grabbed Denim's list. She meant to return it and get back to the business of writing, but the words seemed to shout, "Read me!"

*Officer.*
*Judge.*
*Silence.*
*Politics.*
*Evil.*
*Harm.*
*Indigent.*
*Nepotism.*
*Entangle.*

She read the list over and over and tried to remember the clues Denim gave. The only thing she could remember was him saying something like his daughter's friend could figure it out if she kept first things first. *First things first.* First things first. His words rolled around in her head. She scanned the list again. First things first. *That's it! The first letters! First things first.*

She wrote all the first letters down: OJSPEHINE. Jope shine? Josh E. Pine? Jones H. Pie? *Josephine.*

"Josephine!" When she said it out loud like that, she could hear the "Sephie" in it. Jo and Zady Winningham. Jo was her mama, short for Josephine, also known as Sephie.

Forgetting her letter to Camilla, she raced to the kitchen where Zady was pulling ribs out of a Red Heifer sack. "My mama. Her name was Josephine, wasn't it?"

"Where'd you hear that?" Zady snapped.

"I figured it out, that's all. Jo and Zady. Jo was never Jo

with an *e*, *he* was a *she*. Josephine. And Sephie is short for Josephine, right?"

Zady waved a rib in front of Mara's face. "Don't say that too loud around this house, you hear? The name makes Mr. Winningham feel guilty, and believe me, he don't like to feel his guilt."

"Why would he feel guilty?"

"When he hears that name he thinks about his own failures, child. Simple as that."

"Why?"

Zady placed the steaming ribs on a platter. "You know I'm a caged bird, Maranatha. Some things are too difficult to set free. Besides, my job here keeps my family fed. Raymond's furniture—don't get me wrong, it's beautiful and all—it just doesn't pay the bills. I'm paid to clean this house and cook this food. But I'm really paid to keep Burl's dirty little secrets."

Mara could almost see the weight of the secrets boring into Zady's soul. She pictured an elephant wearing a banner that said, "Secrets." The elephant raised his leaden foot and thudded it down onto a sturdy wooden crate. The crate was strong, sure, but once that elephant pressed its bargelike weight onto it, it would splinter and fall.

She hoped Zady wouldn't splinter.

She prayed Zady wouldn't fall.

# Forty-Five

SNOW—ACTUAL SNOW—CRUSHED THE PECAN leaves to the red earth. Northerners like Denim would probably call it merely a dusting, but to most native East Texans it was a miracle. This time of year there might be an ice storm or two. Mara hated ice storms. Hated how they crackled the tree branches. Hated how limbs snapped and fell to the ground. "It's Mother Nature's way of pruning," Nanny Lynn had said, but Mara hated to see a tree marred even if it was by Mother Nature's icy hand.

This was no ice though. Halfway through school, while Mrs. Armitage was reading a poem by some guy named Robert Frost, J.R. jumped up and shouted, "Snow!" his finger pointing toward the tall windows.

Mara had been in a pity party of her own making because every time Mrs. Armitage read poetry, it reminded Mara of Camilla. Sometimes when the teacher read one poem she'd *have* to go on to the next one, making Mara even more miserable. It didn't matter if the poems rhymed or not, she missed Camilla.

Before J.R. shouted the magical word, Mrs. Armitage had never before stopped reading a poem for anything—said it marred its cadence. Once they'd had a tornado drill midpoem and she'd recited it as they huddled in the center of the school building.

Not this time. J.R.'s "Snow!" had an enchanted effect on the poetry-reading teacher. She set down the poem mid-phrase, leapt to her feet, and said, "Time for recess!"

Snowflakes floated through a sky so gray you couldn't tell where the clouds ended and the earth began. Mara bent her neck all the way back and let the snowflakes kiss her tongue. She licked the snowflakes from her lips, then twirled around and around while the snowflake dance dizzied her.

School closed right before lunch. Mara was thankful Charlie got out early too and offered to walk home with her. Now she wouldn't have to run home. When he said good-bye in front of the big white house, Mara meant to run inside and finish her letter to Camilla. But the pecan tree stopped her. She sat on the cold ground, her spine against its stout trunk. She crooked her neck back a little bit and stared heavenward to see what the snowflaked sky looked like through the pecan's dark branches. The tree seemed to reach out to the sky, begging it for something.

As if in agreement, Mara begged God, *Help me. I'm afraid. I'm alone. Are You up there?*

The damp earth seeped through her jeans. Mara shivered but she could not move from this place. Something held her there. Something she couldn't understand. Just as Mama Frankie's words echoed at night, words swirled all around her now. Words of hope. Words of longing. As snowflakes dotted her jeans, words dotted her mind.

Aunt Elma's skipping Beatles album sang in her head, "I think you'll understand. I think you'll understand. I think you'll understand."

*God, I do want to understand. I want to know where I came from—who my parents are. Why am I here?*

"You are mine. You'll *forever* be mine." General's voice, not the snow, made her shiver.

*Bishop Renny says it isn't right to hate folks—and he's one of Your friends, God. Since I'm pretty close to hating General, is that why You don't listen to me?* Mara took a deep breath, remembering Bishop Renny's words about telling the truth. *I wish he were dead. That's the truth.*

Right now Mara was doing what Camilla had told her to do. "Watch the tree limbs, Mara. Watch the tree limbs."

The limbs stretched out, welcoming the virgin snow. *I've watched too many tree limbs, God. It seems You aren't very good at protecting me. Are You real?*

"I knows you'll grow up to be someone amazing. God told me." Mara couldn't remember Nanny Lynn's face as she said those words, only the look of her rough hands reaching for Mara's sleepy cheek. *God, I wish she could've lived forever.*

"Come, Lord Jesus." Mara pictured Mama Frankie, greens dribbling down her chin. She was never one to waste words. She meant every one of them. Mama Frankie told her what her name meant, something no name book in the library was able to do. *Why did my mom name me Maranatha? Why was Maranatha her prayer for me?*

"Come, Lord Jesus."

*I know something about Jesus—what Bishop Renny says on Sundays, what Zady sings, the way He shines through the lives of the church people, the painting of Him at Mt. Moriah.*

Mara thought about His dark skin and His eyes of love. *I could use some love like that.*

"Someday, God will make your life beautiful again." Zady's words warmed Mara as the snow chilled her toes. Of all the things Zady said, this made Mara's heart sink and sing at the same time. *I'm afraid that You can't put together the puzzle of my life and make it beautiful, God. But I'd like to have a beautiful life. One where I don't feel unwanted or in the way. One where General no longer does what he wants to me.* Mara shook her head. Not even God could do that. It would take a miracle.

Mara could hear Eliot's voice intermingle with the soft dance of snowflakes, "If God painted little brown dots on your face, best wear 'em proud-like." She touched her freckles as the snow kissed them. The freckles had faded a bit—something she used to long for. Now it made her sad. *I miss Eliot, God. Are You happy he is there with You? I'm not. I miss him.*

Under the pecan tree, watching its stark limbs, Mara found no further answers to her questions. The questions seemed to hang in the colorless sky. All she knew was that she was alone and she needed to be loved. When she found Nose Bunny in the vacant lot she'd convinced herself that if she had something *to* love she'd be okay. She'd poured her heart into Nose Bunny, gave her everything, but Mara felt hollow. The more she gave to the stuffed bunny, the more empty she felt, like a glass pouring all its water out, never to be filled again.

Whenever Zady tried to pour love into Mara, her first instinct was to run away. It made no sense to her. Down in the smallest part of her heart she knew she needed Zady's hugs and she longed for them. Still she kept Zady at arm's length—away from her puzzle-piece heart that needed Zady's tender hand.

Mara wanted to scream, "I need to belong to someone," but the words caught in her throat. Mara shivered, not so much from the cold, but from the emptiness of her heart. She took a deep breath and let it out. A puff of steam rose from her exhaled breath. "I need to belong to someone," she whispered.

Steam from her whisper rose like a prayer to the heavens.

*The sweet Lord Jesus says to you, Maranatha, "You are beautiful. You are Mine. You'll forever be Mine."* The sweet Lord Jesus that grew trees from pinecones and painted dots on her nose had a voice that sounded a lot like Mama Frankie's.

Although she didn't pray a prayer the way the TV preachers prayed, she knew one thing. The Jesus hanging on Mt. Moriah's wall spoke to her under the pecan tree using Mama Frankie's voice. It was really more like Jesus picking her out of a lineup. "I'll take that poor thing," Mara envisioned Jesus saying. "She needs to belong to someone."

Mara stood. She looked up at the pecan's tree limbs. From behind the gray haze, the sun burst through, giving the tree something bright to grab for. Mara smiled. For the first time, she also smiled in her heart.

She belonged to God. He was her Father now.

She belonged.

# Forty-Six

MARA WALKED UP THE PORCH STAIRS and went inside. Whoever built this house didn't think much about winters. Space heaters ran full force and couldn't warm it all the way to the corners. The house seemed to echo more in the winter, which added to its cold emptiness.

Mara took the stairs two at a time. At the top she noticed her bedroom door was open. She'd been careful to close it ever since Mr. Winningham scolded her about it at dinner. Said something about winter and heat and letting cold air into the center of the house. It had been one of the longest conversations they'd had, if you could call it a conversation—Mr. Winningham lecturing and Mara saying, "Yes, sir."

She peered around her doorway. Mr. Winningham stood by her bed.

"Mr. Winningham, what are you doing in here?"

He said nothing.

Mara walked to the bed. Mr. Winningham stood anchored to the floor. On her bed was another obituary, this time with a red circle around it and some writing. Next to the obituary was an old book.

Mara looked at the man, now hatless, and met his gaze. "The books were from *you*?"

"Yes."

His measured doses of kindness were almost too much. *Mr. Winningham thinks of me!* She noticed how he combed his silvery gray hair neatly to the side.

"All the newspapers?"

"Yes."

Mara picked up the *Burl Atlas*. Above a circled obituary were the words, "You don't have to be afraid anymore." She turned and again met Mr. Winningham's gaze that in the pale light of afternoon seemed to have softened.

"My brother. Judge Hawkins Winningham. He's dead."

"I'm sorry, Mr. Winningham."

"No need." He looked down at his shoes.

Mara did too. They were caked in red dirt.

"My brother was your father, Maranatha."

Mara sucked in a gasp. Denim's JOSEPHINE words were beginning to make sense.

"Your brother? My daddy? A judge?"

"Burl's only judge, and he was right proud of it."

"My mama's husband?"

"Never her husband. No."

"Then, how——?"

"Enough questions," he said. He cleared his throat. "I've let Zady know that she can tell you the story. I think it's best coming from her. He—my brother—wanted you gone from this town."

The word *gone* hung in the cold room. It didn't shout. It didn't whimper. It just was. *Gone.* Someone—her daddy, apparently—wanted her gone from Burl. In Mara's quest to find her parents, she might have expected a parent who didn't want anything to do with her. That had been her life. But *sent away*? What kind of man wanted to send his child away?

Mr. Winningham touched a wooden hand to her shoulder. "I want you here."

"But—?"

"No one deserves to be hated." A look passed between them—a look of empathy and sadness from Mr. Winningham, and a look of confusion from Mara. He walked through the open doorway. "I've got to clean my shoes. Don't be late for dinner."

Mara read the obituary. Questions jumped wildly in her head like popcorn kernels thrown on a fire.

THE HONORABLE JUDGE HAWKINS WINNINGHAM III LEFT THIS EARTH LAST WEEK. HE IS PRECEDED IN DEATH BY HIS MOTHER, JUDITH WINNINGHAM, AND HIS FATHER, HAWKINS WINNINGHAM JR. HE IS SURVIVED BY HIS BROTHER, JONATHAN ZANE WINNINGHAM. IN LIEU OF FLOWERS, PLEASE MAKE DONATIONS TO THE BURL PUBLIC LIBRARY FUND.

Mara sat on her bed. She didn't know whether she should cry or scream. She had found her father on earth the same day she had found her Father in heaven. Two fathers couldn't be more different. One wanted to send her away. Why, she didn't know. One gave her life. One despised her. One loved her. One was dead. One was alive. The only thing she really knew about Judge Hawkins Winningham III is that he wanted to rid the town of her, that he was handsome, and that he wanted Mara's mama. Denim never had anything good to say about the Honorable Judge, but what he said she hadn't understood. Mara only knew Denim didn't like the man.

The hole she had hoped her parents would fill now grew bigger. Knowing her daddy was an indifferent man made the hole raw. More than ever Mara wanted to know who Josephine/Sephie really was and how she got tangled up with a man who couldn't stand the sight of his own child. She shifted her weight on the bed. Her hand rested on something hard—the book.

*Great Expectations* by Charles Dickens. She opened it, expecting the first page to be ripped out, but it wasn't. On the page was scrawled, "J. Zane Winningham. This is my book. If you are Hawkins, you can't have this book. It's mine." Below the chicken-scratch writing was a crudely drawn scull and crossbones and the words, "God doesn't like stealers." It wasn't until she read J. Zane's words that the realization took root. *Mr. Winningham is my uncle.* The man she knew as some sort of relative was her *uncle.* Her daddy's brother. It tendered her heart toward the quiet man and at once she wanted to fly downstairs and wrap her skinny arms around him—really love on him. As she started her flying she flew into Zady, who stood outside the door.

"Heavens, child. You being chased?"

"Mr. Winningham—he's my uncle," she said, hoping Zady would take this as a logical explanation for running in the house.

"I knows it, Maranatha. I've known it all this time." Zady pulled Mara close and hugged her from the side. "We's needs to talk, you and I. Want to take a walk in the snow with me?"

"But, Mr. Winningham—"

"He'll be here when you get back, child. Now let's get you some warmer clothes to wear. I've brought you some mittens and a hat."

Zady made Mara put on so many clothes that she felt like a giant marshmallow. The hat drooped below her eyes. When she pushed it up with her mittened hands, it fell again. Zady took it off her head, rolled the bottom up, and placed it back on.

"There, now you can see *and* be warm. Let's go."

Snow fell in a delicate waltz onto the sidewalks, and the streets were whiting. "I bet we have a good inch," Zady said. The snow hushed the outside, even making Zady's voice seem quiet.

As they crunched their way past the criminal part of town Mara's stomach churned. If they crossed over the Loop, staying on this road, they'd walk right past General's house. "You sure you want to go on this side of town?"

"All that stuff about the black part of town and the white part—well, I think that's going to change someday. Besides, I want to see the park."

*The park!* The last time Mara had been to Burl's Central Park was the day Aunt Elma died, and before that, well, she didn't want to think about it. "I'm too tired."

"Don't be a party pooper, Maranatha. Don't you want to see the Burl dogwoods all decked out in silver?" Zady grabbed her mittened hand. "Come on, it'll be fun."

When they got close to the pink and green house, Mara asked, "Do you mind if we cross to the other side of the road?"

"Not at all. Why?"

"No reason. I like the other side better. Prettier houses."

She looked at General's house, expecting to see him peering at her from behind a curtain, but the house was dark. Mara sighed.

"You okay?"

"Yeah. . . . Zady?"

"Mm-hmm?"

"You gonna tell me about how my mama and daddy got to be my parents?"

Zady nodded. "Let's walk a little longer."

When they reached the entrance of the park, Mara froze. Memories that she had carefully pushed way down deep blew in her mind like a blizzard.

General.

Standing above her.

Unbuckling his belt.

Nine times.

Mara squeezed her eyes tight, hoping the darkness behind her lids would fade the memory, but even with her eyes closed she could see General's John Deere hat and the tree limbs beyond it. A silver tear warmed a trail down her cheek. She wiped it away. Zady handed her a hankie. Mara had to take off one mitten to use it. When she did, the cold bit her fingers.

"No need to cry, child. I'll tell you about your mama. Don't you worry your sweet little head. But first, let's pray."

"Out here in the park?" Mara heard the voices of laughing children nearby. She surmised they were sliding down the park's long hill. Zady was walking away from the children's laughter down the trail General used to drag Mara.

"Yes. Your mama loved to pray outside. She thought she was a bird sometimes, singing to the Lord in this very park. People would make fun of her singing like that. When she walked here with me after we met, they called her a half breed, even though her skin was as white as this snow here."

"Did that bother her?"

"None 't all. Whenever folks made fun of her, she sang. That was your mama." Zady shook her head. Tears laced her plump cheeks. "I need my hankie back."

Mara handed it to her, not sure how to respond.

They walked deeper into the park, snow crunching under four feet. Every time Mara exhaled, her breath made steam that swirled to the sky.

"Let's pray," Zady said.

Mara stopped, looked at her feet, and closed her eyes.

Zady laughed. Her laugh echoed all around. "No need to close your eyes and stop, child. We can talk to God and walk at the same time." Zady put her arm around Mara, and Mara let it rest on her shoulders. "Sweet Lord Jesus," she prayed. "I've got hard things to say and I don't know how to say them. Make my words tender. You've freed me from my birdcage, Lord, but I don't know what to say. Protect Maranatha from anything the Devil would want to do to her. Help her to know You love her."

"Zady?"

"Mm-hmm?"

"God answered that prayer—today."

"Which prayer?"

"The one about me knowing God loves me. I belong to Him now. We talked under the pecan tree."

"Sweet Lord Jesus. Sweet Lord Jesus!" Zady dotted her face afresh with the hankie. "Maranatha, that's the best news I've heard in years. Bless Jesus."

Mara smiled as they continued on the path and wound their way through the snowy forest. She expected a sermon, or at least a lot more exclamations of "sweet Lord Jesus" from Zady, but instead they walked in silence. Zady's broad grin illuminated her face. Every few paces she tried to begin saying something, followed by a "mm-mm-mm" and throwing her arms to the heavens.

After ten minutes of Zady's waving arms and "mm-mm-mms," Mara broke the silence. "Why did my mama give in and be with Hawkins Winningham?"

"At least you're to the point. Sounds like Mama Frankie filled you in on some things."

"Only that my daddy was handsome and he liked my pretty mama, but she didn't like him."

Zady filled her chest with cold air and let it out slowly. "Mama Frankie's right. Hawkins wasn't a judge when he started pursuing your mama. He was going to law school, but would come home in the summers. Every summer he'd chase your mama something fierce. Flowers. Candy. Jewelry. Your mama sent back every gift. Hawkins' brother, Zane—your uncle—warned him to stop. Told him Josephine wasn't interested and to leave her alone.

"Mr. Winningham said that?"

"He loved your mama too, but in his own quiet way. Hawkins was younger, more handsome, more talkative. Zane was a reader—very quiet—and much older. But he admired Sephie. And he could tell that Sephie hated Hawkins' constant attention. Zane wanted to protect your mama. But by the time Hawkins graduated from law school, he decided he would have your mama, whether or not she'd have him."

"Why didn't Mr. Winningham step in?"

"A man can only do so much, especially when his brother is obsessed. He did kick Hawkins out of the house. Told him to make his own way in the world. Hawkins ended up living with a crooked preacher while he studied for the bar exam." Zady clapped her gloved hands together. "I'm getting cold. Are you?"

Mara nodded.

"Let's walk faster. Get our blood circulating." The faster they walked, the more regular the steam puffs exhaled from their mouths, making them sound like a Burl steam engine. "One day your mama was walking in this here park, probably singing with the birds. Hawkins followed her, grabbed her, and pulled her into the woods."

"These woods? In this park?" *Is there some sort of mark on my mama and me?*

"Mm-hmm. Your father—I hate to call him that—raped your mama."

"What does *rape* mean?" Mara had never heard the word before.

Zady walked faster. Mara had to walk and run, walk and run to keep up. Zady stopped. Mara ran into her. "Hello there," Zady said, breathless.

General stood in front of Zady. His appearance was so sudden he must've come from the outer woods off the trail. "Hey."

When he saw Mara, his eyes narrowed.

Mara trembled from the inside out.

Zady looked at Mara. "You know this boy?"

Mara nodded. Oh, how she wished she didn't know him.

"Yeah, she knows me. We're good friends. Used to play together when she lived on the *good* side of town." He sneered. He had a double-edged way about him; he could cut down two people at once with his words.

"Enjoy your walk in the park," Zady said, and then walked past General. Mara would've been frozen to the sidewalk in fear had Zady not grabbed her hand and pulled her away.

"I will," he shouted after them. "You'll come around the house and visit me, won't you, Beautiful?"

"Don't answer him," Zady whispered. "Keep walking."

After five minutes of more brisk walking, Zady stopped and turned to look at Mara. "How do you know that boy?"

"Like he said. From this side of town." Mara hoped Zady couldn't hear the quivering in her voice.

"That boy's no good, you hear me?"

"Yes, ma'am." She wished she could tell Zady everything.

"His daddy and Hawkins and that police officer, Gus, were in cahoots, they were. Hawkins raped your mama but never got charged. The preacher gave him an alibi. Gus refused to gather evidence. Hawkins had sexual intercourse with your mama, but she didn't want to have it. That's what rape is. Do you understand?"

"Yes." Mara swallowed hard, her eyes wide. Now she had a word to describe the unspeakable things General had done to her in this park. *Rape.* She felt sick to her stomach.

"I wish you didn't understand. These are things for grown-ups to know, not little girls. Hawkins, he beat your mama up. It wasn't enough to rape her; he slammed her head against a rock."

"Then what?"

"He left her there to bleed to death."

"What happened next?" Mara could actually see her mama in the woods, bleeding and crying, the tree limbs dancing above her.

"I found her. Raymond and I were walking in the park that night. We weren't allowed to be in the park during the day since we were black folks, so we took to strolling under the night sky. In the wide field beyond this bend, we'd sit on the grass and look at the stars. God saw that we took a different route that night. We rounded a bend and heard moaning. Raymond, he had a flashlight, so we started walking toward the noise. Thought some animal was caught. Raymond panned the light back and forth as we climbed a steep hill through some underbrush. And then we saw your mama. Whimpering. Holding her sides. Head bleeding. Dress torn off. She was rocking back and forth like she was in a rocking chair. Raymond, he took his jacket off and covered her up."

"Was she shaking?"

"She was, come to think of it. She shook like a leaf in the wind. And Raymond's jacket didn't stop her shaking. We tried to get her up, but she was too weak. Then we thought, *What if someone finds us with her like this? They'll think we did something to her.* Raymond, he had his wits about him and prayed. Said, 'Lord, You need to show us what to do. Need to give us a sign.' No sooner had he said the prayer than Sephie whispered, 'Winningham.'"

"Why?"

"She was trying to tell us who did this to her, but we misunderstood. We didn't know many white folks. The only Winningham we knew was J. Zane Winningham—the man who denied my Raymond a loan for his furniture business. We figured this was her family, so Raymond picked up Sephie and carried her clear to Mr. Winningham's house. When Mr. Winningham saw Sephie, he shook his head and cried."

"Mr. Winningham cried?"

"Like a baby."

"He took her from Raymond and brought her to the room next to yours. It had a big bed in there. Must've been a guest room. He laid her down like she was Snow White and then called a doctor. He asked us what seemed like a hundred questions. We stayed in the parlor downstairs while the doctor took care of her. Right before we left he asked how good we were at keeping secrets. We told him we were fond of secrets. That's when he offered me a job keeping his house. Really though, I believe God sent me there so I could become your mama's friend."

"What about Hawkins?" Mara was careful not to call him father.

"I didn't know about Hawkins until much later. Mr.

Winningham, even though he hated his brother, protected him. Sephie's the one who told me about Hawkins. When Mr. Winningham got wind of my knowing, he made me swear I wouldn't tell a soul. Told me I'd lose my job. Since his bank held the note to our house, he said he'd take the house too. Mr. Winningham's a powerful man—practically owns this town. When he spoke, I listened."

"Why didn't he ever loan Raymond the money to start a business?"

"Not sure, child. I think he was concerned enough that he hired me. Any other connection to us worried him. He didn't want it to look like he favored us."

The snow clouds blew their last flakes; the sun appeared through the Burl dogwoods, warming Mara. "Can we walk back to the house now?"

"Sure," Zady said.

"When did you know my mama was going to have a baby?"

"Mr. Winningham told me a month after I started working there. Told me to take care of Sephie and make sure she ate. Sephie injured her head so bad she couldn't barely walk around without feeling dizzy, so she needed me to feed her, bathe her—everything. We got to be the closest of friends. She didn't mind I was black. She loved me. We cried through Central Park together, asking for Jesus to heal her. I took her to church with me. She felt safe there—at home, really. And Mt. Moriah loved on her. Mama Frankie especially. She wasn't so loud then, hadn't lost her hearing. Sephie told her everything, and Mama Frankie, she prayed for Sephie."

"I think Mama Frankie prays for me too." Mara's feet didn't crunch the snow anymore, it slushed. The sun, low in the afternoon sky, cast long shadows across the trees—trees that now *drip-drip-dripped* melting snow.

"I'm sure she does, Maranatha. I'm sure she does."

They crossed over the Loop. No cars to dodge today. No one dared venture driving on the slippery snow. Instead, an army of snowmen populated the streets. Old men and young children, mothers and teenagers all joined together to create their own version of Frosty the Snowman. The snow, only an inch deep, had a red hue to it. No matter what someone did in Burl, it was christened with red dirt.

Zady opened the gate and motioned for Mara to join her on the green porch swing. "Mr. Winningham kept your mama from Hawkins. Protected her. When she had you, he had the doctor come to the house so she wouldn't have to be afraid in the hospital. Your mama insisted we put my name and her shortened name on the birth certificate to keep you from knowing who your father was."

"Zady and Jo Winningham."

"Yes. When you were born your mama came alive again. Her head was swimming, but she loved you, Maranatha. She used to sing songs to you. Sung that hymn about His eye being on the sparrow."

"So you were there when I was young too? When my mama swung me on this swing?"

"Yes."

"I don't remember you."

"Probably because I did the diaper changing and the feeding. It was your mama who played with you, hugged you, loved on you. She was very weak, but she used every ounce of energy to play with you. Every once in a while, Mr. Winningham petted your head. He cringed when he saw you, though. Felt guilty that he didn't prevent his brother's crime. You were the reminder of his failure to protect Sephie."

"I think I'm still that reminder."

"True. But, Maranatha, he loves you. He simply has an odd way of showing it."

"Like the books?"

"What books?"

"The books in my peach crate. I wondered if it was you who gave me all those old books, but it was him. New ones kept showing up. And for Christmas he gave me a dress."

"He did?"

Mara smiled. "A beautiful dress, like one my mama would wear."

"He often bought your mama dresses. She wore a different one each week to church. It must've nearly killed him to go to Ellen's Fashions and ask the salesgirl for a new dress. Mr. Winningham shrinks around women. But he loved your mama so much, he'd even conquer his shyness to keep her safe and make her happy."

"Did they ever marry?"

"He asked her, and she said yes. But she died before they could. Mr. Winningham was going to adopt you, but when she died, he had no legal rights to keep you."

"How did she die?"

"She faded away real slow-like. She stopped going to church. Mr. Winningham kept buying her a dress a week, but she never wore a one. She spent all day lying on her bed while you played on the floor. She sang to you when she had enough breath. Eventually her singing stopped. Right before she died she had me lay you on her chest. You were asleep from playing so hard. She sung you a lullaby, tears in her eyes. She looked up at me." Zady's voice choked. She took a breath. "She looked up at me and said, 'Zady, you take care of my baby. You tell her about Jesus. Tell her I loved her and that I'll miss her.' Sephie took in a long breath. 'Tell Zane thank you. Tell him I love him,

okay? And Zady? I love you too. Tell the church . . . I love them.'
She took one last breath and whispered, 'Maranatha. Come,
Lord Jesus.' "

Mara welcomed the tears that coursed down her face.

Zady handed her the wet hankie. "The hardest thing I ever
did in my life was take you off her cold chest. When I pulled
you away you started crying like you knew your mama was
dead. For weeks you asked for her. During that time Mr. Winningham's hair turned gray. And then Gus stole you."

"He stole me?"

"Somehow Hawkins found out that he had a child, so he
had Gus take you on his behalf. By now Hawkins had passed
the bar and was pressing the city council to elect him judge.
Figured if he was judge he could be the most powerful man in
Burl—even more powerful than his brother. Your existence
threatened his plan, so he decided to hide you. From what Mr.
Winningham said, he was getting ready to take you again. Far
away.

"The day you were kidnapped, Gus pounded on the door
and pushed right on by Mr. Winningham. You were asleep. He
found you in your bed, snatched you up, and zipped out the
door just like that." Zady snapped her fingers. "He plopped
you at that Elma woman's house—his girlfriend—and renamed
you Mara Weatherall. Soon after, Elma moved in with her
mother in Little Pine to keep you far away."

Emotions tumbled in Mara's stomach like a too-full dryer.
Sad that Nanny Lynn wasn't her grandmother. Wondering if she
knew Mara had been stolen. Secretly glad Aunt Elma wasn't her
aunt. Angry. Confused. Loved. Not loved. It was too much.

"Do you know how Aunt Elma died?" she blurted.

"Cancer, child. Had her the cancer. Took her fast."

# Forty-Seven

MARA WORE HER NEW DRESS TO church. She'd invited Uncle Zane to go when she modeled her dress, but he declined. Said he had a headache. Mama Frankie called her Sephie again. Mara didn't mind a bit. Somehow through the grapevine of Mt. Moriah, folks knew that Mara knew about her past, and everyone seemed to heave a sigh of relief. People were freer around her. They laughed more.

And somehow the greens started tasting like heaven.

When Denim's voice crackled over KBBQ that Mars Bars were in danger, Mara dismissed it. *Denim doesn't know that because Hawkins is dead, I'm safe from being nabbed.*

When Mrs. Armitage read poetry Wednesday in class—even rhyming poetry—Mara's sadness was smaller. Sure, she missed Camilla, but she knew two things. She belonged to God. And so did her mama. She dreamed her mama winked at her through the trees on the way to school and smiled when the sun spotlighted Mara on the way home. The truth, like Bishop Renny said, set her free—even though the truth was ugly. Maybe Zady was right. Maybe Mara's life would turn out beautifully.

Mara sang while she skipped home. The snow from last

week was a distant thought—quickly replaced by seventy-degree days. So the trees were naked but the sun was shining as though it were spring. Mara smiled. The Dodge Aspen wasn't the only thing that had its seasons mixed.

She took her coat off when she walked in the door. "Mr. Winningham? You home?" No answer.

Her bedroom door was open again. *He's probably bringing me another book.* "Hi, Mr. Winningham," she said as she stepped into her white room. Someone in a big coat bent over her bed, but it wasn't Mr. Winningham.

General turned around. "Hi, Beautiful."

Mara looked around, frantic.

"Not here. I made sure. The old man is off somewhere—took his big white car—and the fat black woman ain't here either. It's just you and me. Let's go."

"No," Mara said.

"You don't have yourself a choice." From beneath his coat, General pulled out a knife. "It's a switchblade. With one flick . . . " He pushed a button and a blade snapped alive, long and silver.

Seeing the knife made her shivers shiver.

"Now, let's take a nice walk to the park. To our special place. No funny business, you hear? You act normal while we walk there. Remember the knife."

General pushed the blade back inside its sheath and walked toward her. He closed his hand around her upper arm. "Walk."

General's grip grew tighter—something Mara didn't think possible—when he pushed her toward the stairs. She planted her feet, drug them—anything to slow progress. If he got her to the park, she'd be dead.

Through his clenched teeth General gritted, "We're leaving the house, and all this foot draggin' will stop, you hear me?" He pulled out the knife with his free hand in the same smooth motion his mother did when she lit a new cigarette.

Mara feigned cooperation as they walked from the porch. The green swing swayed in the gentle breeze. *I'm like you, Mama. And I'll be seeing you soon.*

General pushed her through the gate. They walked under the pecan tree's gawky shadow. Mara wished its shadow would reach down and rescue her.

Across the Loop Mara's shaking increased. Her teeth chattered.

"It ain't cold out here, Beautiful. Stop that chattering."

She shut her mouth, but her jaw kept jumping up and down to the rhythm of an invisible woodpecker. Nearing General's house, she looked down the side street where Denim lived, hoping to catch sight of someone there. She strained her eyes to see inside the radio room. It was over a block away, and from her angle, she couldn't see anything. Every window along that street was lifeless—a black inky void.

*Help me, Jesus. Help.*

She took one last fleeting look behind her. No one.

"What're you looking at?"

"Nothing."

"Hurry. We're almost there."

When they reached the park Mara panicked, digging in her heels. "I'm going to scream. I can scream real loud." The hand that squeezed her elbow cupped her mouth, muffling the beginnings of her screams, stifling her breath.

"Not so fast, Beautiful. Remember, I've brought me a friend." He looked around, pressed the button, and stroked its blade across her cheek. "No more dragging."

He pushed her off the trail, through the familiar brush,

only in winter it wasn't so tall. Instead of their usual spot, General pushed her farther into the thicket. Thorny branches thwacked her legs and tore into her arms. She wished she hadn't removed her coat.

"Here." He pushed her down. "Right here."

Mara tried to inch away, but he slammed a boot into her ribcage. "Stay put and shut your mouth." He closed the knife, took out a cigarette, lit it, and inhaled. He bent low to her and blew the smoke into her eyes and face. Mara coughed. "Don't like that, huh? I tell you what, my mama's been frightfully lonely without you coming around. Too bad you won't be able to visit her anymore." He sucked in another long drag. He blew it again into Mara's face. "I hear you've been talking about you and me."

"I haven't. Not a soul. I promise," she managed to say, smoke stinging her eyes.

He shook his head. "Now don't be lying to me. I know more than you think I do." He rocked back on his heels, taking her in. "I'm good at that. Just ask your aunt."

"You didn't kill my aunt." Mara pulled herself onto her elbows and felt her voice grow stronger. "Cancer did. *You're* the liar." *The truth will set you free.*

*Smack.* His heavy hand hit the side of her face, forcing her backward. "Don't you be calling me a liar, Beautiful. It's time your own lies were silenced. You keep talkin' 'bout me and I'm liable to end up in Juvie. That'd kill Mama. It's up to me to make you quit talking, 'specially to all those blacks."

"Go ahead. Silence me." Mara's shaking stopped. *I need Your strength, God. . . . Mama, I'm coming home.*

General fumbled with the knife. The button seemed to be stuck. He fell to his knees, messing with it, and then looked right at Mara. "No matter. First things first. You're mine. You'll forever be mine." He unbuckled his belt, threw his green cap to the earth, and dropped his pants.

Mara looked up. The bare tree limbs reached for the leaden sky. A thick blanket of clouds rolled in and obscured the sun. She remembered all her nightmares—the ones where General chased her and she couldn't scream or elude his grasp. She took a deep breath, pulling air over her mute vocal chords, and prayed God would give her a voice, one last time.

"HELP!" she screamed, clear and loud. "HELP ME!"

# Forty-Eight

GENERAL CUPPED HER MOUTH AND NOSE with his hand. She tried to breathe in another breath, but couldn't. She kicked. She squirmed. But he kept her pinned.

*I'm coming, Mama. Come, Lord Jesus.*

As her eyes rolled backward from lack of air, she heard a commanding voice.

"Let go of her."

General sprung to his feet, his pants circling his ankles.

Mara sucked in a breath. *Denim!*

"You gonna do anything about it?" General challenged. "This here's my girlfriend. We're having us a friendly romp in the park." General bent down to retrieve the knife.

"No!" Mara's voice startled General, enough to make him turn and look at her. In that instant, Mara grabbed the knife. She opened it with the swift push of a button and pointed it at General. Instead of shaking, her hands held steady.

"Put that thing down, Beautiful," General said with a mixture of amusement and fear. When he reached to grab it, Denim closed his hand over General's forearm.

"I wouldn't be calling her that, Robert E. Pull your pants up, boy. I'm taking you to the police station."

"That won't do you no good. Who's going to believe some black guy over the word of Robert E. Lee Townsend? No one will listen to you. Not in this town."

Denim laughed, something that seemed to unnerve General.

General quickly gathered his composure. "I have a friend there," he boasted.

"Good ol' Gus, you mean? Well, I'm afraid he's in custody—for questioning. Something's a bit fishy about the judge's sudden death."

Mara lowered the knife and let it fall to the ground. As she stood, the sun broke through the blanketing cloud. Behind Denim and General appeared Mr. Winningham. Mara was too tired and much too frightened to worry about ruffling the old man. She ran straight into his chest. Mr. Winningham wrapped his thin arms around her and held her tight. He touched her hair. "It's going to be all right," he whispered. "I'll protect you."

They walked together to the white Cadillac, Mr. Winningham with his arm around Mara, Denim gripping General's wrists and pushing him forward, making him stumble. General's pants kept falling down.

Mr. Winningham spoke. "We'll take him to the station, Denim. Then I've got to take Maranatha home."

"Anything you say, Mr. Winningham."

Mara looked at Denim, then at Mr. Winningham. "How'd you find me?"

Mr. Winningham opened the front passenger door for Mara. Denim forced General into the rear of the car and sat next to him, holding General's hands behind his back.

When Mr. Winningham settled behind the wheel, he looked at Mara, then in the rearview mirror. "Denim called me. Knew my phone number at work and told me he saw you with Robert E. from his window. Said it looked suspicious. I met him at the park entrance, but you were nowhere in sight. It wasn't until we heard you scream that we were able to find you. Denim saved you, child. And all along, I thought he was my white menace. Turns out he's our black savior."

Mara, who'd kept General's secret far too long, spilled all of it at the police station. Seated next to Mr. Winningham she first spoke in stuttered sentences, too ashamed to say what General had done to her. She knew the words he used for what he'd done were swear words, so she struggled to describe what he did in a way that wouldn't make her swear. Whenever she stumbled over her words, she looked at her uncle and remembered his love for her mama.

"General raped me nine times," she finally said, and that's when most of the spilling started. She told the investigator everything she could remember from the first day she met General to his meeting her in her bedroom. She had held the secret as long as she could, as long as she knew that keeping it would protect the ones she loved. With Gus out of the picture, and General behind bars, she knew that holding onto the secret would protect no one but him.

*I will not protect him anymore.*

"He threatened to kill me if I told," she said, her voice gaining strength. "And everyone I loved. Said he'd go after them. I suppose he was fixing to kill me today."

The investigator had tears in his eyes while his assistant wrote furiously.

"He followed me. Watched me walk home from school. Chased me."

When she was out of words she looked at her hands folded in her lap.

"That's all we need for now, Mr. Winningham." The investigator turned his face from Mara and blew his nose into a hankie, then put his hand on her shoulder. She didn't shrink from his touch. "I am so sorry. So sorry."

"Let's get Denim home, all right?" Mr. Winningham said.

Camilla was sitting on her front porch when the white Cadillac produced her father from its back door. Mara tumbled out after Denim. Mr. Winningham followed.

A taller Camilla ran to meet Mara. They embraced and laughed at the same time.

"Well, if it isn't Mara coming to visit in the white car-a," Camilla rhymed.

Mara smiled. "Call me Maranatha, Camilla. It's my real name." She said it to Camilla, but really, she was saying it to everyone in Burl, Texas. She was no longer Mara—*bitter.* From now on, she was Maranatha, a plea for Jesus to come, to shed light and truth on her life and the lives around her.

Camilla hugged her neck, practically choking Maranatha. "All right, Maranatha, but that's an awfully hard name to rhyme with."

# Forty-Nine

MR. WINNINGHAM PROMISED TO LET MARANATHA play with Camilla forever and a year. He even said he'd pull a few strings at the radio station and try to get Denim an actual job at the KBBQ station. "No more sneaking around, you hear?" Mr. Winningham told Denim.

Denim smiled. Rose peeked through the front screen door, saw Mr. Winningham, and withdrew.

"It's okay, Rose Salinger. It's me—from the bank," Mr. Winningham said.

She poked her head from around the screen door. "Zane?"

Mr. Winningham nodded. He tipped his hat.

Rose kept her head poked out, but nothing more. Camilla later told Maranatha that Zane and Rose had been coworkers at the bank—Zane as the owner, Rose as a teller in the days before she married Camilla's real daddy.

"I need to take Maranatha home," Mr. Winningham said. "She needs rest."

"Thanks, Maranatha," Denim said. He took her white hand in his. "Thank you."

"For what? I'm supposed to thank you for saving my life."

"You saved mine, beautiful Maranatha. Sure, I speak for

those who have no voice, but I was afraid to let people see who was attached to mine. Some kind of honest journalist, huh? I let Rose's fear eat at me until I seldom left the house. Rescuing you is the best thing I ever did. You gave me a voice today, Maranatha. I only wish it wasn't your tragedy that brought my voice back to me. I'm so sorry."

Maranatha didn't know what to say to Denim's apology. Didn't have the words. So, she smiled.

Camilla motioned to her from under their live oak tree. She shot Mr. Winningham a *may I?* glance. He nodded.

Camilla was crying. And whispering.

"I can't hear you," Maranatha said, while Denim and Mr. Winningham chatted near the front porch.

"It's all my fault," she hushed.

"What do you mean?"

"The stranger danger. When you told me about the bully, something deep down in me knew something was terribly wrong. But I couldn't talk about it. Not then."

"Why?"

"You know how things are if you keep 'em hidden? If I talked about *your* bully, I'd have to remember another bully, and then it'd be out there."

"What?"

"My secret."

*Camilla has another secret?*

"I needed to keep it way down inside. So, I told you to watch the tree limbs." Camilla sat beneath the tree. Maranatha joined her.

"Because I had to once," she said.

"You did?"

"Yep." Camilla wiped a fat tear from her cheek.

"I'm sorry," Maranatha said, looking up. Sitting next to

Camilla that way, the limbs shadowing her face, she felt like she'd lost a funny friend and gained a sister.

"I know." Camilla took a deep breath and looked up toward the sky. "It's not so scary sitting under the tree limbs with you."

"Yeah." Maranatha wiped a tear.

"It's not the limbs that are bad," Camilla said. "It's the bad folks doing bad things. But now that we're here—together—well, it's not so awful anymore."

Mr. Winningham stood at the gate.

"I need to go," Maranatha said.

"After a while, crocodile," Camilla said.

Mr. Winningham opened the front passenger door for Maranatha. She slid in and waved good-bye. Denim and Camilla waved from the front steps. Rose raised a tentative hand from behind the screen door.

"Let's go home," Mr. Winningham said. "And Maranatha?"

"Yes, Mr. Winningham?"

"Call me Uncle Zane."

"All right, Uncle Zane."

The first time she saw the big white house, she dreamed she'd live there someday with servants and grandeur. When she moved under its eaves she called it the big white *house*, not her *home*. Now, when Uncle Zane crossed the Loop to the town's "criminal" side, it was the pecan tree Maranatha saw first, its dark limbs contrasted against the blue sky. The Confederate flag had ceased its clanking. The front gate hung crooked like always. Uncle Zane parked the Cadillac out front, in a rare change of routine.

He opened the creaky gate for Maranatha and tipped his hat. Zady swayed on the porch swing, her broad smile showing her missing teeth. The front door gaped open, letting in the breeze. She stood, waving her hankie at Maranatha.

Maranatha stood underneath the pecan tree—its shadow-limbs reaching clear up the high walls of the big white house.

She tucked her thumb inside her fist. "I'm home," Maranatha said. "I'm finally home."

# A Meal at Zady's Table

### Not Too Sweet Tea

3 cups water
1/2 cup white sugar
8 teabags standard tea (Luzianne, the only kind Zady would use. "All other brands taste like bitter sawdust," she said once.)

Bring water to boil in a saucepan. Add sugar and tea. Boil for five minutes. Let cool.

Add condensed tea mixture to half-gallon container. Fill with cold water and ice cubes.

### Chicken Spaghetti

1 whole rotisserie-cooked chicken (Zady would've loved the convenience of this, but she had to roast her own.)

Place chicken in large pot of boiling water (8 cups water). Cook for 2 hours. Remove chicken. Let cool. To the stock, add 8 cubes chicken bouillon and stir through. Set aside on simmer.

In medium saucepan, melt 2 tablespoons butter over medium-low heat. Add 2 tablespoons flour and stir until combined. To this add:

1 1/2 cups milk
1 1/2 cups broth (from stock pot)
1/2 teaspoon garlic powder
Salt and pepper to taste

Bring to a boil and stir until thickened. Turn heat off. Meanwhile, turn the chicken stock to high. When it's boiling, add 16 ounces spaghetti noodles. Boil for 10 to 12 minutes until al dente (still have a bite to them, not mushy, as Zady would say).

Once noodles are boiling, attack the chicken carcass, removing as much meat as you can from the bones, setting aside. ("Waste not, want not," Zady would say.)

Turn heat on under milk mixture. Add:

2 cups cheddar cheese

1 small can mild green chili peppers

Stir through. When noodles are finished, drain and place in a large pasta bowl. Drop chicken pieces on top. Pour sauce over. Toss and serve. Serves a hungry family of five.

### Whole-Wheat Corn Bread

2 eggs

1 cup milk

1/3 cup sugar

1/4 cup oil

1/4 teaspoon salt

1 cup corn meal ("The yellowest you can find," said Zady.)

3/4 cup wheat flour

1 tablespoon baking powder

Mix eggs, milk, sugar, oil, and salt in medium bowl. Combine corn meal, flour, and baking powder in large mixing cup. Pour into wet mixture and whisk until smooth. Pour into 9 x 11 greased pan. Bake at 400 for 25 minutes or until a toothpick poked in the middle comes out clean.

Serve with honey butter:

1/4 cup butter, softened

7 tablespoons honey

Whisk together and serve with a spoon.

## Black-Eyed Peas the Only Way

2 cups dried black-eyed peas

Place peas in a large bowl and cover with cool water, two inches above the top of the beans. Let sit overnight.

The next day at lunchtime: Pour beans over a colander and rinse, running your hand through the beans, looking for small stones. ("I cracked one of my teeth on one once," Zady said.) Pour into large pot, covering with water by two inches. Add 6 to 8 chicken bouillon cubes and 1 ham hock or left-over ham bone. Bring to a boil. Test the water. If it's still tasteless, add more bouillon. Cover and cook on low for 3 to 5 hours until beans are tender. Ladle out in heaps and serve with Ranch dressing.

## Sweet Potato Pie Like Heaven

11/4 cups all-purpose flour

1/4 teaspoon salt

1/3 cup shortening

3 to 4 tablespoons very cold water

Cut shortening into salt and flour with two knives or use a pastry cutter. (Zady prefers pinching the dough together with her fingers.) Add water and stir with wooden spoon until moistened. Form into a ball. Cover with plastic wrap and let cool in fridge.

2 pounds sweet potatoes

Peel potatoes, cut into eighths, and steam in a basket over boiling water for twenty minutes until tender. Place in food processor and blend until smooth. (Zady doesn't have one, so she presses the sweet potatoes through a sieve.)

In a large bowl, mix 1 1/2 cups sweet potato puree, 4 large eggs, and 1/2 cup brown sugar.

Add:

1/2 cup milk

1/2 cup heavy cream

1/4 cup melted butter (Don't you dare use margarine!)

1 tablespoon lemon juice

2 teaspoons vanilla

1 teaspoon cinnamon

1/2 teaspoon ground nutmeg

1/4 teaspoon salt

Mix until creamy.

Preheat oven to 325. Bake pie shell for ten minutes. Pour sweet potato mixture into warm crust. Bake for 40 minutes until the filling is set, like JELL-O. Let cool, then refrigerate overnight. Serve cold with real whipping cream ("None of that white glop you find in the frozen section will do!" Zady encourages.)

# Reader's Guide

1. When we meet Mara, she is nine years old. What in the story suggests her innocence before she meets General? What shows her world smarts?

2. What, if anything, do you find endearing about Aunt Elma? What specific things does she do that show compassion?

3. If you could create Aunt Elma's backstory, what would it be? Why? What kinds of secrets would she have?

4. Recall a time when you shared a secret with a friend and then regretted it.

5. Why do you think Mara gravitated toward books? What about the books helped her cope with her life? Have you run to the pages of books for similar solace?

6. When should the people around Mara have been able to figure out that she was being abused by General? When should someone have intervened? What kinds of symptoms was she displaying that indicated her abuse?

7. Describe your first impression of Mr. Winningham. How does he change throughout the book? Or does Mara's perception of him change?

8. How would Mara define the word redemption at the beginning of the book? Would she understand it? How would she define it after she met Jesus under the tree limbs?

9. Discuss this verse: "For consider your calling, brethren, that there were not many wise according to the flesh, not many mighty, not many noble; but God has chosen the foolish things of the world to shame the wise, and God has chosen the weak things of the world to shame the things which are strong, and the base things of the world and the despised God has chosen, the things that are not, so that He may nullify the things that are, so that no man may boast before God" (1 Corinthians 1:26-29, NASB). How do these verses relate to Mara? Zady? Denim? Camilla?

10. What do you wish you knew about Camilla? In what ways is she mysterious? Why do you think she hid Denim's identity from Mara?

11. In what ways does General represent evil?

12. This book takes place in the late 1970s and early 1980s in a fictitious Texas town. Did the instances of prejudice surprise you? Why or why not? In what ways do you see racism in your city today?

13. List several character traits of Zady. Which ones do you most admire? Why?

14. Fear plays a large part in this story. Describe the devices the author uses to show Mara's fear.

15. How is Mama Frankie a help to Mara? How does she hinder Mara's search for her identity? Can Mama Frankie be trusted? Why or why not?

16. Contrast Zady's view of God and church with Nanny Lynn's. How do they differ? How are they similar?

17. Who plays a positive role in Mara's life? Do these people realize they are playing this role, or is it accidental? Does Mr. Winningham play a positive role?

18. Why does Mara think the deaths of Aunt Elma and Eliot are her fault? How does this reflect the thought patterns of a child?

19. In the beginning of chapter 1, we see a vignette of Maranatha as an adult. Why can't she tell the story in first person?

20. Describe Camilla and Mara's friendship. What did Camilla gain by her friendship with Mara? Why did she instantly call her "best friend"?

21. How would Mara's life have been different had she had siblings?

22. Discuss the author's use of the big white house as a metaphor. How does Mara see her life as being similar to the house? What about fixing it up seems to help her cope with life?

23. Mr. Winningham is a man of routine. Describe his eating habits and mannerisms. Why do you think he is like this? Does knowing what happened in the past help you empathize with the enigmatic man? If so, how?

24. Recount all the gifts Zady gave Mara. Which gifts were the most significant? Why?

25. Why does Mara have an affinity toward Nose Bunny? Who in her life has taken pity on her? How?

26. If Mara were to choose a career as an adult, what do you think it would be? Why?

27. If you were Zane Winningham, what would you have done when your brother stalked and obsessed over Sephie? What kind of regret does he live with?

28. At what point in the story did you realize that Mara would figure out who her parents were?

29. The author uses trees and tree limbs to symbolize both violation and salvation. How are trees a symbol of pain in this story? How are they a symbol of hope?

30.  What inside Mara changes so that she exemplifies her new name—moving from "bitter" to "Come, Lord Jesus"? What is significant about her name throughout the book?

# Recommended Resources

## Healing for the Past

Cloud, Henry. *Changes That Heal: How to Understand Your Past to Ensure a Healthier Future.* Grand Rapids, MI: Zondervan, 1994. This was one of the first books I read that helped me see that real change is possible, that people don't have to be enslaved to the haunting memories or voices of the past.

Crabb, Larry. *Inside Out.* Colorado Springs, CO: NavPress, 1998. Much of what we do, we don't understand. Those who have experienced trauma or pain, like the character in this book, grow up wearing masks, hiding the pain inside. This book helps people make their insides match their outsides.

Hansel, Tim. *You Gotta Keep Dancin': In the Midst of Life's Hurts, You Can Choose Joy!* Colorado Springs, CO: Chariot Victor, 1998. I picked up this book in college at the recommendation of a friend. On page 39, these words convicted and comforted me: "Pain can either make us bitter or better."

Stoop, David, and James Masteller. *Forgiving Our Parents, Forgiving Ourselves: Healing Adult Children of Dysfunctional Families.* Ann Arbor, MI: Servant, 2004. Those whose journeys include a difficult upbringing will appreciate the wisdom and balance of this book about forgiveness.

Tada, Joni Eareckson, and Steve Estes. *When God Weeps: Why Our Sufferings Matter to the Almighty.* Grand Rapids, MI: Zondervan, 2000. Though we may not be suffering physically, victims of abuse suffer emotionally. This book helps anyone who is in pain gain an eternal perspective in the midst of it.

Wangerin Jr., Walter. *The Book of the Dun Cow.* San Francisco: HarperSanFrancisco, 1978. The story of Pertelote in this book is the story of an abuse victim, afraid to trust, almost mortally wounded. I wept when I realized how similar my heart was to hers, how I mistook love and beauty for evil.

### Healing from Sexual Abuse

Allender, Dan B. *The Wounded Heart: Hope for Adult Victims of Childhood Sexual Abuse.* Colorado Springs, CO: NavPress, 1990. This is not an easy book to digest in one sitting. It's best utilized in small chunks, over months, with perhaps a therapist alongside. I found the workbook to be extremely helpful.

Tracy, Steven R. *Mending the Soul: Understanding and Healing Abuse.* Grand Rapids, MI: Zondervan, 2005. A well-researched book about the rampant problem of childhood sexual abuse.

# Sneak Preview of
## *Watching the Tree Limbs*' sequel,
## *Wishing on Dandelions*

I STILL CAN'T TELL MY STORY up close, like it was me in it, breathing the tangled wisteria on the fence posts of Burl, Texas. There are times I still can't bear to say it was me. The movie of my life continues to flash before me, painful episode by painful episode, like a malevolent comic strip. I get real close to retelling my story, where the screen and I coincide somehow—but only when Camilla and I are across from each other, a jug of sweet tea between us in that comfortable place called friendship. It's Camilla who keeps me honest, who reaches for my wrist when a tear slips through. "It hurts," she says. "The memories hurt." She reminds me that I survived that story, and her presence reminds me of its horrid validity. Reminds me in a kind, wild way that this is *my* story. And that I cannot run from being Maranatha. No matter what I wish.

Maranatha Winningham. You'd think the name would roll off her tongue, that it would undulate like lazy East Texas hills. Not today. As she pumped the pedals of her overused ten-speed, she staccatoed her name. *Mara-natha-winning-ham.* *Mara-natha-winning-ham.* Over and over until there lay more road behind her than loomed before her, thank God.

The hot Burl breeze tangled Maranatha's hair so that it whipped and wrangled about her face. She didn't mind, didn't even brush a casual hand to her face to clear the hair from her field of vision. At seventeen, she welcomed the wildness, wearing her tangles like a mask. A gust of sideways wind whipped the mask from her face. Now she could see. In front of her bike tire beckoned a serpentine of gray pavement radiating heat. She stood in anticipation of the journey, pumping her pedals until her thighs ached and her lungs yelped for cool air.

Maranatha passed the out-of-place costume shop on her left, a dilapidated home with faded Santa suits and sequined twenties dresses in the cracked front window. She pedaled past the farm implement shop whose yard was dotted with ancient, rusty plows, leaving the suffocation of Burl behind her. The highway was seldom traveled this time of day, particularly in the 105-degree heat that assaulted her forehead with river gullies of sweat. She longed for water and chastised herself for forgetting something so obvious.

This strip of road held most of Burl's broken dreams—a turn-of-the-century white farmhouse, now converted into a bed and breakfast that no one visited, a hand-painted For Sale sign declaring the dream dead. A mobile home set way back on a fine piece of property tilted oddly to the left where the cement blocks had deteriorated. A goat stood on its roof, claiming it for himself. Maranatha felt the weight of the slashed hopes. She had seen it all before. Burl held a spell over its occupants, what her English teacher called a fatalistic attitude that permeated every pore of life. Once in a while, someone would get a hair-brained idea to improve his lot in life, speculate on some property, and buy a new piece of farming equipment, only to have bad luck rust it over like old barbed wire.

No one left Burl. No one dared. Life stayed predictable

and easy here. Sure, For Sale signs attested to the pain of try-ing to improve life, but at least it was knowable. Folks even remained after the oil boom crash of the mideighties, prefer-ring to work the registers at Value Villa than to risk life out-side Burl's boundaries.

But Maranatha was destined for something bigger than that. She knew it. A dream needled into the back of her mind, always elusive, never clear. A passion locked up inside strained to shake hands with the world, but Maranatha didn't dare explore that joy. She might unearth terror instead. "Joy and pain, they's married," Zady had told her just last week. "A gal-lady has to embrace the pain to feel the joy."

*I'll choose neither.*

She looked down at the bike beneath her—a sorry excuse for transportation. Uncle Zane had swung on a wild pendu-lum from disinterest to overprotection the day her name changed from Mara to Maranatha. "No gal of mine's gonna be driving a car. Might as well just throw yourself off the Burl theater. Cars are danger, Maranatha. Pure danger." The bike had a crudely shaped bow tied about it on her sixteenth birth-day. Hooked around the bike's frame was a hockey helmet. Propped near the kickstand were soccer shin guards "in case you fall," Uncle Zane said. If he only knew how many times she'd swerved away from tractors on this stretch of road. She'd wanted more freedom in the form of bigger wheels and greater responsibility, but he granted her none. This summer she begged for a job, any job, but he refused, saying he pro-vided enough and she didn't need to be slumming around for money. Needed to tend to the house with Zady.

Like a caged bird.

As she pedaled past a quaint farm, a farmer raised his shovel as a hello, and she nodded. *I could always marry a farmer and live a happy life.* In this, she realized she wasn't much different than the scared Value Villa workers. She felt her heart willing to settle, to become like Neville Chamberlain of her history book—peace at any cost. The tyrant of difficult memories would have to be pacified. Or ignored.

Covered in salty sweat, Maranatha slowed her pace as she rose up one of Burl's piney hills. To her right was a happy grove of crepe myrtles in flaming pink, signaling the entrance to another broken dream. She veered onto the gravel driveway and stopped, straddling her bike. She listened for cars, but heard only the labored noise of a tractor far away. She hated that she always looked behind, like some phantom crouched there in the immediate past, ready to overtake her. She'd been running since before she could remember, running from monsters bent on destroying her. Even though she was sheltered in the big white house and safety was no longer elusive, she felt the presence of evil five steps behind her. Ready to suffocate her. The silence of the day roared at her. It should have blessed her with peace; instead, she worried that something would burst from the silence and grab her.

She steadied herself in the day's silence, seeking refuge in another sense—the sense of smell. Faint hints of tea roses calmed her racing mind for the moment. In front of her stood an iron gate, black and foreboding, with an out-of-place silhouette of a squirrel at its arched top. It reminded her of Willy Wonka's gate, the gate that held children out of the mysteries within. She laid her bike in its familiar dusty place behind the crepe myrtles and approached the gate. It was locked.

As usual.

Heart thumping, she tried the frying-pan-hot handle, a ritual she had performed over the past several years. Why she thought it would magically open today, she didn't know. When she tugged at it, the gate creaked in protest, like a warning. Looking back toward the road, she listened again. Nothing. Just the sound of a dove calling to its lover and the hot crackle of too-dry grass rubbing against itself like a fiddle against its bow. She breathed in the warm smell of roses and touched the angry steel, but it was too hot. She returned to the bike, unzipped the pouch behind her seat, and stretched on her bike gloves. Attacking the gate again, she pulled herself up, up, up until she could swing her leg over the gate's pointed top. She scampered down, preferring to jump the last three feet.

Refuge.

Maranatha smiled. Before her was an open field littered with dandelions past their prime. Bits of dandelion white floated in front of her like an idle snowfall, only these flurries drifted away from the ground toward the sun, in lazy worship. Beyond the field was a charred mansion, burnt when Maranatha's name was Mara and she lived the mystery of her identity. Nearly a decade ago. She could still smell the smoke.

She glanced at her wrist and smiled. Circling it was her name. MARANATHA, each sterling letter separated by a bead. Zady'd given it to her a year after she found out her real name. Part of her quest in learning her identity so many years ago was a need for a name that meant more than "bitter." When she found out her real name meant "Come, Lord Jesus," a part of her heart enlivened, as if it knew she was named that all along. She touched each letter, thanking God that He added *natha* to the end of her name, that He changed her heart from bitter to a place where Jesus could live.

Now under the house's shadow, she remembered the day she discovered its charred remains. Four years ago, she met the house on a day much like today. She was thirteen. She and her best friend, Camilla, had begged Uncle Zane for a ride to the county fair, but he had business to attend to. Still, they pestered. In a rare flush of words, he said, "If you're so bent on going—walk! It'll do you good to know how far five miles is. Take Highway 78 outside the Loop, and just start walking. You'll be eating cotton candy and wasting your money on Styrofoam-filled stuffed animals in no time. Now, git!" They never made it to the fair. When Camilla saw the iron gate and the burnt house, she smelled mystery and promptly named the house "Black."

"All scary houses have names. This one's Black, sure as night." In lieu of cotton candy, they "investigated" the scene, pretending to be arson investigators, and concluded a cat had set the fire to take revenge on an evil master. Camilla pestered Maranatha to return, misquoting AC/DC: "Let's go back to black." When she said it, she wailed and screamed like Brian Johnson. Maranatha pretended indifference, hoping Camilla would forget about Black and get on with life. She did. And Maranatha had been visiting her refuge ever since.

She ran to the middle of the field, letting her hair tentacle itself around her head, and stood still. She picked one dandelion, held it to her mouth, and blew a warm breeze over its head, scattering her wishes toward the had-been mansion. "Jesus, You know my wishes, my heart. You know my name. I want to live up to it. I want my heart to be a place where You *want* to come. Would You show my heart today that You love me? I'm sorry I'm so needy, but I just have to know, have to know it in my gut. Please show me Your love."

It had been her wish for so long she couldn't remember not wishing it. She met Jesus under the pecan tree at her home, the big white house owned by Uncle Zane and home-sweet-homed by Zady, its housekeeper. Zady had dished out helpings and helpings of His love every day at the Winningham table, but Maranatha never seemed to be able to digest even a scrap. She experienced Him at church, surrounded by Mama Frankie and faces darker than her own. When Denim spoke or his daughter Camilla rhymed, she thanked Him for making unique folks, for giving her friends. Still, Jesus' love seemed far away, unattainable. She didn't know how long she could exist without having that knowing Zady seemed to possess.

A portion of her little girl's heart had been abducted by General, the boy-turned-man who violated her so many years ago. His pocked face visited her in nightmares where she had no voice, no safety, no escape. He seemed to lurk behind every stray noise. He didn't haunt Burl anymore, but he lived firmly in her mind, igniting dread. She feared he had stolen the only part of her that could understand God's love, like he held the missing piece to the puzzle of her life.

*Am I wishing for something I'll never have?*

Maranatha shielded her eyes from the pursuing sun and walked toward the burnt house. Four once-white pillars stood tall, blackened by angry flames. She remembered when she'd first seen Uncle Zane's home nearly a decade ago how it loomed large on its street, how she'd longed to be the matriarch there someday. But, as in life, reality was more complicated than that. Sure, she lived there now. Little by little, she was renovating it to splendor, but lately the joy of transforming it had waned thin, like a pilled swimsuit at summer's end. Fixing things was hard. She'd painted and painted until her fingernails were permanently speckled. Then the pier and beam foundation settled further, cracking the new paint.

As she gazed upward at the four pillars that kissed sky where the abandoned house's roof once lived, she wondered if she'd ever have a home of her own, children about her legs, a husband to love her. The thought of marriage both repulsed her and pulsed through her. Hatred and longing—all in one girl.

She walked through the rubbish, darkening her red-dirtied shoes, looking for a sign from heaven. She played this game sometimes, asking God for signs, for sacred objects that showed her that He saw her, that He knew she existed. That He cared.

Just then, something glinted off and on as the sun played hide-and-seek through the pecan trees. She bent low to the ashes, her body blocking the sun. The glinting stopped, so she stood and let the sun have its way again. There, spotlighted beneath the gaze of the pillars, was a simple thick-banded ring. She retrieved it, dusted the ashes from the gold, and examined it, turning it over and over in her hand.

Inside the ring was a faint engraving. *Forever my love*, it said.

"Thank You," she whispered, but her words melted in a hot wind. Dark clouds obscured the sun just like that, and the sky purpled. She slipped the ring into her pocket and ran to the gate, climbed it like a criminal pursued, and dropped on the other side.

She mounted her bike. From behind she heard a bustled scurrying, like the furious bending of too-dry alfalfa.

Then darkness.

Someone's hands suffocated her eyes, obscuring the day, stealing her screaming breath. She kicked her leg over the ten-speed, struggling to free herself from the firm grip, and tried to holler. Just like her nightmares, she was mute from terror. Though she knew General's presence was illogical—he'd been shipped off to some sort of juvenile-offender boot camp—she could almost smell his breath as she gasped for her own. She heard a laugh, but couldn't place it. It sounded familiar, like family.

She kicked and elbowed like a kindergarten boy proving his manhood against a playground bully, but the hands stayed enlaced around her eyes.

More laughter. Even more familiar.

She took a deep breath and screamed. Real loud.

Thunder answered back.

# About the Author

MARY E. DEMUTH HAS SPENT THE last thirteen years as a writer. Her weekly column appeared for two years in the *Star Community Newspapers* in Dallas. She now splits her time between writing women's fiction and nonfiction books about parenting and risky faith. Her titles include *Ordinary Mom, Extraordinary God* (Harvest House, 2005) and *Building the Christian Family You Never Had* (WaterBrook, 2006). Mary lives in Le Rouret, France, with Patrick, her husband of fifteen years, and their three children, Sophie, Aidan, and Julia. Together, they are planting a church.

# EXCITING NEW FICTION FROM NAVPRESS.

## Chosen
**Ginger Garrett**       1-57683-651-7

What really happened in Xerxes' palace? Queen Esther's secret diaries tell all. From her days as a poor market wench through her rise to queen, she recorded it all—the sights and scandals—hoping that one day, others would learn the truth.

## Chateau of Echoes
**Siri L. Mitchell**       1-57683-914-1

As proprietress of one of the most exclusive bed-and-breakfasts in Europe, Frédérique could well afford to be choosy about her guests and thus remain a reclusive widow. But when an insistent American writer arrives for an extended stay, she finds her carefully constructed world turned upside down.

## Stealing Adda
**Tamara Leigh**       1-57683-925-7

It had been a long time since *New York Times* best-selling author Adda Sinclaire had experienced more than a fictional dose of romance. But when publisher Nick Farnsworth walks into her life, everything changes.

Visit your local Christian bookstore,
call NavPress at 1-800-366-7788,
or log on to www.navpress.com to purchase.
To locate a Christian bookstore near you, call 1-800-991-7747.

NAVPRESS®
BRINGING TRUTH TO LIFE
www.navpress.com

5/09 | 3  1/09
3/14  (19) 12/13
2/16  (20)  9/14